mattie spyglass

and the Curse of Ashurnasirpal

Shoba Sreenivasan

HOLYMOLYPRESS

HOLYMOLYPRESS

For more information visit www.holymolypress.com or www.mattiespylass.com

Sreenivasan, Shoba
Mattie Spyglass and the Curse of Ashurnasirpal/Shoba Sreenivasan/Holy-Moly Press
Cover Illustrator Dan Ungureanu

ISBN: 0985360429
ISBN: 9780985360429

Printed in the United States of America

CONTENTS

characters and terms

Key Characters

Spyglass: an ancient entity trapped in a Babylonian archaeological artifact who seeks a pure soul to occupy

Mattie O'Reilly: eleven-year-old girl from Hackensack, New Jersey, in 1968, who finds the Spyglass in her deceased father's archaeological effects and is transported onto the Path of the Virtuous

Geeta Raghavan: eleven-year-old friend of Mattie's, bookworm, who became princess of gypsies; she recently immigrated to the United States from India and also finds herself on the Path of the Virtuous

Eddie Petersen: eleven-year old friend of Mattie's, whose father is in Vietnam; he longs to be a soldier and also is on the Path of the Virtuous

Herman Biddle (aka Dmitri Gneezy): an old wizard who was long in hiding as a furniture salesman at Sears, brother to Uri Gneezy

Uri Gneezy: the evil twin of Herman Biddle, now in snake form

L. Rufus Wigglesworth, PhD: aged professor of Assyriology at Columbia University in New York City, friend of Biddle's and a sorcerer

Gilgamesh: ancient king of Uruk, who is three-quarters god and one-quarter human, who seeks his lost friend Enkidu

Ashurnasirpal: once brutal king of an ancient kingdom, now servant of Marduk; he lives in the form of a hairy, ugly, bull-like beast and is the master of the tunnels beneath Kurnigi

Other Characters (Alphabetical)

Abaddon: rodent-faced satanic creature of the underworld, once a subject of the mortal Ashurnasirpal

Asaru-alim-nuna (old demon gods): gods of death, cave gods, and the primeval sea shark-snakes, once worshiped by man, now obscure and buried by Marduk beneath the Corkscrew of Terror

Austen Henry Layard: British archaeologist and discoverer of the Seven Tablets of Creation in Nineveh in the mid-1800s at a mound called Kuyunjik

Crone: an ugly hag, once holder of the Black Book of Magic, now servant to the snake Uri Gneezy; longs for her lost beauty

Daughter of Tiamat (aka the Hidden Daughter or the Hidden Sister): the sister of Marduk; holds the other Twin Tablet of Destiny and has been lost to time

Dottie O'Reilly: Mattie's mother, a former student of Dr. Wigglesworth's; she left Columbia University after her husband perished and works at Sears in ladies' hats and accessories

Duke of Muscovy: a member of the Brotherhood of Evil and master of cruelty in the underworld

Enkidu: Gilgamesh's friend and fellow warrior, lost in the forest of Humawa

George Smith: British clerk with a genius for deciphering cuneiform; in 1872 he translated the Babylonian story of the great flood (also known as "The Epic of Gilgamesh") from the Tablets; died in Nineveh on an expedition at age thirty-six

Grim Reaper: hooded figure of Death and holder of Death's scythe

Humawa: a giant who guards the forest of death, where the Grim Reaper lives; he is under the dominion of the beast Ashurnasirpal

Iron Knight: known as Goering and once second-in-command of Adolf Hitler's forces, now a servant to the snake Gneezy

Keke: Stal's mother, pious and long suffering

Khan of the Huns: a member of the Brotherhood of Evil and a bloodthirsty titan now in the underworld

Marduk: Dark Master of the underworld, holder of one of the Twin Tablets of Destiny; son of Tiamat and brother of the Hidden Sister

Mrs. Elmwood: Mattie's fifth-grade teacher at Fairmount Grammar School in Hackensack, New Jersey

Nanshe: ancient Mesopotamian goddess of light and life

Paddy O'Reilly, PhD: Mattie's father who died mysteriously in Nineveh while attempting to find the elusive Eighth Tablet of Creation

Prince of Wallachia: bloody impaler and member of the Brotherhood of Evil, lurks in the underworld

Rasputin: charismatic monk in the time of Tsar Nicolas II

Sergeant Petersen: Eddie's father, a US army sergeant who is fighting deep in the jungles of Vietnam in 1968

Stal (aka Iosif or Pocky): pockmarked son of a Georgian cobbler and washerwoman destined to become a brutal dictator

Tiamat (aka Tiamet or Tiamut): the Mother Spirit, thrown into obscurity by Marduk, her wicked son

Trina: one of the wandering spirit children, knew Stal in his boyhood

Tsar Nicolas II: martyr and last emperor of Russia

Utnapishtim: the old man who holds the secret to eternal life in the story of the great flood

Vengeful spirits: souls tricked by Abaddon in mortal life who are now trapped in the underworld and seek revenge against him

Wandering spirit children: the souls of children caught in the underworld

Terms and Places

Assyriology: study of ancient Mesopotamia, Akkadia, Assyria, and Babylonia as well as the deciphering of cuneiform

Black Book of Magic: the book of dark magic held by Uri Gneezy

Book of Life: the story of the creation of humankind

City of Condemned Spirits: a city deep beneath Kurnigi, within the Corkscrew of Terror

Corkscrew of Terror: the horrific circle of terror within the bowels of Kurnigi

Cuneiform: written language of the ancient Mesopotamians, one of the earliest known systems of writing, distinguished by its wedge-shaped marks

Death's scythe: an instrument to reap the souls of the living

Dup Shimati: the Babylonian Twin Tablets of Destiny

Enuma Elish: Babylonian tale of creation held in the Seven Tablets and a chant used by Biddle to invoke White Magic

Kurnigi: land of darkness, the underworld

Muktablu: term for "warrior"

Nineveh: ancient city in antiquity of great wealth in the kingdom of Iraq, settled possibly as early as 6000 BC on the eastern bank of the Tigris River

Path of the Virtuous: the mysterious and treacherous Eight Stones of Suffering that must be crossed

Ša nagba īmuru: story of the unknown mysteries, of He Who Saw the Deep in the Babylonian tale of creation

Space-Between-Two-Seconds: Herman Biddle's chant of protection

White Book of Magic: the book of the magic of light held by Herman Biddle

CHAPTER 1

the third stone

On Tuesdays Mattie's mom, Dottie O'Reilly, didn't work late at the Sears in Hackensack, New Jersey, because there wasn't much customer traffic in her department, ladies' hats and accessories. The department wasn't doing so well on account of how in 1968 there didn't seem to be a whole lot of girls wanting to wear fancy hats. "Modern times," her mother always would say with a disapproving look. "All those girls wearing pants with patches instead of dresses, looking like vagabonds and caring not one whit about elegance!" This caused her mom a whole lot of worry, because Mattie's dad, who had been an archaeologist, was dead ("Deceased, Mattie," her mother always would correct her and add sadly, "while on a very important archaeological quest in Nineveh in the kingdom of Iraq"), and Mattie's mom had to earn a living for them. As Mattie herself was only eleven, she wasn't expected to wear fancy hats, though her mom would have liked it if she had combed her frizzy red hair back into a neat ponytail. Mattie's mom also wanted to make sure she didn't end up like "those hippie girls so barren of manners and etiquette." This meant that on Tuesdays at dinner her mom could work on "refining comportment and conversation" with Mattie, areas in which she said she was "alarmingly lacking."

Mainly this involved eating liver and onions in the dining room. Mattie looked down at her plate. Yup. Still a lot of liver and onions left. There was no getting around it. She pushed around the onions a little bit into her green beans, which tasted every bit as revolting as they looked.

"Mattie, stop playing with your food," she heard her mother say. "And use your knife, not your fork, to cut the meat."

Mattie looked up from her plate. Her mom's shiny blonde hair was pinned back in a smooth bun as usual, but there was something remote about her eyes—like she was there but wasn't. Puzzled, Mattie tilted her head. Usually, at this point, her mom would want to talk about something in the news that was interesting, but not something serious like the Vietnam War—that was always on the news—because "serious conversation doesn't mix well with digestion." But her mom wasn't saying anything at all; she was just sort of staring off.

Then Mattie felt a soft whoosh in her ears, like the rush of water through a pipe. There was something wrong, but she couldn't figure out what it was. Maybe she was dreaming. Her mind felt kind of woozy. She hoped this wasn't a dream and it wasn't a school day, because she just knew she couldn't get up lickety-split and get ready. *It couldn't be a school day*, her mind told her. It was as if all her thoughts were jumbled up in a soupy mess, everything kind of blending together. Mattie saw her mom was still there, right across the table, still staring off.

Mattie picked up a slimy green bean from her plate and tried to put it in her mouth. The bean stretched in front of her, right out of the fork. The greenish color now had yellow streaks in it as the bean stretched and stretched toward her! Mattie wanted to say something to her mom about how the green bean was stretching, but her tongue was frozen in her mouth. She couldn't even get out gurgling sounds. The strange bean was growing and growing and coming right toward her mouth, and Mattie couldn't even move away. Then suddenly her head jerked forward toward the bean, as if whatever forces that had held her back had let go.

Mattie opened her mouth to bite the bean. As she did, it changed into a wormy, slithering thing with a head and eyes. *Mommmmm!* Mattie struggled to say, "Mom," but nothing came out. She tried to scream, but only a sound like a faint whistling came forth. The wormy bean was now a shiny iridescent green, a bean with a mouth and a long forked tongue that darted out. *A snake!* Mattie shivered in fear. *A snake! Mom! A snake is on my fork!* She tried to yell this out but couldn't. Her mom looked frightened, her eyes open wide, but still like she was very, very far away instead of right across from Mattie in the dining room in their house on Andersen Street in Hackensack, New Jersey. The snake had elongated beyond the fork, its tail touching the ground. In a quick movement, it was off the fork and on the table, and now up in the air, launched right toward Mattie's mom. Mattie thought she was screaming, "Mom! Look out!" but not a word came out. It was all like the whole thing was slowed down but fast at the same time.

The snake now had Mattie's mother in its tail and held her tight. Mattie tried to jump across the table and stab the nasty creature with her fork, but the more she tried, the more frozen she was. *No! No!* she cried out in her mind. *Mom!* The snake's body wrapped around and around her mother. Then her mom turned to Mattie and whispered, "Look for the flying frog to find me," and she disappeared slowly into a mist until there was only a blank space where she had been. This was an awful dream! Not a dream, a nightmare. Mattie commanded herself, *Mattie O'Reilly! Open your eyes! Wake up!*

𒀭𒀭𒀭 𒀭 𒀭𒀭 𒀭

Mattie's eyes snapped open. But it was like looking up into the sun through eyelids—all bright and yellow, warm but not comforting. Images took focus in front of her. Was that Eddie over there? And Geeta? And Mr. Biddle? Mattie realized she was falling downward, tumbling really. Eddie and Geeta looked like they were falling too. She threw her hands out to achieve some kind of balance. Her legs were akimbo. The whooshing sound in her ears grew louder, and the yellow light grew brighter. Mattie could see, however, that she was wearing her green-checkered pants, the ones her mom said were unsuitable for church, even with a skirt over them. *Mom!* A sharp pain shot right through Mattie's heart, and the realization hit. She wasn't sleeping in her bed in Hackensack, New Jersey. And her mom wasn't downstairs listening to the CBS morning news on the radio. And today wouldn't be normal at all—no Fairmount Grammar School, no Mrs. Elmwood yelling at her and all the other fifth graders. *Oh, no! Oh, no! Oh, no!* Mattie cried out to herself. The image of her mother clasped tightly in the tail of that evil old snake Gneezy on the Second Stone filled her mind. *Mom!* She had to rescue her mother!

Mattie saw that the Spyglass was in her hand, its eyes looking up at her in fear. *Spyglass.* Oh, what trouble that Spyglass had been ever since Mattie had pulled it out of that trunk in the attic.

Oh, you rat-fink Spyglass! Mattie thought. *You'd better help me save Mom!* The yellow light blinded Mattie as she braced herself for the fall.

Eddie plummeted to the hard ground below. There was no thud, only a heat that enveloped him. He had assumed the airborne position by instinct, like his father, Sergeant Petersen, Special Forces, stationed somewhere in the jungles of Vietnam, had taught him. Eddie looked over and saw that Mattie had landed too and was standing up but appeared unsteady. Her hair was all frizzy, and her chubby face was red. She looked dazed. But not Eddie. He was combat ready. With his yellow military crew cut—though the cowlick in the back always stuck out— and with his keen scanning eyes, Eddie kept himself on alert on their dangerous mission. When the evil Uri Gneezy had captured Mrs. O'Reilly—and Mattie's dad too—Eddie had vowed he would take on the mission to rescue them. He also would find his own dad, who was hidden somewhere in the jungles of Vietnam, somewhere in time. Eddie set his jaw in determination. If anyone could complete this rescue mission, it was his dad. That was what his dad did—take on dangerous ops that no one else could or would.

Eddie stood up, or tried to, for the stone under them was slippery—red and seething, undulating light and heat. He saw Geeta tumble to the ground just ahead of him and right next to Mattie, whose round face was streaked with tears.

Geeta fell on her back. Her glasses lay crookedly on her serious brown face; her black braids were loose. As she stood up, her owl eyes looked like they were trying to focus. She peered at the terrain. *It must be the Third Stone of Anger,* she thought. Then her heart panged when she considered that Mrs. O'Reilly and Dr. O'Reilly were trapped on the Second Stone, within the clutches of the evil that was the snake Gneezy. Geeta thought of the journey thus far, from the First to the Second Stone, of the lessons the Path of the Virtuous had thrown their way. She thought of her grandfather, her old ThaTha in Bombay, India, and how his rheumy eyes dimmed with age-held wisdom, how he spoke of the illusion of life, also known as *Maya.* "Remember always, Geeta," he'd told her, "that which appears so never is." But Geeta had argued with him. "How is that possible?" she'd said. "The material world is what I see and touch. How is that an illusion?" Her old ThaTha had said only, "The soul cannot be seen or touched, yet it is more real than the body." And now Geeta yearned for ThaTha's counsel. *ThaTha, the evil snake holds Dr. and Mrs. O'Reilly,* she thought. *That is real, not illusion! How can we rescue them?* But ThaTha was silent.

Eddie saw Mr. Biddle had landed on the stone just ahead of the three of them and was silhouetted against the horizon. His cape fluttered around his shoulders; the dark-brown boots that stopped at his knees somehow served to anchor him to the ground, though he also leaned on a gnarly wooden staff.

Mr. Biddle was looking up into the sky, if you could call it that, for it seemed as if the air around them was lighter than mist. His white hair was long, flowing down his back; his blue eyes were bright with tension. He turned his head back toward Eddie, Geeta, and Mattie and pointed the wooden staff toward the sky. The three children tilted their heads up.

There in the sky, the figure of a gaunt Buddha formed through the haze just above the horizon. As the Buddha spoke, more and more Buddhas filled the sky: some fat, some thin, some male, some female, some with faces that could not be seen—all in a meditative pose, covered in saffron-colored robes. Then the chant rose and vibrated through the air over and over.

Eight precious stones,
eight matters of the soul,
rise like the wind of wrath.
Eight stones of suffering.

When Herman Biddle's boots had hit the Third Stone, he felt its treacherous slipperiness. The admonition of the Buddhas held an increasingly portentous tone as their chants rang repeatedly through the sky.

Fear, hate, anger, bitterness, envy, duplicity, greed, and despair.
Six stones remain.
If you can cross them,
you will find the Seer of Truth.

The Third Stone of Anger. Herman Biddle shivered at the task ahead of them—traversing six more stones of suffering. Suffering. The Path of the Virtuous wasn't for the faint of heart. It was true, all that was said of it—that the Path tested its sojourners severely and yielded only to those with purity of purpose. And Biddle also knew that the magic held in the White Book of Magic—the spells he knew as a wizard—would be strained. For as the journey up a mountain begins with the ease of steps up the foothills, but quickly rises and strains the heart with its steepness, so too was the ardor of the journey of the Path of the Virtuous.

Behind Mr. Biddle, the three children, unsteady on the slippery stone, remained mesmerized by the Buddhas as the chants boomed across the land. Slowly the Buddhas faded into the hazy sky, the sound of their chants echoing in their ears.

Geeta adjusted her glasses. "The Third Stone of Anger," she whispered to Mattie. Geeta by instinct was quieted by the ominous feel of the atmosphere. "We are now on the Third Stone."

Mattie saw this was true. "But my mom's on the Second Stone with my dad!" she said, her heart breaking. "We've gotta go back and get them."

Geeta nodded. Yes. They must rescue Mrs. O'Reilly. And Dr. O'Reilly too, of course. But how? Geeta glanced back and saw Eddie, whose keen eyes were scanning the land. Eddie would know. She hoped fervently that Mrs. O'Reilly had caught the Small Book of Spells she had thrown down. *Oh, please, please, let it be so,* she prayed.

Herman Biddle turned toward Mattie, Eddie, and Geeta. His face was long with worry. He thought of Paddy and Dottie held in the tail of Uri Gneezy. *Uri.* Biddle knew his twin brother's heart like no other, having felt its beats as they had grown together in their mother's womb. And because of that, he knew Paddy and Dottie were in the gravest of danger. Gneezy would stop at nothing to get what he wanted—unending power that the Spyglass would open up through access to the Twin Tablets of Destiny.

"Mr. Biddle," Mattie said. He saw her chubby, tear-stained, innocent face look at him expectantly. "We're going to find mom and my dad too, right?"

Geeta watched the emotions that crossed Mr. Biddle's face and knew he was in torment.

"Yes," Mr. Biddle said after a long pause. "They will be found." *But how?* he wondered. *How?* His shoulders, slumped in defeat, told another story. They had traversed two stones, true. But at what cost? Though his feet moved forward in starts and fits on the slippery surface, Biddle knew it would be only moments before the Path's harsh lessons would be upon them. He felt the immensity of the task ahead of them. The fact that no one who had attempted to cross the Path of the Virtuous returned to the world of the living caught Herman Biddle's heart. It was a journey he never had been brave enough to try himself. But now, in his avoidance of his own fate, he had pushed an innocent girl, Mattie, into it. And he had endangered her, Eddie, Geeta, and the ill-fated Paddy and Dottie O'Reilly as well.

"Mr. Biddle." He heard Eddie's voice behind him and turned. "Wait up." Eddie's analytic eyes had Mr. Biddle in his range. Herman Biddle felt the gaze and knew at once that Eddie, young warrior that he was, would not be kept from his mission to rescue Paddy and Dottie. He also knew Eddie most certainly would perish if he tried. Biddle felt anguish stab his heart in sharp thrusts. No. He could *never* let that happen.

Biddle's white hair flowed down his back in waves; his beard was longer now and covered the front of this cape. He held up his wooden staff against the wind. The cape was a cobalt blue, shining and shimmering against the hazy yellow light—a contrast to the red stone at his feet. The words of Mother Tiamet, the Woman with the Robes like the Sun, spoken to Mattie on the Second Stone, echoed in Biddle's mind. *You, daughter, have changed the River of Time and cheated the Dark Master of that which is his—the souls of ancient Nineveh. Go, daughter, and hide, for your brother of darkness will kill you, and I cannot protect you.*

Your brother of darkness will kill you. These words rung in old Herman Biddle's ears. *Daughter.* How could Mattie—a mortal— really be Tiamet's daughter? Or was it, as Biddle believed, that the mother had said that because all mortals were her children? Still, Mother Tiamet had warned, "Your brother of darkness will kill you." The Dark Master was a brother to no one; he was a master alone. Still it was Mattie who had found of the Tree of Moreh, the enchanting, ethereal vision of branches with seven blue orbs that had rescued the ancient souls of Nineveh from Marduk's hold. As a result, the River of Time had been thrown into chaos and with it the story of creation.

Biddle knew the puzzle of the Hidden Sister of Marduk, who was the daughter of Tiamet, held a mystery that only deepened with each page of its story. Where and how had she disappeared? Where were the Twin Tablets of Destiny? These were the Tablet of Light that the daughter was said to have held, and the Tablet of Darkness, the other destiny, which her brother Marduk held. Herman Biddle knew the Spyglass was at the core of it, the core of the mystery of the disappearance of the daughter of Tiamet and the Tablet of Light she held, the Tablet that the power of darkness—called by many names, Satan, Devil, Marduk—sought. Biddle trembled at the weight of the possibility—Marduk as the holder of both Tablets of Destiny. Humanity's free will would disappear at once.

A hot wind rose from the Third Stone. Abruptly Biddle was drawn from his thoughts, for a rumbling that was furious in tempo was suddenly gathering force; it filled the air and stopped the four in their path. It showed the old wizard that Marduk was watching and waiting for the Path of the Virtuous to ensnare Mattie, and then he would kill her as well Eddie and Geeta. With horror Biddle realized that the Dark Master knew exactly where they were. He knew their journey and would hurl Marduk's legions of the underworld at them to thwart them. For himself and his own life, Biddle cared not. But the three children—anxiety clutched at his heart. Mattie felt the Spyglass grow cold and heavy in her pocket. Then a sound that chilled the soul, loud and harsh like the clanging of chains of those held imprisoned, echoed through the Third Stone.

Mattie gasped, for above them the sky turned ominously dark, and then she saw two red orbs gleaming in fury. Mr. Biddle called out in alarm to the three, "Keep your eyes down! Don't look at the sky!"

Mattie put her hand up to shield her face, as did Geeta and Eddie, so blinding was the dreadful red light. Biddle at once knew the danger; mortals couldn't dare look at the eyes directly, for the power of their evil would blind them. The red orbs were those of the Master of Darkness himself. Satan. Devil. Marduk. Beams of searing hate fell from the two eyes upon Mattie. She felt the heat, followed by coldness—one that immediately filled her with fright.

Thief!

The word detonated the air. The ground beneath Mattie, Eddie, and Geeta shook and lifted them. The sound of the Master of Darkness's displeasure rang through the underworld. Groans of agony rose in a stream of sound from the undulating red ground. Mattie felt the Spyglass grow colder and heavier with fright in her hand. Herman Biddle steeled himself, pushing away the fear that stabbed his consciousness. He thrust his wooden staff into the air and swirled his cape against the hot wind. As he did, the cobalt blue of the cape lifted and hovered above it. The cloak itself was now white, not a color so much as a bright white light.

Mr. Biddle now spoke an incantation, his eyes shut. He whispered it first, and then his volume increased with each word.

From the dark lands of the east,
and the churning sea of the west.
From the treacherous mountains of the north.

The sky turned dark, and the red orbs began to dim in response to the force of Biddle's magical chant. Herman Biddle cried out:

And the parched plains of the south,
before you bore a name
and destinies were determined
in the midst of heaven.

Herman Biddle was surrounded by the bedazzling white light that grew from his cape as the raging red orbs dimmed behind it. Mattie lifted her hands to her eyes—so blazing was this gleaming white light. Geeta looked away, and Eddie, determined not to lose intel, squinted his eyes into the glare.

Biddle cried out, his long hair streaming behind him against the hot winds that lashed his face. He arms were spread, the gnarled wooden staff stabbing the air as he bellowed:

Oh, Great Mother,
open the doors of time!

Instantly the four travelers of the Path of the Virtuous were lifted into the air and disappeared into the white light of Biddle's cape.

Mattie, Mr. Biddle, Geeta, and Eddie now floated inside the Space-Between-Time, where they hid. But a menacing growl, the voice of the Dark Master, followed them and vibrated in their thoughts.

Thief! Betrayer! Traitor!
You cannot hide long or well.
Soon that which is mine
will be restored,
and you, sister, destroyed
forevermore.

Herman Biddle shivered at the threat. No, it wasn't just a threat—it was the Dark Master's prophecy. A deep shame filled him, for in his heart was a sorrow so strong, so deep that he could barely raise his head. Oh, what had he done in avoiding his own fate? He should have taken hold of the Spyglass and traversed the Path of the Virtuous alone and found a way to destroy the wretched thing. Memories from the cold Siberian lands that were once his home filled him. He remembered that evil knot in time as the century turned from one to another, and in the moment when the clock struck midnight on 1900, how the gypsies told of a large yellow moon that rose over the Siberian landscape and cast a sallow light where horrendous events that would follow would fall like shadows over the frozen ground. There in Russia, across the lands, Marduk's followers would rise everywhere, whispering in the ears of the people false promises and turning their hearts from love to hate, from forgiveness to anger. And so the people would turn a deaf ear to goodness and eternal life and choose instead the trinkets of earthly power and dominion over others. They, those whose chose Marduk as master, would turn neighbor upon neighbor with anger fed by envy, anger that would rise to a pitch of righteousness that allowed evil to grow unfettered. One drop of black ink would spread and contaminate the clear waters. Kindness couldn't grow on such parched earth. Goodness would die on the vine. Oh, how

Herman Biddle had tried to undo that knot time and time again. He and Rufus Wigglesworth had traveled the distance of horror and evil again and again but always had failed. The River of Time had held firm—until now, until Mattie had opened the doors to chaos. Biddle's shoulders slumped under the weight of these thoughts.

The image of the martyr Tsar Nicolas II, in all his great majesty—his gleaming blue uniform, his kindly bearded face, and the gossamer gold wings that showed him to be an angel now, as he had appeared above them in the ghastly sky of the Second Stone—haunted Biddle. Tsar Nicolas's words regarding the task before them loomed large in his mind—*Before death and Hades can be cast into the fire forevermore, before the Book of Life can be written again, the Path of the Virtuous must be crossed.*

Before the Book of Life can be written again, the Path of the Virtuous must be crossed. Biddle flinched at these words. Oh, what a task to be placed upon the shoulders of Mattie, a child! Not just Mattie, but Eddie and Geeta too. A trio of innocence. Biddle set his mind in firm resolve; he couldn't place such a burden upon them. He wouldn't shirk his fate, his duty. Not now. He would rescue Dottie and Paddy and take up the Path of the Virtuous himself—alone, as he should have from the start, when the treacherous Spyglass had entered his life when he was just a boy; when he should have killed Uri in cold blood, brother or not; before Uri rose, before his soul was given to Marduk and the dark powers of the Black Book of Magic.

Glancing back, Herman Biddle saw the three and was struck again by their vulnerability: Mattie, her chubby face sweaty and red, looking at him quizzically; Geeta, gazing around thoughtfully; and Eddie, his eyes alert and in military scan mode. Biddle's heart rang with tenderness for the trio, and then the familiar stab of fear followed. How could he ever protect them? He came abruptly to a decision; it would have to be done, for their own good, and quickly. There was no other way.

Inside the confines of the Space-Between-Time, Mr. Biddle tossed his gnarled wooden staff into the air like an arrow. The staff flew up in a dark streak that split in two. From it fell a large, glistening, egg-shaped object.

Eddie looked at the weird object. It was coming right toward them! He tried to move, but he just floated right into the path of the egg-shaped thing. He felt its magnetic force pull him up and toward it. "Hey!" he yelled.

Mattie was just below Eddie, looking up at the egg-like thing; she was puzzled, for though it was big, it also looked like a soft, transparent, glowing balloon, and not particularly dangerous, as she saw Eddie being pulled closer and closer to it. "What is that?"

Geeta turned to her to answer that it appeared to be something that Mr. Biddle had conjured from a spell, but before she could, the egg enveloped them in its light. Mattie, Eddie, and Geeta were trapped inside a gleaming transparent egg of light that rose up and stayed suspended in the air.

"Hey!" Eddie said. He charged to storm out but fell back. "What the heck!"

"Mr. Biddle! Help us!" Mattie cried out, for Mr. Biddle was floating outside the egg.

His tone was stern, but his eyes, now the blue of a light sky, couldn't be anything but kind. He shook his head. "I can't, Mattie. I've locked you inside a vessel that will keep all of you here, in the Space-Between-Time. It'll keep you safe from Gneezy and the Dark Master until I return."

Eddie's face contorted in indignation. That wasn't what a warrior did—run from the enemy. He shouldn't be trapped inside an egg, hiding with two girls!

"What about Mattie's mom and dad? Who's gonna rescue them?" Eddie yelled.

"I am, Eddie," Mr. Biddle replied, though his eyes revealed his anxiety.

Eddie thought about how Mr. Biddle ran a mission, all zigzagged. Uri Gneezy would make mincemeat of him. Mr. Biddle couldn't go this alone. He knew nothing about search-and-listen procedures, defining mission ops, or conducting action reviews! Plus, Mr. Biddle was no warrior.

Eddie tried again. "How are you gonna rescue them, Mr. Biddle? You need us! And Mattie! Remember, *she's* the Mistress of the Spyglass!"

"Mr. Biddle!" Mattie said, her hands pressed against the shimmering wall of the egg. "Eddie's right. Let us outta here! Please!" Mattie thought Mr. Biddle could never make it by himself, and she also thought about what a good person he was, how he'd listen so nicely to all the old ladies in the Sears furniture department who never bought anything but just came by to gab. Oh, poor Mr. Biddle could never go against that horrible snake Gneezy by himself! The snake would kill him! Mr. Biddle needed her and the Spyglass, and Eddie and Geeta!

"Please, Mr. Biddle!" Mattie pleaded. "Let us come with you!"

Herman Biddle shook his head. "No, Mattie. It's not possible."

"Mr. Biddle, is this the wisest course?" Geeta asked solemnly, her dark eyes reflecting disapproval. She thought back to when Mr. Biddle was little Dmitri and how fear had held him tightly. Did Mr. Biddle not need their assistance? And what of Rasputin and the gypsies who followed Geeta? Were they not needed too?

Together they could defeat evil, but could Mr. Biddle do it alone? No, it was impossible. Tsar Nicolas had said that the Path of the Virtuous must be crossed before the Book of Life could be written. Geeta felt certain this meant that all of them had to take on the journey together, not just Mr. Biddle.

"Yes, Geeta," Mr. Biddle said. "It is best."

Eddie shook his head and tried to charge out of the egg again but hit the wall and fell back. Herman Biddle felt Eddie's anger rise, and that would only attract evil. He had to act fast before the forces of evil knew where he had hidden them, for Biddle knew that to allow the three to continue on the Third Stone would be sheer folly. The Path of the Virtuous set its own journey, and he already had see that he was helpless to its force and that he could offer the three no protection whatsoever from what fate it held in store.

This *was* the best course, Biddle told himself. It was the only course—to imprison the children inside the egg, suspended in the Space-Between-Time, a vacuum in time.

"No, Mr. Biddle!" Mattie pleaded, "Let us out!" She pulled out the Spyglass and yelled, "Spyglass! I command you to let us out!" However, the Spyglass lay heavy and inert in her hand. Fear had frozen the Spyglass in a cocoon of paralysis, for the memory of the snake Gneezy's force still surrounded her, and the words of the Dark Master silenced her.

Herman Biddle shut his ears to Mattie and Geeta's continued pleas and Eddie's angry shouts. He flung open his cape, which flowed about him like waves upon the shore, filled with energy and light. Into this magical cape, he thrust his hand and pulled out three Cards of Time. Then he flung them toward the strange egg that held Mattie, Eddie, and Geeta. The three Cards of Time melted into the egg, and one by one they landed into the children's hands.

Over the shouts of Mattie, Eddie, and Geeta, Mr. Biddle called out, "These are three Cards of Time."

Geeta gingerly held her card, all black and shiny, and observed, "These are black, Mr. Biddle. How are we to use them?"

A wind rose outside the egg, swaying it. Herman Biddle knew that time was ebbing. "The cards have no magic powers inside your vessel. I give them to you as protection, should the vessel break." As Biddle said the words, a pang stabbed his heart. *Should the vessel break.* It couldn't; it mustn't, for should that happen, all would be lost. Oh, what a risk he was taking! But there was no other way, for the Path of the Virtuous threw them about hither and thither, and was becoming ever more dangerous. It was safest to have Mattie, Geeta, and Eddie held in abeyance within the egg in the Space-Between-Time. But if the egg-shaped vessel broke, Biddle knew he may never be able to find them, thrown as they would be onto the will of the Path.

Eddie kept running inside the small space and hitting the sides with his shoulders, trying to break the egg, which was now hard and transparent but didn't give. He gave his best kickball kick to the egg's concave side but to no avail. It held firm.

Geeta considered the black Card of Time in her hand and the foreboding tone beneath Mr. Biddle's words, *As protection, should the vessel break.*

Outside the egg the wind grew stronger and propelled Biddle back. His blue eyes glistened with both fear and determination. He lifted his hands, veined with time, and the cape moved about his shoulders as if it were a living thing, now blue and green. It glinted like the ocean under bright sunlight but hinted at the layers and dark depths below.

Mr. Biddle's voice rang out:

So they shall dwell,
three innocent souls,
until there is peace from the enemy—
the Great Beast, the poisonous scorpion,
the mighty dragons,
and all who bow to the master of blackness,
Marduk.

Mr. Biddle swirled the cape. Mattie, Eddie, and Geeta fruitlessly beat at the egg's concave sides. The wind then gathered into a hurricane force that spun the egg. It spun faster and faster and faster. As it did, the egg became a whirl of light with the faces of Mattie, Eddie, and Geeta inside becoming a blur. Then the egg disappeared.

The wind stopped, and Herman Biddle stared into the space where the children had been. If he failed and perished on the Path of the Virtuous, Mattie, Eddie, and Geeta would be eternally trapped in the Space-Between-Time, or until Gneezy found them and a way to break the spell of protection. Herman Biddle shivered. No. He could not, would not fail! He prayed that his incantation held firm.

He thundered:

Enuma elish la nab u shamanu
shaplish ammantum suma la zakrat.

The White Book of Magic materialized, and Herman Biddle flew up into its pages as it closed and disappeared.

CHAPTER 2

the sounds of treachery

The Great Beast, once King Ashurnasirpal II, now just a servant to the Dark Master Marduk, felt the quake of the land beneath him. The horrific wails of the underworld rang through the air. Ghostly images of scores of bodies writhing in pain filled the sky. The sky above Ashurnasirpal churned angrily. Two red enormous eyes filled it, and a growling sound rumbled through the air, the raging displeasure of the Dark Master Marduk for the snake Uri Gneezy.

Blood streaked the sky, and the anguished moans of those in the deep tunnels of hell vibrated up through the ground.

Uri Gneezy felt the trepidation surge through him. Large lightning bolts fell from the sky and pierced the snake's body. "Master!" Uri Gneezy called out. "Please…" He raised his arms above his head in an ineffective gesture to deflect the punishing lightning bolts. "I have these vermin who are precious to the child who holds the Spyglass."

Ashurnasirpal looked toward Gneezy, as the snake shifted his serpentine body toward the sky and with his tail lifted the doomed prey, Dottie and Paddy O'Reilly, who shivered in fright high in the air.

The voice above seethed with anger. In the sky the red eyes gave way to a creature with three dragon faces whose colors changed from a blinding yellow to a blood red to an oily black. The creature opened its mouths, and from them ghastly images poured out—scores upon scores of monsters, some male, some female, some young, some old, all with maggots that bit into their writhing bodies.

The dark-red eyes glowed, and the Dark Master's words rang threateningly.

> *You, snake,*
> *whose blood is shared*
> *by he who aids the thief,*
> *will stop the River of Time!*

The plaintive sounds of those who had displeased the Dark Master and were trapped for an eternity in the dark netherworld filled the air. Their pained cries clearly sounded out in warning.

> *Capture she who is a thief*
> *and hides on the Third Stone.*

The red orbs glowered. The Dark Master Marduk's voice bellowed, striking Gneezy like lashes across his serpentine form.

> *You will bring me*
> *that which is rightfully mine!*

I will be the begetter of eternity,
holder of the Twin Tablets,
holder of all destiny.

An icy rain fell over the land. A giant dragon-like creature, with black wings like those of a bat, spanned the sky. From its mouth fiery hailstones rained down. Ashurnasirpal held his hairy hands above his head. Sharp knives of pain filled the snake Gneezy's body as fiery flames pounded him.

The oily land beneath them was like quicksand; the more they moved, the more it pulled them down. The Iron Knight was slipping into the oily ground, flailing under the assault of the hailstones and barely holding on to the reins of the black stallion he rode. Beyond them the legions of the army of the Third Reich were slipping and falling into the slick substance. Somewhere in the recesses of agony, the cry of the Crone could be heard, cursing Uri Gneezy for his ineptitude.

Then the ghastly flames of pain stopped as the images disappeared in the sky. The words of the Dark Master thundered again in the air as the dragon faded from view.

Should you fail,
beware your fiery fate
of the pit and snare.

A deafening sound fragmented the air as the two red eyes disappeared. The Great Beast, once the mighty and powerful King Ashurnasirpal II, knew that the Dark Master was ruthless toward those who failed him, for eons ago Ashurnasirpal had been trapped in the foul body of an animal for his treachery against the master. The Great Beast's fiendish heart now filled with hope. Yes, he would break the fangs of the snake Gneezy and take his power and bring the Dark Master what he desired. Ashurnasirpal, whose savagery once had been so feared that men dared not look him in the eye—yes, he would be king once more. He, Ashurnasirpal, destroyer of rebels, he whose blood ran through the ancient kings of Assyria. The Great Beast snorted in triumph at this thought. He, Ashurnasirpal, would again be great! No longer beast but king!

The oily substance that had held them receded into a slimy residue under Ashurnasirpal's hooves. He grunted, and small flames flew out of his nostrils. The snake Gneezy—how had Ashurnasirpal allowed the snake to get the upper hand? His face was hard with ire as he watched the Iron Knight bow in obedience to the snake, as if the snake were a true master! They would find out soon who was master and who was slave. The beast shook, and his hooves marked deep grooves of contempt into the slick ground below. The words of the Dark Master rang in his ears.

Capture she who is a thief
and hides on the Third Stone.

The Great Beast could see that the Iron Knight had Gneezy's full attention. Now was the time to act. Ashurnasirpal dove into the muddy darkness, disappearing into the ground below.

𒀭𒈨𒌋𒂖𒈨𒌋𒁹

Uri Gneezy heard but did not fully register the disappearance of the Great Beast. It was the Iron Knight, now fully supplicant, who raised his head in the direction of the Great Beast and said, "Master, the beast disappears." The Iron Knight then bowed again, to emphasize that he knew his place, before he remounted his black stallion. He, who once was known as Goering and had lived like a baron, had been second in command to Adolf Hitler. His blond hair had been like that of a movie star and his face as handsome as one; he had cut a dashing figure. He also had been a German hero in the First World War; how far he had fallen. Now, as the Iron Knight, he had much experience playing the role of the sycophant, having so recently kowtowed and scraped in false humility to the wretched Hitler, the stupid man who had given up everything for lust for a woman. A scowl crossed the Iron Knight's face. Behind him lay the ruins of the Third Reich: the SS, the Nazi soldiers, Hitler himself, all writhing in the oily slime of this forsaken place.

"Yes," Uri Gneezy noted, looking toward the horizon.

The Great Beast of the Master of Darkness was indeed gone. The snake looked pleased, as the Great Beast had been far more hindrance than help. His malodorous presence and ever disapproving pronouncements had grated on Gneezy, for was he, Uri Gneezy, not the master now? And was not the beast to be *his* beast of burden? But the Great Beast wouldn't submit, for too strong was the memory of power in his mind. The snake shook his tail, which held Paddy and Dottie captive. The two luckless victims of the snake looked pale and frightened.

Uri Gneezy smiled at their fear. Fear was a commodity with which he had full familiarity; in fact he had found it to be a very useful emotion. He also had seen that the red-haired girl would willingly trade the Spyglass for these worthless creatures. He smiled a greedy sneer. It would all end soon. No more chasing Biddle across the eons of time in an endless cat-and-mouse game.

Capture she who is a thief
and hides on the Third Stone.

That would be easy enough. Gneezy would find the Third Stone and capture the Spyglass. He would crush Biddle, and no longer would that sniveling fool be a presence to consider. Stop them in the Path of the Virtuous, treacherous on its own—that too should be easy. Trap them in the Path—that would be their Fortuna's wheel; they'd be stuck forever on the stones. *Soon. Soon.* He, Uri Gneezy, would grasp in his hands the Spyglass and would receive all power from the Master of Darkness! The snake Gneezy quivered in anticipation.

𒁹𒌋𒊓 𒂖 𒁹𒌋 𒁹

The Great Beast dove deep into the tunnels under his palace. It was a labyrinth of torment that he had constructed and where he once had held the ancient souls of Nineveh. Ashurnasirpal's beast face registered anger. *Once held,* for the souls were lost because of the snake. But the tunnels still held his armies— those who had displeased the Dark Master and were given to Ashurnasirpal as slaves over centuries upon centuries of time as tokens of appreciation. They were creatures who were repulsive beasts like him, human and animal at the same time. They came from the annals of history—those who had wished to hold power, who had made their pacts with the Dark Master and failed. They were minions like him, condemned to serve until such time as the Dark Master saw fit to free them from their tortured bodies. The tunnels were dark, but the beast knew them well. From his nostrils he snorted flames that lit the cave walls. Here and there the walls were marked with messages written in blood—BEWARE, BEWARE, BEWARE.

A great foreboding gate the color of dried blood rose before Ashurnasirpal. The beast stopped. From the dark iron gate a hand shot out, a skeletal form that then emerged to reveal its body—a body of bones held together with thorny branches, blood dripping from each finger. This horrific figure stood before the beast and bowed in obeisance.

"Master," the creature said. Its skeletal face was streaked with black ash; it was a partial face, the flesh burned from the flames of hell. It held out a large key of tarnished gold to the Great Beast.

Ashurnasirpal grunted as he took the key. His hooves again marked the slimy, swampy ground. He flung his hairy head back and roared. Then he inserted the key into the lock of the rusty gate, and as he turned the key, he bellowed:

Scorners, blasphemers, corpses,
who hang from thorny bleeding branches
of endless sin,
from the City of Condemned Spirits,
where hope died east of elsewhere,
rise, rise, rise!

The bloody iron gates flung open, and from them poured creatures of the underworld: some with wings like bats; others like large rodents, faces ensnared in greed, their mouths ever nibbling at nothing; creatures that were half dragons, half scorpions, with their human faces stained with tears of regret, of avarice, of duplicity; creatures with three faces, all eyes bleeding, and wasp wings upon their bodies.

The Great Beast roared with satisfaction as he and the creatures flew up to the tunnel's ceiling—up and out but under his full control.

𒀭𒌷𒌷 𒂍 𒀭𒌷𒁹

When the ground below him had given way. Uri Gneezy hardly realized it at first, so engrossed was he in his thoughts of power. His body shook, and he saw that the Iron Knight had fallen next to the black stallion. Behind him the legions of the Third Reich were haphazardly tossed about. The ground below them erupted with Ashurnasirpal's gruesome creatures of the caves. These monsters flew about the Iron Knight and the denizens of the Third Reich, as all put their hands up over their heads to avert the blows rained upon them by the doomed creatures of the Dark Master's circles of hell.

Uri Gneezy's eyes narrowed as his serpentine body shook. The black eye upon his cape glowed: traitor. Gneezy smelled treachery. His great mouth opened, and the forked tongue sprang out like an antenna to find the traitor.

From the earth below, as if to answer his question, the Great Beast emerged, charging toward Gneezy, the oily mud a slimy cover over his hairy body.

Gneezy hissed, and his tongue sprang toward the Great Beast. "What are you doing?" he roared. "You dare challenge me!"

The Great Beast snorted flames in response. He bellowed, calling forth the ancient dead kings and warriors, "Tukulti-Ninurta! Shalmaneser! I call on you, Ashur-uballit, Arik-den-ili, Tiglath, Pilser! Conquerors of Canaanites and Phoenicians! Conquerors of Babylonia! Destroy the snake!"

Kings and rulers of ancient Kalhu, enslaved Hittites, and Aramaean soldiers rose from the oily mud, their bodies covered with shields of tarnished gold, their hands bony with decaying flesh falling. Those enslaved by the curse of Ashurnasirpal rose from the ground with a deafening cry of the pain of years of being held captive. They charged upon Uri Gneezy as one, some on chariots and others on strange half beasts—horse and man, bull and man. Dragons blew fire from their nostrils; giant scorpions, with their many claws, inflicted gashes upon Gneezy's large reptilian scales.

Uri Gneezy gasped at this treachery as he fell beneath their blows, hard strokes from swords and iron poles. He saw the Iron Knight failing in his fight against the flying creatures, his soldiers of the Third Reich falling beneath the hideous onslaught of the great bats with claws that flew into their bodies, piercing them mercilessly.

"It will be mine, snake!" the Great Beast bellowed. "It is written that only I am to be capturer of the Spyglass, and our Dark Master will restore my kingdom to me!"

Held aloft in the grasp of the tail of the snake Gneezy, Paddy and Dottie were helpless to escape; such was the strength of the grip around their waists. They wrapped their arms around each other. Paddy O'Reilly thought of how he had found Dottie so strangely in time—in 1938, decades before he would meet her in real life. In the tunnels of the evil Ashurnasirpal, he had found his love, who had fallen, literally, from the sky! And the child, Mattie, *his* daughter. Oh, how the lures of academic greatness paled against the love he felt for Dottie! *Dorothea...in the long form!* He now knew that theories formed in the safe confines of his academic archaeological perch at Columbia University were not theories at all. The Eighth Tablet. Paddy thought of

* Chapter 2 *

Dr. L. Rufus Wigglesworth, esteemed chair of the Columbia University Department of Archaeology. Even in the dire circumstances he was in, Paddy ruefully thought about how Wigglesworth was well past his academic prime, and decorum surely dictated that the old man step graciously aside and offer the helm to a younger academician, such as himself. Oh, how Wigglesworth had vigorously opposed Paddy's exploration in Nineveh in this year of 1938! Paddy recalled Wigglesworth's derisiveness when he had broached the topic of the Eighth Tablet, the dire prophecies of what had happened to the ill-fated George Smith, the amateur British Assyriologist who, in 1872, first translated from the cuneiform the ancient tale of the great flood held in the Babylonian Tablets of Creation. Seven Tablets Smith had found. Paddy thought of the words of the Old Testament—*The Spirit of God was hovering over the face of the waters.* The Eighth Tablet, which told the story of the writer, the Spirit of God, surely lay somewhere under the yellow dirt of Nineveh! Despite all the terror unfolding before him, his fingers itched to dig. Paddy thought of Biddle and Wigglesworth's pronouncements regarding the Twin Tablets of Destiny, Dup Shimati, the division of light from darkness. Paddy was jerked out of his thoughts by the tightening of the snake's grasp around his pudgy frame. The land beyond them, the strange land of Nineveh writhing with strange creatures, flew about them, and Paddy shut his eyes against the fearsome sight.

With closed eyes Dottie whispered a prayer. *My God, my strength in whom I will trust.* Oh, to have found again her great love, Paddy! But now they were at the cusp of being destroyed. And where was her daughter Mattie? Was she safe? Were Eddie and Geeta safe too and still with Mattie? And Herman Biddle and Dr. Wigglesworth—how their dire prophecies haunted her. *Myths,* she thought with irony. *Which are the myths and which are real?* Dottie thought of her life in Hackensack, working in Sears after Paddy had died (oh, but he was alive now; he was here with her in this ill-fated land—true—but with her and young!). She knew that the story of Sears and that life was just a veneer, a covering of the real story of battle of the dark forces against those of light. Herman Biddle had been wrong, as had Dr. Wigglesworth. One could not avoid fate. One could not dismiss the currents that ran under him or her, for the force was too strong. Dottie's thoughts stopped at the sound of hooves close by.

"Paddy!" she called out in alarm. "Look!" Ashurnasirpal's great bull mouth opened, and they saw teeth yellow and long as the mouth bit the tail.

Gneezy cried out in pain as the ancient kings and the enslaved of Assyria pummeled his body. His tail gave way under the assault and loosened its grasp on its prey. Ashurnasirpal greedily grabbed Dottie and Paddy, one in each arm, and dove into the murky, oily slime.

The flying creatures of the circles of the doomed also dove into the muddy slime, as the chariots and slaves disappeared into the ground as quickly as they had appeared.

Gneezy lay stunned and broken on the ground, his serpentine body shrinking into his human aspect until he was only his cadaverous form. From his mouth the snake tongue, which remained, shot out. His face was bruised; his green eye and blue eye glittered in fury.

"Beast Ashurnasirpal!" he roared. "You will pay dearly for this treachery."

Mounted once again upon the stallion, the Iron Knight rode forward then dropped off the steed to greet Gneezy. Behind him the moans of the Third Reich could be heard. "Master," he began. The Iron Knight then gasped at the skeletal form of Gneezy.

Gneezy's head turned until it spun and spun. His face transformed from green to gray. His body shook, and his head fell back. His mouth opened, and from it flew a black tongue that arched long into the sky. From the black tongue arose a sound—a hellish sound, curses from the underworld. Then a streak of black appeared in the sky and transformed into the Black Book of Magic.

The book opened, its reptilian cover undulating, the scales emitting the sounds of the torment of the condemned across the ages. Gneezy was pulled into the Black Book, followed soon by the Iron Knight and the legions of the Third Reich. When the book shut, its blackness disappeared into the sky.

CHAPTER 3

the spell of prophecy

The office lay in tatters, with papers laid to havoc by the Winds of Doom that had taken L. Rufus Wigglesworth, PhD, from his academic nest in the university. Now Wigglesworth had a unique viewpoint, as he lay on his back upon a heap of the detritus of decades of scholarly labor. Though his head was pounding, Wigglesworth retained clarity of thought, coming as it did from long years of forced discipline. His old body, corpulent as it was, did not allow for quick movement. He was back in his office at Columbia University, where he still was the chair of the Department of Archaeology, where even in 1938 he was being pushed by the younger bucks—those upstart PhDs grasping for power, like Paddy O'Reilly—to leave his post and be relegated to emeritus status. *Paddy! Dottie!* Wigglesworth thought of the two held in the tail of evil. *On the Second Stone on the Path of the Virtuous!* Wigglesworth's face was clean shaven, his head balding, and therefore the three chins were visible and shook in fear.

Wigglesworth's thoughts were held by the past as his eyes focused on the yellow water stain on the ceiling of his office—yellow like the soils of Nineveh. Oh, what had the Tablets of Creation unleashed but danger? But what year had he returned to? For in the dizzying travels through time—begun so long ago at the turn of the century, when his wizardry was first awakened in the excavations at Nineveh—he had been batted about here and asunder. Moreover (a Wigglesworthism if there ever was one, for *moreover* was such a useful introducer to topics, he pontificated to his graduate students, a word that brooked no protestations, that held forth strength and resolve; Wigglesworth dearly loved the word), the room clearly showed the effects of the hurricane-force winds, an interesting phenomenon, for in the past, their excursions (for what to call the travels through time with Herman Biddle but "excursions"?) had never revealed themselves in the present. So, Wigglesworth deduced, staring up at the ceiling—for he was loath to get up, as this was an endeavor that took much effort, given his girth—this was indeed different. The River of Time had been changed.

"Harrumph. Harrumph." Wigglesworth made the grunting sounds as a sort of encouragement to his body to make the effort to rise.

"Rufus," Wigglesworth heard to the side, as a helping hand came into view. He grabbed it and heaved himself up.

It was, of course, Herman Biddle, his cape aglow, his boots showing the faintest patina of red dust upon them, and his face furrowed with worry. Biddle immediately began to pace. "It is much worse than we had anticipated," he said, looking out of the grimy windows of Wigglesworth's office.

Wigglesworth steadied himself against his desk, a bit wobbly from the sudden change from the prone to the upright position but mostly worse for the wear from the events during the Night of Broken Glass and especially those on the Second Stone. The memories flooded him again with the shocking realization—Paddy and Dottie were ensnared in the grasp of the snake Gneezy!

"Where are the children?" Wigglesworth asked, seeing that Biddle had come alone.

The old wizard turned to face Wigglesworth. "I've placed them in a vessel held in the Space-Between-Time."

Wigglesworth was alarmed. "But from where?"

Biddle paused then said, "From the Third Stone."

Wigglesworth's heart stopped for a second, and his next words were suffocated in a gasp. "The Third Stone!"

Biddle nodded grimly. "I had to, Rufus. We must now go back to the Second Stone, somewhere in ancient Nineveh, to find Paddy and Dottie."

Wigglesworth interrupted the quivering of his chins. "You feared that Mattie with the Spyglass in hand would follow you, along with Geeta and Eddie. And that the Path of the Virtuous wouldn't allow this but only scatter them apart to traverse it separately." He shook his head. "That is one path of logic, Biddle, but I fear you've underestimated the power of the Path. And you've forgotten the consequence of actions on the Second Stone—that the River of Time itself has been plunged into chaos, that what was is not and what will be may not be correctly seen."

Biddle's blue eyes were bright with fear as he spoke slowly. "I have neither underestimated nor forgotten. It was the only way I could conceive that would ensure their safety."

"The Second Stone," Wigglesworth said. He felt the words on his tongue like sharp stings. "You've already moved forward to the Third Stone, Biddle. Now you ask to move *back* on the Path?

Even if we could, how would we find Dottie and Paddy? Gneezy could have hidden them anywhere."

"And we shall see where that is and change what will happen." Biddle held Wigglesworth in his gaze. He knew that what he was about to ask him next would court the wrath of the Dark Master. "Help me call the goddess Nanshe and cast the Spell of Prophecy," he said.

Wigglesworth felt his breath leave his body, and the blood that ran through his portly frame seemed to freeze in fear—Nanshe, she who could reveal through visions and dreams what was yet to come or could come. Again the mysteries of the ancients of Babylonia swirled in his mind, those of the gods and goddesses now relegated by modern man to the realm of myth. When called upon by the ancient peoples, these gods and goddesses could alter the wheel of fate—that is, before the god of science had reached its ascendancy to blacken out man's vision to the possibility of the impossible. Wigglesworth's memories held him—his dusty days among the yellowed books and how by chance his own life had been diverted from the obvious, how he had lived both in the flesh and through the travels of his dreams. He thought about Nanshe and the dreams of what was to come.

The Spell of Prophecy! To cast such a spell! Wigglesworth's rotund body shook with fright. How much Biddle was asking he knew full well. Casters of the spell only served to enrage the Dark Master, he who was given the spoils of man and was tempted by his base instincts and had given away his free will. Fate was written by man as he traversed his life, not rewritten by the caster of the Spell of Prophecy, and fate couldn't be thwarted even if the spell was successful. And there also was the other uncertainty of the effect of having knowledge of what is to come. A man who knows what is to come only knows what he sees in that moment, and time isn't linear, and the seer into the future changes it as surely as a flowing stream is diverted by logs that roll into its midst. These thoughts ran through Wigglesworth's mind, but he cast them aside. Then he grimly nodded his assent.

Wigglesworth raised his fleshy arms and shut his eyes. He chanted haltingly the first words of the Spell of Prophecy, calling to the goddess of creation herself to intercede. She had been maligned by the followers of Marduk as a five-headed dragon, a demon, and enemy of the gods. She was sometimes called "Chaos," and her water was sweet and not bitter, as the followers of Marduk had said; her very name had been met with derision through the ages. Through the eons she was known to her secret worshipers as the goddess of light, whose robes shone like the sun, who was not chaos but order, whose name was whispered in secret sacred sounds—*Tia-me, Tia-mu, Tia-ma, Tia-met, Tia-mut, Tia-mat*. These worshipers had to remain hidden—that is, as long as the ancient lies remained in the memories of man.

Wigglesworth's voice rose in strength, his three chins shaking upon his tubby body, which trembled under the exertion.

> *O holder of light,*
> *mother of our dual wills,*
> *you who hath given*
> *Dup Shimati,*
> *the Twin Tablets of Destiny,*
> *I call on you!*

He now called forth the secret ancient Mesopotamian names of the goddess whose aspect was often splintered like light through a prism into many forms of light and creation.

Tia-me, Tia-mu, Tia-ma.
Tia-met, Tia-mut, Tia-mat.
In your three sacred forms
of body, of mind, of spirit,
O exalted one,
Aja, Antu, Aruru, Nintur,
giver of life,
send us Nanshe!

Wigglesworth stopped in anticipation, his body still quivering. The stillness in the room was deadening. The spell hadn't worked. Wigglesworth breathed heavily, his body clearly worn by the effort the incantation had taken. He looked at Biddle, his eyes saying there was little else he could do.

Biddle saw very clearly the exhaustion that had fallen upon his old friend Wigglesworth's face and the toll the incantation had taken upon him. Biddle steeled himself. He began his own incantation, his voice strengthened by resolve. Wigglesworth joined him, their voices rising in a chant of desperation and pleading.

They who sought to slay you,
they who cast their spears
to split your body,
to scatter you to the evil winds—
they are tellers of lies,
calling that which is light
dark
and that which is dark
light.
Marduk is

the deceiver, he who is
Master of Darkness,
who cloaks himself in false light.
We call you to
send us Nanshe!

Still there was silence. Wigglesworth and Biddle cried out again, their eyes shut, their hearts united in purpose.

O Goddess of Light,
send us Nanshe
to show us where the servants
of the Dark One
hold the two.

Suddenly the room plunged into a deep darkness. Then emerged the face of the goddess rising like a beam of light through a dark mist. Her robes held the colors of sunlight as it shines against the bluest of skies. Biddle and Wigglesworth raised their arms to the goddess and pleaded and sang thrice the ancient secret names in its three sacred forms.

Tia-met, Tia-mut, Tia-mat.
Tia-met, Tia-mut, Tia-mat.
Tia-met, Tia-mut, Tia-mat.
O Goddess
of senses, reason, conscience
of body, mind, spirit,
we beseech you!
Protect that which you have
borne!

At these words Wigglesworth's small office shook, and blinding silver light filled it. The papers rose from an unseen wind and propelled Wigglesworth and Biddle back. The goddess herself sang out the name.

Nanshe! Nanshe! Nanshe!

Wigglesworth and Biddle joined in the cry.

Nanshe! Nanshe! Nanshe!

A great streak of light—a path of milky stars—formed, and Mother Tiamet's shimmering robes and figure melted into the starry path, which then disappeared, leaving only the black sky.

Then a moon rose in the midst, and the figure of a woman appeared; she was clad in iridescent and moving robes, a living thing itself, made of the silvery-blue scales of fishes of the great oceans. A smell of sweetness filled the room, and the mist that fell upon Biddle and Wigglesworth's bowed heads was composed of droplets scented with roses.

Biddle and Wigglesworth cried in relief, "Nanshe!"

Nanshe's long hair, the color of a green sea, cascaded down her back. Her deep eyes moved with knowledge like the ocean's waves and were filled with sorrow. Her voice sounded in admonition.

Mortal man,
who seeks to see
and to alter
past, present, and future?
The fates and the furies

know now that
what has been seen
may never be unseen and
what is done
cannot be undone.

The words rained upon the heads of Wigglesworth and Biddle, bowed in supplication, and Nanshe spoke again:

See now, mortal man,
what may be and will not be.

The room then shook with the sounds of prophecy: of voices telling and retelling the future that mingled and mixed so no one word could be heard. Nanshe's face changed and held mercurial images of time as man had lived it, would have lived it, or could have lived it: the wars, the small peace that followed, and more wars; those of evil hearts and those of kind ones; dark clouds of storm and tempest. Dragons with fanged mouths spewing fire filled the air, and sharp white bones flew from these mouths. The demon dragons swirled around and through the poor figures of Wigglesworth and Biddle, who were tossed up here and there like flotsam upon raging waters. Dark tunnels snaked through the room.

And at last the words of Nanshe rang out:

They who you seek,
whose fates you wish to unravel,
are hidden deep
beyond the tunnels
of the Dark Master's servants,
within the bitter City of the Condemned.

The images receded and disappeared. Wigglesworth opened his eyes slowly. His heart was beating fast, and he gasped for air, so worn out was he by the spell.

Herman Biddle's face was white, and his blue eyes shimmered like bright stones with realization.

Wigglesworth whispered, "Hidden within the City of the Condemned."

Biddle shivered at his next words. "Beyond the tunnels of Ashurnasirpal, where evil can hide, impervious to the White Book of Magic." His shoulders slumped at the immensity of the task. To travel into the bitter City of the Condemned would mean to walk into the mouth of danger. But to even find this godforsaken place of the blackest of evil…Biddle choked back his fear again.

He exclaimed, "How, Wigglesworth, could we ever travel beyond Ashurnasirpal's tunnels to reach the City of the Condemned?"

Wigglesworth didn't respond. He fully knew the daunting nature of the journey, but they had no choice but to act, for Paddy and Dottie would suffer torments he couldn't bear to consider if they were left there. Wigglesworth busily dug through a pile of documents. "Here," he said, at last pulling out a yellowed sheaf of papers. He held up the manuscript and said, "'Discoveries in the Ruins beneath the Tunnels of Ashurnasirpal.'"

Biddle reached up, took the yellowed document, and read the name of its author. "Austen Henry Layard." He looked at Wigglesworth in puzzlement. "I thought his work was confined to the discoveries in the libraries of—"

Wigglesworth commanded, "Open the manuscript."

Biddle did as ordered. Sheaf after sheaf of yellowed paper, all blank, followed. Confused, he looked up at Wigglesworth. "Blank papers? I don't understand, Rufus."

"Blank," Wigglesworth declared, "to all but one. We need Henry Layard to help us."

Herman Biddle knew now what Wigglesworth meant. "Let's go."

Biddle raised his cape to swirl it, but Wigglesworth stopped him. "A warning, Biddle—I can come with you but have meager wizardry of my own. Can you chance it?"

"Rufus, bring with you the gift of Ninazu, the Small Book of Spells. That will recompense for any diminishment of your wizardry." Biddle started to swirl the cape, but Wigglesworth stopped him again.

"It's gone," Wigglesworth said.

Biddle paused. "You're certain?"

Wigglesworth nodded. "It disappeared in the chaos that was the Fourth Wind of Doom. Lost to time. And in whose hands it's in now, friend or foe, I can't say."

Biddle said no more. "I'll protect you. Come."

Biddle swirled his cloak, lined with the Cards of Time. The cards flew out from the confines of the cape; hundreds upon hundreds like white wings fluttered above the heads of Biddle and Wigglesworth. Biddle pointed his arm like an arrow toward one, and a beam of blue light pierced the Card of Time as the old wizard pulled it toward him. The other Cards of Time merged back into Biddle's cloak in one fell swoop. A wind came through the walls of Wigglesworth's office, and once again the papers whirled about. Wigglesworth clutched the yellowed manuscript to his chest.

The Card of Time in Biddle's hand grew larger and larger and fell away from his hand. The room was consumed with a blinding light into which Wigglesworth and Biddle disappeared.

The darkness obscured any ability to see, and therefore, though her eyes were open, Dottie felt as if she were still grasped in sleep. She shook her head to shake away the wobbly feeling but still felt the disorientation of awakening, as if from a deep slumber. She felt the stain of the dream world lingering upon her conscientiousness. Little bits came to her: she and Mattie in Hackensack at home in the dining room; snakes and worms; and something she told Mattie, something to tell her where they were. Oh, if only she knew that Mattie was safe! Dottie's heart clutched when she recalled that her child Mattie held in naïveté the Spyglass, sought by evil and with only two old men, Herman Biddle and Dr. Wigglesworth, to protect her. And Eddie and Geeta were with them, all innocents traveling into the unknown, sought by the horrifically evil forces of Marduk. Dottie thought of how many of the ancient secrets she had arrogantly dismissed as myths told a very real tale of creation and destruction. This was a tale she and Paddy had to understand and unravel to save their child. Dottie felt herself strengthen in her resolve. Paddy, armed as he was with his knowledge of the Enuma Elish, and she with her knowledge of the myths of Gilgamesh and ability to decipher cuneiform—all this would hold them in good stead.

A pungent, foul odor filled the darkness and stopped Dottie in her thoughts. She wrinkled her nose against it. *Where is Paddy?* she thought in alarm. As she felt about her and hit Paddy's pudgy arm, relief filled her. No longer were they held in the clasp of the snake, and Dottie could feel that some movement was possible.

"Paddy," she whispered. Paddy grasped her arm in response. As their eyes adjusted to their chamber of imprisonment, they saw they were in a small, dark, dank cave. "Paddy," Dottie whispered. "Look." Paddy's eyes widened.

The Third Stone lay empty and silent. From its hard ground rose a heat, that of a simmering anger rising like steam. Herman Biddle had failed to consider that it was arrogance to think that he, a mortal man, could alter the course of the Chosen One and that of the Twin Tablets of Destiny. Desires that spring from man's inner wants—his fears—do not direct destiny. Fate was stronger than Herman Biddle's will to protect, and the River of Time was in flux. The story was being rewritten. And here Biddle's magic held no sway and couldn't halt the journey on the Path of the Virtuous. Fate had overpowered his intention to sway the three children away from their destined journey. And it was clear that Mattie, Eddie and Geeta were to traverse some part of it alone. Biddle, with his interference, was but a small hand held up against the hurricane winds of fate.

The egg that held Mattie, Geeta, and Eddie in the Space-Between-Time careened downward from the sky. When it hit the solid ground of the Third Stone, it shattered, tossing out the three figures.

Mattie, Geeta and Eddie tumbled to the ground, surrounded by the tiny shards of the egg's shell. The three gazed at the emptiness of the Third Stone, where no other being was present. Then they looked at each other in realization. Mr. Biddle was gone.

Mattie yelled, hoping against hope for a cry back, "Mr. Biddle!"

But there was no Mr. Biddle, only the heat from the stone, which rose like a warning around them.

Geeta shook her head solemnly. "Mr. Biddle's plan to protect us has failed. And now we are alone."

Eddie stopped her. "Listen," he whispered.

The stone quaked under them, and the ground split. The thunderous sound of the ground shattering in the quake followed. The earth rose beneath them and catapulted them into the air.

Eddie shouted to Geeta and Mattie, "We're in the middle of a volcano!"

Hot waves of lava flowed beneath them, throwing up flames of heat. All three screamed as the flames licked below them, and they were pulled into the depths of the volcano.

Mattie cried out, "Spyglass! You rat fink! Help us!"

But the Spyglass lay inert. She couldn't stir herself, so deeply frozen was she in fear. Oh, what had Mattie done in rousing the wrath of the Dark Master! And what had she, the Spyglass, done! And why? For the Spyglass didn't know what tied her fate to this child, this insignificant child, like no other who had held her in their possession. But tethered together they were, at least until the Spyglass could break free and save herself from the confines of her metal chamber. That was all that mattered. Oh, but if she only knew how it had happened! If only the shadowy memories would form clearly again so she could undo what had been her sin and be free. But what was it? What had she done? And who was she?

All the Spyglass knew was that fate had given her power without knowledge, that it had bound her into the metal, that her very soul was trapped here and would be through the eons until the Chosen One was found. She had been drawn to Mattie, had held herself in the dark recesses of the attic until it was time. Was she right to have done so? "Daughter," the Great Mother had called Mattie. The Spyglass remembered what the Great Mother, the Woman with the Robes like the Sun, had said to Mattie on the Second Stone. *You, daughter, have changed the River of Time and cheated the Dark Master of what is his—the souls of ancient Nineveh. Go, daughter, and hide, for your brother of darkness will kill you, and I cannot protect you.* Even the Great Mother could not help, the Spyglass thought gloomily.

This goddess whose name was hidden, the very vowels of which were altered and re-altered through time to protect those who kept her alive in their souls and chanted only to themselves— the three sacred words that spoke of the three forms, *Tia-met, Tia-mut, Tia-mat*—what power did she have? The Great Mother, the Spyglass felt instinctively, was an uncertain and weak ally. She didn't trust the goddess and saw how her power had dimmed through the ages as more and more followers turned away from her and toward the Dark Master. This the Spyglass knew from having been held from eon to eon in the clutches of those whose souls had darkened with greed from the power the Spyglass gave them and soon became the Dark Master's slaves. Each time the Spyglass had fallen away from those hands as they came nearer to the Dark Master, who wanted possession of her.

But...but! Back then she had three gold bands. Only two now remained, and those two bands were all that separated her from the clutches of the Dark One. The Spyglass had done the unthinkable; she had given Mattie one of the gold bands that protected her to rescue her from the Dark Master when Mattie had eaten the forbidden fruit of the Tree of Knowledge. Perhaps worst of all, she had aided Mattie in releasing the trapped souls of the ancients of Nineveh into heaven. And the Spyglass herself was weakened; the imprint of Gneezy lay upon her. But what choice was there but Mattie? If the Dark Master prevailed, it would mean her eternal doom to this prison, this dreadful metal prison that had held her through the ages. The Spyglass felt the weight of these realizations. She shivered, and her eyes fell deeply into the recesses of her metal prison.

The flames rose higher and higher as they consumed Mattie and Eddie and Geeta. The glowing red of the embers of wrath and anger ran deeply like veins into the earth. These veins then grabbed the three travelers. Mattie, Eddie, and Geeta were lassoed tightly and flung into the recesses of the volcano.

CHAPTER 4

the british museum in the year 1880

Sir Austen Henry Layard moved slowly and with great trepidation down the first narrow hallway and then a second one that led to a back office in the British Museum. He held a candle against the darkness. Sir Henry had a stern face, old now but with the remnants of a handsome outline hidden under a gray beard. He came to the office door and paused. Slowly he pulled from his coat pocket the key and inserted it into the lock. The door opened to his touch quickly, as if it had been waiting for him.

The old man shivered. He entered the room and saw the letter that had been slipped under the door. The small reading room in the British Museum held various manuscripts and books—all related to Nineveh, all from his own discoveries there, all jumbled haphazardly upon the shelves that lined two of the walls. It was musty, and a fine film of dust coated the edges of the shelves and the small table by the side of the armchair. Though there was no reason others couldn't use it, the reading room had evoked such superstitious fear that all those in the museum avoided it, for it was said that the room's contents were cursed. This was the curse, it was said, that had befallen George Smith. The young engraver, drawn like a moth to flame, had blithely entered the reading room, studied the manuscripts, and learned to decipher the ancient texts of Nineveh. Others, scholars whose study never gave them the greatness of Smith, whispered that he had made a pact with the devil so that he would be directed to where he would find the missing story of Gilgamesh and bask in the glory that followed. Sir Henry had last ventured into the room almost a decade earlier, in 1871, and then only to retrieve that wretched manuscript regarding what lay beneath the tunnels of Ashurnasirpal in order to give it to Wigglesworth to keep away—away in the future and from the ever curious eyes of George Smith, now the *deceased* George Smith.

Sir Henry stooped to pick up the letter, and as he did, the door to the reading room slammed shut behind him, startling him. *Drafty old building,* he told himself. *That's all it is. Someone likely has a window open, and the wind has shut this door.* But Sir Henry knew otherwise. The ancient forces, the winds of evil, lurked here. He gazed at the envelope that he held in his veined and brown-spotted hands. It was faded yellow and shook in his palsied hands. Should he drop the cursed missive and leave? *Why did I come here at all?* he chastened himself. *Why?* What were Smith's communications to him now, now that Smith had been dead more than four years? But Sir Henry had come, drawn he knew from some force that held him firm to Nineveh. Whatever it was that Smith had written to him would be revealed one way or another. It was best to read the letter here and be done with it.

Sir Austen Henry Layard seated himself in an overstuffed armchair and placed the candle on the small table at the side of the chair. It was dark, and the candlelight was just enough to begin the task that he so dreaded—to open this letter, the last communication of the late George Smith. Sir Henry recoiled. All who touched the Seven Tablets were surely cursed! He pulled from his coat pocket a small silver flask and took a sip of brandy to give him fortitude. The brandy didn't steady him; the letter shook in his trembling hand.

It was now 1880 and many years since Sir Henry had left excavations for politics and diplomacy. He had learned of Smith's death in Aleppo on August 19, 1876, on yet another expedition to Nineveh. Sir Henry had known at once that Smith's passing wasn't as it seemed. And now, upon his return to London, he had been told a letter had been found at the British Museum, a letter written to him by George Smith, apparently shortly before his death, secreted among Smith's manuscripts. These boxes of material recently had been donated to the museum by Smith's widow. *Oh, what happened?* Sir Henry wondered, and quivered at what must be the real truth—the truth beneath the story of dysentery as the cause of Smith's death in Nineveh. Sir Henry nervously combed his fingers through his long, grizzled, gray beard. He put down the letter and looked out the small window of the reading room into the dampness of the dimming dusk. Why couldn't he have stopped Smith? Why had he let him persist in the treacherous task of pursuing the tale of Gilgamesh, one he knew would kill him?

Sir Henry thought of the dream he had dreamt on the banks of the River Tigris in 1845, before he lay his touch to the dirt of the land. How he had not heeded it! The dream tantalized first with the glory of the great palaces and sculptures, but then he saw gloomy monsters, dragons that pulled him underground to a labyrinth of caves, of chambers upon chambers, where he heard the cries of the tortured souls there. The Great Beast, the appalling beast that was half man and half bull with fire that came from his nostrils, rose before him, and the stench of death clung to that beast Ashurnasirpal, who roared a curse that curdled Sir Henry's blood and awakened him, grasping for air, drenched in sweat. But he wasn't deterred, for he had been young and rash then, willing to tread on the neck of danger with reckless abandon, looking for intrigue and battle.

Sir Henry was old now and had long left his interest in all things of antiquity that were once his bailiwick to younger men—men with stamina to excavate under the broiling sun of the deserts of what was once Babylonia, men with courage, for Sir Henry knew he didn't have the fortitude to confront the dark mysteries. And there also was the hostility of the natives in the desert, which was well known to him, simmering under the deceivingly cooperative countenance of those who lived in that benighted land. Some were said to be secret worshipers of the goddess, in defiance of the ancient god Marduk, the goddess whose name Sir Henry had heard in secret chants—*Tia-met, Tia-mut, Tia-mat.* He knew that the ancient battle of good and evil rose again and again in the undercurrent of their chants, that it was real and not to be toyed with.

Still Sir Henry did toy with the dangerous battle, for there was the cursed mound Kuyunjik. It was the venerable Sir Henry himself, just a few years after his first excavation in 1845, who had discovered the shattered thousands upon thousands of pieces of clay tablets in the library of ashurn-Bani-pal at the king's palace, the king whom scholars credited as having had the foresight to collect the writings of the ancient tales in tablets and who, by modern calculations, perhaps reigned between 668 and 626 BC. Foresight! Sir Henry's face paled at what the esteemed Assyriologists did not know, could not know, for the truth of the fate of the king and the consequence of his cursed library was known only too well to Sir Henry through premonitions and dreams.

What these admonitions from the underworld meant, Sir Henry understood but had chosen, at least at first, to ignore. He had told himself that he wouldn't fall prey to timidity and brashly proceeded to turn a deaf ear to the warnings from the underworld. As to the alarm in the eyes of the villagers whom he attempted to recruit to be his laborers, who turned way in fear and whispered warnings, Sir Henry in his arrogance as well dismissed them as the superstitious rants of simple desert natives. So it was that he disregarded his own premonitions against continuing his expedition, for in Nineveh he had felt the whiff of evil rise from the Tablets as they were lifted from the mounds. But he plunged ahead and had transported them from the excavation site to the British Museum. However, the pungency of evil is strong, and its scent lay in Sir Henry's nostrils—the aroma of death and decay. And the visage, that vile face of the beast Ashurnasirpal, stabbed his waking moments with fear and left no peace in sleep, for his dreams were riddled with horrific images of the fate of those who tampered with the secrets within the Tablets. And for these reasons the Tablets lost appeal and their secrets remained sealed within the mystery of the undecipherable slashes and lay in a dark underground chamber of the Assyriology section of the British Museum—until George Smith found his way to it and pieced the wretched, cursed thing together. The fragments, when whole, would reveal the secret of Dup Shimati and break Smith's life.

Sir Henry again pondered the value of the discovery of the cuneiform tablets in the mound of Kuyunjik and cursed his decision to unearth them from their home and transport them to the British Museum. He knew that others didn't think the

Tablets were contemporaneous at all to the historic warrior king Gilgamesh but a sort of popularized version of the original, copied and recopied through the centuries until they were found and saved in the library in Nineveh; but there were other ancient secrets within those Tablets, mysteries that were best left to crumble, unread, in the desert ground. This Sir Henry had known even then when the blood of youth had run impetuously through his veins. Still he had excavated and removed. But to what end he did not know, for they had served to rouse the curiosity of the eccentric young Mr. George Smith. Sir Henry sighed deeply as he fingered the edges of the letter. The *late* George Smith, dead on expedition, as predicted, or perhaps as foreordained.

He looked out his window into the foggy mist that was London. His eyes then took in the words written by George Smith in the earlier letter written just months before his fated trip to Nineveh in 1876.

I have discovered in these ancient tablets a curious reference to Dup Shimati, tablets of some sort, I have surmised, and ones that were the subject of much debate by the ancients, thought by some to hold two separate narratives of destiny, one of the living and one of the underworld, and by others the fixed fate of mortal man and the fate of the gods. But the passages I have constructed from two central fragments say something much different. This Dup Shimati is actually Twin Tablets, each of which holds the promise of destiny and how it is to be written. Incredibly the holder of both Tablets would receive secret knowledge and in turn control all souls and win forevermore the battle between good and evil. But in which direction?

Sir Henry wondered, *Which direction indeed?*

Mattie's mind was spinning, as she, Geeta, and Eddie plunged into the depths of a chasm of the volcano then deep into its blackness. The grasp of the veins of heat of the volcano fell away and no longer wrapped Mattie's body. Suddenly she found herself falling through a ceiling of a large room and crashing into something that shattered loudly as it broke into pieces.

"Good God!" Mattie heard someone say in the distance in an English accent. "The bust of Lord Pemberly is ruined!"

Mattie felt a hand reach out to her and pull her up urgently.

"Run!" said Eddie. Eddie, who had landed in front of Mattie, saw there were men close behind them, ready to grab Mattie.

Mattie jumped up and ran behind him. She saw that Geeta, who had landed next to her, was breathing hard as she was catching up to Mattie. Geeta and Mattie hurried toward Eddie.

As they turned a corner, Mattie heard voices yelling, "The vandals are over there! Catch the ruffians!"

𒈨𒌋𒁲𒈨𒌋𒐠

Sir Henry heard the shouts of men and their thunderous boots outside the reading room. He also heard the directives of the senior curator. "Percy! Over there!"

He wondered at the sounds and shook his head in disapproval. Stomping about like cattle in the British Museum! Why would the senior curator allow such departures from decorum? But it was none of his affair, Sir Henry resolved. None. The sooner this newly found letter from the late George Smith to him was opened and read, the sooner he could leave it in this cursed room, locked away from him forever. That he should have even stayed in the room to read it—Sir Henry now thought this was a grave error.

𒈨𒌋𒁲𒈨𒌋𒐠

Mattie and Geeta followed Eddie, who was zigzagging through large halls, turning down one then another. Eddie darted through an open door and quickly motioned for Geeta and Mattie to follow. Behind them they heard a cacophony of sounds—shoes hitting the hard floor, voices raised in their direction. "Go there!" someone said. "I see them turning into the Assyrian collection!"

"We must be in a museum," Geeta said, her voice a whisper interspersed with gulps of air as she tried to catch her breath. Her eyes widened behind her glasses as she attempted to see what surrounded them now, but the light was dim. Geeta considered the accents of the men who were chasing them.

Mattie heard Geeta whisper her hypothesis, "Perhaps in England?"

Eddie, who had flattened himself against the wall, motioned for Mattie and Geeta to be quiet. He was on alert, listening for the sounds of the approaching enemy.

𒀭𒁹𒈨𒀭𒁹

Sir Henry was now held deep in reverie; he thought of the strange rumors about Smith and his increasingly eccentric behaviors. His arthritic hands grasped the unopened letter from Smith. He again wondered about the short life of George Smith; he had been self-taught in Assyriology, with no formal education, and had been from the working class; keeping with the rigidity of the British, that fact should have relegated him at best to the duties of a clerk. His detractors wondered how he had deciphered cuneiform so adeptly. He surely had formed a pact with the devil; this is what was oft said behind Smith's back. These were the whispered accusations, most dismissed as born of jealousy of Smith's peers, who with the right credentials had toiled for years but failed to discover anything of worth.

It was after all George Smith who, after painstakingly putting together the many pieces of the Tablets into coherent form, had deciphered the cuneiform script. He had discovered in those very tablets in 1872 the Chaldean tale of the great flood, which had plunged some into a crisis of faith and strengthened the faith of others. Was it the pagans who had borrowed and altered the biblical tale? Or, if the great flood was described in the ancient tales of Babylonia, did it precede the Old Testament account in Genesis? Sir Henry didn't wish to broach such religious heresy, but George Smith bravely did, speaking as he did when the British prime minister William E. Gladstone himself was present at the 1872 seminal lecture.

Sir Henry thought once more of the whispered accounts by his colleagues of Smith's strange behavior when he had deciphered the Chaldean tale of the deluge, how he had torn off his clothes, as if he were imprisoned by the cloth itself, as if heat had held him. Oh, how he had howled like a creature—half beast, half man—right there in the dignified confines of the British Museum's library of Assyriology. Three expeditions—one too many. And Smith's words in the last letter written to him rang again in Sir Henry's mind. *Incredibly the holder of both Tablets would receive the secret knowledge and in turn control all souls and win forevermore the battle between good and evil. But in which direction?*

Sir Henry's face trembled at Smith's question, and he was brought back to the present. Sir Henry knew that the direction of good or evil was left to the holder of both Tablets. So it became known as well to the naive King ashurn-Bani-pal in the reading of the ancient Tablets in his library that the Dark Master of fifty names, but known best as Marduk, was *not* all-powerful, Marduk who held only one Tablet of Destiny. And the other Tablet? Where was it? Who held it? The doomed King ashurn-Bani-pal didn't know but sought it for himself, but he only became the prisoner of another king now of the underworld, and the Dark Master's beast, Ashurnasirpal II. The pitiless and cruel Ashurnasirpal had once been a king in the mortal realm and even crueler in the netherworld. The warnings were whispered to Sir Henry in 1845 in the nightmares that had awakened him each night on his first venture into excavation. Ashurnasirpal II's ancient reign of suffering was such that his very name still shook the souls of the denizens of the desert, and they spoke in barely audible tones of his curse and the secrets that mortal man should not know, which were held in the Seven Tablets of Creation. These secrets were a deep mystery that could not be understood by mortal man who could only read the surface. For hidden beneath the cuneiform slashes of the Seven Tablets, beneath the words they formed, the grim story of man's fate and Creation. A story that could not be read by mortal man's eyes. and written beneath the tale.

Sir Henry again remembered the terrifying apparition, the creature in his dream on the banks of the Tigris River that appeared before him at the mound of Kuyunjik—the large beast with the stench of death, like a bull with fire that came from its nostrils—but with eyes and aspect of a man's face. The Great Beast had stood on two hooves and barked curses upon him for his theft of the Tablets. *Ashurnasirpal.* The natives digging at the mound had run, and only those from villages afar could be convinced to resume the dig. Sir Henry had let Rassam and others, those who hadn't seen the apparition, persuade him otherwise, dismissing the vision as a hallucination born of the desert heat.

Sir Henry knew better then and in his old age now knew keenly that there was evil within the Tablets—secrets that shouldn't have been unearthed. He hadn't been able, even with his formidable authority, to stop the task George Smith had proposed—to find the missing Twin Tablet, the counterpart to the one Marduk possessed. Smith had said he felt certain that the secret was within the elusive Eleventh Tablet that finished the tale of the great flood and of Gilgamesh and would lead to the other half of Dup Shimati.

With much reluctance Sir Henry had kept his silence in public. Privately he had vociferously argued with Smith to think of his wife and children. He had warned Smith severely. But Smith was young, impetuous, and persistent; he was on a meteoric assent from clerk to curator to sensation of the archaeological world in discovering the tale of the deluge, which would give physical proof to the biblical tale. Smith had declared confidently that he would find the missing pieces of the Gilgamesh tale and the Eleventh Tablet among the ruins of the excavation site and, most important, would become holder of the knowledge of the missing Twin Tablet. "No, Smith. That is precisely what you do not want," Sir Henry had warned. Even the thought sent currents of trepidation through his old body. Sir Henry now thought of how much tragedy through time had followed those who had sought the missing Twin Tablet, forever having the Dark Master at their heels.

𒀭𒌋𒁹𒀭𒁹

Mattie was still catching her breath when Eddie motioned for her and Geeta to follow him into a large adjoining room. All this running around was hard—and scary too with those men chasing them. Mattie herself didn't really like museums a whole lot, and this one sure wasn't changing her opinion. It wasn't that museums were bad or anything, just kind of nerve-wracking. That was it. It was party manners time, walking around in a museum. You had to talk real quiet like and pay attention to speeches about old paintings. Even if you ran into something interesting—like, say, dinosaur bones, not that Mattie ever did—you couldn't touch anything, because everything in a museum was old and rickety and could break, even if you didn't even come near the thing! Like what had just happened! And why were they here? Mattie's heart sprung with a sudden hope; maybe that horrid snake had hidden her mom and dad here! That must be it!

"I think Mom's here," she whispered to Geeta, who leaned farther in to hear as Mattie added, "'Find the flying frog,' Mom said."

Geeta looked at her quizzically. Mattie was about to explain about the dream, but Eddie made an impatient signal for her to be quiet. *Oh, that Eddie!* Mattie thought. *Always so bossy!* Eddie's yellow cowlick stuck up as usual, and his sharp freckled face held determination of purpose. He tilted his head toward the hallway, alert for the sound of their pursuers. But everything was still. For the moment.

Eddie scanned the chamber they were now in, which was dimmer even than the others they had just run through. He could barely see the outlines of Mattie and Geeta nearby. The room was cavernous, with high ceilings and a width that intimidated rather than welcomed. It held a number of glassed cases with books and manuscripts. There was an eerie quiet, as if no one had been in here for years and years. The dust on the glass cases bore witness to the room's lack of use. Mattie and Geeta followed Eddie softly.

In the shadowy light, Eddie spotted what looked like a small door at the side. He went toward it and opened it. It was dark below, but there appeared to be stairs leading downward. "Come on," he said, motioning Mattie and Geeta to follow him down. Once they were in, Eddie grabbed the door to shut it. As he did so, the little illumination they'd had from the large outer room was lost. It was almost pitch black, with the only the dimmest of flickering light coming from somewhere at the bottom of the strange circular staircase. These stairs were stone wedges and not at all like normal stairs; they were flat and deep, so that to go down you had to jump from one to another. Musty smells enveloped them.

Mattie reached for the Spyglass to ask for some light. It lay heavy, cold and silent, within the deep recesses of her pocket. She tried to pull it out, but it wouldn't budge. Mattie shook her head in irritation. What good was it to be Mistress of the Spyglass when the darn thing never listened to you anyways?

They were down four stairs when suddenly the door above flung open. Eddie, Geeta, and Mattie flattened themselves against what there was of the concave wall. Two men, whose silhouettes could be seen against the doorway, were lit by the yellowing daylight that streamed through heavily curtained windows behind them.

They heard one of the men speak. "Take the candle, Percy. Go down and see what you can find."

"Hooligan children, I'd imagine, sir. Tryin' to find a spot o' shelter from the rain. Nothin' more." The man's voice was hesitant, as if he were frightened to venture farther. The weak light from the candle cast shadows down the stairs but fell short of where Eddie, Geeta, and Mattie hid, holding their breaths, their hearts pounding hard.

"Go on, now Percy," they heard the man say. "We can't be letting Sir Layard's collection be vandalized."

They could see the other man's hesitation in the flicker of his candle as it hit the wall. "I dunno know, sir...they say it's haunted down there—curses from them ancient kings for stealin' their sacred tablets. Look how Mr. George Smith died...choked by a... giant fanged monster they say...out in that godforsaken desert!"

"Flights of fancy and sheer nonsense! Smith died of dysentery. There are no ghosts down there. Go on, Percy!"

The children heard Percy's boots on the first step. Mattie felt the dust caught in her nostrils tickling her. Oh, boy. She had to sneeze! Her sneezes weren't quiet or ladylike, like her mom often said, shaking her head. "Just like your father's, like the roar of an angry bull!"

When the sneeze came out, indeed more lion than bull, the sound ricocheted within the small confines of the staircase. Percy yelped in fear and dropped his candle down the staircase as he fled back up. The door above them slammed shut.

Eddie ran up and grabbed the candle that had fallen on its side, the flame faltering but still lit.

Above them they heard the boots of the men as they ran out of the room. Then everything was silent again. Geeta and Mattie looked up at Eddie, who held the candle. His face was lit from below and highlighted the outlines of his skull; he looked more skeleton than boy. "What?" he said. "What's the matter?"

Then behind him appeared bony hands getting ready to push Eddie down the stairs. Eddie saw the frightened look on Mattie and Geeta's faces as they screamed. The skeletal hands grew and grabbed Eddie, and fear was trumped by astonishment. Then the hands flung Eddie down the stairs toward the girls.

Mattie and Geeta lurched as the stone stairs beneath them gave way. Eddie was in a downward nosedive toward them. Together the three were plummeted down the spiral staircase, hitting the walls as they fell. The disembodied skeleton hands followed them, hitting Geeta, Mattie, and Eddie, and plunging them down, down, down.

𒀭𒌋𒐖 𒁹 𒀭𒐖 𒀀

Sir Henry turned to the disturbing last missive of Smith's that now lay in parched sheets in his hands. Much of the letter was written in the slashes of mangled cuneiform, and its content was only known to Smith himself. But one piece was decipherable, read and reread by Sir Henry who trembled, at the message.

I have found the ša nagba īmuru, the story of the unknown myster-
ies, and know now that it is the story of Dup Shimati. It is not as it
was thought. The dark underworld lives. And I fear that I will soon
be plunged and imprisoned beneath the black earth, for the forces of the
Dark Master surround me. I feel the evil breath of the curse of the King of
Ashurnasirpal upon me, his hooves treading on my neck as I awaken in
sweat each night... and see the shadow of the snake behind him.

CHAPTER 5

the seventh king of uruk

When they hit the bottom of the stone stairs, dazed, Mattie looked up first. The bony hands were gone. The stairs melted right in front of them, oozing a greenish light but with bits of red, orange, and purple—a lot like the colors of the crayons Mattie used to melt on the hissing radiator in her room when she was little, just to see what would happen. And now the stones melted into a waxy, oozy hodgepodge of colors, just like her old crayons, until there were no more stairs. Then even the oozy wax was gone.

All three lay sprawled on the cold concrete floor with a great black emptiness between them and the door high above. Mattie was frozen to the ground. She wanted to say this to Geeta, whom she felt was nearby, for she heard her breathing but couldn't see her. Mattie wished desperately that she was smarter, that somehow she could understand what she was supposed to do to find her mom. "Look for the flying frog to find me," her mother had said, but what did that mean? Frogs didn't fly. Mr. Biddle

would know, but who knew where he was? No, Mattie had to figure it out. She scrunched her forehead. How did she, Mattie, who
only just became milk monitor at Fairmount Grammar School
for the fifth-grade lunch, end up Mistress of the Spyglass? Maybe
it was all a mix-up. But no. Mattie thought of the golden sheen
of her skin, of the exquisite robes she had worn. She thought
of how the ancient peoples of Nineveh had called upon her to
lead them, how the enchanting woman spirit had come to her.
She remembered the king in the blue uniform, whose voice was
loud and imposing but whose face was so kind, and the little
shriveled-up old man, whose large ears had veins like blue rivers crossing and crisscrossing. *Daughter.* Mattie heard his faraway
voice before it faded. *Beware.*

Eddie had tried to stand but was held flat to the ground by
a magnetic force. The more he struggled, the more it held him.
He felt the surge of fear; they were trapped! When in enemy
territory—and this was it if there ever was such a case—Eddie
knew from his father the worst thing was to let your guard down,
which is exactly what would happen if the soldier gave way to
fear. Eddie stopped struggling against the force that held him.
The candle had fallen from his hands. There was no light, so he
couldn't see. *But there is another sense, Eddie,* he heard his father's
voice fill his mind, *that a warrior must always make use of.* Sergeant
Petersen told him from afar, *It is the sixth sense, the inner radar. Still
your mind, Eddie, and the answers will come.*

Geeta, nearby, was glued to the ground, just like Mattie and
Eddie. She thought how the atmosphere defined the phrase
"The silence is thick." She had read that before but wondered
how the lack of sound could be described as being thick. But
here it was—silence that filled the air like a dense presence. Her
old ThaTha had told her once that this was what the yogis who

lived within the caves tucked into the snowy mountains knew—
that silence was a presence; it was not the absence of sound. In
fact it was vibrations beyond sound, the call of souls to hear, to
understand what the mind wouldn't allow one to hear, what the
mind with its chatter obscured to the ordinary person. But what
was the message of this silence? Would it lead to Mrs. O'Reilly?
And Dr. O'Reilly? To Mr. Biddle? Geeta strained to understand.

The thoughts of the three came to an abrupt end as the force
that held them to the ground suddenly released them. Mattie,
Eddie, and Geeta were thrown to their feet. The blackness of
the chamber gave way to the light of a full moon—a smoky,
silvery-blue glow that enveloped the cave-like chamber.

The earth below stirred and heaved; the quake flung Mattie,
Geeta, and Eddie back. Then seven giant clay tablets the color
of mustard and streaked with dried blood wrenched themselves
from the earth and rose and formed a circle that trapped the
three in the middle. The engraved writing upon these Seven
Tablets quivered then lifted off the clay itself, freed from the confines of the slabs. The symbols hovered over the Tablets then flew
like swarms of black gnats, attacking Mattie, Geeta, and Eddie.

Instinctively Eddie threw his hands into the air, hitting the symbols as they rushed toward him. Mattie and Geeta wrapped their
arms over their heads as the cuneiform letters thronged around
them. The symbols gave off weird whirring sounds. Mattie's eyes
were wide as saucers; she was afraid, for though she couldn't
understand what the symbols were saying, she felt the full force
of their anger. Geeta's black braids flew back, her thick glasses
askew on her face, and the strange blue light that surrounded
hit her brown face almost smudged it of details. Eddie was in an
attack pose, his knees bent, his fists up, though he flailed helplessly against the onslaught of the swirling ancient words.

The sounds now formed into words of the ancient language of Babylonia and echoed harshly in rage.

Bu-ú šá-ma-mu e-nu-ma e-liš la na
mu-um-mu ti-amat mu-al-li-da
at gim-ri-šú-un
e-nu-ma la šu-pu- e-nu-ma.

Geeta looked puzzled, for she heard the first words and knew they were off in some manner. But how?

The symbols turned and twisted, forming words in an ancient tongue, words that had a chastising tone. The symbols hissed as they swirled around and around Mattie, Eddie, and Geeta, forming an impenetrable force around them. The words now rose into a feverish pitch of wails and scrambled before them again and again.

From the reaches of a deep memory, the Spyglass was now awakened by a grim realization. The Seven Tablets and the story as set forth when time was made—that story of creation itself was in flux! In her inner sanctum, the Spyglass knew that this journey, whatever it was, that had begun with Mattie could only spell her destruction. But the Spyglass was now powerless to fight the fate that was set by the Path of the Virtuous. How the Spyglass bemoaned her decision to choose Mattie as her Mistress! She had given Mattie one of her precious gold bands to save her when the stupid girl had eaten from the Tree in Moreh in Nineveh. Saved her. This, Spyglass realized now had been a mistake. Why had tied herself to this girl. *Mattie Spyglass!* Oh, why! Oh, why! The Spyglass felt the full force of her actions; she had controlled so many people and left them in tatters when they were of no use. Now to be in the grasp of this...this...child!

If only the Spyglass could remember who she was, how she had been imprisoned, and where lay the daughter and the other Twin Tablet of Destiny—then she could be free and escape the chilling destruction that was surely to follow.

The words flew at them again.

> *At gim-ri-šú-un*
> *bu-ú šá-ma-mu e-nu-ma e-liš la na*
> *e-nu-ma la mu-um-mu*
> *šu-pu- e-nu-ma*
> *ti-amat mu-al-li-da*
> *ti-amat mu-al-li-da.*

Hearing the scrambled words, Geeta turned in panic toward Mattie and Eddie. Her memory had clicked. She remembered at once the chants of Mr. Biddle and Dr. Wigglesworth and their correct order.

> *E-nu-ma e-liš la na-bu-ú šá-ma-mu*
> *šap-liš am-ma-tum šu-ma la zak-rat.*

"The words are wrong!" Geeta whispered. "They are not in the right order!"

Eddie heard this intel. "What does that mean?" he whispered back.

In alarm the Spyglass answered through Mattie, whose eyes were closed and whose lips moved as if she were hypnotized. "Chaos."

As if in response, the ancient symbols, now sharp black knives, launched themselves toward the three children who were trapped in the middle of the seven giant Tablets. But the black slashes stopped suddenly before hitting Mattie, Eddie, and Geeta; the symbols turned toward the clay tablets and sunk back into them in haphazard order.

"Cover position!" Eddie barked the order. "Backs to one another!"

Mattie, Geeta, and Eddie formed a tight circle, backs to one another, each facing the immense fortress of the Seven Tablets, which were slowly circling closer and closer toward them.

Eddie cried out, "Down! Get down!"

A great wail sounded. Mattie felt the pain of that wail, a sound coming from anguish and heartbreak. Then from within the Tablets that imprisoned the three emerged a cyclone of words, sounds that turned and twisted and flew over the figures of Mattie, Eddie, and Geeta, who were crouched close to the ground. The words shook them, deep guttural sounds with the force of thunder.

Mi-ttu!

Mi-u-saa-uu!

Eddie tilted his head up from his crouched position, for not to see what was happening was to lose intel, but what was forming in front of them astonished him.

In front of Mattie, from the cyclone of sounds, an image formed. It was a warrior, a man ten feet tall, whose muscular body was clad in gold armor, his legs bare from the knees below, and whose large feet were clad in sandals of a living substance that moved about his feet like sea anemones under murky waters. His face was the color of blue flames. His hair and beard were black ropes that twisted and swayed as he roared at the three and held a golden spear whose tip ended in a pale-green flame; this weapon was pointed right at Mattie.

Mattie's eyes were wide open with fear in the face of the large man; the tip of the spear was so close that she felt its heat. Mattie sensed Eddie quickly move out of their protective circle as he shot up toward the man to deflect the spear away from Mattie.

Geeta cried out, "Eddie, no!"

The warrior grabbed Eddie in one large hand, lifted him by his shirt collar, and shook him like a rag. He pulled Eddie close to his large face; his white teeth were bared and bright against the deep blue of his skin, and his shining brown eyes seethed in fury.

Mattie struggled to pull out the Spyglass, which was lodged tightly in her pocket, and finally wrestled it out, her will overcoming that of the Spyglass. In a panic she pointed the Spyglass at the warrior and screamed, "Back! Back!"

The warrior froze at the sight of the Spyglass. He backed away two steps but held Eddie firmly in his grasp. He roared sounds of the ancient tongue that formed into words that penetrated the minds of Mattie, Eddie, and Geeta.

Mi-ttu!
mi-u-saa-uu!
Divine weapon.
Ma-ttu.
Weak no more!
I rise now, and Enkidu will be avenged!
Ashurnasirpal!

Eddie was shaken; his face paled so much that the freckles stood out like little mustard seeds on a white plate.

Geeta cried out, "Help him, Mattie!"

Mattie screamed, "Spyglass! Destroy the giant!"

From the Spyglass came a beam of light, first faint then strong, that hit the warrior's enormous arm. The giant roared in pain and dropped Eddie.

Eddie scrambled toward Mattie and Geeta. Mattie was breathing hard, her face flushed and sweaty. "Stay behind me, Eddie," she said. "He's scared of me."

The blue warrior swung his huge spear in a half circle, his large feet stomping the ground and shaking it. The Seven Tablets continued to encroach upon them ever closer, encircling them all. Mattie again pointed the Spyglass at the warrior's golden spear, and the beam of light hit the tip of the flame, which sputtered and made horrific hissing and crackling sounds, like those of bones being crunched, before it extinguished.

The warrior cried out in alarm. The beam of the Spyglass now hit the wall of the Seven Tablets, which began to shudder. The Tablets then trembled and shattered into a thousand pieces.

The giant lifted his large hands in despair as pieces of the Tablets rained upon his head, pushing him to the ground. He shouted strange sounds that then formed into words the three understood. "See what it is you have done!"

Eddie yelled at Mattie and Geeta to drop down. The pieces of the Tablets bombarded them as they smashed to the ground. Mattie was crouched beside Geeta and Eddie. She felt the shards hit her arms like pellets.

Eddie called out to Mattie and Geeta, "Roll down! Keep your hands over your head!"

He thought of his dad, way out in Vietnam, deep in the jungle, surrounded by the enemy. He remembered his father's stories of shrapnel falling like rain upon his platoon when they'd hit a booby trap set by the enemy. He had said that going into an area you hadn't reconned first was about the same as walking right into a trap. And this was exactly what Eddie had done, wasn't it? He had led his small platoon of Geeta and Mattie down the stairs and smack dab into a trap! Eddie's heart sank. He had failed to follow the core directive of a leader—to keep his platoon safe.

𒁹𒌋𒁹 𒂍 𒁹𒌋 𒀉

Sir Henry still held George Smith's letter in his hand when the books on the shelves trembled and the artifacts it held shattered to the floor. Beneath him the armchair shook. He stood up in resignation as he greeted the two figures who appeared in succession before him.

"Good afternoon, Wigglesworth. And Biddle."

Sir Henry neither wished for nor wanted wizardry in his life. But since the last excavations of the mound of Kuyunjik in 1854, his life was no longer the ordered set of events a superficial glance might have suggested. In innocence he had removed the Tablets deep from their earthly grave for scholarly study and brought them to the British Museum. But another forbidding thing he had found buried in the mound of Kuyunjik was the strange Spyglass. He would not touch it; in fact he had pushed it deep under the dirt with his shovel, prompted by some primeval instinct that warned him of danger. And he had told no one of his discovery. Then the Spyglass haunted him in his dreams, an apparition at once alluring and horrific that tempted him with unlimited powers, if only he would take possession of it.

Sir Henry had succumbed to the urging of his dreams. He woke in the dead of night and left his tent with soft steps so as not awaken the others, and grabbed a spade from the workers' tools. Then he went to the mound, his head turning furtively backward with each step to make sure he wasn't being followed. Finally he stood at the spot where he had buried the Spyglass. Under a bright moon that lay flat against the black sky, Sir Henry plunged his spade into the earth. There in the kingdom of Iraq, standing on the mound above the ancient city of Nineveh, Austen Henry Layard unearthed the Spyglass. He saw it lying there innocuously, a small metal tube, just a spyglass, and he pondered for a moment his silliness in avoiding this artifact. Then the tarnished metal that was the Spyglass transformed as Sir Henry watched in amazement as it shed its dark patina and three gold bands shone. He heard the voice of the Spyglass beseeching in tone, beckoning him to hold it and to place the glass to his eye. At once Sir Henry felt the magnetic force of its power, which pounded with strength like the currents of a river before it plunges into the falls.

His free hand reached out to touch the Spyglass but then stopped. Unlike the many others the Spyglass had tempted in the centuries upon centuries before, he knew it at once to be the mark of evil, for a great trepidation filled him. Sir Henry knew how wickedness tempted man, how the Dark Master lured through the promise of power and then grabbed one's soul. Stung by the Spyglass's potential for evil, he immediately dropped the spade that held it; to this day he swore he had seen eyes looking out from the thing—eyes that beseeched him, that tried to enter and capture his heart. But Henry had turned away at once. He grabbed sticks and, from his excavation gear, pulled out matches and lit them to the parched wood and watched the flames grow. He then gingerly picked up the Spyglass with the spade and threw it into the flames, watching the sparks of its death, and thought the wretched thing gone, for the Spyglass never appeared again in his dreams. But the memory of its evil lay vivid in his consciousness.

The Tablets from the mound, as promised, were sent to the British Museum. Sir Henry gave up excavation and left the tablets he had unearthed in the bowels of the museum, for he had no stomach for their mysteries. He kept afar from all who talked of the Tablets. Then he learned of George Smith piecing them together from their broken bits. He wondered whether Smith had taken possession of the Spyglass and whether what Smith's detractors had said was true—that the devil had given him the astonishing and sudden brilliance that had led to his discoveries. Sir Henry had kept away from the Tablets and Smith and all that they portended as long as he could—kept away, that is, until the portly professor from the future, L. Rufus Wigglesworth, appeared in his dreams. Then Herman Biddle and Wigglesworth both had beseeched him to help them keep safe a young woman and her child, the wife and issue of an Assyriologist, Paddy O'Reilly. This Paddy O'Reilly had sought the dangerous Eighth Tablet of Creation, the tale buried by the foes of Tiamat...buried by Marduk. And this Paddy O'Reilly had met his death, fatefully similar to that of George Smith, in the year 1957, more than eighty years following Smith's demise in 1876, having found something.

Wizards. Sorcerers. How had Sir Henry so entangled himself with magic? But he had, for he was shown the future in the form of the fate of the young widow and children of George Smith—how they would suffer despite the 150-pound annuity they would receive from the Queen of England; how a shadow would fall upon them and upon the very earth of England itself; how malice was emerging, growing first as the smallest of seeds in the hearts of man, but how it would blossom to sheer evil that was too much to even consider in one thought. The great evil of two apocalyptic wars started by the Dark Master's servants would come. Through their seemingly endless travels in the River of

Time, Biddle and Wigglesworth had tried to stop the onslaught of the chilling events but had failed each time. So often, after one of their visits, Sir Henry had sat deep in his armchair, wondering whether he was slowly going insane. Were they real or hallucinations, these phantoms from the future?

And now it had happened, as Biddle and Wigglesworth had prophesized. George Smith was dead, despite Sir Henry's warning to Smith regarding what could happen. Smith's last letter bore no doubt that he was the victim of the Dark Master.

Sir Henry held out the letter. "From Smith."

Wigglesworth read it and wordlessly passed it to Herman Biddle.

Biddle gazed at the letter, the words registering slowly into his consciousness. His white hair and beard lay flat, his cloak limply about his neck; his expedition clothing, the brown vest, the boots to his knees, were still covered with the red dust of the Third Stone. All of it spoke of resignation. "The shadow of the snake," Biddle read, then thought, *Uri.* What had George Smith found in Nineveh? Something that had angered the Dark Master and invoked the curse of the Great Beast.

Biddle silently handed the letter back to Sir Henry. There was no time for subtleties, as in their past contacts, when Sir Henry had required a patient dissertation upon why he was needed in their efforts. Biddle said plainly, "The Spyglass has reemerged, and our friends are trapped by Marduk's servants in the City of the Condemned that lies below the tunnels of Ashurnasirpal."

Sir Henry took a sharp breath. Of all of Biddle's words, one phrase sent a shiver of primeval fear through him—"The Spyglass has reemerged."

Wigglesworth held the yellowed manuscript out to Sir Henry. "Your study of what is beneath the tunnels of Ashurnasirpal."

Sir Henry quivered and wouldn't touch it. "Please, I have implored you to keep it away, in the future."

Biddle closely watched Sir Henry's reaction and kept to himself the fact that they were now on the treacherous Path of the Virtuous, for it was becoming apparent that with age Sir Henry had greatly lost fortitude, ruled instead by terrors both real and imagined.

Wigglesworth said, "I've done as you asked, Henry. But now we need the knowledge to find our friends."

Sir Henry turned away from the two. Herman Biddle said softly, "Only you have that knowledge, Henry. You must help us."

"No," Sir Henry said vehemently but in a trembling voice. "No more wizardry! It has done no good. Smith lies dead...or worse. I am finished."

Wigglesworth harrumphed his displeasure. "Henry..." he began.

Sir Henry turned toward Wigglesworth, his tone resonating with the finality of his decision, "Do not bother, Wigglesworth. I am firm in my resolution to let the events unfold as they may. My meddling has altered nothing. Perhaps it has hastened or even caused poor George Smith's death. Please leave."

Sir Henry turned his back to Wigglesworth and Biddle. He looked out the small window in the reading room as if intently studying the mist that covered the glass.

Biddle and Wigglesworth exchanged glances. A willing assistant was best. However, best wasn't always possible. Biddle began to swirl his cape when a frantic series of knocks stopped him.

The door opened, and a middle-aged man, with a bushy black mustache and large mutton-leg sideburns, and who was clearly sweaty with exertion, peered anxiously into the room. "Sir Henry!"

Sir Henry was startled by the panic on the man's face and recognized him as the museum's senior curator. "Yes, Carlton?"

The man gasped for breath, "Sir Henry! You must come at once. There's been a disastrous accident—an explosion within the Assyrian antiquities, destroying everything below." The curator now stammered, "In the haunted bowels…deep within the chamber."

The blood drained from Sir Henry's face as he whispered, "Where the Seven Tablets of Creation are held."

𒀭𒇲𒄑𒇲𒁹

Eddie's disappointment at having led his small platoon of Mattie and Geeta right into the jaws of danger loomed large in his mind, but these thoughts soon were swept away by what was forming from the pieces of the shattered Tablets that had disintegrated into a fine dust.

Above them they saw the darkness lift to reveal raging dark water—water that swirled and lifted and hit the walls of the deep chamber. Then from the waters rose a giant creature, a dragon with massive thorns upon its back. The creature writhed in the water and grasped in its tail a small vessel with animals of all sorts teeming from it and a man with a wooly white beard at the helm. "Utnapishtim!" the dragon creature roared at the old man with the white beard. It then flung the vessel into the water, and the old man cried out in agony as he was plunged into its depths. "Gilgamesh," he said, "find me you must, or mankind is lost!"

Mattie felt a coldness rise from the Spyglass within her hands—the coldness that comes with deep fear, and the word again rose from the Spyglass to Mattie's lips, which she unconsciously mouthed. "Chaos."

Geeta heard Mattie and knew at once that it was the Spyglass who had spoken the word again. The images disappeared as quickly as they had come, leaving only a deep blackness above them. But in the dim light of the chamber, Eddie, Geeta, and Mattie saw that the warrior remained. He stomped his monstrous feet and cried in despair as he pulled at the dark ropes of hair that hung to his shoulders.

The giant blue warrior pointed to Mattie and cried in anguish, "You! You have turned the sacred Seven Tablets and their secrets and story of truth into dust! You have caused Utnapishtim to be lost forever!" Sobbing, the huge man fell to his knees, dropping his golden spear and burying his face in his hands. "I who am Gilgamesh, king of Uruk, will never return to save my friend Enkidu, lost now forever to the terrors of the curse of Ashurnasirpal, the Great Beast of the Dark Master!"

The giant—he who called himself Gilgamesh, the king of Uruk—stayed on his knees, his body wracked with sobs. Great tears splashed to the dust beneath his gargantuan feet. Mattie kept the Spyglass pointed at him, but now she felt bad as the giant cried and cried. Mattie really didn't think she had anything to do with that old man on the boat—Mr. Ut...whatever—being lost. That was kind of unfair; she'd never even met him. And those Tablets—she had nothing to do with them breaking; they just fell down all by themselves. That was kind of on the unfair side too. But boy, this giant blue man, this king, sure was upset. The only adult that Mattie had seen cry—and even then it was just tears running down her face—was her mom. But Mattie's mom was a girl, and boys—men—don't cry. So this was unusual and made her feel super, super bad.

Mattie heard her mother's voice from afar. *Be kind to those in pain, Mattie.* She stepped forward without thinking, hearing

Eddie in the background shouting at her, "Stay back! Don't approach the subject," and put her hand on the giant man's wooly head of ropes and patted him like he was a great big Saint Bernard.

The giant warrior felt the child's concern, but it could not ease his distress, so enveloped was he in the tragedy of his fate and that of his dear friend Enkidu, who was forever lost.

Geeta considered the scene of the flood, the dragon, and the small vessel with the creatures and the old man that had come before them and disappeared. The word that Mattie had spoken—coming from the Spyglass, she was sure—was *chaos*. Geeta's mind reached back to when she had been enrolled at the Auxilium Convent School run by Catholic nuns in Bombay, India, before her family had moved to Hackensack. She thought of the lessons in the Old and New Testament that even the Hindu students at the school were taught. In Genesis, God was sorry that he had created man, whose heart was evil, and sought to destroy his creation—all but one man and his family, Geeta remembered. It was Noah and his family who were spared. This must be the tale of Noah and the Ark and the great flood, Geeta thought, but wasn't Noah supposed to survive so that mankind lived on? Her eyes widened with the sudden knowledge of the meaning of the scrambled tale of creation and the word uttered by the Spyglass—*chaos*. "The flood," she said, turning to Mattie. But Mattie didn't hear her, as she was absorbed in the plight of the giant.

Eddie was too flabbergasted to say anything. Leave it to Mattie to pat a giant enemy like he was some sort of big friendly dog! Eddie maintained his defensive pose, his fists up, and bemoaned that yet again he had no weapons whatsoever.

The warrior's humongous body shook in grief.

"It's OK. I'm sure that old man isn't really lost at all," Mattie said in soothing tones, as she continued to pat the giant's wooly head. "And there's gotta be more of those clay things around here—museums collect that kind of junk. Right, Eddie? Geeta?"

Geeta's mind took in the word *chaos* and considered it once more. This is what she remembered Dr. Wigglesworth had said on the Second Stone, that time was set asunder and that order was no longer possible. If the story of creation didn't exist, how could they exist? Geeta thought of the gypsies and Rasputin, of the figure of Tsar Nicolas as martyr and his words—that the story of creation was to be rewritten. Time and events were now scrambled, not following one after the other but turned topsy-turvy, maybe even overlapping one another. Geeta's mind took in this thought and its implications. How would they ever find Mattie's parents and Mr. Biddle? Chaos! Geeta's owl eyes registered now in shock at the recognition of the enormity of the events. "But Mattie—" Geeta said, before her words were cut off by Eddie.

"Sure, Mattie," Eddie said slowly, a plan forming his mind. He eyed the giant warrior's fallen golden spear, the flame on the tip now extinguished, lying there for the taking, if only Eddie could get to it.

Eddie saw that the warrior giant wasn't paying attention to his fallen weapon. Now was the time to act. He swooped in and, in one quick move, grabbed the spear, which was long—maybe even eight feet, he estimated—and thick around. The gold of the spear shimmered under his hands, and Eddie felt a power, a current run under his fingers. He grunted, for the spear was heavy. With some difficulty he lifted it, being tilted forward by its weight, but still in triumph, and pointed it at the warrior giant.

"Stay back!" Eddie commanded. "And don't make any sudden moves."

The king of Uruk looked up, astonished. The yellow-haired boy was a *muktablu*, a warrior! For only true warriors could touch the sacred spear given to him by Kingu and not be killed, formed as it was in ancient times by the gods and strengthened in power through eons by the bravery of the pure hearted.

"Oh, Eddie!" Mattie said. "Cut it out."

The warrior's face formed a small smile at Eddie's temerity; he felt the admiration one does for another brave soul; still the boy was a young *muktablu* with much to learn, for despite his fierce determination, he was weighed down impossibly by the heavy spear.

"Young warrior," the king of Uruk said, amused, "do you plan to impale me with my own spear?"

Eddie paused. He really didn't know what he was going to do, but he didn't plan to give up the advantage. He struggled with the golden spear as he pointed it at the giant. "Back!" Eddie barked.

Eddie balanced himself as much as he could. But the spear was awkward and way too heavy for him. He stumbled back from the weight and fell onto the dusty remains of the Seven Tablets, his feet up in the air.

The warrior king laughed—a laugh that rumbled through his body, though it wasn't enough to overcome his sadness. He stood up and helped Eddie balance the gigantic spear.

"Young warrior, *muktablu*," the king of Uruk said. "I, Gilgamesh, king of Uruk, also was as stubborn and filled with valor as you. But no more. For I have failed in every task given to me—to restore the story of the truth of the sacred Tablets, to save my people of Uruk, and to rescue my friend Enkidu—as I have lain trapped within these stones for the eons while all have perished."

The king of Uruk's eyes brimmed again with tears as he wailed, recalling that the sacred Tablets were now only dust and fragments and Utnapishtim was lost within the deep seas. "Oh, Enkidu! Friend, how I have failed you!"

Eddie kept his eyes unwaveringly on the warrior as he grappled again with the spear. The giant had said he was a king. "King of Uruk," he had said, for Eddie, despite his tumble, still held on to the intel. What was the king of Uruk?

Eddie pulled the spear back and fell right onto his rump again. He felt the sting of Mattie and Geeta's laughter; leave it girls to think battling with the enemy combatant was funny.

"Ouch!" Eddie cried out, as he felt something pierce his back and stick to his shirt. He pulled the thing off.

𒁹𒁶𒁺𒁹𒁶𒁹

Biddle and Wigglesworth hurried behind Sir Henry to the antiquities section of the British Museum. Sir Henry saw a middle-aged man trembling in the hall and guarding the closed door to the room that led to the chamber below that once had held the Seven Tablets.

"Percy!" said Carlton, the senior curator. "Tell Sir Henry what happened."

Percy said miserably, "All ruined, sir."

"How?" Sir Henry, asked turning to Carlton.

"We thought at first vandals, but the explosion was too fierce," said Carlton. "Three hooligan children ran this way: a red-haired girl, a yellow-haired boy, and a brown Indian girl, all dressed most peculiarly."

Herman Biddle's face fell in realization. Wigglesworth gasped.

"What is it?" Sir Henry asked, turning to the two.

Biddle turned toward the closed door that led to the chamber. "We must go down there. Now!"

𒐖𒀯𒐖𒀯𒐖 𒐖

In the blue light of the chamber, Geeta gazed at the small stone piece in Eddie's hand. "What is that, Eddie?" she asked. "May I examine it?"

Eddie handed the piece to Geeta as he stood up.

Mattie peered at the fragment in Geeta's hand. "That's that funny writing," she said.

Geeta continued her examination of the fragment. "It is in cuneiform." She held it up.

The king of Uruk bent forward, and his giant brows knit in together.

"Look," Eddie said. The small stone piece flew out of Geeta's hand and hovered in the air high above them.

The king of Uruk tilted his head up. "It is a fragment from the sacred Tablets."

The cuneiform letters rose from the small piece and formed words in the air.

𒐖𒀯𒐖𒀯𒐖 𒐖

Carlton and Percy moved away from the door, as Sir Henry, Herman Biddle, and Wigglesworth went toward it.

Percy cried out in warning, "There's ghosts there, sir!"

The door flung open on its own accord to reveal a deep blackness. In an instant the blackness rose like a substance, enveloping Wigglesworth, Biddle, and Sir Henry, then plunged them into darkness. The door then disappeared, leaving only a blank wall where once there had been an opening.

Dumbfounded, Percy and Carlton stared at each other. "Sir Henry!" Carlton called, as he banged on the wall. The room quaked and heaved, and the two men were hurled to the floor, hitting it and falling unconscious.

𒁹𒌋𒌋𒁹𒌋𒁹

"Dup Shimati," Gilgamesh, the warrior king of Uruk pronounced, and his face turned first the purplish blue of ripened plums then was drained pale by fear. "Dup Shimati," he whispered.

Mattie was drawn to the words that floated above them, first slashes then a whispering magical chant that hypnotized her. She felt her feet lift off the floor toward the cuneiform slashes that glowed beckoningly.

Geeta tilted her head back. *Dup Shimati.* She had heard these very words uttered by the old woman when she had torn the page from the Small Book of Spells in the gypsy encampment.

"Hey!" Eddie said, trying to reach Mattie to pull her down, but as he did, a current of air lifted him toward the words. He saw Geeta floating beyond him, up toward Mattie. The chamber that had seemed so cave-like now had no ceiling, only a dark and unending starless sky. Even the king, the great giant, with all his weight and heavy spear, was lifted by the current of air as if he were nothing more than a piece of fluff and flew toward and into the black night sky.

Herman Biddle, Wigglesworth, and Sir Henry landed with a thud onto the floor of the chamber, which was covered with the dust of the Tablets. All three saw Mattie, Geeta, and Eddie, and the strange blue giant flying above them, being sucked up into a dark vortex.

Biddle attempted to lift his cloak to fly up but was held down by a force that pinned him to the chamber floor. He struggled, and even the chant he tried to call out stayed lodged in his throat. Wigglesworth's three chins shook in frustration as he tried to lift his flabby arms to call a chant, but it was to no avail, as each attempt only further pinned him to the floor.

Eddie, the last of the four flying up, looked down and glimpsed Mr. Biddle, Dr. Wigglesworth, and some other old man below. It was important that Mr. Biddle have their grid coordinates. Eddie yelled to Mr. Biddle, "Coordinates—Dup Shimati! Enemy combatant—king of Uruk," as he disappeared into the black sky above with Mattie, Geeta, and the king.

The black sky suddenly disappeared, and in its place all that was left was the ceiling of the chamber within the bowels of the British Museum. Beneath the feet of the three old men were the crushed remains of the Seven Tablets.

Herman Biddle's face trembled in agony. Wigglesworth knew at once the thoughts that crossed his old friend's mind—the treacherous and unrelenting whims of the Path of the Virtuous that threw one like flotsam upon raging waters, an arduous path that Mattie, Eddie, and Geeta would each face alone.

"Wigglesworth," Biddle said, his words quivering with anxiety, "you must find Dottie and Paddy without me. I must search for the three innocents whom I have let become lost on the Path."

Wigglesworth shook his head dolefully. "Biddle, do you not understand?" He glanced at Sir Henry to see if he was listening, but Sir Henry was in another world, his face furrowed as he knelt on floor, his trembling fingers gingerly touching the powdery remains of the destroyed Seven Tablets. Wigglesworth whispered, "The Path of the Virtuous sets its own course. You cannot alter it."

Biddle hurriedly began to untie his cloak. "Please, Rufus, don't argue with me. Take this for protection. I have a few Cards of Time in my pockets, and I also have my staff."

Biddle continued to grapple with his cloak, whose color now turned from drab gray to a vibrant brown of the rich earth, then green and yellow, and glowed. However, it wouldn't fall from his shoulders, struggled though he did to remove it. Herman Biddle then stopped. It was futile; the Path of the Virtuous wouldn't allow it. He turned to Wigglesworth and said, "Rufus, let us chant the incantation, the Spell of Prophecy. Perhaps it will lead us to the children."

Wigglesworth again looked to see whether Sir Henry had heard, but he hadn't, so engrossed was he by the dusty remains of the Seven Tablets. Wigglesworth shook his head glumly and whispered, "The Path of the Virtuous can't be read by prophecy. It is written as it is lived." Biddle's shoulders fell in resignation.

Sir Henry was pondering the fate of the Seven Tablets. He scooped again the fine dust that remained of the Tablets and held in it in his hands. "All of which remains of the Seven Tablets that told the tale of man's creation," he murmured to himself and thought of the toil it had taken to unearth the Tablets and bring them to the British Museum, the agony of body and mind. Beyond him Sir Henry heard the urgency but not the words in the whispered communications between Biddle and Wigglesworth; it was something dire, he knew, for what else would the destruction of the ancient Tablets of Creation mean for the fate of humanity? Sir Henry knew the Tablets were more than just artifacts; they held power. No, they held magic—dark magic. And what did this mean to those who had perpetrated their destruction? Sir Henry felt the current of dark forces vibrate from the dust of the Tablets and shuddered. He knew that whatever the content of the whispered discussion between Biddle and Wigglesworth was, there was no doubt that it spoke of both the seriousness and treachery of the journey. He tilted his head toward Biddle and Wigglesworth and heard their words.

Biddle pulled out a Card of Time. "Wigglesworth," he said, "we must find Eddie, Geeta, and Mattie somehow, maybe traversing these Cards of Time."

Wigglesworth unhappily shook his head again. "Time is in chaos. It may no longer exist as depicted in your cards."

Biddle's shoulders slumped, and he said in anguish, "How will we ever find them now? No. I can't leave them lost to its horrors. I can't!"

Clapping his hands free of the dust, Sir Henry stood. He turned to Biddle and Wigglesworth and said, "You seek the children as well now?"

Biddle and Wigglesworth turned to him, their eyes holding apprehension. "Yes," Biddle said.

Sir Henry paused then said, "The boy mentioned something about the king of Uruk. If he is with this king, your paths are the same."

Biddle said to Sir Henry in puzzlement, "The king of Uruk searches for the City of the Condemned?"

"Yes," Sir Henry said. "It is what is deciphered in *that*." He trembled as he pointed to the yellowed manuscript that Wigglesworth clutched to his chest. He continued, "To find his lost friend, Enkidu."

Wigglesworth said immediately, "Let us not dawdle then."

Biddle began the chant, joined by Wigglesworth, and cried out:

E-nu-ma e-liš la na-bu-ú šá-ma-mu
šap-liš am-ma-tum šu-ma la zak-rat.

Sir Henry remained resolutely silent. Then, in his bosom, he perceived a rising shame. "*Your* journey," he had said, clearly informing Biddle and Wigglesworth that he would have no part in it. Oh, how had he become such a coward? A coward who would shirk duty when the fate of three children lay at risk, and the fate of good as well. Sir Henry felt a sharp desire to be brave again, as he had been in youth. He felt in his blood something stirring, something akin to an aching longing to move beyond the confines of cowardice, where he had hidden for so many decades. As if in answer to this longing for bravery, from his throat suddenly sprang the chant and the deep sound of his voice adding to the force of the chant begun by Wigglesworth and Biddle.

E-nu-ma e-liš la na-bu-ú šá-ma-mu
šap-liš am-ma-tum šu-ma la zak-rat.

The dust on the ground rose like a tornado of wrath and surrounded the three in a whirlwind of grayish-yellow powder. A flash of light enveloped the room, and into this light, Sir Henry, L. Rufus Wigglesworth, and Herman Biddle disappeared.

CHAPTER 6

the forging of stal

Uri Gneezy's sleeping bony frame stirred as the cold Siberian winds blew through the shack where he lay. The cold was nothing to him, for death had chilled the blood that flowed in him long ago. But the skeletal body of his human frame (or even when he was in it, the serpentine one, whichever he inhabited) was still subject to the curse of physical pain. This pain shook his body and slowly brought him back to consciousness. It was a torture he'd endured through the ages, a punishment for his failure to capture the Spyglass set before him by the Dark Master. Hate now crossed Uri Gneezy's thin face. His one blue eye and the other green glowed in anger. This victory had eluded him because of his *brother*, a word he spat out. *Dmitri, Biddle, or whatever name you go by now, I shall destroy you. Mark my words—you shall live no more.* Gneezy thought of how sweet the capture would be and how the deepest and worst of the circles of hell should be reserved for Herman Biddle.

Gneezy realized that the game had changed. Now that Biddle had been flung upon the Path of the Virtuous, he had no more control than Gneezy over time. The Cards of Time that the sniveling and cowardly Biddle had thrown to hide from him were no longer protection. The red-haired child had turned the tide in the first battles, bringing to the forces of light souls that once had belonged to the Dark Master and worse yet turning time asunder. Gneezy felt the current of uncertainty surround him. Time was in flux. Events that were may not be. But the story, all of it, could be rewritten to the Dark Master's favor. But first Gneezy needed to capture the Spyglass. And to do so, he realized, his mind reeling now at all these thoughts, he would need to enter the frightening lair of the treasonous beast Ashurnasirpal, for the red-haired child would be lured there by the prey, her precious parents. To do so, Gneezy knew he needed forces to battle those who served and protected the Great Beast in the City of the Condemned.

Uri Gneezy writhed, twisting his head, which now shed its human face and turned serpentine in form, the terrifying triangular form of a cobra, but his body remain human in form. Gneezy's snake eyes, the blue and the green, narrowed in thought. How? If time could be changed—*was* changed—where and how could he harness the wicked? They were many in form, but they were scattered over history. Some, Gneezy knew, lay in the power of the beast Ashurnasirpal, for the snake had heard faint whispers that those held within the City of the Condemened were ruled with not one but four fists, the biggest of which was Ashurnasirpal. But there was one whose heart beat like his, for he had seen this one as he had traversed the Path of Time, chasing Biddle when he thought he'd had the Spyglass. He cursed Biddle and that fat man with the three chins who had tried to meddle with time in order to undo the flourishing seed of evil planted in the heart of man but never succeeded. There was one whom he knew could be controlled but only if brought under dominion when young and raw. But the window of opportunity was narrow—one time, one place. If this one could be brought under Gneezy's rule, then the millions upon millions that had followed him would be under Gneezy's control. Surely this would be enough of a force to defeat any opposition provided by Ashurnasirpal and his minions.

Gneezy's form, that of a snake head over a bony, old human body, was slight, and he stood unsteadily on his frail human legs as he tilted his snake head back. From his mouth the black snake tongue sprang out, its forked tip dripping with evil. Leathery, undulating reptilian scales flew from it and formed into the large Black Book of Magic. It fluttered open over Uri Gneezy, its pages emitting the stink of decay and death. And from it was hurled the Crone, who fell to the ground on her knees.

"Master," she said sneeringly, as she looked upon the form before her, her gnarled hands clawing at the dirt floor as she tried to rise. The Crone saw the snake head over the thin and weak body of an old man, with its blue eye and green eye glittering at her. The Crone's back was humped, her mouth open with one snaggly yellow tooth sprouting as she spoke. If ugliness could reach a peak, it had done so surely in the visage of the Crone, whose face oozed yellow puss from numerous erupting boils about her chin and forehead and whose hair was a grizzled mass of gray. The Crone never had accepted Gneezy as her master; she held him still in her mind's eye as the small Russian boy greedy for power who had come to her hut by the gypsy camp, seeking her counsel and bowing to her authority. She who once had held the Black Book of Magic and whose

spells were once under her command now had to bow to this...
this snake. In her heart she had felt the tantalizing closeness of
breaking free of his hold when the Dark Master had spoken,
for if Gneezy could capture the Spyglass, she could have both
her beauty and freedom back. Here the Crone sighed.

Gneezy's blue eye and green eye took in the Crone. Her
thoughts were known to him, for he possessed her and was her
master. She couldn't act in treachery against him like the Great
Beast, much as she might want. For that reason she was an instrument he could use without fear.

"Crone," Gneezy said softly, but under the softness was a
sharp viciousness. It cut through the Crone, for she knew whatever the snake asked of her she would be compelled to obey,
and the snake's soft voice only belied his cruelty. "You shall go
forth, backward into the blackness of time, to find a Georgian
cobbler's son, one who is called Iosif."

The Crone said nothing, though she stood now, her body
reflecting a bent supplication to the snake. She kept her humped
back down and lowered her face even farther into her sagging
chest. She thought of how the snake had tortured her with giving
her beauty back to her only to snatch it away. A thing yearned for
but not actualized dims in memory, but to have it again, as she'd
had her beauty, and then to be robbed of it—the heartache of it
was almost too much for her to bear. She moaned, almost unconsciously, a small murmur of pain.

Gneezy saw all of this and was pleased, for here in the Crone
he had full control. There seemed no dimming in the foolish old
woman's yearning for such a trivial thing as physical beauty. Oh,
how cheaply he had purchased her soul!

"We must make certain this boy's heart turns black, as it was
written," Gneezy continued, "for before the River of Time was

set to chaos by the red-haired child—she who now possesses the Spyglass stolen from our master—it was written that this boy Iosif, when he became a man, would boast he was made of *Stal*. It was written that this Stal would rule with brutality and turn one against another, and our master would reap their souls to fill the Book of the Dead."

Gneezy began to change form again. His body slowly extended and turned a sickly sleek green as the scales of his serpentine self emerged; his human legs writhed and formed into the long, undulating shape of a giant snake.

Stal. The Crone raised her eyes now to the snake Gneezy, whose reptilian form was loathsome to bear witness to. "Stal," the Crone said aloud and knew whom Gneezy meant—a boy who had been much like Uri himself. It was a wonder, the Crone thought, that it wasn't Iosif and Uri who had shared a womb, so alike were they. It was written that this Stal one day would grip the people of Russia in fear, turn one against the other, and the master would grow strong in souls under Stal's reign of cruelty. She shivered with sudden knowledge as the realization hit her. The River of Time was roiling in chaos. What was written may not be. Stal could be diverted by the currents of time into obscurity; if so, the hold of the Dark Master upon the souls of the earth would be lost. And if the Crone failed in what the snake had asked, what then? She knew the depths of the Dark Master's anger and how depraved and cruel his punishment could be.

Gneezy's face was a mass of scales, and the blue eye and green eye in turn flashed their evil glares upon the Crone. The snake hissed, "He, this Stal *must* belong to our master. His fate cannot be altered."

Gneezy loomed over the humped body of the Crone, his snake head twisting about, and his tongue hit the Black Book of

Magic, flipping page upon page, some muddled and smeared, others still clear, until it stopped. A page lifted from the Black Book and filled the small shack with its images—that of the town of Gori in the Russian province of Georgia in 1890. The church steeples, the small buildings, the cold winter of Gori as people bustled against the wind. The images took over the small wooden hovel until the Crone felt snake's presence recede.

She gasped in pain as her body shrunk, and then her consciousness emerged from the eyes of an eleven-year-old girl. The girl's soul pushed back as the Crone asserted her will over the child. The Crone looked down and noticed she was wearing a long, dark, wool skirt and a coat with a fur collar as she stood on a street outside a small church. She was holding a woman's hand as they walked along briskly.

"Don't dawdle, Trina," the woman said, in response to the girl's jerk of her body as the Crone full took control over the child.

𒀭𒅅𒁹𒀭𒁹

A short boy at the cusp of adolescence, with a pockmarked face, his dark hair combed back to one side, was cornered in the church school room by several other boys who mercilessly taunted him. The boy's fear was so strong that it rose like a stink that filled the room with its scent. This boy, Iosif, in worn and tattered clothes, swallowed his fright, and a fierce expression of defiance crossed his face. His hands were in fists at his side, but he didn't raise them to defend himself. The voice of his mother, Keke, rang in his ears. *He who is slow to anger is better than the mighty, so say the Proverbs, Iosif. Keep still in anger, and turn the other cheek, and the Lord will bless you.* Iosif attended the Gori Church

School only through Keke's begging to the church, which had relented and allowed the boy into the school, in exchange for which Keke scrubbed the school's floors each week.

"Pocky!" one of the taunters yelled out.

Iosif pushed his head down and drove through the clot of boys, their fists hitting him on all sides. He heard their laughter. "He's nothing but a filthy, lice-ridden coward! He drinks the dirty water his mother brings home after cleaning the floors!"

Iosif felt their blows, but they were nothing to a boy whose young life knew only the steady fall of beatings from a drunken father. *Be strong as steel,* he told himself, as the blows fell upon him. *You are Stal...steel.* And with that he withstood the pain, let it bounce off his body and away from his psyche. He would be strong, he resolved; he was Stal and wouldn't become a sniveling beggar for mercy. His mother also had been a victim to her husband's foul temper and brutal rages. But she bore it with piety. And often, after the blows, she'd sit close with Iosif, bathing his wounds in cold cloth and whispering to him that he would one day be a bishop, that like Job they had to bear the trials that God threw their way. *Behold—happy is the man whom God corrects; therefore do not despise the chastening of the Almighty.* And it was true that Keke had found a way to place Iosif in the Gori Church School, among the children of the rich, where his tattered clothing and dirty nails marked him as different. He bore their taunts, for they were nothing in comparison to what his father's rages held. But Iosif couldn't hold in his heart Keke's piety, for why did they have to have so much misery while others had so much fortune? "He who heeds the word wisely will find good, and whoever trusts in the Lord, happy is he," Keke would say quietly. Still, Iosif kept his doubts to himself and studied hard in the Gori Church School—studied and endured the daily mockings from the schoolboys.

He knew that to relent to their taunts and turn a fist against them would only mean expulsion. *Be strong. You are Stal,* he told himself. *Someday you will crush them with your strong hands.*

Iosif ran and pushed open the door at the front of the church school. He barreled outside, and as he did, he crashed into a young girl then fell to the ground. Iosif looked up and saw for a moment only the girl's angelic face. *Trina.* Her name floated in his mind, and his eyes took in her enchanting, pale, oval face; the light-hazel eyes with dashes of green; and her hair, sheening like polished dark wood, so smooth, thick, and luxuriant, held back by a ribbon. *Trina.* Iosif was mesmerized.

The girl's governess frowned at the boy. "Iosif!" she barked, and the girl herself looked startled. Iosif gathered himself up as the other boys tumbled out of the school.

"Trina!" the Crone heard one of the boys call to her. "Pocky wants to marry you!" Loud peals of laughter erupted.

Iosif scrambled up and turned to Trina, his eyebrows arched in suspicion. What the boys had said was true. The Crone, now looking out through the eyes of Trina, could readily read this in the boy's face; Iosif's eyes showed that he was enamored with her. Though the Crone couldn't see her face, she knew she must be beautiful again by the manner in which Iosif stared at her longingly. And she must also be rich, for the wool of her skirt was fine and well woven. She was a lovely rich girl who was loved by this small, poor, ugly boy. The Crone felt a wave of relief. She wouldn't disappoint the snake Gneezy. A slight smile formed on her lips. Soon her own beauty would be restored. This would be easy.

Inside the dingy wooden Siberian shack, the ground shook, and from the pages of the Black Book of Magic, the Iron Knight, once known as Goering, second-in-command of Hitler's Third Reich and now just a slave to the snake, was hurled out of the book to the dusty floor of the hovel. The Iron Knight scrambled up. He still wore the uniform of the Nazis: the medals upon his breast, the dreadful band with the swastika circling his forearm, the tightly cinched broad black belt across his waist—all of which spoke of his imperious nature; he was once commander of the Gestapo. His body had been running to fat, but the uniform covered the obesity well, or so the Iron Knight in his conceit believed.

"Master," he declared simply, and bowed to the snake Gneezy, whose cobra-shaped head loomed above him. The snake's tail coiled around the Iron Knight and lifted him into the air.

"See!" the snake screamed. Then images fell from the Black Book of Magic: deep, dark tunnels and beneath them darker caverns; dreadful beasts, half humans who clung screaming to the walls of dark chambers; locusts and leeches feasting upon their wasted bodies; dark and oily waters rising beneath the prisoners; snakes and creatures with octopus arms grabbing and choking them; then, deeper still, chambers upon chambers of tortured souls in circle upon deeper circle of horrors.

The Iron Knight recoiled. The images fell away. Gneezy squeezed the body of the Iron Knight, whose face reddened. His handsome features were marred by the marks of lashes upon his cheek—lashes he had taken upon his person by the army of the beast Ashurnasirpal.

"The City of the Condemned," Gneezy spat out, "controlled by the treacherous Ashurnasirapal. He has stolen our prey and keeps them imprisoned deep in the chambers of the City of the Condemened, where there is no escape, waiting to ensare the red-haired child who holds the Spyglass and will surely come to rescue her parents. Then he will capture the Spyglass, and the Dark Master will bestow upon the beast all that should be mine!"

The snake strengthend his grip upon the Iron Knight, who resisted the urge to scream in pain. He saw the snake register this and appear pleased, for the reptile loosened his grip.

"Master," the Iron Knight gasped. "It will not be so."

Gneezy's cobra head swiveled again. "Speak," he hissed.

The snake uncoiled itself and flung the Iron Knight to the ground. He stood up and gazed at the hideous, sickening, green-scaled specter of the snake right in the eye. The Iron Knight knew that to succeed he had to be forceful—he, hero of the Great War, one of the noble race. He, Iron Knight, once president of the Reichstag, ace fighter pilot, Blue Max. He was a warrior and strate-gist, the Iron Knight thought with his usual arrogant self-satisfaction, and the snake wasn't. Uri Gneezy read these thoughts with his own satisfaction. Arrogance and ego were easily manipulated; he could readily control the Iron Knight through flattery.

"The beast believes he has the upper hand. Let him think that," the Iron Knight said decisively. "We'll let him lure the red-haired child who holds the Spyglass into his trap." He paused then continued, "I plan to storm of the City of the Condemned, but to achieve success, I need more forces. We must be enlarged beyond that of our remaining regiments from the Third Reich."

Gneezy narrowed his eyes and hissed in agreement, "Yes. All the Russian forces—they shall be taken." The snake took in how the lure of great power shook the Iron Knight and added with a small manipulative smile, "For your command." He saw how the Iron Knight responded to this prospect of power and thought it was well that he had kept him at his side. This fool would be useful to him; he was so easily read and controlled.

The Iron Knight thought of the thrill of commanding an army again; the swelling waves of adrenaline through his body strenghtened him. He had done this before and would do it again. He was born for war, and now he would command all of the Russian army, instead of that pompous, backstabbing little man—"Stal," he called himself, made of steel. Ha! Steel! He, Goering, was made of iron and would hold the reins of the power of the Russian army, gathered across time and under his command. That was the plan—the grand plan.

The Iron Knight spoke, pacing now in the small space of the hovel and invigorated by the thought of the hunt for the prey, for the hunt was the best part. "Good. We'll build our strength from the Russian army, forces a thousand—no, ten thousand—times the strength of the beast and storm the City of the Condemned! We will capture the Spyglass and crush the beast, and all will be yours, Master." The Iron Knight now added a bow, a touch of drama he felt subtly underscored the point of his brilliance with the show of a small gesture of humility.

Uri Gneezy's blue eye and green eye in turn glittered at the anticipation of crushing the beast Ashurnasirapal and imprisoning him in the worst of the chambers of the City of the Condemned; Ashurnasirpal's treacherous behavior would be severely punished.

The snake hissed his pleasure. "Ten thousand times strong," he repeated. The long, black, forked tongue lashed the air and hit the Black Book of Magic. From its pages flew out a baton— a long tube of ivory, covered with gold-and-silver knives and embedded with gold snakes and scorpions that were inlaid with precious stones. On each end was a black snake, entwined to form the symbol of the swastika. The baton flew down and landed in the Iron Knight's hand.

"Commander," the snake hissed.

The Iron Knight grabbed it tightly, and his eyes shone with pride. "The reichsmarshcall's baton." He snapped to attention, holding the baton at an angle across his chest, his eyes bright with the anticipation of the conquest.

"Come," the snake Gneezy said. He snatched the Black Book of Magic with his mouth and swallowed it whole. Then he grabbed the Iron Knight with his tail as he dove into the dirt floor, deep into the earth.

𒁹𒐀𒁹 𒄩 𒁹𒐀 𒉀

Iosif saw the fetching Trina's eyes upon him as he stood up. He felt the red heat of shame, for he knew the boys' taunts were true. How could he—poor, small, pockmarked, and ugly—hold such thoughts about the rich and lovely Trina?

Trina's governess had let her hand go and was walking into a nearby shop. "Come, Trina," she said from the shop's door as she was stepping inside. "Look at these gorgeous frocks!"

The Crone smiled at Iosif and remained where she was, instead of following her governess.

One of the boys, seeing the opportunity that the governess's absence provided, pushed Iosif against Trina and laughed as he bumped clumsily into her yet again. Iosif felt the shame.

"*Bodishi.*" He muttered "sorry" in Georgian to Trina, his head down.

The opportunity to ensare the boy couldn't be lost, thought the Crone, for time was short—who knew when the snake would come for her? But this boy, Iosif, surely had a fierce scowl, for he wasn't melting under her smile. The Crone, as Trina, frowned. It had been a long time since she had been a young girl, and charming a boy like this, an undomesticated wild one with rage surging through his veins, was proving to be difficult. The Crone needed to hypnotize this boy into a lovesick swoon. "Iosif," she said in her most melodious voice and fluttered her eyes.

Iosif felt his heart jump...could it be that the beautiful Trina could love him? Trina was smiling *at him!* Iosif saw another boy—a rich boy, Koba, with blond hair and good clothes—look at Iosif with jealousy, and he knew Koba also had seen Trina's look of love cast at him, the lowly and poor Iosif! Perhaps it was as his mother, Keke, had said; God would now cast good fortune upon him, and Trina's love was the first sign. Iosif's heart beat with hope that Trina indeed had returned his love.

"Look how he loves her! Like an ugly dog licking at her feet!" Koba sneered. The other schoolboys made woofing sounds like dogs. Jeering laughter followed. Koba then savagely kicked Iosif in his back. "Pig," he said to Iosif.

He heard Trina cry out in alarm. As Iosif dropped to the ground, the boys' laughter rang out and stung like whips on his ego; anger flooded his veins, and he could take no more. To be humiliated in front of Trina was too much, especially when there was the hope that she could love him. He couldn't be weak and passive like a lamb; that would only spur Trina's contempt. No. He must act with strength. Iosif jumped up and pushed a boy named Pavle near him, who, startled by the act from the always passive Iosif, pushed back hard. Iosif butted his head into the chin of this Pavle, who was bigger than him, and hit the target hard. He heard the mocking tone of the boys, their words in snippets—"Dirty Pocky thinks he can love Trina!" Anger flowed through him at these words. And all the anger he had held back when the blows of his father had fallen over him, when he'd had to sit meek and mild in the face of bullying at Gori Church School—all of it broke loose. *I am as strong as steel! I am Stal!* Iosif punched Pavle in the face, hitting his nose hard, and heard the satisfying crunch of his nose breaking. The boy howled in pain as blood poured down his face. Iosif then brutally kicked the boy in the stomach and beat him and beat him, the sound of his fists pounding hard upon Pavle. *I am Stal!* he thought. *I am Stal!* He felt the other boys kicking him, yelling to stop, but Iosif couldn't. He jumped up and held up his fists, waving them wildly at the boys, as the bloody Pavle lay at Iosif's feet. Iosif felt only anger surging through his ears, the blood pounding hard. *Stal!* The other boys looked at Iosif warily, for he was like a wild dog foaming in rage, his fists in the air, readying for attack.

"*Policia gamoidzaheth!*" Iosif heard Koba say in Georgian. "He should be locked in a dirty cell and beaten!"

The word broke through his consciousness. Iosif felt fear now. *Policia!* He saw how much blood had fallen from Pavle's face and ran into the street.

He heard Trina call out, "Iosif! Look where you run!" The Crone panicked. If this boy were to die before his soul was the master's, all would be lost. *Oh, stupid idiot!* She ran into the street yelling, "Stop!"

But Iosif was blind with fear and ran, his head turned toward the injured boy and the other schoolboys to see whether they had moved to bring the police after him.

"Stop, you stupid boy!" Iosif saw the words form across Trina's lips, and they stung his heart. Then he saw Trina's face but was startled, for beneath it was such ugliness; the Crone's own aspect was now visible beneath the beauty of Trina's face, like shadows of fearsome creatures swimming under the surface of a placid lake.

So startled was Iosif and pulled by the transformation of Trina that he didn't look forward but instead ran right into the galloping horse hooves of an oncoming carriage. The sound of the screams as he fell and the crunch of his left arm beneath the wheel of a carriage were the last sounds that Iosif heard before he fell into unconsciousness.

The Crone was now trapped inside Trina, for she struggled in the body of the girl, pushing her forward into the street as she saw Iosif fall under the wheels of the carriage. *The boy must not die!* The Crone felt waves of fright. What would the snake now do to her? Where would the Dark Master imprison her in the terrifying rings of hell? She must reach the boy Iosif before his soul left his body and push it back. The Crone fought to move Trina's body into the street, but Trina's soul fought back, and they struggled. So strong was Trina's will that the Crone felt the weight of it hold her, and the Crone cried out in fright as Trina fell to the curb in a faint.

Keke's face was intense in concentration, so focused was she upon washing the floor in the elaborate home of a wealthy Jewish trader in the town of Gori. Her expression was haggard, her dark hair hidden under a black scarf. But when the long afternoon light hit her face, one could see the lost lines of loveliness now smudged by poverty and ill luck. She looked like an old woman, though she wasn't in reality. She had suffered the fate and circumstances of a poor marriage to a brutal drunkard, the heartache of losing one child after another in childbirth, and the unyielding fist of poverty that beat upon her soul. But the poor suffered only on this earth, for it was told it was easier for a camel to go through the eye of a needle than for a rich man to enter the gates of heaven. Keke scrubbed the floor with vigor. The toil of women brought forward the blessing of the Lord; this she believed fervently. And to this ancient Christian community, a people and country near Russia but not Russian, the word of the Bible had been brought by the ministry of a woman, Saint Nino, who had grown up in the Georgian Orthodox Church.

A mother suffered for her child, and now Keke thought of the Virgin Mary and said a silent prayer—*Mother, help me be strong.* And had God not given her Iosif, a brilliant boy? For this boy, her only child, she would stop at nothing. It didn't matter that her knees hurt, bent as she was day after day upon the floors of the homes of rich traders, or that her hands were red and cracked from laundering the clothes of her employers, Keke thought. It was all toward one goal—Iosif would become a priest. Keke's tired eyes lifted, as she silently beseeched, *Lord, let it be so.* All her toil would be well spent. Iosif was in the Gori Church School; he would then go to the Georgian Orthodox school, Tiflis Theological Seminary. Look how all the schoolteachers spoke of the boy's genius; he had learned Russian so effortlessly, speaking Georgian to Russian to Georgian with dizzying ease. Ah, to have only one child was a sorrow after so many had been taken from her, but the Lord had blessed her indeed. And she kept her boy strong—yes, beating his disobedience with a stick. Yes. But it was for strength, so that Iosif would grow up strong and righteous. And he also would someday become a bishop.

"Keke, please rest, dear woman." She saw the kind mistress of the house and looked into her hazel eyes, which were filled with concern.

Keke shook her head. "No, Mistress. I wish to finish this work today."

The trader's wife felt a deep sadness for Keke, whom she knew was often brutalized by her husband. She placed a parcel by Keke's side and waved her hands at it as if it were nothing special. "This is for you. Some left-over pieces of meat we cannot use, some odds and ends of vegetables, and a small loaf of bread."

Keke looked at the bundle. She knew it was anything but leftovers, but the trader's wife knew that Keke didn't accept charity, that if it were the Lord's wish for her to suffer, she would. Still Keke knew the trader's wife gave these gifts from love, and a growing boy such as Iosif needed good food.

"Thank you, Mistress," Keke said, and kept scrubbing the floor. The trader's wife sighed. Her heart ached for this good woman. But Keke was proud and couldn't be kept from working hard.

The thumps on the door and cries of panic startled both women. They ran to the parlor, and the trader's wife opened the door. There at the threshold was the grocer, a hefty man with a thick beard. The trader's wife gasped. "Trina!" she exclaimed. The man held the limp body of her daughter in his arms.

The governess trailed behind the grocer, her face panicked. "I left her for only a moment outside the milliner's! I swear it!" she cried out to the trader's wife.

The trader's wife turned pale as she rushed to the grocer and directed him to bring her child to the parlor. She said to the governess, "Fetch the doctor at once!"

The governess ran out of the house as directed. The grocer carried the prone body of Trina into the parlor and placed her on a couch. Keke said silent prayers as she fetched smelling salts and brought a bowl of cold water and some rags to the unconscious child.

Trina's mother looked at Keke gratefully for her resourceful-ness and dipped the rags into the bowl, kneeling by her child, smoothing her brow and placing the wet rags on the child's fore-head. "Oh, my Trina! How did this happen, Mikhail?" she asked the grocer in anguish.

Grim lines moved across the grocer's bearded mouth as he gazed upon Trina. "There has been a serious accident," he said, not knowing how he would tell Keke of the fate of her precious son Iosif falling under the hooves of the carriage and hearing the sound of the *policia* in the distance. He stared tongue-tied at the pathetic figure of Keke. The trader's wife at once noticed his expression and said, "Mikhail, tell us what has happened!"

Trina's eyes suddenly snapped open, and she stared out. Her mother let out a gasp and fell back in horror. The grocer also stepped back in revulsion. Keke stared at the face of wickedness forming before her, her lips mouthing silent prayers to the Lord to cast out the evil that had possessed the child. Trina's eyes weren't the innocent ones of a child but windows into evil, and the sinister ugliness that was the visage of the Crone now mate-rialized over her face. The child's body vibrated in convulsions.

𒀭𒇻𒌋 𒂍 𒀭𒇻 𒆤

As Iosif awoke, his nostrils were assailed with the stench of misery that filled the air. His left arm lay in a funny angle to his elbow, and a sharp pain ran through his small body as he turned on the floor.

"You!" he heard a stern voice call to him. It was the *policia,* Iosif realized with a sinking heart, and he was being held in a jail. He turned his head and from the floor looked out through the cell's bars at the man's boots, black and hard. His eyes then turned upward to the red face and dark bushy eyebrows and mustache. Beyond the policeman, he saw the schoolboys pointing at him.

He heard Koba say to the officer, "For no reason, he beat Pavle 'til he was bloody."

"This small pockmarked boy? You are certain he is the one?" the officer asked.

"Yes, it is him, Pocky."

Iosif heard the derision and felt a slow anger override the pain. He pulled himself up, his face set in determination not to lay in the filth like a dog but to stand up like a man. *Stal,* he reminded himself. *You are as strong as steel! Stal!* The intense pain of a broken arm held him in its grip. Sweat poured from his brows. *Stal!* He looked at the policeman in defiance.

The officer's face turned stern. "You are accused, Iosif, of a brutal beating, for Pavle now lies near death. You also are accused of the theft of Koba's gold watch."

"Liars!" Iosif said between waves of pain and bared his teeth like an angry dog.

The officer shook his head. He held up the gold watch. "It was found upon you."

One of the schoolboys looked at Iosif with a wicked grin. "Who is a liar now, Pocky?" Koba said.

Iosif knew at once what had happened, for Koba also had looked with longing at Trina and had seen that she regarded Iosif with love, and he wished for Iosif to be removed. Iosif knew Koba had planted the gold watch upon him and saw the sneer of triumph in his eyes. It was one thing to accuse Iosif of a schoolboy's fight, no matter the injury to the other boy. But this? The theft of a gold watch? That was entirely another matter. And even for a boy of twelve, the punishment for such an offense was severe—the tsar's prison camps in Siberia.

The officer opened the cell doors, and two muscular guards roughly grabbed Iosif; pain shot through him like a current.

"Come, boy," said one of the guards. "It will be easier if you do not resist."

Iosif stared at the rich blond Koba, who looked triumphant as Iosif was dragged out of the cell. *Someday, you vermin, you will bow at my feet and beg for your life,* Iosif thought, and the idea of revenge strenghtened him and fortified his anger. He snarled at the men who held him. "Vermin!" he spat out.

The men savagely pulled his arms. "They won't be as nice to you in Siberia as we are, you stupid boy."

One of the guards laughed and viciously hit Iosif in the head and pulled at his broken arm again. Iosif felt the excruciating pain but pushed it aside. *Stal!* One day he would rule over them, these nothing nobodies as they begged for *his* mercy. Yes, like cockroaches beneath his shoe, he would kill them one day and think not another thought about it. The longing for the power over another filled him. In that moment a door to his soul was opened to the powers of the underworld, a door that parted wide through his anger.

The ground beneath the small jail began to shudder. The dirty floor shook, and a wail could be heard, a wail that seemed to Iosif an answer to his longing, for it suddenly took away his pain. From the cracks in the floor, ten thousand black snakes with sharp tongues—small like worms at first then growing large—shot out. The officer and the schoolboys screamed in alarm. The two muscular guards tried to keep hold of Iosif, but the black snakes twisted and turned about their legs and moved up, biting their bodies, necks, arms, and faces, causing the men to cry out in pain and agony. The men dropped their hold on Iosif. The guards and the schoolboys struggled to escape the confines of the jail, but the hold on them by the black snakes that writhed around them like living ropes was too strong.

Then one of the black snakes elongated and opened its mouth. From it sprang a tongue, and then another form emerged, splitting the body of the black snake in two. From this materialized a fearsome image, that of a dragon with a back that held spikes like swords and spewed flames that fell upon the boys and the guards.

"No!" they screamed as the flames enveloped them. "No!" The cries of anguish of those around Iosif filled his ears like music. As he watched the destruction, his face wasn't filled with fright, for no snake touched him. Rather there was about him a clearing, and his pain was gone. He didn't feel a whit of pity for the schoolboys. Instead he felt in his heart something close to purity—that of undiluted hate.

Then the dragon turned to him, its large and fearsome head with eyes of red embers fixed upon Iosif. He beheld the appalling vision but didn't flinch. There was something growing in Iosif, a power he felt moving through his veins. The dragon's mouth opened, and from it emerged not flames but a creature—a creature both man and snake with a cobra head—as the dragon disappeared. This creature with green scales was now on the floor in the clearing that grew around Iosif like a protective circle, the cries and screams of those drowning in flames around the perimeter. Though the flames and screams of agony, the smell of burning of flesh assaulted his senses, still, it was as if he and the snake were alone.

"Iosif," the creature hissed, staring at him with one blue eye and one green eye. The snake then reached into the periphery with his tail, and from the flames, he pulled out Koba. The boy screamed in agony as the snake tightened his hold, and his face shook with fear. The boy's face was scarred now by flames, his handsome features forever marred.

"Shall he live?" the snake asked Iosif, his eyes glimmering. "Or die? It is your choice."

Koba screamed in pain in the snake's grasp. But before Iosif could speak, the image of his mother, Keke, filled him with foreboding, and her words came at him. *Judgment is without mercy to one who has shown no mercy.* But then Iosif thought of the fulilty of his mother's life, how it was steeped in misery that no amount of piousness alleviated and how Keke reveled in her suffering. *The meek shall inherit the earth, Iosif.*

"The meek do not inherit the earth. Only the strong do," the snake hissed, reading his thoughts. The stupidity of Keke's faith filled Iosif with sudden revulsion; he saw her as passive and meek, bent and old before her time. For what? Iosif saw Koba's face shake with fright as the snake constricted around him. "Please," the boy begged, "Iosif."

And this last word hit him with all its hypocrisy. "So I am Iosif now, am I? Not Pocky!"

The snake smiled, his cobra face shifting at the boy's anger.

Iosif turned to the creature. "Kill him." He felt his heart soar at once with pleasure; so soon had his wish to subjugate been fulfilled! Of course there would be no mercy for Koba. "But make him suffer in pain first," Iosif added.

"As you wish," said the snake, as he flung Koba into the flames beyond. Iosif heard the boy's agonized screams shatter the air before he perished. And he felt again pure pleasure. Gone. How wonderful life would be if all who stood in your way could be eliminated so easily.

The snake turned to Iosif. "The master will give you such power."

The flames beyond were gone, and Iosif was only aware of the space where he and the snake stood. The snake hissed, "For your soul."

Beware! Satan! It is Satan! Iosif, he deceives those who dwell on the earth, the words of his mother rang in warning. This snake, the dragon—they were creatures of the underworld, Iosif realized fully. But what had God done for him when he lay in the jail cell just moments before? Nothing. What had being dutiful and accepting suffering done but nearly lead him to be sent off to the dark dungeons of Siberia? What had praying done for those who sat bent in agony in the church pews, poor and hungry and shivering with cold winter after winter? And who had come to save him? Was it God? No. God was nowhere to be seen. If this snake hadn't appeared, Iosif would be on his way to a cell in Siberia, to die in his own filth like a mangy dog. His heart hardened. He would give his soul to the Dark Master who gave power, not to God who only stood by and watched as he flailed under blows of cruelty.

"Take it," Iosif said.

𒁹𒅀𒌑𒁹𒁹𒀭

From deep beneath the earth, the snake Gneezy slithered up then through the carpets of the rich trader's parlor. He broke through with a thunderous sound as the floors gave way to his being. The gigantic reptile's green scales shone as he loomed over the prone figure of Trina as the grocer tried to hit the snake with a stick. Keke spoke, the words choking her heart. "Evil has fallen upon us!" The snake's tail whipped forward, grabbed the grocer, and hurled him against the wall. The trader's wife screamed in terror and clung to her child, who lay limp in her arms, her life ebbing.

The snake's tongue shot out, and its forked tip fell upon the face of Trina. From it, like a magnet, it pulled out the image, the ugly face of the Crone, and swallowed it whole. The snake turned to Keke, and his face was wicked in triumph. *Satan!* she thought. Keke saw the image of her boy Iosif now reflected within eyes of the snake—her boy Iosif, who looked out through the eyes of the serpent in triumph. Keke's heart gave out as she collapsed dead to the floor.

CHAPTER 7

east of elsewhere

"Look!" Paddy heard Dottie whisper again, as she pointed toward the man crawling out of the wall, his expedition clothing tattered and in the fashion of the 1870s.

Paddy O'Reilly's eyes took in the sight before him. His first reaction was that it couldn't be. But it was. Oh, but what a find this chamber—lugubrious though it was—was promising to be! Why, it was even better than that first tunnel with its cuneiform inscriptions, for here now was the man himself who knew the untold ancient tales of Nineveh! Paddy's bushy red mustache bristled with anticipation. To think of the academic papers that could follow—perhaps "The Chaldean Flood Revisited by Paddy O'Reilly, PhD"—and now in the flesh here was the great George Smith himself! Though Paddy also thought perhaps "great" was a bit of an overstatement, given the amateur status of the man, and really how was it that an almost supernatural force had opened for Smith the doors to archaelogical discovery? Still perhaps Smith could be a coauthor on the paper; Paddy would be first author of course; a dead man couldn't be the lead on a scholarly publication. Surely Columbia would grant full professorship, and perhaps a position as department chair would follow!

These thoughts spun about irrationally in quick flashes within Paddy's mind until the grim reality of the chamber asserted itself into his consciousness; academic accolades really ought not to be of foremost concern under their present bleak imprisoned circumstances, Paddy chastised himself. Still, frankly for Paddy, all the events staggered his mind, and keeping track of the dizzying forays into time and places ancient and modern was almost more than he could bear. Look at all that had followed since the volcanic burst of the mound at Nineveh right below his feet, including the appearance of Herman Biddle and the strange children, one of whom he was to realize was his daughter—from the future, of course, for Paddy was in 1938 an unmarried man, but was it still 1938? And here was the attractive Dottie, his wife… but not in '38 but in some other future time! Good God! How was he to keep these dates clear?

Paddy held out his hand to the man before him who had fully emerged from the hole in the wall and was standing up, his tall thin frame stooped a bit given the low ceiling. "Mr. Smith, I am Dr. Paddy O'Reilly, assistant professor of Assyriology—"

"Shh!" the man said abruptly, his ears cocked toward some faraway noise, perhaps heard only in his own mind, Paddy thought, for there was a whiff of madness about Smith, what with his eyes darting about wildly. Certainly, as well, 1876, the year of George Smith's death, had been many decades prior—if it was indeed still 1938—and the years clearly hadn't been kind to Smith's sanity; his thin was face drawn, his dark beard and hair shaggy and embedded with dirt, his eyes brimming with lunacy. Still a cave wasn't the most salubrious of environs, and therefore perhaps allowances should be made for Smith's manner, Paddy thought.

Dottie appeared puzzled by Smith's reaction. She and Paddy exchanged glances. She'd heard no noise. Their chamber was small and confined, the darkness relieved only by a dim light exuding from a slimy fluorescent substance that oozed against the cave's wall. All was eerily silent. Then Dottie heard it—a whoosh sound.

"Jump!" commanded George Smith, as he made a wild flailing leap onto the slimy substance that held him magnetized to the wall. "Jump, you fools!" he screamed.

Paddy felt the sting of the word *fools*, especially as it included Dottie. "Really, Smith—" But before he could finish his retort, beneath their feet a torrent of water rushed through. George Smith grabbed Dottie's arm and roughly pulled her up to the wall to safety. Beneath them the water was rising quickly and was already up to Paddy's knees. It churned and made hissing noises, buffeting him about.

"Paddy!" Dottie screamed, her hand out to him. "Jump!"

Paddy's stout frame was such that jumping was almost out of the question, at least any jump of worth.

"For God's sake!" Smith yelled. "Jump!" Paddy's face dripped with sweat as he made a futile effort to leap to the wall.

The water was now at Paddy's waist. Dottie held out her hand again in panic. "Paddy!" she cried out. The water gained force as it began to pull Paddy down. "No!" Dottie screamed, and struggled to jump into the water against the hold of the wall and Smith.

George Smith pushed Dottie back against the wall and flung himself away from it. He jumped into the raging water, grabbing Paddy with surprisingly strong arms, and threw him with some force (perhaps exceeding that which was necessary, Paddy later thought) against the oozing green wall, where Paddy stuck to the side like a chubby worm.

𒀸𒌋𒈠𒀸𒌋𒐏

The first thing Mattie noticed when she opened her eyes and looked up was that the forest was really, really green. But that wasn't quite right. No, she thought, as she beheld the glittering, gleaming leaves of the trees that were canopies above them. It was a lot more than just green. Mrs. Elmwood, way back at Fairmount Grammar School, would have just the perfect word for it plucked right out of that Vocabulary Garden of hers, Mattie thought. And Geeta probably already knew the word! This thought brought Mattie back to the painful realization that her mom—and her dad too; she shouldn't leave him out just on account of not really knowing him and all because he was dead…*deceased*…but not anymore—were still being held somewhere by that horrible snake.

Deep within the recesses of her metal chamber, the Spyglass yet again considered her plight. Oh, this child Mattie! What horrendous events were now to follow here on the Third Stone? How could she rely upon this child to protect her? She couldn't. Most important, Spyglass thought, she needed to overcome the girl, take her over. If she, Spyglass, had an innocent soul to inhabit, she could find a way out of this prison. Yes, the child Mattie would be overthrown at the first opportunity, she resolved.

Immediately as he stood up, Eddie saw that they were in a clearing in a forest, but who knew where? He had assumed proper airborne posture, of course, before landing. He saw they were wide open and were vulnerable to a frontal assault; the flanks were uncovered; and they had no defense in the rear. That king of Uruk was nowhere to be seen. Mattie was talking to herself, and Geeta was gazing up at something. Eddie reached into his back pocket—maybe that Spyglass had given him a weapon—but came up empty. All told, the assessment was this—completely defenseless, or situation normal all fouled up as usual.

Geeta thought she heard something and tilted her ears toward the canopy of trees. She straightened her glasses, which lay crooked upon her nose, and peered up. *What is this forest?* she wondered. It was silent, but there was a noise. Not a noise, no. A whispering presence. Her knowledge of ancient myths was limited to what they had learned about Nineveh. And the king of Uruk—who was he? And what did the man whom the king of Uruk called "Utnapishtim" have to do with all of it? Was he really the biblical Noah as she had thought? But if that were the case, and he had drowned, what was the fate of humanity? And what were the Seven Tablets? The Seven Tablets, the king had said, had trapped him, but he mourned their destruction. Why? Geeta pondered these questions. ThaTha would know perhaps, for he often said there is only one tale of truth, one that humans told and retold it, but the message was the same. "But what is that message, ThaTha?" Geeta had asked. ThaTha had merely shut his watery old eyes and seemed to be seeing something from within. When he opened them, he'd said, "If you listen, your journey will tell you."

The leaves above them moved like waves upon the water. The rustling sound was like a stream over rocks, peaceful, soothing. Mattie felt her eyelids drooping. She yawned. It would be so nice just to take a catnap. She looked back and saw that Eddie was shaking his head like he was trying to force himself awake. Geeta felt the powerful desire to lie down on the soft leaves that were at her feet. They beckoned her, and she found herself bending down, down.

"Stay awake!" Geeta heard Eddie command, though his voice sounded like it was filled with sleep. "Maaaattie! Geeeeeta!"

Eddie was alarmed. He knew from his father that within the silence of the jungle lay the deadliest danger. He heard his father cry out to him from somewhere in time, *Don't lie down! Danger! Stay alert!* Eddie cried out to Mattie in words that were slow and stretched out. "Pullll out…the Spyglasss….daaanger."

Mattie didn't see the danger, but something in her sensed a presence. She pulled out the Spyglass from her pocket in her green-checkered pants, but to do so was difficult, for the Spyglass seemed to be glued to her pocket. *Oh, that rat-fink Spyglass, always misbehaving.* But Mattie prevailed and in slow motion saw her hand stretch out to show Eddie the Spyglass. The Spyglass's eyes blinked at Mattie slowly and angrily.

"Edddie," Mattie said. She wanted to ask what order to give the Spyglass, but the words stayed in her mind. She saw Geeta blinking her eyes, trying to fight off sleep. The sound of the leaves was mesmerizing, its melody as sweet as that of a lullaby. Each rustle of the leaves seemed to say, *Close your eyes, close your eyes, close your eyes.* Mattie was the first to fall to the ground. There the soft green leaves immediately covered her curled body like a blanket, the Spyglass in her outstretched hand. The Spyglass also felt her awareness ebb, in keeping with her Mistress, and her plots and plans to overthrow Mattie became mere whispers in her mind. Then Geeta yielded to the lure of sleep as she snuggled deep into the eiderdown softness of the leaves. Lastly Eddie, who had made a mighty effort to resist, succumbed. In short succession all three children lay on the bed of soft leaves sound asleep, and the Spyglass too was deep in slumber, grasped within Mattie's hand. The leaves stopped rustling.

From beyond the soft bed of leaves that covered the three sleeping children, black water burbled from the ground. It formed into a placid pond that was smooth as a mirror, reflecting perfectly the green canopy of the forest. A wind rose and swirled the pond's surface. It shifted in response, the ripples causing the reflected canopy to swirl. The pond's surface rumbled in turmoil, faster and faster, until the reflected images of the leaves were like a rising green tornado. From the depths of this dark, whirling water emerged a sinister black hooded figure—with darkness where there should be a face—riding upon a large, flat, winged sea creature. This hooded figure, known as the Grim Reaper, rode upon the writhing flying creature from the dark waters, covered with seaweed and slime that fell from it as they rose from the water into the air. The sea creature's body was scaly and flat, and the Grim Reaper rode it like an evil magic carpet. This sea creature had fins that were like huge wings on either side of its body; its skin was gray and green, and from its ends shot out octopus arms. The sinister figure who rode this creature was holding a scythe. This scythe's handle was made of a long twisted wooden branch, and a long, sharp, curved, bloodstained blade lay perpendicular to the handle and projected to the left. A fierce wind blew, taking away the covering of the soft leaves that had blanketed Mattie, Geeta, and Eddie, leaving the three sleeping children in the open.

The Grim Reaper turned the flying creature to hover low over the three sleeping figures. The sea creature's long octopus arms twisted over Eddie, Geeta, and Mattie, then over Mattie's outstretched arm, encircling it and the Spyglass. From the end of each of the octopus arms was a small hooded head that shot out little flames of dark smoke. From these small hooded heads a whispered sound rose. The heads softly hissed their chant of death.

> *Your blood and bone*
> *you keep.*
> *Your soul we*
> *we reap.*

The Grim Reaper swung its lethal instrument of death—the scythe—toward the sleeping children. It was wielded by a skeletal hand that poked out of the heavy dark sleeves of the robe. The hooded being then directed the scythe's sharp blade with precision as it hovered right over Mattie's forehead, ready to harvest her soul.

𒀭𒌷𒄀𒀭𒈾

Sir Henry Layard was tossed from the deep-blue sky onto the parched and cracked yellow earth of mounds that rose like small hills upon the land. As he scrambled up, he looked about the land from the mound's perch, and memories of his youth flooded him. Nineveh. The capital of the cursed and cruel King Ashurnasirpal, who sought to capture the Dup Shimati, the Twin Tablets of Destiny for himself and became the cruel beast Ashurnasirpal. The mound at Kuyunjik was where Layard now stood. The ground was covered with low brown grass that sloped innocuously to the dry land below. Beneath this mound had been the thousands upon thousands of fragments of Tablets. It was he, Sir Henry Layard, who had directed the mound to be unearthed. He now thought of the terrifying night when the beast Ashurnasirpal had appeared in his dreams and pulled him below the tunnels as a warning. Sir Henry had seen how the tunnels had lain deep below the earth but above the fires of Hades, and also noted the labyrinthine path that led to the City of the Condemned. The impetuousness of youth, however, had prevailed. Sir Henry had a photographic memory for the visual and had drawn in his diary what he had seen in his dreams, the map of the tunnel and the path downward to the City of the Condemned. He dismissed the dream and forged ahead with the excavation, keeping the small diary he called, "The Tunnels of Ashurnasirpal," directly referencing the beast. Only then did he realize the enormity of the evil of Ashurnasripal and how he, Sir Henry, had tampered with the dark underworld. However, a bell once rung cannot be unrung, so he had discovered in the ensuing years. And misery had nipped at his heels ever since.

Sir Henry shut his old eyes in pain. Oh, to unring that bell! If only he could. His lined face and gray beard told the tale of an old, worn-out man drained of courage and valor. The call to bravery that had swelled in his veins in the bowels of the British Museum and that had prompted him to call out the chant with Biddle and Wigglesworth was gone. Sir Henry immediately regretted his action; he shouldn't have called the chant. No, he should have stayed an old man, safe in his nest of cowardice.

The atmosphere of the dusty mound was alluring, and the memories of Sir Henry Layard's youth flooded him, for in his youth, even before the excavations of the mound at Nineveh, Sir Henry had brandished pistols, alternately fought and befriended Persians and Turks, been chained and captured, and thought once he would be murdered in cold blood by barbarians. He had fought back bravely and overcome exceedingly impossible odds. He had escaped deadly fates and had walked on bleeding feet upon the scorched land to the gates of Baghdad. All this had exhilarated him. Courage and the quest for adventure had flowed in his veins.

The memory of it all washed over Sir Henry, and he felt fear, not exhilaration, at his impetuousness in those days long gone. As he stood upon the mound, he closed his eyes in pain and reminded himself sharply that he wasn't the man he was then. *You are an old man.* And again the vigor drained from his veins, as if a tap of courage was being turned on and off. *An old man,* Sir Henry told himself, as dust from the mound rose from the gentle breeze into the air and sparkled like small flakes of gold. *An old man,* he repeated to himself. The small pieces of dust glimmered in front of his eyes as the light grew dazzling in strength and split into two beams.

Sir Henry's mouth flew open. Each beam held the story of his life, each a different story telling the tale of the path taken and that not taken. Each flowed out into the air, strong strands of light with the palpable force of an electric current. These beams held his life in different forms: of Henry Layard turning from bravery to cowardice, of the graying of his beard and soul; of Henry Layard strong with youth who chose courage over cowardice and in turn whose beard never grayed, for the days of his life, though short, ended in vigor. Each beam sprung out and called to him. Sir Henry knew he had again a choice—of cowardice or courage, of the safe and known or the unknown. He could save himself with just one grasp of the beam; he knew could be instantly back in the safe confines of London and leave behind this foolhardiness that Biddle and Wigglesworth had brought upon him. Yes, he would do it. This journey was not his. Sir Henry flung his arms up, and the trembling palsied hands with the brown spots of age ending in gnarled fingers grasped toward the beam of the known path, the path of safety and old age. The fingers so close to the beam of safety paused. From the beam the old beaten Sir Henry looked at him, lying upon his deathbed, gray in face and soul. He saw in the beam himself in the path that cowardice had forged for him—old, bent, beaten—and the sight brought a moan of deep regret to his lips. Then suddenly his fingers receded from it, and Sir Henry flung his grasp toward the other beam, the unknown and dangerous path of courage. As he did the beam wound around and over him until he was enveloped by it and felt the heat of it in the blood that rushed through his veins. The light was so dazzling that he shut his eyes against it.

When Sir Henry opened his eyes again, the world was different. He saw the mound from a different prism; his brown eyes sparkled with curiosity; and his body bristled at the anticipation of the quest as the blood of youth now flowed in his veins. The old man Henry Layard was no more. The gray beard was gone, and its place was a trimmed dark brown mustache. Sir Henry's face had shed the lines of age, and they were replaced by the smooth face of youth. He was once again what he had been—a handsome man, tan, strong, and full of bravery. His dark eyes were deeply set, his nose a long aristocratic one that presided over the mustache and was followed by a strong jutting chin. His cheekbones were prominent, and his jawline was well defined and square. Beneath his white shirt, the outlines of his muscular form could be seen. Sir Henry wore his brown hair parted on the side; his dark locks fell over his forehead to give him a dashing air. His excavation boots were dusty as he stood jauntily upon the mound. He touched his face and found it to be smooth, and looked at the strength in his brown hands. He raised his arms into the blue sky of Nineveh and shouted in triumph.

Sir Henry saw the portly figure of Rufus Wigglesworth and the thin, caped one of Herman Biddle plummeting down from the sky and landing with a thump on the mound. He moved toward the fallen and scrambling figures at a brisk pace. He held out his strong hand to Wigglesworth and pulled him up, and picked up Biddle's staff. As he handed it to him, he remarked, "So I am in youth again. But you, gentlemen, it seems have not fared our journey in time as well."

Biddle dusted his cape and smiled ruefully. It was true. Both he and Wigglesworth remained old men. "Layard," Biddle said, "your memories called you, and you responded. This is good, for in this journey we'll need your youth and strength."

Wigglesworth looked at Sir Henry. He recognized how youth was in his body and wondered how completely it was in his psyche. "And we'll need your bravery too, Henry."

The handsome face of Sir Henry was now set in a frown, as he recognized there was much danger in the journey they would be embarking upon, this travel into the City of the Condemned, right into the lair of the Great Beast Ashurnasirpal. He said grimly, "You understand that we are standing on top of the tunnels. And beneath them is where we must go. It is a path I have traveled only a small distance and only in a dream."

Biddle nodded his assent. "We understand. Let's go then." He began to wave his cape, but Sir Henry interrupted him with his palms up.

"Stop," Sir Henry said, as he strode over the mound, no longer hesitant in manner or speech. Though he knew the peril of the journey, the invigoration of the land and his return to his youth filled him with nerve. He thought of how he had first seen the great cone-shaped mounds rising like apparitions against the setting desert sun.

Sir Henry turned to Biddle and Wigglesworth and said in warning tones, "There is a deep mystery here, where the tale of creation was first told. Great nations rose and fell, and cities remain under mighty ruins, shadows now obscured by time. If you listen you will hear the tale of prophecy, the voices of the long dead, the once mighty who roamed these lands. They now whisper their pain in the wind."

A wind rose from the mound, raising its yellow dust in sparkles into the air. Wigglesworth's eyes gazed upon the mound below his feet, as he thought of the agony that lay below, within the netherworld of the City of the Condemned. He whispered a verse from the Bible, "'For thou hast made of a city a heap…a ruin.'"

Looking sternly at Biddle and Wigglesworth, Sir Henry said, "You have asked for my help to traverse into the depths of terror. For me to do so, there cannot be secrets among us. Before I take a single step into the horrors that will surely greet us in the Ashurnasirpal's lair, tell me the truth. Where is the other Tablet of Destiny? I know we seek it so as to keep it from the clutches of evil. But who holds it?"

Biddle and Wigglesworth looked at each other, for they had held the secret closely to their hearts and hadn't spoken the truth aloud. Sir Henry looked at them and demanded, "Tell me."

Biddle began, "As there is day and night, as the light is divided from darkness, so too are there twin destinies." His blue eyes glittered in fear. The wind grew stronger as it flew into the faces of the three men on the mound, their hair swept back, their eyes watering from the increasing force. Sir Henry strengthened his hold on the mound, his muscular legs like trunks that had sunk into the earth.

Wigglesworth picked up Herman Biddle's thought. "Twin Tablets given by the Great Mother whose name is held in the sacred sounds *Tia-met, Tia-mut, Tia-mat*; the Great Mother who gave one Tablet of Destiny to her son, Marduk, and one to her daughter as holders of fate. It is said that the Twin Tablets hold destinies to guide mortal man. Marduk was given darkness to hold; the daughter received light. Marduk and the daughter each held only one Tablet so that the destiny of one's soul lay in one's choice, for if only one held both, mortal man would have no choice, no free will. Then the holder of both Tablets would rule supreme over all souls. And the Great Mother in her wisdom did not wish that."

Wigglesworth paused; the telling of the story was draining him, and his chins quivered in exhaustion. Herman Biddle saw this and picked up the tale. "Perhaps because mortal man dared to eat of the Tree of Knowledge in defiance of God, or wished for eternal life to be like the gods, as the ancients wrote—I cannot say which—man was given free will, the choice of his destiny, good or evil. To be of light or to be of darkness. Marduk the Dark Master wasn't always so. Marduk who held the Tablet of Evil—that of darkness and death—turned evil when he saw that his own power grew with the souls he had gathered into the clasp of evil. And so it was that Marduk became greedy for power over all, greedy to hold all the souls of mortal man. Greedy to become even more powerful, to be the holder of the sky of heaven. He yearned to be the supreme lord over all gods and man. The daughter of the Great Mother, the sister of Marduk, was the holder of light, life, and goodness and—"

Sir Henry interrupted impatiently, "This is the tale of the Enuma Elish. I know too that the Great Mother's name was defiled by Marduk and said to be degraded to 'Tiamet,' a fragile body that could be destroyed and not 'Tiamat,' all-powerful over body, mind, and soul. But this daughter of the Mother Tiamat, the sister of Marduk...she...I have not heard of her. Where is she, and where is this other Twin Tablet of Destiny?"

"The other Tablet of Destiny..." Herman Biddle paused, for he felt anguish in just thinking about where the other Tablet lay.

Wigglesworth said solemnly, "The daughter of Tiamat, sister of Marduk, who holds the other Tablet of Destiny, has been lost to a mystery. She is lost, hidden in time, trapped somewhere in a tale of deceit—a tale, it is said, woven by the Spyglass."

Sir Henry whistled a low sound of realization. The Spyglass. He recalled how he had found and then thrown into the fires the Spyglass, having known it at once to be an instrument of the wicked.

Biddle said softly, "The Spyglass holds the secret to where the daughter of Tiamat lies, and therefore where the other Tablet of Destiny, that of light and goodness, is held. It is said that Tiamat's daughter wears the Twin Tablet close upon her body, like a shield." Herman Biddle continued, "The Spyglass is an entity without a soul. How and why that is the case, I don't know. I only know that it has sought through time to capture a soul to inhabit. But the soul must not only be a willing vessel, but also must be pure for the Spyglass to take it over. The threads of treachery run strong in the impure soul. So it is that the impure soul serves the Spyglass no purpose. Thus this metal temptress, through the eons of time, glitters like a diamond to lure the unsuspecting into its trap and has destroyed and discarded each soul it cannot use."

Sir Henry's eyebrows knitted in puzzlement. "Biddle, there is an error in your logic. If the other Twin Tablet of Destiny, that of goodness, is lost, how is it that Marduk, with the Tablet of evil, has not overcome all with his temptations? The tales of the ancients are rife with superstitions. Perhaps we're best directed by Genesis. Goodness still exists upon the earth, Biddle, so surely the power of the Twin Tablet of good remains. And therefore mortal man still has free will."

Biddle said quietly, "I don't know these answers, Henry. I can't say with certainty that free will still exists or, if it does, that it will do so for long. The dark forces have grown in strength as man readily surrenders his soul in exchange for the allures of the earth. The mystery is deep, and each unraveling produces yet another layer of murkiness. The River of Time is in chaos. Destiny is not set; events coil upon one another. Those written as great in history are lost to obscurity; pettiness and anger reign, for there is no order, no rhyme or reason to existence. The rivulets of the eons swirl in confusion. The tale of creation is undone."

Here Biddle paused, for though Sir Henry was now strong with youth, should he be told? He looked to Wigglesworth.

Wigglesworth nodded and said boldly, "Chaos must be undone for the story of creation to be rewritten. And it can only be rewritten once the Path of the Virtuous is crossed."

Sir Henry looked at the two old men with incredulity. "The Path of the Virtuous!" He knew the myth of this Path well— that no one who began it survived. So that was what Biddle and Wigglesworth had been whispering about in the bowels of the British Museum! Sir Henry's brown eyes turned shrewdly upon Biddle then Wigglesworth. "Gentleman, the task is of double impossibility then—rescue the children and your friends in the City of the Condemned and then move merrily across the Path of the Virtuous? It is, of course, sheer madness."

Wigglesworth's eyes shut, for the mystery of this land was great; so many ancient tales had fallen and risen for thousands of years between the life-giving and life-taking rivers of the Tigris and the Euphrates. But there was something well beyond that. Wigglesworth opened his eyes and looked at Layard intently, his three chins shaking as he spoke. "Layard," he said, "you have given us George Smith's words."

Wigglesworth pulled the yellow missives from his pockets, adjusting his glasses as he peered at one yellowed sheet and read the last sentence. "'For this Dup Shimati is actually Twin Tablets, each of which holds the promise of destiny and how it is to be written. Incredibly the holder of both Tablets would receive the secret knowledge and in turn control all the souls and win forevermore the battle between good and evil. But in which direction?'" He looked up at Sir Henry with penetrating eyes.

Sir Henry look unmoved, his handsome face still registering the enormity and impossibility of the tasks. "Wigglesworth, you tell me nothing I already do not know. We're embarking on a journey right into the lion's mouth. Then, you and Biddle add that we embark it on the Path of the Virtuous, which has been crossed by no mortal man."

Herman Biddle feared that though Sir Henry had shed the body of the old man, vestiges of the old man remained in his psyche, and Sir Henry's intellect asserted itself over his emotions and the call to plunge into danger; "caution be damned" was being silenced. But they needed Sir Henry fully and completely, for this doubt that rose in his soul would serve only to harm them, the stench of cowardice like that of a decaying carcass that would attract the vultures of evil.

Wigglesworth heard Biddle's thoughts in his mind and said in a fierce tone, "Layard, listen! The Dark Master seeks the Spyglass, held now in the hands of a child, Mattie. All the forces of the underworld conspire to kill this child and capture the Spyglass. If the Dark Master Marduk succeeds in this, George

Smith's question will be answered—destiny will be written in the direction of *evil*."

Sir Henry paced on the mound against the wind. Only a fool ventured into danger without knowledge. He was no fool. He turned to Biddle. "When we are within the City of the Condemned, tell me, does your wizardry have any power?"

Biddle said truthfully. "I don't know."

Sir Henry shook his head again in disbelief. "Sheer folly." Youth, yes—he had impetuously chosen that beam. Youth, but not this…this…utter folly!

Wigglesworth held open the tattered pages of Sir Henry's manuscript. "Henry, only you know these contents. You must help us. Please."

Sir Henry looked at the manuscript and paled. He swallowed hard then stared at the two old men—all that lay now between him and the unspeakable horrors residing within Ashurnasirpal's City of the Condemned. Even in his regained youth, Sir Henry felt the currents of fright run through his blood, and the courage began to bleed out of his veins.

Biddle and Wigglesworth immediately saw how Sir Henry was changing again; the first bolts of gray were forming in his brown hair, and the lines of worry were starting to burrow in his forehead. They had to act quickly before Sir Henry was lured back to his old self. Biddle's blue eyes were filled with anxiety. He looked again at Wigglesworth and said, "Rufus…"

Wigglesworth spoke again to Sir Henry. "Only you can read these blank pages to lead us into the City of the Condemned. Layard, do not be a coward! You must help us!"

Sir Henry's eyes turned toward the dust that was rising from the mound. The gold sparkles formed, in concert with the fear in his heart, and a dim beam began to rise like a rainbow of shades of gold. The old path was forming once more, the path of his safe life. Biddle and Wigglesworth saw the beam and saw how Sir Henry leaned toward it and how the youth that was upon him was fading quickly. He was turning again into an old man. Sir Henry hadn't chosen the Path of the Virtuous to traverse, but he could traverse it if he chose to do so.

Sir Henry fell under the beam's enchantment. Images held in each particle of gold dust mesmerized him: the beam of the safe life, the life that was long in years but short in bravery that was unraveling before him; of his old age ensconced in the safety of his armchair, where he could write his books, the tales of his captures and escapes, the miracle of quinine that had saved the Bakhtiari chief's son, the battles on the Mesopotamian plains, tales that had another tale that Sir Henry dared not tell that lay within the dirt of desert. It was a story that was wound to his heart. And the memory of this pain shot another image through the gold beam: the long chestnut-brown tresses, the golden eyes that beseeched him from an oval face like that of an angel. *Lady of my soul!* Sir Henry cried out in his mind, and his heart beat the song of heartbreak. No! He wouldn't abandon her again! And as soon as he made this resolve, the spell of safety shattered and the beam vanished.

Sir Henry turned toward Biddle and Wigglesworth. The vestiges of the onslaught of old age fell away, and he was once more the young and hardy Sir Henry. But this time it was whole; both mind and body beat the sound of vigor, youth, and bold-ness. Biddle and Wigglesworth knew there was something that Sir Henry held fast in his heart, and whatever it was that he had seen as he stood in a trance before them would never be told to them. But whatever it was had strengthened his resolve, had returned to him bravery. Sir Henry held out his strong hands, which held the blood of youth and impetuousness, and said, "Give me the manuscript."

He studied the manuscript briefly then said, "It is written that to enter the City of the Condemned the spell of ša nagba īmuru—deep mysteries—must be cast."

Wigglesworth and Biddle felt their blood run cold; casting the spell that challenged the Dark Master's control of the underworld was what this spell meant. Sir Henry saw Wigglesworth's reaction; the brown of his eyes glittered with challenge, as if asking, "Who is the fearful one now?" Sir Henry commanded, "Cast the spell of ša nagba īmuru."

Biddle's arms suddenly flung up, his staff piercing the sky as he called out:

O Ereshkigal,
Mistress of the dead,
you who hold the
decay of death!
O Mamitu,
once caster of the
dark winds,
we beseech you
to guide us
to the underworld,
once yours!

In response the winds gathered upon the mound, mounting in intensity into a gale force. The gusts threw even the corpulent Wigglesworth back. Sir Henry's eyes were sharp upon Biddle, and he withstood with sheer determination the winds that beat upon him. Biddle's cape had fallen back as it glittered against the blue of the sun-dappled sky. The cape now reflected the sky like the ocean and took its color, but deeper, richer, with melancholy undertones. The cape drew the color of the sky into it as the sky paled. Biddle's cape swept back in the wind, away from his shoulders like a giant sail.

Then the face of the Ereshkigal, Mistress of Decay, took form in the sky—one half of her face divine with deep yellow skin and orange eyes streaked with hazel; the other decayed, showing bone and blood—and opened her mouth in a mournful wail. Sir Henry gasped as the once powerful goddess of decay enveloped the sky around them. Wigglesworth's chins quivered under the force of Ereshkigal's wail, for it was the call of suffering, of every instance of the pain humanity has inflicted one upon another. The wind, now bitter cold, blew across the land. Then in the sky appeared Mamitu, once the goddess of the fate of the underworld, her face like that of granite, gray and hard with eyes that were black pebbles and whose mouth lay shut in grim silence and judgment. The two faces, that of the goddesses Ereshkigal and Mamitu, mingled and melted into each other as they spoke as one.

Beware, mortal man!
Darkness in all its power
lies beneath your
feet and pulsates,
greedily answering
the call of man for
petty dominion!
Beware,
for if you call the words,
you open the
way to your destruction!

Biddle's eyes were shut tightly against the bitterly cold wind, its force strong and challenging. It threw back his white hair and his old hands, veined with rivers of time and stark against the now pale sky. He opened his eyes as he raised his staff to the goddess.

Mistress of the Underworld,
Mistress of Decay,
we beseech you,
open the way!

The goddesses' faces, turning from stone to blood to bone, shook in the sky and said:

Only he who was visited
in his dreams
by Zakar
can speak the chant.

Biddle and cried out to Sir Henry, "You were given the god of dreams, Zakar's, message to open the way. Say the chant!"

Sir Henry's eyes reflected courage, and his voice boomed against the ominous sounds of the wind.

Ša a nagba īmuru!
Dark story of the
unknown mysteries!
Open your pages
to our eyes!
Ša a nagba īmuru!
Open story of the unknown mysteries!

Their arms held up to the sky, Wigglesworth and Biddle echoed Sir Henry's words.

Ša nagba īmuru!
Open story of the unknown mysteries!

At these last words, the sky turned dark, and the visages of the goddesses disappeared. Thunder rattled the earth. Bolts of lightning shot across the blackness as raging winds shook the earth. Sir Henry then cried out the chant.

O winds of the south,
warm with sickness.
O winds of the north,
of cold and fear.
O winds of the west
of dampness and dire.
Blow away from us.
It is the unlucky, dry, hot
winds of the east
we call to!

A hot wind borne of the heat of the flames from hell blew from the east. It lifted the mound upon which Biddle, Wigglesworth, and Sir Henry stood and shook it as the three men faced the furious winds. Sir Henry chanted the spell.

Let the wind carry our blood
into the secret places of evil,
where the duplicitous
Dark Master is king,

deep into the land
of treachery and deceit
that lies
east of elsewhere.

A wail echoed upward from deep within the bowels of the earth, and the sky shook against a dust tornado and flung the three men to the ground. From the dust tornado emerged giant arms the color of red earth—with hands that were broad and palms that were blank—that told no tale of the future. The hands then spread out and grasped Biddle, Wigglesworth, and Sir Henry. All three were plunged into the parched and cracked earth below.

Within the forest of Death, the Grim Reaper again swung its scythe, the sharp point falling near the center of Mattie's forehead as it swung down low. The octopus arms wound tightly over Mattie's arms and over the inert Spyglass in her grasp. The leaves in the forest now sung a dirge in deep and sepulchral tones in the somber anticipation of the reaping of a defenseless soul for its Dark Master.

Blood and bone
you keep.
Your soul he
reaps.

With each mournful note, the leaves changed colors: mustard yellow, burnt orange, blazing red. The whole of the forest was backlit into a melancholic beauty by an unseen sun. Mattie remained hypnotized in immobility, frozen out of awareness as the piercing blade hovered, ready to reap its fruit. Controlled by the faceless hooded being, the scythe's blade moved with the precision of a surgeon as it edged closer to the sacred third eye, the holder of the entry to one's soul.

Somewhere within the depth of their frozen states, Geeta and Eddie, lying so close to Mattie yet immobile to help her, felt the enormous awfulness of what was happening seep into their marrow and saw the whole scene in their minds. Eddie shouted out in his thoughts, *Mattie, don't surrender! Keep your shield up!* He struggled against the spell of sleep, exhorting his body up but to no avail. *Dad! Give Mattie your warrior strength!*

Geeta also struggled against the hypnosis of the nightmarish forest to open her eyes. If only she could awaken—then she could shake Mattie awake. *Mattie! Mattie!* Geeta cried in her mind again and again. *Oh, Rasputin! Oh, Tsar Nicolas! Can you not help us?*

The colors danced about the forest, a visual to the doleful sound of the ballet of the hooded reaper's extraction of the soul. The scythe's sharp blade pulled at Mattie's third eye, as a glimmer of golden light, pure and immense in beauty, began to rise out of it. Then the reds, yellows, and oranges of the leaves began to lift, leaving dark-brown brittle leaves.

Geeta and Eddie saw in their mind's eye the alarming fate of their friend as the scythe moved toward Mattie. *No!* they cried out in their minds again and again. *Mattie! Wake up! Wake up!*

Mattie sensed something hot in the middle of her forehead, but she couldn't move.

Paddy felt the oozy green slime keep him magnetically glued to the wall above the raging waters. Dottie was just beyond him, similarly mired in the goo. They saw George Smith, embroiled within the raging currents of the water below.

"Oh, Paddy! We have to help Mr. Smith!" Dottie cried out.

"Smith!" Paddy shouted, and felt no little shame, for it had been George Smith who had rescued him, flinging him like a sack of potatoes onto the slime but rescued him nonetheless. Paddy struggled against the slime, his arm outreached. "Smith!" Paddy shouted again. And rather than reach out, incredibly Smith scowled at him! Paddy let out an involuntary yelp as he teetered into the water. "Aaagh!"

Smith flung himself out of the water with the agility of a frog, for his back legs now were indeed more amphibian than man, ending as they did in webbed feet, right into the slime. Dottie's eyes were wide, and the words *Find the flying frog* entered her mind. That was what she had told Mattie! And now a hope rose in Dottie; somehow she was able to communicate with Mattie, and she hoped fervently that Mattie had heard her. If so, then Herman Biddle and Dr. Wigglesworth could find them.

Smith roughly grabbed and pushed Paddy back into the safety of the wall. "Imbecile!" he snarled. "How many times am I to rescue you?"

Paddy huffed. Really! Before Paddy could give way to his indignation, the oozing slime that had held them so firmly began to dry into brittle threads that quickly gave way. Paddy, Dottie, and Smith tumbled into the raging stream below. In the water they were battered about by what seemed at first glance to be large boulders. But on second glance... *Oh, horrors!* thought Paddy, his heart pounding fast. He felt a sharp nip at his arm. No mere boulders were these but huge decapitated heads, their mouths open wide, with teeth large and yellow, some with hair long and tangled, others bald, others with gashes upon their foreheads, jaws snapping at them with hunger.

"Dottie!" Paddy shouted, buffeted about in the water between the ravenous heads, as he saw his beloved fast approaching the open jaws of a giant head. "Turn!"

With his amphibian agility, Smith leapt right out of the water onto something that had floated down. It was a raft of sorts—or, as called by the ancients, a *kelek*—made of wood branches that lay upon long banana-shaped balloons that were made of animal skin. Smith grabbed Dottie up into the sinewy raft just as the great jaws had sprung open to devour her. Dottie gasped in fright, her hair wet and plastered about her head, giving her the sleekness of a seal. From the roaring water, Smith seized a large branch, which he used to fend off the hungry heads.

"Paddy!" Dottie cried out, then turned to Smith as she saw Paddy floating like a well-fed tasty morsel in the midst of the heads that gathered around him. "Help him!"

Smith narrowed his eyes and said sardonically, "Yes, madam. Naturally." He then maneuvered the raft toward Paddy, who sputtered, flailing about as he tried to strike out at the great teeth and snarling heads. Dottie grabbed from the water a gnarled stick that floated by and struck at the heads surrounding Paddy.

"Back!" she screamed, as the stick hit a head, its jaws turning toward her and yellow teeth snapping the stick in half. "Oh!" Dottie exclaimed in alarm.

"Onto the *kelek*!" Smith commanded Paddy. Paddy felt the nip again of the yellow teeth within the voracious jaws of a large head, its black, dead eyes bulging. Smith maneuvered the raft while simultaneously using the branch oar to hit the heads. "Now, you fool! Jump!"

Dottie had her arms outstretched into the raging currents toward her beloved, risking the danger of the heads that now leaped out of the water to bite her. "Paddy!" Smith growled, as he saw that Dottie would soon plunge into the waters herself. The *kelek* was moving fast, hurtling between the monstrous heads. Paddy looked to be hopelessly in the grasp of the unrelenting currents. The rushing currents pulled him farther into the churning waters and away from the raft.

"Here!" Smith said to her. "Grab the oar." He thrust the oar into Dottie's hands. "Keep the *kelek* near us." Dottie stood precariously on the raft and thrust the oar forcefully into the water as George Smith jumped in. Dottie opened her mouth in surprise, for George Smith's back legs were decidedly froglike; what showed of his legs from the tattered expedition khaki pants was green skin ending in webbed feet. Smith leaped on top of one snapping head to the next, the suction of his frog feet giving him stability, using them as steppingstones toward Paddy. The yellow teeth chomped at Smith but to no avail.

Smith saw Paddy being carried farther and farther down the rushing river. He saw too that Dottie was moving the raft down the stream, but the distance between her and Smith seemed to be increasing rather than shortening.

Paddy's fear had reached epic proportions as he felt the pain of being bitten by the heads. He saw only the jaws, the fearsome teeth in the decapitated heads, their faces inhuman, blood dripping where there should have been a body. And oh, the sounds they made—the terrifying sounds of their lips smacking in anticipation of the meal.

Garrumph! Garrrumph!
Harrumph! Harrumph!

Oh, to end in this ignominious manner! Paddy thoughts whirled about as he was battered and bitten by the petrifying heads. He heard in his mind Wigglesworth's chastising eulogy of his demise in tones of admonition, as the learned faculty of Columbia University listened. *Into the jaws of failure, so the benighted Dr. Paddy O'Reilly met his death, eaten alive on a fruitless expedition.*

CHAPTER 8

holder of the scythe

Gilgamesh, king of Uruk, thudded to the ground just beyond the foreboding forest as it began to change colors. The blue of his face immediately deepened in color as he recognized where he was. His muscular body shook under his golden armor, and his hair and beard, those black wooly ropes, swayed back as the earth beneath him rumbled. Gilgamesh instinctively tightened his grasp upon his spear. The mournful notes of the dirge echoed through the forest and filled his ears, sending panic into his heart. He knew where he was—the horrid, dark forest of Death, guarded by the fierce giant Humawa, once master of the gloomy forest but now under the dominion of the Great Beast Ashurnasirpal—Humawa, in whose forest lay the Grim Reaper, where all who dared enter fell victim to the seductive sounds of the leaves, the call to death. Death. And it was happening now, as the colors of death fell upon the forest, first in a blaze of splendor before the nightmare of emptiness descended.

The great king of Uruk felt his courage seep out of him as each death note rang out from the gloomy changing forest. His thoughts turned back in time, across the ages and thousands of years back, for Gilgamesh had attempted once before, in the time of the ancient past, to enter this forest with his friend Enkidu. They had tried to do so when Gilgamesh's kingdom was weakened by Death, who had stolen entrance into Uruk on a warm, soft whispering wind and lain to dust two-thirds of his subjects. And so it was his task to find the antidote to the brutal Death and the secret to immortality so that his people should not suffer the despair of mortal life. Into his dreams, those many eons ago in Uruk, came the answer in the form of a vision. It was a beautiful woman whose eyes shone like the stars and upon whose golden head were seven bright moons and who spoke to him but whose words he couldn't understand. Gilgamesh spoke of the dream to the ancient woman priestess of Uruk, Nana, who had lived through the waves of the deadly fever, whose face was kind, whose thoughts were wise and who had counseled him. She had nodded and understood that it was the Great Mother who had come into his dreams. The old woman whispered the three sacred names, *"Tiamet, Tiamut, Tiamat."* She then called upon those of Uruk who were not enfeebled by the fever to come at the midnight hour to the sacred center of the kingdom. And so they came, the old and the young who could still walk, though their faces were gaunt from the ravages of the deadly whispering wind. They gathered around their king, who stood tall upon the hard ground, and beyond whom were the walls of Uruk.

The wise priestess, Nana, had stood next to Gilgamesh, her face like a walnut, brown and with sharp lines, her eyes black like wet pebbles and holding in their depths both wisdom and kindness. She was ancient in age, and therefore her knowledge held the tale of Uruk, some said across the seven kings, of which Gilgamesh was feared to be the last king. Her hair was both black, like that of a raven, and the color of rubies under a bright sun. The black and the ruby-red strands lay coiled in a large bun at the nape of her neck. She was tall, but not as tall as the ten feet of Gilgamesh. She was slender and fragile in build. Upon her person she wore robes whose color was like the changing sky—now gray, now blue, now a velvet black, then a mass of colors: orange, blue, pink, yellow, green, and tan that sharpened in focus and told the story of the people of Uruk, then turned back to blue then black. The magic robes were said to hold her spirit and those of all the ancestors of Uruk. So it was that the people of Uruk believed Nana to be their goddess and one who could speak to the Great Mother herself. The robes moved about Nana like a soft whispering wind as she walked toward the sacred center of the kingdom. There she took seven brittle twigs from the great folds of her robe and placed them on the ground. She pointed downward, and a droplet of blood, not red but the deepest of blue like a sapphire, dropped slowly, shimmering from an internal light. Gilgamesh saw that as the blue droplet hit the twigs, a great silver fire rose, its flames like silvery waves of the ocean. The faces of the citizens of the kingdom of Uruk were alit with wonder.

The old woman Nana then looked up into the darkness of the night sky, whose blackness was weakened by the tendrils of silvery fire reaching upward. She whispered, "Evil wind, tempest and hurricane, whirlwind that blows seven times upon the face of man and four sides that were said to have held our Mother Tiamet...Tiamut...Tiamat." Here a great wind began to blow strong and angry and swayed almost to the ground the enfeebled, the few left of Uruk. Gilgamesh himself had swayed, the dark-black ropes of hair swinging about and whipping his stern face, but he had rooted his feet, large and flat, upon the ground. The fire grew greater against the wind, the silver tongues hitting the sky in defiance.

Then Nana whispered again, calling upon the Great Mother, using the most sacred name, which signified the spirit, "Tiamat, oh, Mother Tiamat, whose blood the evil winds of the worshipers of Marduk have thrown to secret places, we, your loyal worshipers, call upon you!" Sounds as strong as thunder shook the fire as the old woman said the words. Then Mother Tiamat appeared within the silvery fire, translucent in form, the seven moons shining above her head. The evil winds blew fourfold now, from all sides, and the weakened people of Uruk were flung about the ground. But the people of Uruk did not care. They rose in defiance, though the winds battered them, for the Goddess Tiamat was again with them. Their faces were flushed with awe at the sight of the Great Mother. Gilgamesh flung out his arms in supplication toward the silvery fire. "Mother Tiamat! Oh, supreme being! We speak thy word. We obey thy commands!" And the people of Uruk sang out, "We obey thy commands!" The vision of Tiamat flickered within the silvery flames, but she remained silent.

Then Nana whispered, "Mother, Death follows the mortal people of Uruk upon these evil winds. We beseech thee for help."

Mother Tiamat's voice rang out through her form in the silvery fire, her face sad with resignation.

Seven sacred
Tablets lay hidden within the earth.
Those tell the tale of truth,
but the followers of

Marduk
write a tale of lies.
When the lie is undone,
I shall reign
supreme
over these evil winds.
Until then
I am powerless.

Nana stood firm; there was too much to lose for her people, and though the Great Mother's tone was such that she should not speak, Nana nonetheless spoke once more. "Mother," she beseeched again into the flickering silver flames, "is evil to reign supreme? Can good hold no sovereignty?"

Mother Tiamat saw the pain in the old woman's face and knew how well Nana had served her people. Tiamat spoke now to the king of Uruk.

Gilgamesh, king of Uruk,
to conquer Death,
through the forest of Humawa
must one traverse,
though none who venture
into Humawa's forest
ever leave.

The silvery vision of the Mother Tiamat was slowly fading from the fire. The old woman's shoulders were bent in resignation, so great was the task. Gilgamesh saw his people, whose faces, lit by the silvery fire, drained of hope. It wasn't just the ravages of death—that was the only the shell of mortal form. No, for the people of Uruk, alarm lay in the knowledge that as evil reigned supreme, their souls would belong to Marduk, and they would be enslaved within the menacing dark underworld for eternity.

Gilgamesh knew he had to act. He then boldly called out as the last flames of the silvery fire were extinguishing, "Mother! Goodness must reign once more! Fashion me a weapon that you bless, and I will go forth into Humawa's forest. I shall conquer Death and restore the Seven Tablets to your glory." Into the fading flames Gilgamesh threw his ancient warrior spear, the weapon of mighty metals forged by the six kings of Uruk before him, each strengthened by the valor of the warriors before them. The flames caught hold of the spear and gained strength.

The Great Mother's face appeared, her face again shimmering within the shining silver flames. In her hand she held the ancient spear of the King of Uruk aloft.

> *Gilgamesh, king of Uruk,*
> *shall you go forth*
> *against those*
> *who are sharp of tooth?*
> *Merciless of soul?*
> *Whose vipers and dragons*
> *and raging beasts*
> *overcome all with terror?*
> *For it is into this den of horror*
> *you must travel.*
> *Know this, Gilgamesh,*
> *before you answer.*

Gilgamesh did not hesitate. "Mother Tiamat, I am willing. Though I am one-quarter mortal man as son of Lugalbanda, and my blood holds death within it, so too am three-quarters god as the son of my mother, the goddess Ninsun, priestess once of Shamash. I say to you, Great Mother Tiamat, my soul will not be so easily trampled under the merciless viciousness of Marduk. But my people, those of the kingdom of Uruk, their mortal bodies and souls do fare not so well. I beseech thee, forge me a weapon!"

The fire was so strong that the silver flames grew large, and the people around it scattered back. The face of the Great Mother was gone, replaced only by even stronger flames, their silvery tongues reaching out into the black sky. From the flames eleven warriors—six male and five female, all mighty in strength—rode forth on white horses with wings; one of the eleven, the largest, was Kingu, the warrior helper of Tiamat. Each warrior held a spear. Kingu, whose face was bearded and hair long and lustrous like a mighty river of power falling from his head to his back, roared the battle cry of the warrior. And the ten warriors clashed their mighty spears with that of Kingu to create one enormous spear. Kingu flung the spear down, and it appeared in the hand of Gilgamesh—the spear whose metal was ancient and powerful, born not just of silver, gold, and bronze but of the substance of strength that came from the valor of the mighty warriors of the past. It was eight feet in length and gleamed a golden color with a tip that held a sharp green flame. The spear glimmered in Gilgamesh's grasp as he looked upon the magical weapon in wonder. And Kingu spoke:

Go forth, Gilgamesh,
son of Lugalbanda and Ninsun,
born of mortal man
and immortal goddess.

Know that
only the warrior pure
of heart
and of spirit
shall be able to hold
this mighty spear.

The eleven warriors upon their winged horses faded into the black sky, and the silver flames died back into the ground.

Nana and the gaunt people of Uruk looked at their king, Gilgamesh, who held the mighty spear with a powerful pale-green flame flickering at its point—a sacred weapon crafted by the warrior gods now in their king's hand—and felt hope for the first time.

"Go forth, Gilgamesh, king of Uruk," said the old one, Nana, her voice wavering in pain and her eyes shining with tears, for she knew now she may never see Gilgamesh again, so treacherous was his path and impossible the journey. "Go, Gilgamesh, and find the secret to eternal life. Bring it to us that we, the last of the peoples of Uruk, should not fall into the clutches of evil."

From the circle of the people, one man, whose face and body showed lines of strength but clearly was weakened by fever, came toward Gilgamesh. "I shall go with you, Gilgamesh, that you should not travel alone," he said, his voice hoarse.

"Enkidu," Gilgamesh said to the man, who was tall, but not as tall as the ten feet of Gilgamesh, and whose body was a muscular form and whose brown face showed the resolve of a warrior. His hair was coarse and deep black, and there was about him the tension of a wolf, for Enkidu bore the signs of both man and beast. Still, though the force of warrior and beast flowed in his veins, it was apparent that much effort was needed for him to stand tall and straight, as he was enfeebled by illness. His eyes, bloodshot and weary, told the full story of his long fight with the deadly, evil disease of the winds.

Gilgamesh saw how weakened was Enkidu and said, "Brother, you are not strong for such a journey."

But Enkidu shook off Gilgamesh's protestations. "Do not argue, my friend. I will come with you."

So it was that Gilgamesh took his leave of the kingdom of Uruk, accompanied by his friend Enkidu as the whispering winds of death blew across the land. The story of their journey—and how it would come to be that Enkidu would meet Death when he ventured first into the forest of Humawa while Gilgamesh stood at its edge—would be told again and again in the sorrowful thoughts of Gilgamesh's mind when he lay trapped for the eons within the Seven Tablets, only to be released now by the red-haired child.

These thoughts ran through Gilgamesh's mind as he looked upon the forest once again with fear. Humawa's forest was treacherous. Then a vision from deep within the forest shimmered before his eyes and showed him Death's victim. And the knowledge hit the king of Uruk with full force as he saw the sinister hooded figure, its dark robes flying over the prone red-haired child, the looming octopus tendrils of the creature it rode wrapped around her arms. The servant of Death was poised over the red-haired child with his malevolent scythe, the instrument that reaped sleeping souls.

𒁹𒌋𒌋𒁹𒌋𒁹𒌋

Mattie's thoughts were like pieces of dust scattered by a breeze. She heard faraway voices, those of Eddie and Geeta, but couldn't make out their message. She felt the pull of sleep again, the mournful song of the leaves reaching her, beckoning her toward them. As she began to fall back to the lure of the leaves, as she started to slip into a deep slumber again, she thought, as one does sometimes right before unconsciousness beckons, of the last thing that had happened—of how sad the king of Uruk was because he had lost his friend, like she would feel if she lost Geeta or Eddie. She hoped the king could find his friend.

𒀭𒄑𒉈𒈦

A roar, the strength of that of ten thousand lions, filled the forest as Gilgamesh, king of Uruk, swung his spear at the Grim Reaper. The ground shook beneath the sinister flying sea creature upon which the hooded figure rode as it hovered over Mattie. The Grim Reaper turned its evil carpet and guided the flying creature's octopus arms toward Gilgamesh to ensnare him.

"Leave the child be!" Gilgamesh shouted to the Grim Reaper. "She is not yours!"

"Do not interfere, Gilgamesh, king of Uruk!" the hooded figure snarled, as it again turned its skeletal arms holding the scythe and moved toward Mattie to reap her soul. "Or be destroyed!"

Then Gilgamesh, king of Uruk, roared again his roar of ten thousand lions loud and strong. The force of his roar flung the Grim Reaper, and the bony death hand that grasped the scythe and had been poised over its victim fell away from Mattie. The hypnotic hold of the scythe on the third eye, the entrance to the soul, was broken. Mattie stirred. The sound of death was interrupted. The dark foreboding forest of Humawa quavered in confusion. Never before had the refrain of death been thwarted in

Humawa's forest. The colors of the leaves—the bright oranges, yellows, and reds—shimmered uncertainly above the dark brittle leaves. The notes of death's wails rang out in broken and discordant notes, and as such broken too was the hypnotic slumber that had fallen upon Eddie and Geeta. Eddie's eyes snapped open first, and he immediately leapt up in a defensive pose—fists up, scattering the leaves that had blanketed him. Geeta struggled up, with brittle brown leaves embedded in her disheveled black braids and her glasses askew. She gazed myopically out then pushed her glasses down to see.

"Oh!" she gasped, as she saw that Mattie lay prone, one arm outstretched, grasping the Spyglass, as a flying sea creature ridden by a dark hooded figure hovered just beyond her, its octopus arms reaching to envelop her. Geeta then heard Gilgamesh roar. This time the might of the roar was that of the earth splitting. Gilgamesh savagely plunged his spear's point into the body of the flying sea creature. The creature writhed in pain as the warrior giant pulled his spear back and tore the body of the creature in half and flung it away from Mattie. The hooded figure fell to the ground, now that the flying carpet that was the sea creature was torn in two; its bleeding remains carpeted the forest floor beyond as it turned into a mass of desiccated skin.

Eddie barreled toward Gilgamesh to help him. He called to Geeta, "Wake Mattie up!"

Geeta ran toward the still sleeping Mattie. "Mattie!" Geeta shook her friend. "Mattie!"

Mattie was still deep in slumber, her body limp like a ragdoll. She saw a glimmering image of the little shriveled-up old man from Nineveh whose large ears had veins like blue rivers crisscrossing them. *Daughter, beware.* And somewhere beyond, Mattie heard Geeta's voice too. What was Geeta saying?

"Oh, Mattie!" Geeta cried out. "You must awaken!" Geeta's heart pounded with fear, as she saw with wide eyes the two figures facing each other in battle—the sinister hooded figure and the king of Uruk.

The Grim Reaper, Death's ambassador, let out a baleful wail as it stood upon the ground. The wail went to the marrow, its sound sharp and ominous with the horrors to come. The reaper stood tall, taller than even the ten feet of Gilgamesh, and wielded the scythe in large circles, the black of its robes flying about and revealing the skeleton figure beneath, though there remained blackness where a face should have been. The scythe's blade hit the golden spear of Gilgamesh, splitting it in two as it flew from his hands.

The Grim Reaper snarled a sound that emerged from its dark faceless aspect. It wielded the scythe toward the king of Uruk as it hissed in a raspy voice, "Gilgamesh, king of Uruk, you who dare to interrupt Death's song, will now hear it ring in your ears!"

At this the sound of death again rang out in the forest, the glittering multicolored leaves singing their lugubrious melody. Gilgamesh's eyes fluttered as he tried to keep them open, but the pull of the song was strong. He immediately fell under its hypnotic lure, falling to the ground in unconsciousness like a great tree that had been felled. The Grim Reaper now positioned the scythe's sharp blade over Gilgamesh's forehead, as the songs from the leaves grew louder and louder.

Eddie keenly observed, as he came running, that the dark hooded figure beyond, its back to him and hovering over the unconscious king of Uruk, was intent in its purpose. *A distracted enemy is a weak opponent,* he heard his father's voice. Eddie grabbed the portion of the fallen half of the spear that lay on the ground. The spear was still some four feet in length and heavy, made as it was of an ancient alloy of metals that gave the possessor warrior strength, as long as the heart remained pure. As Eddie's hand grasped the spear, the purity of his warrior soul was felt by the metal skin of the spear, and the ancient strength of warriors who had lived in the eons before him seeped into the small blond boy's body. *Act now!* He heard his father's directive, the sergeant's command to the soldier. Eddie let out a warrior's cry as he ran straight toward the back of the Grim Reaper, who was still bent over the fallen figure of Gilgamesh. Eddie had been a good hitter in Little League. He wielded the half spear like a bat and swung it hard, hitting the hooded figure about the middle. It was a good hit, sharp, strong, and filled with fury. It swung the Grim Reaper to the side, its dark robes a black blur as it spun. *Again!* Eddie heard his father. *Strike again!* Eddie's face furrowed in determination; he charged again and swung the broken spear at the skeletal hand that held the scythe and hit it hard and strong. He heard the gratifying sound of the bones of the hand break into pieces as the scythe fell to the ground.

The forest vibrated, and its cry of alarm rang out, for twice now the song of death had been interrupted. The Grim Reaper was now disarmed; as the dark robes fell to the ground, what was revealed was a headless skeleton. The bones of skeleton then disintegrated and sprinkled to the ground as a dirty white power. Death's servant lay in a heap upon the brown and brittle leaves on the forest floor. The forest stilled to a shocked silence.

And here Eddie did the incredible—a thing that had never before happened, and he would never know why. But he did it. He dropped the ancient half of the spear and picked up Death's scythe.

Gilgamesh, king of Uruk, opened his eyes and lifted himself up groggily to see, with blurred vision, the small boy with yellow hair, the young *muktablu* holding Death's scythe!

Mattie, now awake, grasping the Spyglass to her chest and sitting next to Geeta, heard the ominous wail of the forest ring out again. They looked at Eddie as he held the large scythe. "Oh!" Geeta gasped. And the Spyglass in Mattie's hand also made a sound, a moan of fear.

Eddie was surprised by the fierce power of the heavy scythe, which he held in both hands. A warning gurgled in Gilgamesh's mouth, but nothing came out. He struggled to stand up, the hypnotic effect of death's song fading but slowly. "Young *muktablu*... warrior...drop...drop it."

Eddie shouted in alarm, for his hands, which held the scythe, were slowly turning to bones, the skin drying and shedding. And now the scythe held him; it was glued to his skeletal hands. Beyond him the dark mass of robes rose and flew toward him. A strangled scream of fear rose in Eddie's throat, and the scythe suddenly jerked him into the air. He saw that his hands were bones, and his skin was falling off his arms.

Eddie was turning into a skeleton.

Mattie cried out in alarm as she looked up. "Eddie, drop it!" She pointed the Spyglass up, but no beam shot out. The Spyglass had buried herself deep within the recesses of her metal prison, terrified by the events—chaos and death. "Spyglass!" Mattie shook the inert Spyglass in frustration.

Geeta's upturned face showed her fear. "Oh, Eddie!" she cried out. "Ungrasp the scythe!" Geeta pulled out Mr. Biddle's Card of Time, and Mattie, seeing what she was doing, followed. "We will throw them up to Eddie!" Geeta cried. Both girls flung their cards up, hoping they would cover Eddie and take him to safety. But the cards just boomeranged back into their hands, slick and black and blank. Geeta felt her heart sink. "Oh, Mattie," she said, and saw that Mattie's eyes were filling with tears as well. They looked up into the sky helplessly as Eddie turned more and more into a skeleton, arms and hands now bones. His face was peeling off and his head was turning into a skull.

The scythe yanked Eddie up by higher and higher over Humawa's forest; so high above was he that didn't hear Gilgamesh's warning or Mattie and Geeta's cries. The girls ran toward the Gilgamesh, who had shaken off the sedative effect of the chant and was slowly standing up.

"Can't you help him?" Mattie pleaded to Gilgamesh.

"Yes, please, king of Uruk!" Geeta beseeched. "Please help Eddie."

The black robes of Death had flown up from the ground and were hovering over Eddie. Like dark clouds the robes began to descend upon and envelop Eddie into their folds. Eddie felt his skin drop off him and felt a darkness seep into him.

Eddie was now almost fully within the dark robes of the Grim Reaper, and they could see he would soon be lost. But the king of Uruk only hung his head in shame, as he stood on the forest ground. With his ten feet of strength, he knew was meager in proportion to Death's grim workings. Gilgamesh saw how the boy was being taken over by the scythe, to be killed soon and his soul reaped.

The king of Uruk helplessly held up the two broken pieces of his once mighty spear and said dolefully, "I do not know how."

CHAPTER 9

the Brotherhood of evil ⚲

Deep within the dark robes of the Grim Reaper, Eddie felt the skin of his body falling off. A slow, sorrowful chant began in the forest, the multicolored leaves shimmering in anticipation of a new reaper. Eddie's arms were gone, and only the bones underneath showed as the malignant scythe pulled him about. He felt the blood and flesh leave his body as the dark robes of the Grim Reaper fell over him. Beneath the robes, darkness, death, and the musty smell of decay surrounded him. Beyond he heard the doleful chords of the forest ring out. The forest's leaves stayed the colors of autumn, and their song rose, still the chant of death, but with no power. It was instead a melancholy sound, a sound of beauty and pain but no bite.

Little master, little master, command us now, the forest cried out, but one more ruthless event had to happen before the forest could have its wish.

Eddie felt his face, still in flesh, become hot as the scythe he held in his hands of bone turned toward him, poising its sharp point over his forehead. Death's reaper could not be of the living. And Eddie was still a living being whose soul was still in his body, and the scythe was going to reap his soul. Eddie felt a spiral of heat emerge from the middle of his forehead, the third eye, as the sharp point of the scythe moved closer. Once his soul was reaped, there would be no head, and Eddie would become faceless and fully Death's servant.

Control the weapon! Eddie suddenly heard his father's voice from deep within. *Don't let the weapon control you!* And then he felt a surge of power coming from his father and running through his body, and words came from his mouth, "Ooorah...ooorah"— a great battle cry formed. Then words that Eddie didn't know he knew came forth. It was the ancient battle cry of warriors that he heard in his ears. *Alala! Alale!* Eddie felt his father's voice come through him. "*Alala! Alale!*" These words came from the memories of warriors before him. "*Alala! Alale!*"

Below him on the ground, Gilgamesh heard the ancient battle cry of the pure-hearted *muktablu*, the cry of the warrior. He threw his head back, the dark ropes of his hair falling away as he roared the warrior's cry, "*Alala! Alale!*" The strength of the warriors' chant resounded through the forest. "*Alala! Alale! Alala! Alale!*"

High above in the sky, the scythe suddenly became docile in Eddie's hands and fell back from his forehead. *Declare your victory! You are master!* Eddie heard his father's words. "I am master!" Eddie cried out to the scythe, and the voices of warriors of pure heart from times past rang out and echoed his call. Eddie's voice vibrated through the forest, and again he felt the might of ten thousand warriors pure of heart across the eons surge through his body. "I am master!" As he commanded the scythe, the dark robes dropped off him and fell to the ground, disintegrating into a dark black powder. Eddie was transformed again, the bones of his body quickly covered with blood and flesh.

Deep within the tunnels below the Palace of Ashurnasirpal, within the recesses of the City of the Condemned, the sounds of Eddie's triumphant cry as he held Death's scythe—

I am master!"—reverberated. The cry rang loudly inside the shadowy cells of the souls that inhabited the tunnels: liars, cheaters, murders, assaulters, and those whose souls were robbed of them in the forest of Humawa. All had been condemned to the many circles of terrors for eternity. Then above the imprisoned creatures, the sound of the rusty iron gates swinging open echoed through the deep tunnels. The dark underworld shook in confusion as the sound of the gates to the City of the Condemned flung open from the cheating of the Grim Reaper. Then from beneath the gates, from the miserable burrows where they had been held bolted, the creatures of the underworld rose up: the silent flying creatures with wings like bats, others like large rodents, faces ensnared in greed, their mouths ever nibbling at nothing; creatures that were half dragons, half scorpions, with their human faces stained with tears of regret, of avarice, of duplicity; creatures with three faces, all eyes bleeding, and wasp wings upon their bodies, ghosts of the ancient and evil warriors who wished to cheat death, their tarnished armor clanging about. All rose through the tunnels, up and out, wailing in confusion. Their souls were like tattered clothing upon them, as the ghastly spirits floated upward like balloons.

And the beast, once the great King Ashurnasirpal II, raised his hairy bull head, and flames of anger shot out from his nostrils as he galloped toward the open bloody gates to the City of the Condemned. When the beast heard the triumphant cry of the living boy holding Death's scythe, he felt his power diminish at once. He was no longer holder of Humawa's forest, where mortal men were lured in their dreams and where a deep slumber would overtake them, dead to the world, and Death's creature reaped so many souls.

The Great Beast roared to no avail as the fleeing spirits flew past:

Scorners, blasphemers, corpses!
Return, I command you,
to where you belong,
into the City of the Condemned!

Ashurnasirpal roared again and again, "Return, I command you, to the City of the Condemned!" But his call went unheeded. The beast bent his head down as the escaping spirits of the underworld rushed around him, beating him down to the ground. There was no world for them, they whose souls had been reaped by Death, whose instrument now lay within the hands of a boy, a living being. Their souls shook in bewilderment as they flew upward and out of the Great Beast's lair through the roofs of the tunnels. Some in life had been good but had entered the evil forest of Humawa, only to be captured in slumber. Others had evil upon their person, like a sheen, and they too had entered the forest of Humawa, arrogant in their hopes of finding treasure and power. These souls—the blasphemers, the scorners, the liars, and cheats—hadn't sold their souls to Satan but could have redeemed themselves in their mortal lives. So it was that these escaping spirits were composed of the innocent, whose balance of good and evil lay in the range of good; those whose balance tipped toward evil; and those who were whispers away from pure evil.

The rusty iron gates remained open, and the Great Beast rose, looked up, and could do nothing. He, holder of the keys to the City of the Condemned, saw the spirits rise up and through what was the bottom floor of his palace, the great Palace of Ashurnasirpal. The tunnels lay beneath the grandeur of the palace in labyrinthine coils that went deep below into the ground, to the gates to the City of the Condemned. Here, for eons, Ashurnasirpal first in his cruel mortal reign, then as the ruler of the City of the Condemned, had imprisoned the captured souls from the forest of Humawa. *Lost. Lost.* The beast felt doom fall upon him as he stood by the open, bloody, rusty gates to the City of the Condemned, the air foul and dank with his defeat.

Behind the beast rose a red glow, the angry glow of the two red orbs of Marduk, which soon surrounded him. The beast's hairy body quailed as the red glow grew into flames and he felt the full searing displeasure of the Dark Master, Marduk.

Who is master?

The Great Beast shook his body and mustered the strength against the excruciating heat of the flames to speak, "It is you, Master."

The red orbs of the Dark Master's eyes flashed as the flames around the beast grew.

Tell me, beast,
if I am master,
who then holds
Death's scythe?

To this Ashurnasirpal could not respond. Humawa was his servant, and his servant had allowed Death's scythe to slip away, to a mortal boy no less. Incensed that this should be, the beast bent his hairy head and shook it. "Master, all shall be again under your dominion."

Marduk's voice shifted the earth under the beast's hooves, and he fell, hitting the flames.

A boy now holds Death's scythe.
The dead rise out of
the City of the Condemned,
and the girl who holds the Spyglass
has thrown time into chaos!
And you dare say
that all shall be under
my dominion?

Then four demons in the form of giant gray horses with a black horn in the middle of their foreheads rose from the flames and surrounded the Great Beast, their teeth bared and a yellow foam forming on their lips. The beast cowered and tried to back away from the demon horses, but there was nowhere to go.

The Dark Master spoke, his words sounding the first tones of the punishment to come.

Ashurnasirpal,
once a great king,
shall you be lower
than the maggots that feed upon the dead?

The four demon horses charged toward the beast, their hooves stomping upon him, their black horns plunging into his hairy hide. Ashurnasirpal was enveloped in fright. These were the Four Demons of Destruction, who rode over their victims and pummeled them into the ground, so nothing remained of their will but dust. Ashurnasirpal shook himself. Terror was what he threw upon others. He, Ashurnasirpal, wouldn't be clothed in the whimpering garments of the cowering. The beast, with a strength that came from eons of having controlled others, rose up against the demon horses. He snorted flames from his nostrils and charged toward them. The demon horses rose up on two legs, and Ashurnasirpal roared in rage, the flames from his nostrils striking their faces. The Great Beast again and again charged at the demon horses, all of his anger now aroused. His fury rose at his servant Humawa for having allowed the loss of the scythe and at his being imprisoned in this beastly body. Ashurnasirpal thought again and again of how great his mortal kingdom had been and how he would rule again, not as a beast but as a king, with all the armament of power. The enraged beast struck out again and again at the demon horses, growing stronger and larger with each breath of rage. His hairy body was now singed by the flames of Marduk's ferocious hell's fire, but the demon horses fell back against the beast's ferocious strikes, hitting the burning ground and dissolving into the flames.

The flames fell away and out. Then there was a blackness, relieved only by the red orbs of Marduk. His voice now entered the beast's ears.

Beast, you have held yourself
against the Four Demons of Destruction,
but I warn you,

though I let you now escape
their hooves,
do not think you are safe
until the scythe is returned
and the Twin Tablets
of Destiny lie upon my breast.

The Great Beast spoke. "It will be as you wish, Master." He stood upon his two hooves, his body uglier than ever, with large patches of hair singed bare. An odor more foul than that of the decay of a thousand carcasses filled his nostrils as the red orbs faded.

Eddie landed on two feet, crouched to the ground in the forest of Humawa. He couldn't fall in the airborne way, as he had the scythe grasped in one hand, large and ominous in appearance but in his hands weightless as a feather. His eyes were wide, for once on the sturdiness of ground, he realized it was he who now possessed this weapon, the Grim Reaper's scythe, which was powerful beyond anything he could have fathomed. He remained in the crouched position. Somewhere in time was his father, still in the jungles of Vietnam, whose presence Eddie felt again. Something in Eddie's soul was now hushed, as if he needed silence to understand the enormity of the change in him. He had changed, and changed forever.

Mattie was peering down at him with squinted eyes. "Are you OK, Eddie?" she asked.

Geeta also was gazing at him, her owl eyes taking in his expressions. She saw the change in Eddie's face, and in her mind, she thought of ThaTha. *Destiny falls upon one and tests the soul.* Eddie's soul would be tested severely by this scythe; this Geeta saw at once, and her brow furrowed. She was worried for Eddie.

Eddie slowly stood up but remained silent. Both girls sensed that Eddie needed space, and the scythe by his side—the large and gnarly wooden handle, the fierce blade that bent inward, large and vicious in appearance—had altered him somehow. Mattie and Geeta felt a sharp shiver run through their bodies, a primeval instinct that living beings feel in their souls when confronted with the instrument of death. Their eyes were mixed with awe and fear—fear not of Eddie but the scythe and what it might do to him.

The king of Uruk picked up the two pieces of his broken spear, and the strength of a thousand warriors flowed through his hands. From his throat sprang the song of the warrior, "*Alala! Alale!*" From his hands rose a heat, and the two pieces immediately melded together, and the magical spear was whole again. Gilgamesh, king of Uruk, was again strong, his weapon restored. He approached Eddie, who had watched the restoration of the spear with silent eyes. Gilgamesh knew the young boy had acted with selflessness but didn't know how he had changed that which he should not have.

Eddie's eyes took in the king of Uruk but said nothing, his voice caught in his throat by all the strange events his mind was still processing.

"*Muktablu,*" Gilgamesh said in soft tones, for he saw that the boy was surrounded by silence and words rang hard upon his ears. "Do you understand how it is that you have cheated Death? That you have stolen the weapon of Death from the Grim Reaper's skeletal hands?"

Eddie didn't speak. All this that the giant king spoke of, he knew, so he remained silent but listening. Somewhere in the periphery of his awareness he sensed that Mattie and Geeta were there, listening as well.

Gilgamesh continued, "And you also destroyed the reaper when you stole his scythe. In doing so you, face the wrath of the merciless Dark Master Marduk, in whose servant Humawa's forest we are now trapped and must journey out of."

The giant blue figure of the king of Uruk paused. "You have fought the enemy with pureness of heart and selflessness of spirit." Gilgamesh, king and three-quarters god, suddenly bent down on one knee like the knights of old, his spear held to one side, with his head bowed to Eddie. "Now you are truly a warrior both in name and spirit, *muktablu.*"

Eddie felt a blush of heat rise to his face as he looked at the bowed head of the king of Uruk. No one had ever bowed to him, least of all a king! Warrior. "*Muktablu,*" the king said again, and Eddie felt the power of the word surge through him. *Muktablu.*

With growing alarm Geeta heard the king of Uruk's words. Eddie had cheated Death, but beyond that, he had destroyed the Grim Reaper. Did that mean that no soul could be reaped? But if so—and here Geeta's head spun—what then? Creation was in chaos, the River of Time in flux, and did Death now not exist? But did not the soul exist anyway? Eternal and unchanging? The dualities, creation and destruction, must both exist, was it not so? Geeta's head whirled in confusion and fear. *Maya, illusion. What is real is unreal, and what is unreal is real. Know that the splendor of the sun that shines forth in the universe, the moon that brightens the dark sky, and the fire that burns brightly are all of the One.* ThaTha's words rang in Geeta's ears. *The ocean of the mortal world has neither real truth nor order.* Oh, but *ThaTha,* she beseeched, *what does that mean for my friends? For me?* But ThaTha's voice remained silent.

Mattie was very happy that Eddie was OK. Still, she saw that he was different now. He was always pretending like he was a soldier, but now...with that weapon of his, he seemed like a soldier—a warrior, like the king had said. Mattie's eyes caught the silence that was around Eddie, something she couldn't put her finger on. Eddie was different now, maybe like she had been different ever since she'd held the Spyglass, and ever since the people—*her people*—of Nineveh had given her golden robes. Yes, she *was* different, and her skin always had a golden glow underneath it now. And Geeta also had changed; the gypsies had called her "Princess" and looked at her with a lot of respect. Mattie knew she was different now, no longer just fifth grader Mattie O'Reilly from Hackensack, New Jersey. And she had to think and concentrate—for example "What was the flying frog and where was it?"—for somewhere out there that snake and his creepy creatures had her mom, and she had to save her. *Oh, and my dad too.* Mattie chastised herself again for continually forgetting about Paddy; still she really didn't know him and all, so maybe she could be excused. They were all different now than when this whole thing had started that afternoon in the basement of Sears, Mattie concluded—her, Geeta, and Eddie. Yes, Mattie was *very* happy that Eddie was OK, she thought again. But she wondered how much a king bowing to him was going to go Eddie's head. He was bossy, sure. Mattie thought of when Eddie would make himself captain of the team when they played kickball in the park on Andersen Street. She kind of smiled to herself. Good ol' bossy Eddie! He'd always be giving orders to her and Geeta—"Go there" or "Kick now!" Just think what things would be like now that a king had bowed to him and he had that scythe! Then the reality of the situation hit her—this wasn't kickball in the park, and Eddie had something that belonged to the dead...to that skeleton, and that couldn't be good. But, Mattie reminded herself, Eddie was OK, and that was all that mattered. Plus maybe now they could find her mom, and dad too; maybe now that Eddie had that...that... thing, they could fight any bad guys like that nasty snake. Mattie now thought of the Spyglass; she was Mistress, and she would have to have a talk with that Spyglass, just like her mom would with Mattie when she went "astray." That's exactly what Mattie resolved she would do—have a long "chat" with the Spyglass about how the Spyglass was supposed to do what Mattie said, for after all Mattie was the Mistress and not the other way around.

But the Spyglass—oh, duplicitous, double-crossing entity that she was—still in Mattie's hand, thought differently. *Very* differently. Now the Spyglass's eyes looked out of her metal prison, and she began to scheme, for always at the forefront of her mind was her desire—to have a soul she could fully control. And a cold-blooded scheme hatched in her mind while she lay clutched in the innocent and unsuspecting hand of Mattie. Now here was this boy, the Spyglass thought, holding Death's pitiless scythe in his hands. Surely, this boy, this flimsy silly boy, could be overcome by all the force the Spyglass had. The boy, Eddie, must be killed, and the scythe must become her property, the Spyglass concluded. Then, with Death's scythe in the Spyglass's control, her escape out of the metal prison would be assured. But first, her Mistress, the child Mattie, must be brought under full sub-mission. No more would she allow herself to be driven from treacherous stone to stone. Once the Spyglass reigned supreme over Mattie's soul, the impenetrable fog that imprisoned her memory would lift. She would know who she truly was. Then, she, Spyglass, also would know the secret—where it was that the daughter who held the second half of the Twin Tablet of Destiny lay hidden. And with the Spyglass in possession of Death's scythe,

the daughter would be easily disposed of, and the Tablet hers. Here a great surge of energy went through the Spyglass at the thought of being equal to Marduk. *Then we'll see*, thought the Spyglass, *which of us rules supreme!*

Mattie felt the heat of the Spyglass in her hands. She saw that it was glowing and felt puzzled. Maybe that disobedient Spyglass had heard Mattie. Maybe the Spyglass was finally going to listen and be obedient to her.

Deep within the ground, in the dark netherworld of the tunnels of the City of the Condemned, the Great Beast Ashurnasirpal angrily marked with his hooves two lines—one for the red-haired child who held the Spyglass and one for the boy who dared to hold Death's scythe in his living hands. He roared his curse, a bloodcurdling roar. "Die you shall!" The beast resolved that they would perish and that he again would have the Dark Master's favor, for Ashurnasirpal still held power, although the tunnels had been emptied of the stolen and blasphemous souls. Under the labyrinth, deeper than the tunnels, were those who freely had traded their souls for paltry earthly power that lasted but a blink of an eye. They had readily and willingly made this trade; they weren't souls stolen in sleep by the Grim Reaper, or taken by fear and torture, or those condemned by their mortal acts—these were lost for now, until the possession of Death's scythe could be again within the Dark Master's dominion. Those who had willingly given their souls to the Dark Master, however, remained in the underworld, and among those were the legions of evil spirits who had burrowed deep beneath the tunnels and whose wickedness was such that when they walked the mortal earth all who came into contact with them felt a wave of terror crawl down their spine. And of these evil spirits that had burrowed themselves beneath the tunnels of the City of the Condemned were the Three.

Ashurnasirpal plunged his head down as he dived deep beneath the City of the Condemned into the cavernous darkness, into and beyond the recesses of the punishing tunnels. Into blackness the beast's singed body was spun as he plunged downward, downward into the murkiness, both black in color and heavy in its bleakness, until he hit a hard surface. There his eyes adjusted to the dimness. He heard wails of pain and felt rather than saw the presence of these spirits of harshness—these wicked ones whose evil had grown through the cruelty they had brandished when alive, sinister ones to whom history had assigned names but whose pages could never really record the depth of their depravity. In this deep black hole where *wickedness* was too mild a word to capture the nature of its denizens were the Three. And there was a clandestine thing known to Ashurnasirpal, and not known to the Dark Master, so surreptitiously was this knowledge held. The Three secreted a resentment deep in their hearts. These Three felt cheated by Marduk, not because he had taken their souls but because their earthly exquisite pleasure of perpetrating pain upon others had been so short. And in this Ashurnasirpal was himself sympathetic, for he too held resentment against the Dark Master. For though Marduk had given him lordship over the City of the Condemned, he kept him as a beast of burden, foul in smell and appearance. The Dark Master had lowered him in rank beneath the vile snake Gneezy, and also, like the Three, the earthly pleasures of his sadism were no longer potent. Ashurnasirpal again felt the sting of the Dark Master's actions. And so it was formed, born of this resentment against Marduk, born of a greed for power—more power, all power—slowly, a dance of loyalty among those incapable of loyalty; a union of trust among the most untrustworthy. It, the union, was formed among the Three and Ashurnasirpal, a covert brotherhood, the Brotherhood of Evil.

It was known that there were seven secret names, seven sounds, that conferred power upon Marduk. It was also known that no thoughts could be held secret in the Dark Master's world, for all was heard and understood by Marduk, as a means to thwart the traitor. But what wasn't known, but came into the knowledge of Ashurnasirpal, was that when these seven secret sounds that conferred power to Marduk were desecrated, the Dark Master would be deaf to the thoughts of those he enslaved. And the story of how the Great Beast came upon this knowledge, of this chant of those seven desecrated names of Marduk, had never been told; it was only known to the beast. But when the Three had formed their union with Ashurnasirpal, he had shared it with them. Ashurnasirpal reluctantly had told the three denizens of the Dark Underworld the desecrated names. The beast had given them this information out of necessity, for the Three had asked to what end such a union would benefit them. And how was it, they asked with their eyes and hands—for to think it, to say it was too dangerous—that the beast could protect them from the wrath of Marduk? It was then that that beast showed them. He uttered the desecrated sounds that enveloped them, made them silent to the prying ears of Marduk. Here now they could have a coalition of strength born of secrecy. They could plan and plot their deceitful enterprises free of apprehension that Marduk would discover their treachery. They could plot and gather power, keep power over the evil souls that dripped down, sometimes in spurts, sometimes like a flood, into their cavern through the ages. They could make certain that they, the Three and Ashurnasirpal, held sway over others beneath them who had served them when they'd had mortal bodies and that others in the time to come would show their evil faces and cruelty in the world above. So it came to be that the Three knew of the seven desecrated names of Marduk through the ritual that the Great Beast performed—where their eyes grew dry and bloody, and where the bodies that held them convulsed in pain so horrific that Three couldn't speak. Then Ashurnasirpal had uttered words, a dark spell, so that each of the four yielded a portion of his strength, so that each was weaker alone then they had been, and if the Three were to join, they would still be weaker than the remaining one. This was to guard against the lure of treachery, which all understood ran potent in each of the four traitors to Marduk. Then, once this portion of each of the four's power was surrendered, they cast another spell and swore themselves into the Brotherhood of Evil. It was then that the words entered and stayed in their minds, and they bore a faint emblem, ⟨𝍦⟩, the Sign of the Four, which lay on their foreheads, invisible to all but one another.

The Great Beast thought of all of this as he stood upon the ground of the cavern of darkness. Then he whispered the desecrated names of Marduk.

Ankia-en-lugal,

Ugug,

Umum,

Tudu,

Udud,

Gar-gash,

Bilulu-en.

As he did, in the darkness of where he stood, a dim light enveloped him in a protective ball, over and under the very ground where he stood so that he was encased and protected from Marduk. Then, around the sickly yellow light, an intricate black web spun and covered the ball. In this black web was now Ashurnasirpal. He called for the Brotherhood of Evil to emerge, in the rank they had devised for themselves, a tacit acknowledgment of the order of their power, though each one knew that the whole was greater in strength than its parts so that none tried to overtake the other. Loyalty to one another was paramount to keeping their strength, for if they fell to their natural instincts of treachery, the Brotherhood would vanish, and without the Brotherhood, the power they held deep in the bowels of hell over the condemned souls also would disappear, for Marduk, the Dark Master, was fickle. Look at the ascendancy of the snake, as the Great Beast had described to them. But the Brotherhood had knit a web of deceitful denizens of the dark underworld that remained powerful and, in truth, under the Brotherhood's submission and control, though they all bowed to the Dark Master. In the living world, an emperor with many thousands of acres and millions of subjects cannot control everything at all times. So too was it in the underworld; Marduk held dominion over all, in theory, but in practice it was the Brotherhood who had held sway over their own servants. And also the force of the Brotherhood kept alive the whispered voice of avarice and yearning for power over others in the ears of the living. Through this, over the ages, the Brotherhood had cultivated those mortals who would lead others to acts of tremendous violence toward their fellow man and have such tarnished souls that it was only inevitable that they readily would surrender themselves to the Dark Master, known as Satan, Devil, Marduk. The Brotherhood met to keep their strength, for as time moved, there were more and more of those with wickedness, men and women who readily gave way to the Dark Master, and without the Brotherhood, the four would have long ago lost their dominion over the underground terrain of darkness.

As was their tradition, in a nod to their pedigree and status, first came out a being who had above his head a wreath of leaves like a crown, but these leaves were dry and bloodied.

"Khan of the Huns." The beast snorted the name and bowed his hairy bull head down.

Khan of the Huns was round faced, and his skin was sallow colored. He had no hair upon his face. His forehead was large and protruding; his almond-shaped eyes were askew, one higher than the other; and upon his head was always a cap of bloody leaves. This Khan of the Huns had been a fearsome leader, so much so that his name had evoked terror. He had a narrow and cruel mouth, and a large neck about which ten small scorpions were entwined like a living necklace. Khan had eyes that had been dead even when he was in his mortal form until the year 453. The gray robes of this man reached to his knees and were stained with blood. In his hands he clasped by the hair the beheaded heads of his enemies, whose bloodshot eyes bulged in horror. The ferocity of his plunder and invasion had spread across the lands of those who had lived by the Ural River, the Danube, the Baltic Sea, and into the very lands that bordered Nineveh. So great had he been in mortal life, so small in death. Khan of the Huns flung the beheaded heads against the wall, the vindictive caves now echoing their howls of pain, and a small smile of pleasure flitted across his moon face; small because he had played this game through eternity, and it had long ago lost its allure.

Then Khan of the Huns said as the beast stood by him, "I will bring forth the others." As he spoke, blood spilled from his mouth, for his last moments in his mortal body were of drowning in his own blood. He then said:

> *Wicked of heart,*
> *cruel of deed,*
> *I call upon you.*
> *Rise for our brother,*
> *for he, the Great Beast, Ashurnasirpal, calls you.*

The walls of the cave fluttered as a dank and foul breeze rose. A distant trumpet sounded, heralding the presence of a great one yet to come. A large dark horse galloped out of the wall. Its rider was a man with a narrow face like a ferret, with a long nose that imperiously presided over a black mustache, a roof of sorts over red pouty lips and a sharp chin. There was a greenish hue and an oily sheen to his skin. Black hair effeminately swirled in long coils about his shoulders, and upon his head was a foppish dark-red velvet hat that appeared to be adorned by pearls, diamonds, and rubies. He wore upon his body a coat made of the same dark-red velvet, with large buttons that if one examined closely were in reality human eyes of his victims—protruding eyes that twitched in fear. The man dismounted the horse. He stood upon two bony legs. In his hands he held sharp and oiled stakes, and threw each one into the ground with a flare. These small stakes signified his penchant for impaling his enemies. He grinned, showing his small, sharp, rodent teeth.

"Prince of Wallachia." The beast snorted the name and bowed, though this prince was known by many names for the cruel pleasure he took in the slow leeching of the lifeblood from his victims with nails and fire, with knives and stakes. *Vlad.* But no one dared whisper this name, or worse, *Impaler.* Among his legion, this prince had control over those who lived in the twilight between death and life, the unliving, those who rose in the night and plunged their fangs into the necks of the living to suck their blood, and who rested in dark tombs through the day. And these unliving the prince held sway over, and in that he differed from the others in the Brotherhood, who had no legions of the unliving that walked the earth. This, the prince felt, placed him above the others, and a resentment had grown in him that he should be called second and not last, for the last to be called was the one that the Brotherhood had tacitly acknowledged held the most power. The prince took off his red-velvet, jewel-adorned hat as he returned the bow. The jewels that glittered were not pearls but the teeth of those the prince had tortured; the diamonds were small sharp blades that had been used to cut his victims, but the rubies were real.

The prince and the khan stood silent and formed a small circle with the beast.

From the walls came the sound of discordant bells, tolling the song of death. And slowly stepped out a pale man with a balding head fringed by coarse hair and a long face that seemed to melt into his beard. He had bulging eyes and a sloping nose. His face was stern, and he held in his hand a pointed staff that poured blood. He seemed quiet and aristocratic in aspect; his power was immense, for he held under his sway thousands of souls, they who had willingly, upon his order, tortured and killed with abandon when in their mortal form. This man was said to have killed his own son, so callous was he—grand duke, but first tsar of Russia once.

"Grand Duke of Muscovy." The beast snorted the name and bowed. The Grand Duke bowed in return, a slight and anemic bow, but a bow nonetheless.

The four creatures formed a circle in the center of the cave. In unison they spoke the desecrated names of Marduk so as to doubly cover their activity against the red orbs of the Dark Master. The chants rose in sound as the symbol upon their foreheads, 𒀭, pulsated a blood red.

Ankia-en-lugal,

Ugug,

Umum,

Tudu,

Udud,

Gar-gash,

Bilulu-en.

Khan of the Huns spoke first, and his flat face held no mercy, "Brother, we have heard that the gates of your City of the Condemned lay open and that your tunnels are empty of the spirits. We have heard this is because Death's scythe is now held by a mortal and also that all of the order of the underworld lies at the cusp of destruction."

With a black look of anger, the Duke of Muscovy declared, "Death's scythe must be captured! We know it is the Dark Master who has commanded you, beast, to capture and kill the yellow-haired boy as well as the red-haired child who holds the Spyglass and those who protect them and whose power comes from the White Book of Magic. It is for this you call us together."

The Prince of Wallachia, who had observed the order of rank, had remained silent. *Fools,* he had thought as he heard the duke and khan speak. *Slow, blundering fools.* But he didn't say this. He merely smiled and shook his black locks. He saw upon the beast Ashurnasirpal's eyes something that spoke of a grander plan. "I think you underestimate the beast, Duke," he finally said.

The Grand Duke of Muscovy's face reflected displeasure at this disrespect, but it was always so with the prince, who thought himself the grandest, that small rodent from Romania who was nothing next to him, once tsar of Russia. However, the prince had an astuteness that Khan of the Huns and the duke lacked; their brutality ran roughshod over others. But the prince—he was elegant in his aggression. He understood the subtleties of torture, and therefore the psychology of control. Ashurnasirpal didn't need the cover of the Brotherhood for tasks the Dark Master would approve of, tasks that would return to him lost souls. No, the beast could have called upon all the souls who still served the Dark Master to aid him.

The khan now agreed with the prince, and his lopsided eyes reflected his concurrence. "No," said the khan. "These things of which you speak, Duke of Muscovy, such things do not need the cover of the Brotherhood. Is it not so, beast?"

The three waited for the Great Beast to speak.

But Ashurnasirpal kept silent. The other three had taken in how the beast appeared, how his body reeked of decay even more than before, how his hairy body was singed and bare in places, signifying that he had been punished for displeasing the Dark Master. The beast said nothing still, his blood-red eyes again scanning the Brotherhood, his foul breath coming out in spurts from his wet nostrils. The cover of the desecrated words he trusted, for they had yet to fail the Brotherhood. But this thought, this idea of the beast's—it was enormously arrogant and injudicious. The Brotherhood of Evil hadn't given him authority over the City of the Condemned, as the tunnels were his, but they had allowed him dominion over the souls they controlled; they had allowed the beast to harness their power with his. But now the beast had come empty-handed, for though there were a scattering of souls within the recesses of the City of the Condemned from his reign as king, much of his power had come from the souls reaped in Humawa's forest, and these were gone. And those who had been condemned to the underworld due to their nefarious mortal acts, but who sought escape from darkness, also had been lost.

Ashurnasirpal saw that the Brotherhood was well aware of his weakened state; he came with little in the way of power. The Brotherhood was forged as four, but would it remain? Could it, even if one of them no longer possessed much in the way of riches—that is, souls, which constituted power in the underworld? The khan, the duke, and the prince, in fact, already had silently concluded that Ashurnasirpal should no longer be their leader—still one of the four, yes, for that was irrevocably sworn, but not their leader. And their thoughts rang out as if spoken. The beast still said nothing.

The prince fluttered his hand up impatiently. "Beast," he said, "speak."

Ashurnasirpal shifted his hairy body, and his hooves marked the ground in uncertainty. Would they accede to the beast all power, give him full control over those who swore allegiance to them? This he did not know, but without this, his plan could not be. There was no other way. The khan, duke, and prince heard these thoughts, but did not understand them, for deeper beneath lay hidden what the beast wanted to say.

Then the Great Beast made a motion, and the four closed the circle, with their heads bent toward one another. "We shall overthrow Marduk," he whispered.

The three were shocked into silence by the audacity of the statement.

The duke spoke first and stated simply, "The Dark Master is all-powerful."

The beast shook his head. He spoke quickly and with passion and hatred, for there was still much anger at Marduk in Ashurnasirpal's heart for his being imprisoned within the foul body of a beast for his treachery in trying to capture the Spyglass for himself eons ago. But nonetheless he spoke his thoughts. Why should they, the Brotherhood of Evil, give away possession of the scythe and Twin Tablet of Destiny to Marduk? If the Dark Master were all-powerful and could overcome the force of goodness, wouldn't he have done so already? What need did the all-powerful have for his servants other than for them to bend in supplication? And also the Dark Master couldn't stop the boy from taking the scythe, so strong was the power of White Magic and goodness. No. The Dark Master didn't hold all power.

The prince nodded and thoughtfully twirled a long black lock in his bony fingers. Though there was a truth to this, he still said, "The Seven Tablets say that Marduk rules supreme. The force of evil reigns at the last in its triumph over good."

Here the beast countered, "What if the tale written in the Seven Tablets has been altered? What if it did not conclude with the battle between good and evil, with Marduk reigning supreme over all gods of the underworld? What if those ancient gods of malevolence have not been conquered? What if their allegiance to the Dark Master is fickle?

The duke and the khan said nothing. The prince, intrigued, arched an eyebrow. His long black locks swayed as he spoke. "Yes, beast, it is true that Marduk is only as powerful as the souls he can hold under his dominion, and this is why the dark undergods bow to him. And with time in chaos, and creation and destruction laid asunder, souls pledged and plunged downward are no longer guaranteed."

The Great Beast nodded and continued, "So it is, Prince. And we have always known that the Dark Master is only half strong. We know his Hidden Sister—on whose breast it is said that their mother, the enfeebled and powerless Tiamet, laid the second Tablet of Destiny—holds the other half of power. The Dark Master seeks sole possession of both Tablets, the Dup Shimati."

The duke nodded in thought. "And do you, Ashurnasirpal, still hold in your trap the two hapless humans that the red-haired child holds precious? The child who clasps the Spyglass?"

The beast nodded and grunted. "The humans are held in the Corkscrew of Terror, the tunnels burrowed deep beneath my city. It is certain that the red-haired child will fall into the corkscrew's trap to rescue them. And the Spyglass, who it is said holds the secret to where the Hidden Sister lays, will be captured."

An idea struck the khan now in all its force, and his lopsided eyes gleamed in anticipation. "Yes," he spoke with excitement. "We have no need of the Dark Master, for now Marduk's power is seeping away, as the trapped souls in the City of the Condemned have risen up and out. It may be another god of the underworld who will rise and take Marduk's place."

"Or," said the prince, his pouty red lips aflame with the tantalizing possibility, "the Brotherhood."

So the plan was constructed. It would be easy, for the yellow-haired boy and the red-haired girl were within the forest of Humawa and with only the foolish king of Uruk to protect them. It also had been seen that the wizard who called for the White Book of Magic—he who had shared a mortal womb with the snake Gneezy—was lost upon the Path of the Virtuous, no longer a protector of the red-haired child. The Brotherhood would capture both the red-haired girl and the boy with the scythe by leading them to the trap of where the two humans were. Once there they would be killed, and the Brotherhood would possess the scythe and the Spyglass and quickly find the Hidden Sister and the Second Tablet of Destiny. Then, holding these powerful objects, they would fight any souls who still swore allegiance to Marduk and overthrow him. Then they would hold to their breasts both Tablets of Destiny. They, the Brotherhood of Evil, would reign supreme. Four heads were better than one, they knew. They would put aside their individual needs for glory and share the power, for such power as this was too much for one; the opposition, that of the gods of the underworld, was too strong for only one to hold both Tablets for long. No, they said, such power needed the unity of the Brotherhood of Evil. Still, in each creature's mind, a perfidious, dangerous, and disloyal thought rang.

Greater than the Dark Master Marduk, I will rule, thought Khan.

Greater than the Dark Master Marduk, I will rule, thought the Prince.

Greater than the Dark Master Marduk, I will rule, thought the Duke.

Greater than the Dark Master Marduk, I will rule, thought Ashurnasirpal.

And when it occurred, each of the four read in the others' eyes the treachery that ran through each mind, and nodded in recognition of their deep, true traitorous natures. But still, without all four there was no possibility of overthrowing Marduk, and so the plan was laid to overthrow him. They would allow the beast full dominion over their horde of souls to overcome Marduk and his forces, for it was he who held the human prey. They would go forth, and when the moment came, when Marduk was laid asunder, it would be all four—the Brotherhood of Evil—who simultaneously would clasp both Tablets of Destiny to their chests, and no one in all eternity would be able to overcome them. The sky of heaven would fall into their wicked claws.

CHAPTER 10

the young *muktaвlu*

In the forest of Humawa, Eddie stood motionless, held in his surprise at the king of Uruk's supplication to him. He turned to king's bowed head. In the stillness of the forest, Eddie heard his father's voice. *With honor comes power, and with power comes duty. And with both comes humility.* Eddie knew at once what to do; he fell to one knee himself, bowing in supplication to the king.

The king of Uruk peered up, startled to see Eddie kneeling on the ground, bowed to him. Then Eddie looked up at the king, and upon the boy's face an image shimmered, for from somewhere within the folds of events that might be or once were, deep within the recesses of time when a war waged in the jungles of Vietnam, Sergeant Petersen sensed the great danger that his boy was now in. It was a danger of which Eddie had little understanding. Gilgamesh saw the square-jawed face of the sergeant flickering under Eddie's face and at once recognized a kindred soul, that of a warrior.

Sergeant Petersen's warrior face shone out from Eddie's face, and he beseeched the king of Uruk, *Great Warrior, Gilgamesh, king of Uruk, I ask you to protect my young son.*

The king of Uruk nodded his assent. Then the sergeant's presence disappeared, and the face of the young *muktablu* returned. Gilgamesh stood up and shook his great ropes of hair. He looked down from his height of ten feet, the plum blue of his skin glowing in resolve. "Young *muktablu*," he said to Eddie, who was still on one knee, bowed in supplication, "stand now, for we are equals. You have saved me, so in turn, *muktablu,* I will serve you."

As Gilgamesh spoke these words, the forest shook in anger. Above them a shrill sound was heard in the distance. Eddie stood up, and the scythe shivered at his side.

Eddie nodded and unconsciously touched the scythe, as if to comfort it. Mattie and Geeta had watched Eddie kneel to the king. Geeta now thought of the king's humility and Eddie's too. She also had seen a flicker, an image, float across Eddie's face, but couldn't be sure if she had really seen it.

As the two girls stood watching the king and Eddie take the first steps deep into the forest, Mattie said, "Geeta, we have to help my mom! She told me to look for the flying frog to find her."

Geeta tilted her head quizzically. "But a frog does not fly."

"*Muktablu*," Gilgamesh said in the first steps deep into the forest, observing how the scythe had taken in the anger of the forest and was trembling in the boy's hand. It was the anger of Humawa, he knew, and the Dark Master too, no doubt. "We must now journey deep into this forest." Gilgamesh didn't say where, but he knew. They would journey to Kurnigi, the land of darkness, and into deep tunnels of the underworld to find Enkidu. Then maybe together they could restore Utnapishtim, the old man with the creatures of the land, sea, and air, and who held mankind's fate but now was lost in the sea of chaos. Gilgamesh knew there would be the forces of evil, ever present, pressing upon them and into them. He also realized the journey may never get that far. Though he was three-quarters god and only one-quarter human, he could well be imprisoned in the dark chambers of the Marduk for an eternity, as he had been imprisoned in the dark basement of the British Museum, guarding the Seven Tablets of Creation, which were destroyed now. Gilgamesh, though ten feet in height and with strong muscles upon his warrior arms, now felt himself to be an ant in the face of the great mountain of fate. He shook his long ropes of hair, as if to shake off the pessimism that had seeped like a fog into his soul. There was much to do, and he, Gilgamesh, king of Uruk, couldn't fall prey to doubts and anguish.

"Come," Gilgamesh said, motioning for Geeta and Mattie to begin the steps deeper into the gloom, for he saw that the girls hadn't followed him forward. In the dark forest, the winds howled in anger as they approached. There the king of Uruk stopped in a small clearing. He stood by Eddie, small next to the vicious scythe, as the red-haired child and the small, brown, owlet child joined them. Once again he willed himself to force back doubt and fear. He held his spear upright and leaned on it for strength.

Gilgamesh spoke of the journey ahead. "We must travel through Kurnigi, the land of darkness, to find Utnapishtim, the old man who holds the secret to eternal life, lost now, captured by the dragons of darkness and death. We must learn the old man's secret before we go deeper under Kurnigi, into the City of the Condemned, where Enkidu lies and where the cruel beast Ashurnasirpal reigns supreme."

The king of Uruk paused, and in his pause, the forest that held them swayed and the leaves rustled. *We shall kill you first. We shall kill you first. We shall kill you first.* Eddie heard the threat of the forest and clasped the scythe even harder.

Mattie heard the leaves and their malicious chant; she saw how sad and serious the king of Uruk looked, probably because going through this forest was going to be a lot of work. But, Mattie noticed, he hadn't said anything about finding her mom (and dad), and Mattie wasn't going to waste time looking for that old guy first, she resolved. They were going to find her mom (and dad) then the old man. Mattie's mouth opened to form these last words, and Geeta, who heard Mattie's thoughts, decided to speak, as she felt that the king in his ten feet of height was more than just a mortal man, maybe even divine—for he was blue like Krishna—and needed to be approached with respect. Into Mattie's mind Geeta said, *Please, let me speak to the king for us.* Mattie nodded; Geeta was a lot better with words than her.

The king of Uruk saw that the girl children were holding a thought. Then the small, brown, owlet girl spoke. "King of Uruk, we too have a quest. We must find our friends, Dr. and Mrs. O'Reilly, whom the evil snake Uri Gneezy held in his tail, and also there was a beast, like a man and bull with fire from his nostrils, who was with him."

Mattie felt proud at how Geeta had spoken. Eddie nodded; his jaw was set firm. "Our mission is to find Mrs. O'Reilly and…" Here he thought, *And that fat guy who was always on my case,* but didn't say it out loud, for a *muktablu* had dignity. "…and Mattie's dad too."

Gilgamesh saw the three children, each with determination in their eyes. "I do not know of the snake, though Marduk is said to be both snake and dragon. But the beast you saw with the snake who held your friends in his tail was surely Ashurnasirpal. And so our quests are the same. I am certain Ashurnasirpal holds both my friend Enkidu and your friends. Come. Let us move forth." The giant blue king took great steps forward, and the three followed.

Mattie came up to Eddie and whispered, "You think the king is right? That my mom's where his friend is?"

Eddie nodded. "That beast was big and looked like a bull and a man, and he was working with the snake, so the intel makes sense. The beast has your mom and dad, Mattie."

Eddie stopped and looked at his two friends—Mattie looking as goofy as ever with her hair all frizzy, Geeta looking like a librarian. These two facing the army of evil! At least he was a *muktablu* and was finally armed with a weapon. Eddie now knew why Mr. Biddle had been so scared for them—how easily they could too become prisoners of the snake and the beast, how they could be killed. He kicked himself for not having tried to keep Mattie and Geeta in that egg somehow and gone by himself. Where was Mr. Biddle? And that Dr. Wigglesworth? Eddie had given them the coordinates deep in the basement of that museum. But would Biddle and Wigglesworth find them? And how much did Uri Gneezy know about where they were? Mr. Biddle had the White Book of Magic, and his cape, things they needed in order to hide from the enemy, protection they needed to venture into enemy territory to conduct the rescue mission. But all Eddie had was Geeta and Mattie and that Spyglass, which was no help at all, given that it was an unreliable weapon. Thankfully he also had the scythe and the king of Uruk. But, Eddie thought, he had to get it into those two girls' heads; that's how serious this mission was.

Eddie whispered now, his face set, saying he wasn't just talking but giving them important intel and operation orders, the

OP-ORD. He held the scythe with the blade pointed toward the ground. "Mattie, Geeta, listen," Eddie said urgently. "The snake is the enemy. We're going right into the enemy's land. The king says it's where that beast—the bull man—rules. And the snake knows we're going to come to rescue your mom and dad, Mattie. He wants that Spyglass, and he'll *kill* you for it."

"I know all that Eddie," Mattie said dismissively. "I'm not stupid."

Geeta saw the intensity in Eddie's face and knew he was worried.

The giant king turned back and saw that the children had not kept up. They must not be separated. "Come!" he called. "Hasten your pace."

Eddie started toward the king. As they walked, Geeta said, "There is more intelligence, Eddie. Mattie's mother has spoken to her. 'Find the flying frog,' she has told her, and we will find her."

Mattie nodded. "That's exactly what she said—'Find the flying frog.'"

Eddie said, "You must have heard wrong. Frogs don't fly."

"That was my initial reaction as well," Geeta said. "But then again, Eddie…" Here Geeta pointed the King of Uruk, whom they were fast approaching. "…kings are not ten feet tall and blue."

Eddie thought what Geeta said was true; this was an operation that had nothing normal about it. They were on the Path of the Virtuous; Mr. Biddle was a wizard and not a furniture salesman at Sears; Mattie had the Spyglass; Geeta was the princess of gypsies; and he was holding Death's scythe!

"OK," Eddie said. "We'll look for the flying frog."

The three caught up to the king of Uruk, and the foursome walked farther into the forest. As they walked, Mattie's eyes turned upward, drawn by the leaves that were a canopy above them, the sounds of the rustling leaves hitting her ears. She heard the woeful song of the forest, relieved only by the sharp tones of anger. All of this Mattie heard, but she didn't listen, for it was the color of the leaves that drew her eyes upward and mesmerized her. The colors were strange—some vibrant colors of orange, red, yellow; others a glistening green; still others another color. It was this other color that held her. What was it? Mattie had no words for it; instead she felt the coldness of those leaves, the color of which she couldn't describe. If she had a word for it—one she knew Mrs. Elmwood wouldn't like—it was *creepy*.

She touched the Spyglass in her pant's pocket as she and Geeta walked toward Eddie and the king. The Spyglass lay dormant. *For now*, the Spyglass seemed to be saying. *For now*. Mattie thought ruefully that there seemed to be way more rat fink in the Spyglass than good guy. Or good girl, seeing as how the Spyglass seemed to be a she. Mattie remembered she had forgotten all about having a "talk" with the Spyglass about doing what she was told to do and made a mental note to do so as soon as possible. The Spyglass also had to help her find and rescue her mom (and dad—drat if she didn't forget all about him again!).

Geeta looked up to see where Mattie's eyes were turned. She took in the strange color of leaves, but she also couldn't place a name on it. The girls couldn't know that the leaves took on the color of shadows of what was yet to come, the portending of a bleak storm of events. Geeta felt the melancholy pull of the leaves upon her heart. She thought of old ThaTha and the tales he had told her of the wise ones, the yogis, who sat in their thin cotton dhotis, their faces marked with three lines, yellow and white. They sat day upon day in the forest, willing their being to escape their bodies. Their spirits would rise up out of their mortal bodies; this journey out was filled first with fright and terror as the mortal body cried out for the spirit to return to its blood-and-bone prison. This journey of the soul, however, led to other places, to something ThaTha had said was enlighten-ment. But this forest, Geeta thought, didn't seem to be a forest of enlightenment but rather one where a dark cloak enveloped and blocked wisdom.

And Eddie, now *muktablu*, found—as one does when great-ness is placed upon one's shoulders—that the burden was both heavy and light. Young Eddie had within him the values of honor and integrity but also had a striving, a desire to be a warrior, to be one that could stand shoulder to shoulder with his father. In Eddie's mind, however, these weren't conscious thoughts. Rather the word *muktablu* rang again and again in his mind. Warrior. Another thought entered from his long-enforced dis-cipline, from his father's wisdom, and Eddie also had gleaned it from thumbing through the old and worn-out army field manu-als his father had left behind when he went to Vietnam. *Know the size of the opposing force. Assess the terrain. Know your weapons.* Eddie thought he knew none of these things, least of all his weapon—only that it was the Grim Reaper's, or at least it had been. Eddie had to acknowledge he knew little—embarrassingly little—about the scythe, but he knew that the Grim Reaper was Death, and the weapon, the scythe, was one of Death. But, he, Eddie Petersen—age eleven from Hackensack, New Jersey; son of Sergeant Peterson, deployed deep in the jungles of Vietnam—knew that his military occupational specialty (MOS) would never be death. The scythe would be a weapon of protec-tion of the weak, Eddie decided. *That's my MOS—protector of the weak.* The scythe trembled in his hands as his thoughts reached it. The forest also heard Eddie, and the leaves shook in opposition, rustling the sounds, *No, no, no, no.*

So it was, each with their thoughts wrapped around them, that the foursome—the three children and the tall, muscular, blue warrior—plunged into the thicket of the forest. Gilgamesh wielded his great spear to cut a path, for there was no cleared way, just overgrown, thorny bushes and the ever-present changing canopy of leaves above them. There were bushes with eyes for leaves and thorns that stuck out like small knives, ready to be plunged into the innocent interloper. But the thorny bushes held back, blinked their eyelids of leaves, and kept encased their sharp blades because the boy held power. He held the scythe. *And who is master of the forest?* they wondered. It couldn't be Humawa, once mighty, once strong. But could it be this boy? This yellow-haired boy who had thrown off the reaper's robe and declared himself a master? The forest and its denizens were quiet, all held as if in a hushed silence, as if the forest had taken a breath, a deep frightened breath, but had yet to exhale. Behind them— just behind them in the forest clearing that they had just left— had Eddie, the king, Mattie, or Geeta bothered to look back, they would have seen a sight that would have frozen their hearts. Gathering upon the ground from the black dust that lay there— gathering like a great, dark storm cloud—was the hooded robe of the Grim Reaper ready to pounce.

CHAPTER 11

entrance to kurnigi, the land of darkness

Sir Henry felt it now as beats of anticipation not fear. *Lady of my soul* rang in his heart; the memory was painful, yet it had surged courage and longing through him. He opened his eyes, surprised to see that he, Wigglesworth, and Biddle were not deep within the tunnels of Ashurnasirpal but instead floating on a large raft upon his beloved River Tigris. But where were they floating to? To Basra? Sir Henry wondered and recalled how in 1847 a raft of his design, much like this one, had conveyed the giant stone winged bull down the river. He remembered the hundreds of men it had taken to pull the figure out of the trench and onto a cart to be dragged from the remains of the Palace of Ashurnasirpal. Here Sir Henry shuddered at his arrogance.

But where were they now? Again floating to Basra? But this couldn't be the city of Mosul, where his friend Rassam lived, where Sir Henry was first introduced to the lures of Nineveh, where he first felt the deep longing to dig where he shouldn't have. Or was it some other evil place, not from his memory but from the prophecies of evil? There upon the giant raft, wooden beams on top of hundreds of inflated balloons of goatskins, lay a colossal stone winged figure of a lion with the head of a bearded man. Sir Henry heard the shouts of the men upon the raft, villagers who lived near the Tigris, dressed in their white robes and turbans, with sharp spears. They stood on top of the stone figure and were guiding the raft. It was a clear evening, with the mound of Nimrud, its conical shape silhoutted against the sky, turning the shades of pink and purple of a setting sun. Sir Henry himself was on the very top of the winged figure. He looked down to see that he held a weapon in his hands, a bloody sword. He saw below him two rather unconventional workers—the heaving and portly figure of L. Rufus Wigglesworth scrambling upon the winged figure to steady himself and, upon the raft itself, Herman Biddle, his white hair flowing back and his cape aglow, reflecting the pinks and purples of the sky.

Biddle recalled the clasp of the giant hand upon him as they were plunged below into the parched earth. But here now they were upon the River Tigris and not deep within the tunnels of Ashurnasirpal! Biddle looked up to Sir Henry to say that the chant hadn't worked, for they had remained in Nimrud and weren't en route to the City of Condemned. But before he could utter the words, the sky above them broke, as it if were made of pink and purple glass. It shattered and splintered. The waters below them roiled, and the villagers were thrown about, some into the river. Sir Henry, on top of the great winged figure, was startled, for the stone figure was moving. The giant statue— whose face was that of a man with a long braided beard, whose head was covered in a golden turban, and whose body was that of a winged lion—now came alive. It stood up on four legs and spread its enormous wings, tossing the figures upon it and the raft like a dog shakes off fleas. Wigglesworth cried out in alarm, as he was in danger of being tossed into the River Tigris, and held himself firmly to the limbs of the winged lion. Biddle now flew up, his winged cape about him as he landed near Sir Henry upon the great lion figure.

The water suddenly turned placid as the winged figure that held Sir Henry, Biddle, and Wigglesworth upon its body flew high into the air and toward a great palace upon the shores. Wigglesworth immediately observed that the palace must be that of King Ashurnasirpal II. That palace had been built, so the legend said, with the blood and agony of leagues of those captured by Ashurnasirpal. It was meant to be an edifice celebrating his cruel glory, though in this Ashurnasirpal had been blinded by ego, for glory could be held only by the Dark Master, not his slave. Ashurnasirpal was in fact a king but a slave too, and this he hadn't understood. But he did understand this once he had been transformed into a hairy, smelly beast. Wigglesworth knew all this but still was awed and stared in wonder at the Palace of Ashurnasirpal, as it was called—three giant stories in height, stretching a thousand feet in length. Sir Henry saw from his perch on top of the winged lion that there were gargantuan columns carved with faces held fixed in terror, their mouths open and chanting a voiceless warning. The structure glowed brightly against a deep clear-blue sky. Carved into them were still more faces and figures that moved in their stone prisons. These columns stood upon engraved walls that told a story of anger, of treachery, of deceit. As they approached the severe beauty of the palace, Biddle readily observed and felt that his magic was small and that goodness was dwarfed by the evil held here. A large wall surrounded the place, and the placid water, gleamed in a green color that shone like a mirror below them. The winged lion flew over the wall and into the fortress. The sky that was so blue turned gray, a flat slate gray.

The great winged lion-man, with its three passengers— Biddle, Sir Henry, and Wigglesworth—flew over the grounds of the Palace of Ashurnasirpal. From the earth rose thousands upon thousands of horrendous beasts—half man and scorpion, rodents with great black wings, and pale, bloody ghosts of ancient peoples—flying up and past the great winged lion-man that held Biddle, Sir Henry, and Wigglesworth, some hitting the lion-man as they flew past. The sound of the wails of the dead released from the tunnels of the City of the Condemened filled the air.

Wigglesworth held tight to the winged lion-man and gasped, "The dead are rising!"

Herman Biddle felt the fear of confusion; order was gone. *Chaos.* But what had caused the captured souls to rise? There was no mistake; the dead were rising from the depths of the City of the Condemned up and out through the Palace of Ashurnasirpal. Sir Henry was the first to see as they were batted about by more and more of the rising dead flying about the sky from the upheaval. "Look!" he cried.

Two red orbs filled the sky as the dead rose like a foul steam from the ground, the eyes of evil. Satan. Devil. Marduk. The gruesome creatures of the underworld continued to fly out of the clasp of the underworld in waves.

The red orbs grew enormous.

Traitors! Thieves! Killers!
Escape you will
but for a moment
before I shall

capture you to
join your brethren!

The three upon the winged lion figure trembled. Even Sir Henry, though armed with the vigor of his youth, felt fear stab at his heart as the sound of Dark Master filled the air then faded. Wigglesworth, Sir Henry, and Biddle clung to the winged lion figure, which broke into pieces under the assault of the flying dead as they plunged headlong toward the ground.

𒀸𒅗𒌋𒂖𒅗𒌋𒁹

The rushing waters surrounding Paddy increased in intensity and almost in proportion to his fear. The dimness was relieved by a green glow that shone against the tunnel's walls. The jarring sounds of the chomping jaws buzzed in Paddy's ears as he batted away the heads that bit him and tried to keep his head above the water.

Garrumph! Garrrumph!
Harrumph! Harrumph!

Dottie panicked as she realized how ineffectual her attempts were to maneuver the *kelek* toward Paddy. Her hands tightened on the oars as she pushed them into the water. The oars hit the heads, which snapped and tried to bite them.

"Paddy! Keep yourself afloat!" she screamed, but the sound of the rushing water and the chomping jaws drowned her cries. She hit the heads around the *kelek* with her oars, beating them back.

Beyond her, with his amphibian agility, George Smith continued his hopscotch from head to rolling head, which turned their yellow teeth to bite him. Smith was trying to gain ground toward

Paddy. His webbed feet deftly used each head as a steppingstone of sorts, jumping just before the jaws opened to bite him.

Then there was a great whooshing sound, and the decapitated heads were flung out of the water and up into the air, their jaws snapping. Smith was tossed into the rushing water, as a maelstrom of decapitated heads flew into the air, sucked up and above. Smith felt the sharp hits of the heads as if they were large baseballs and ducked into the water.

Paddy's face was drained of all color and looked like a large white balloon upon which someone had pasted a wet mustache and fringed it with more wet hair and glasses. His pudgy legs tiredly tread the water, and his arms flailed against the rushing water. He didn't have the strength to resist; the current was taking him where it would. In his mind his death was all but a sealed fate. His life, such as it was, didn't flash through his mind, just the chastising words of Dr. Wigglesworth—*A fool's errand.* Then Paddy's body registered that he was no longer being bitten, and this morsel of information made his way to his brain. The absence of pain brought some color back into his face, as well as a little renewed vigor to assault the rush of the water, though not much. He wasn't dead, after all, Paddy thought.

Smith's frog legs cut neatly through the choppy waters toward the chubby man. He saw the pale face bobbing about, looking dazed. The woman seemed to be managing better, he thought, as he glanced back at Dottie, who was now deftly pushing the raft toward Smith and Paddy and making headway. The water then stopped rushing. It came to a halt, as if obeying some command. Dottie moved the oars easily through the placid water and quickly toward Smith and Paddy, who was just a bit beyond. Dottie saw with relief that Paddy was still alive. Then there was a sound—a strident sound like that of a thousand plates crashing to the floor, a sound of metal upon metal—that echoed through the tunnel. In an instant the water disappeared.

Smith fell to the shallow floor of the stream, which was littered with black stones. He quickly stood on his webbed feet and secured balance. Paddy had fallen splat and painfully upon his buttocks onto the stones that were the bedrock of the stream, his eyeglasses askew, his face confused. Dottie's raft now sat on this same bedrock, not far from Paddy and Smith. She jumped off the raft and ran past Smith to Paddy.

She adjusted Paddy's glasses as she knelt before him. His chubby face bore the stamp of teeth marks, now reddening against the white of his skin. The shock of the events was showing on his face.

"Try to stand up, Paddy. We don't know if the water will come rushing in again." Dottie said gently, her heart aching at the wounds upon his face and his bewildered expression.

Paddy looked at Dottie first in confusion then in recognition, "Dorothea...Dottie in the short form," he whispered, taking her hand with both of his hands, now pale and shriveled by the water.

Dottie's eyes welled with tears. "Yes, Paddy. Now stand up, please. Please." She tried to lift him, but his heft was such that she couldn't.

Smith was upon them. He put two strong arms under Paddy's and lifted him. He spoke briskly, and the undertone of his irritation was clear. "The lady is right. We must make our way back to the side of the tunnel before the water rushes in again."

Paddy stood wobbling upon the slippery black stones beneath them. Dottie took one side and Smith the other.

"Hurry!" Smith said. But before they could reach the side of the tunnel to fling themselves against the oozing glue of the green slime, the black stones beneath their feet gave way. The stones were no longer substance but were turning into bodies, corpses that rose up—young and old, men and women from times ancient and modern. Rose they did, these dead awakened now by the sound of the gates of the City of the Condemned clanging open. Some had bloody faces and bodies; some had daggers in their sides; some had ropes about their necks; some had foam about their mouths; others had the sleep of death brimming in their eyes. They rose up, up. They rushed up through the ceiling of the tunnel in a whoosh.

As the storm of spirits ascended, Paddy, Dottie and Smith were pulled down, as if into a drain. Dottie clutched Paddy's hand as they were flung downward, upside down and topsy-turvy. Smith too was falling, Dottie saw his webbed feet beneath her just before the blackness hit.

𒀭𒅗 𒂍 𒀭𒅗 𒁹

A great dark storm cloud rose behind Mattie, Eddie, Geeta, and Gilgamesh deep in the forest of Humawa. The cloud was in fact a vengeful spirit. Oh, if only the four had looked back to see this presence descending in stealth and foreboding of the evil that was to befall them. But they didn't look—neither Mattie, Geeta, Gilgamesh, nor even Eddie, with all his training to keep his eyes and ears open in enemy territory. That was what the forest of Humawa was; they were in the zone of the enemy. The story of this vengeful spirit was known to Gilgamesh but was so hidden in the recesses of his memory that it didn't reside in the uppermost of his thoughts. Oh, Gilgamesh, king of Uruk—had he only thought! What agony he could have prevented, for this spirit, this darkness looming over the unaware four in the forest of Humawa, had been imprisoned within the hooded black robes of the Grim Reaper. And it wouldn't lie quietly in defeat like dust on the forest ground.

The story of this prisoner of the Grim Reaper—Abaddon, as he called himself—was a tale of foolish grasping for immortality and infinite power. Abaddon was small and bony in stature, with a sharp rodent face and eyes that were small dark-yellow slits, alert and scheming in a face that had an oily sickly gray sheen; his black hair rose like broom bristles upon his head. He had been in life a mediocre magician of the dark arts, one who had begun in the court of the beast when he was the mortal King Ashurnasirpal II. In that ancient time Abaddon was a seer, one who foretold what thoughts rang in those who meant harm to the king. In truth Abaddon didn't have much in the way of prescience, the ability to look into the future. However, he had developed a web of ears, informed by the servants who were foolishly viewed by the masters they served as deaf and mute. Abaddon had bought their favor with bribes of honey and gold, and they poured into his ears what they knew—who was treacherous to Ashurnasirpal and who was faithful. Abaddon used this information well; he used fire and herbs to conjure a scented smoke, pretended to fall into a hypnotic daze, and spoke what Ashurnasirpal's servants had told him.

Therefore it went, until one day when Abaddon happened upon a heap of bodies, writhing in death's throes—they who were the dying enemies of Ashurnasirpal brought there by the very words of Abbadon. The force of dying was strong, and Abaddon was mesmerized by their dance toward death. He then saw the vision—the black hooded robe and the skeleton figure inside as it descended above the bodies and with the sharp blade of the scythe culled the souls of the dying. Abaddon felt a surge of desire to hold that scythe and wield such power!

The Dark Master Marduk heard this cry, this want, and saw that Abaddon would be a good servant of darkness, for his soul was evil. *Abaddon,* he heard the Dark Master in his mind, *bring me ten thousand souls, and you shall be the holder of the scythe.* So, while Ashurnasirpal, still in the flesh, strove for mortal power, Abaddon, through deceit, threat, and treachery, brought more mortals for the Dark Master to turn to evil and take over their souls. Into his thumbs did Abaddon secret the demonic magic given to him as payment by the Dark Master for bringing him souls. And the thumbs grew—they turned blue and black and glowed from his skeletal hands. Soon it was known throughout the kingdom of Ashurnasirpal that there rose a sorcerer whose strength came from Marduk himself. Some whispered that Abaddon's gathered power in the demon thumbs was such that soon he would be greater than King Ashurnasirpal himself and rule as the henchman of the Dark Master. Ashurnasirpal had many eyes and ears that reported to him. Soon enough was Abaddon's grasping for supremacy known, the servant who wanted to be greater than his master King Ashurnasirpal. As a result Abaddon suffered in his mortal body when Ashurnasirpal sliced the demonic thumbs from Abaddon's hands. Now the servant could only grasp in his greedy reach that which four fingers in each hand allowed. Still Abaddon didn't desist, though he harbored wrath in his heart against Ashurnasirpal; instead he worked in stealth, wearing the cloak of subservience. He brought more and more souls to the Dark Master. When the ten thousandth soul was given over, Abaddon waited in impatience for the ruthless weapon, Death's scythe, to be in his hands. But nothing happened. Abaddon was still a puny mortal with no more power than what he could cull like a rat.

A surge of anger rose in his veins at Marduk's deceit and grew in the weeks that followed. He placed his foot on the forehead of the next soul—many hundreds now above the ten thousandth—who died, and blocked the reaper's scythe. The reaper cried out in alarm. And to Marduk, Abaddon said, "Dark Lord! Why does this creature still hold my scythe?" Marduk heard the arrogance and said, "Take it now, Abaddon, and hold it forevermore." The foolish Abbadon didn't know this injunction wasn't a gift but a curse, for the reaper then turned upon Abbadon and, while he was living, pulled his soul from his forehead and threw him into the Grim Reaper's skeleton jaws. There Abbadon lay imprisoned through the ages, looking powerlessly out of the hollow orbs of the reaper, never once the holder of the scythe. So it was that when Eddie had taken the scythe from the Grim Reaper, he had freed Abaddon's malevolent spirit from the black dust that was all that remained of the reaper's robes.

Thus it was this dark presence that rose up behind the unsuspecting four who began their journey into Humawa's forest. The forest's canopy glimmered in gloomy shadows that fell over Gilgamesh, Eddie, Mattie, and Geeta. They felt the cold chill of Abaddon rising from the dust. It was Geeta who turned back, by some instinct, and felt the darkness of Abaddon take form. The creature's outlines could be barely seen within the dusky mist; it was a small bony creature, gray like that mist that enveloped him, with a rodent-like face and gossamer bat-shaped black wings sprouting from his back. This creature within the mist about him flew past her and Mattie and to Eddie. Mattie and Geeta felt the cry of alarm and warning rise then stay stuck in their throats. Gilgamesh, king of Uruk, turned and shot his spear at the creature, but Abaddon, within the dusky mist, was quick, like a whirling dervish, too quick for the warrior's magic spear to touch him. Abaddon flapped his diaphanous death wings then threw out frozen knives from each of his four fingers—so fast that the eye could barely see it other than as a flash—that stabbed Gilgamesh through his arms, his chest, his legs. The king of Uruk felt a thousand cold knives hit his body and fell him to the ground.

"*Muktablu!*" Gilgamesh called out a warning to the boy as he fell to the ground. "Do not lose the scythe!" Beneath him the ground was alive now with maggots biting into his skin and pinning him to the ground. Ten thousand red ants the size of rats rose from the earth and began to crawl over Gilgamesh as he rolled about under the attack of the fiery insects. The forest laughed in glee at Abaddon's triumph! They wished Eddie ill will, as no living being should possess Death's scythe, and they held in their malevolent souls allegiance to Humawa.

Eddie had heard Gilgamesh's cry. He turned to see with horror the fate of his friend. Holding the long wooden handle firmly, he swung the scythe, and the blade went through the misty robes that held Abaddon. Abaddon, however, wouldn't be defeated so easily, as he wasn't of material form but a mist that couldn't be shredded. He was a black vapor, a polluted fog that was attempting to seep into Eddie like a second skin. Eddie jumped back, and Abaddon laughed, flapping his black wings in delight—so easy would be the defeat of this boy! He, Abaddon, would be holder of the scythe, Death's reaper, after all these eons!

Eddie sprung up again and wielded the scythe around and around, slashing through the black miasma but to no avail. Again Abaddon laughed the laugh of glee, and the evil leaves above, their eyes and teeth gleaming in derision in the canopy, joined him and laughed and laughed with him. *Oh, little warrior, how weak you are!* the leaves called out in their glee. *Oh, little warrior, how you will submit to Abaddon!*

Eddie spun around helplessly as the black mist revolved around him. Mattie spotted the nice king just beyond them, immobilized upon the forest ground, moaning in pain under the biting stings of the maggots and ants. "King! Jump up!" she shouted.

Geeta's heart fell as she saw that the black mist, in its trickery, had Eddie going in circles. She saw how it moved to trap Eddie, and yelled, "Eddie! He is around you! Jump up!" But as Eddie jumped, the mist seemed to be over him and under him at the same time, and his face and form were disappearing into the blackness.

Mattie raised the Spyglass. It was cold, which made her angry. Once again when they needed Spyglass, she wouldn't come. Mattie knew that Spyglass wasn't going to help this time either, unless she was told what would happen if she didn't help. Mattie shook the Spyglass and threatened, "I'll throw you into the forest! I swear I will if you don't help Eddie!" Still the Spyglass lay inert as Mattie shook it in frustration, her face turning redder with her mounting fury. Eddie was in scary trouble—he could even be killed—and the Spyglass didn't care. *Selfish. Mean. Spoiled. Two-faced.* These words ran though Mattie's mind. "You horrible Spyglass!" she screamed. "Help Eddie now!"

As Mattie screamed her order to the inert Spyglass, evil leaves, with eyes and teeth, began to rain down upon her and Geeta. Then it became a downpour of leaves that fell and bit the girls with their sharp teeth. Mattie batted at the leaves with the Spyglass. Geeta pulled herself into a ball, nestling her head into her chest. Mattie spun. But whatever the girls tried, it was for naught. They couldn't overcome the stinging leaves that clung to them like thorns, piercing their skin. The leaves were now covering them with their stinging nettles. The more Mattie and Geeta brushed them off, the more fell from the forest to take their place. They were covering Mattie, who, like Geeta, had fallen to the forest floor. Mattie's red face was sweating with panic, and her cries of "Aaagh!" echoed about her. The Spyglass was grasped in her hand firmly, a cold metal burrowed in indifference to her Mistress's cries for help.

Geeta too was being enveloped by a blanket of stinging nettles. She heard Mattie crying out in pain, and though her own body stung with pain, it was the cries of her friend that hurt her heart. Oh, what to do? The nettles were bombarding both girls, and there was no way out. Then Geeta heard another voice, her own joining Mattie's, yelling in the discordant chorus of pain. Underneath her screams, Geeta heard her old ThaTha's voice in the distance at first, echoes in her mind. Then ThaTha's words formed more clearly and rose above Geeta's cries. *Pain is only perception; give it power and it holds you. Calm yourself it, and it cannot harm you. Om, om, om.* She took deep breaths and said to herself over and over the sacred words, *Om, om, om.* If she panicked, the forest would win, and she could never help Eddie or Mattie. Geeta began to feel a calm fall over her. *Mattie,* she whispered to her friend in her mind, *be calm, and we cannot be hurt. Be calm.*

Mattie heard Geeta's words in her mind. *Calm.* She felt the stinging nettles of the evil leaves upon her, but it wasn't calm that ran through her. It was anger that she felt coursing through her hands. She shrieked, "Help us, Spyglass, or I'll throw you away!" But the Spyglass remained still and indifferent to her pleas. As the Spyglass lay inert, Mattie's anger grew. She struggled against the stinging leaves. Her anger now coursed strong; it flowed through the veins of her arms and into the fingers that grasped the Spyglass. The anger flooded her, and Mattie flung the Spyglass up toward the great canopy of the forest. The very branches, the limbs of the trees, now bereft of leaves, rose up like strong muscular arms trying to catch the Spyglass.

Mattie's throw was good. The Spyglass now spun up into a gray sky up and beyond the canopy. The Spyglass had ignored the vibrations of Mattie's anger; the yellow-haired Eddie was nothing to her. She wasn't going to risk the clutches of the evil spirits of Humawa's forest for him. The Spyglass opened her eyes to see that she was flying high in the sky. Below them on the ground, the evil Abaddon, swirling like a foul gray mist, his black wings flapping maliciously over Eddie, cast his rodent eyes up and saw the Spyglass. He immediately recognized it as being something the Dark Master desired. The Spyglass held a powerful force that Marduk couldn't take outright; this was all Abaddon knew. Abaddon's evil spirit leaped in beats of avarice as he flew up, leaving aside Eddie and moving toward the spinning Spyglass. His black tendrils shaped like hands with four fingers swirled up and scratched at the sky to grasp the metal treasure.

As the black fog rolled up and away from Eddie, he stood up unsteadily, holding aloft the scythe, which still struggled against him. He saw what had diverted the malevolent presence away from him—the evil black tendrils were inches away from encasing the Spyglass.

"Mattie!" Eddie screamed. "Call the Spyglass back!" But he saw that Mattie and Geeta were struggling against being buried in the leaves that bit them and that Mattie didn't hear him. And still further, the king of Uruk was rolling on the ground, crying in pain as he battled an unholy trinity of maggots, giant ants, and the evil leaves that had rained upon him and were biting him mercilessly. Eddie flung his scythe at the voracious leaves that bit

Mattie and Geeta. At the approach of the grisly scythe, the leaves instantly fell away. Then they burrowed into the ground with a hissing sound. Mattie and Geeta struggled up.

Eddie ran toward the king of Uruk to rescue him from drowning in a painful sea of ants, maggots, and leaves. "Call the Spyglass!" Eddie cried out to Mattie, pointing to the evil black tendrils that were now encasing the Spyglass in the sky but in a transparent mist that still couldn't grasp the Spyglass firmly.

"No!" Mattie said, her face red and perspiring, small stings from the leaves leaving prick marks on her face, neck, and exposed arms. "I hate her!"

"Geeta! Get her to call the Spyglass!" Eddie shouted, as he swung the scythe toward Gilgamesh, sweeping the air around him. The giant king of Uruk rolled like an infant on the forest ground, helpless against the bites of the ants, maggots, and leaves. Eddie again swung his scythe, this time low to the ground to sweep away approaching leaves, ants, and maggots from crawling over the king. The power of the scythe was such that the leaves, maggots, and ants moved back, and those on the body of the king also began to slowly crawl off, again hissing their displeasure. The scythe they would obey; it was the holder, Eddie, whom they wished to destroy.

Abaddon, rising in the blackness, now high above in the sky, felt luck was turning his way at last. Released was he from the imprisonment of the reaper's robes. Stupendous power lay within his grasp. Death's scythe was nothing. He, Abaddon, would hold the Spyglass, and whatever secret powers it held would be his. *His!* The fog thickened like smoke from a factory chimney. It churned and darkened and spun a web around the Spyglass to entrap her. In mist form, Abaddon couldn't hold the Spyglass, but if he could spin enough, the robes would turn to cloth, and his hands would transform into bones that could clasp the Spyglass. And so, like darkness that begins at dusk in lightness but blackens as the night moves forward, so too spun Abbadon, and from the mist, his hands with four fingers and no thumbs took physical form and covetously raked the air.

Geeta's body was sore with the pain of the sharp leaves, but Eddie's cry of alarm registered through her pain. She saw at once why Eddie was alarmed, for she observed how the dark mist was enveloping the Spyglass and was close to capturing it. Geeta pointed up in panic at the Spyglass. "Look, Mattie! The evil robes are going to get the Spyglass. Please, please, please call her!"

But Mattie remained resolute, shaking her head, the frizz of her hair forming a determined red halo about her angry face. "No," she said. "I told Spyglass that I was going to throw her away if she didn't listen and help us. And she didn't."

Behind her black-rimmed glasses, Geeta's eyes widened at the strength of Mattie's resolve. "Mattie, this is not rational! If we do not have the Spyglass, the snake Gneezy will get it! Then surely he will kill your mother!"

Mattie's face reddened in anger. "It's all Spyglass's fault that the snake took my mom in the first place! Spyglass is nothing but a selfish, two-faced creep. She never helps us, only helps herself. Let's see how much she likes it when the snake is her boss instead of me!"

"Oh, Mattie!" Geeta said, despairing and pointing to sky, which was thickening in blackness around the Spyglass. "That is just foolishness! Call her!" But Mattie shook her head. She'd had enough of the Spyglass and her mean and tricky ways. She would find her mom and rescue her without the Spyglass. Mr. Biddle had been right all along; the Spyglass was bad—bad to the bone.

High above in the sky, as the deep blackness spread over the Spyglass, she heard the voice of her Mistress Mattie below.

She heard the anger but disregarded it. Mattie was still below and within her dominion. The foolish girl and she were one; after all she had given her one of her three precious gold bands. Oh, what an ungrateful child this Mattie was! She would show Mattie what being thrown into the jaws of danger felt like! No misery would the Spyglass suffer alone! No, Mattie would be subjected to whatever agonies the Spyglass was to experience. So the Spyglass turned toward the smallest tendril of light, a pinpoint that still remained within the enveloping black fog, and threw out a beam of light that was like a strand a spider might weave. Down, down it traveled until it hit Mattie on the ground below.

Mattie yelled out in surprise as the Spyglass's tendril spun around her feet first then over her legs and her body, though her arms were still free. The tendril, strong as steel, pulled her into the air, upside down, and into the dark sky above.

"Aaagh!" Mattie cried, upside down, her arms akimbo and reaching out a hand. "Help!" Geeta grabbed both her hands, only to be jerked up with Mattie into the sky. Mattie was upturned, her feet over her head, her body bound tightly by the strand weaved over her. Her face was flushed, her eyes bulging. Geeta held tightly onto Mattie's hands. The two were drawn up higher and higher until they disappeared into the spinning black fog that was Abaddon's lair.

𒀭𒀭𒀭

Eddie swung the scythe over the beleaguered Gilgamesh, who struggled against the bites of the insects. He finally shooed the maggots and ants away; repelled by the force of scythe, they had burrowed back into the earth. Eddie heard Mattie's scream. He looked up in astonishment at the incredible sight above him—Mattie upside down, her body wrapped by a strong thin rope of light, Geeta holding on to Mattie's hands, both being pulled up higher and higher into a dark smudge in the sky.

"Geeta! Mattie!" he cried, and tried to jump up with the scythe in hand, helplessly swinging its blade upward. Eddie remained firmly on the ground. Mattie and Geeta disappeared into a vortex of blackness. Gone. "Mattie! Geeta!" he shouted.

Gilgamesh was stunned by the ferociousness of the insects. The forest of Humawa held much danger, and he, Gilgamesh, king of Uruk, had failed again. Though he was now fully freed by the force of the scythe from the evil leaves, maggots, and ants, the pain of the assault was still there. He stood up gingerly and shook his black ropes of hair in anger at himself. He saw how the young *muktablu* was jumping and wearing himself out to no avail; Gilgamesh also had seen the red-haired child and the owlet disappear into the foul black mist—a mist he knew was Abaddon. Gilgamesh foolishly had forgotten about the evil, vengeful Abaddon, who had lain within the robes of the Grim Reaper. The owlet and the red-haired child surely would perish under Abaddon's capture, and the metal Spyglass would fall easily into the hands of evil. He dropped to his knees in despair. Though he was one-quarter man and three-quarters god, Gilgamesh had failed against the forces of the forest of Humawa, as he had eons before when he had let Humawa capture Enkidu and allowed him to be plunged deep below Kurnigi into the City of the Condemned. Gilgamesh's blue face shook and deepened in color under his shame. He put his hands to his head and pulled at the black ropes of hair.

As Eddie moved toward the king, his heart beat with fear. Mattie and Geeta had nothing to protect them, for the Spyglass was more foe than friend. He'd had Death's scythe but had let

Mattie and Geeta slip right into the enemy's grasp. He should have been standing guard at all times over Mattie, for it was the Spyglass that the enemy sought. But he hadn't; he had lost sight of the mission. He wasn't a protector but was just like those officers in Vietnam, the ones his father said you couldn't rely on to keep you safe. Eddie shook his head in disgust at himself. He didn't deserve a weapon, so incompetent a warrior was he. His heart filled with despair.

"King," Eddie said, his voice trembling with emotion, willing himself not to let the tears well in his eyes, "take the scythe from me. I'm not a *muktablu*."

Gilgamesh looked up and saw the anguish in the boy's face as he held out Death's scythe to him. He stood up and shook his head at the offer. He then spoke with more bravery than he felt, more certainty than he knew was true. "Come. Are you not the son of a warrior and therefore raised to be a warrior yourself?" Gilgamesh said, patting Eddie on the back and gently pushing the scythe back to the boy's side. As he said the words, they strengthened him. "A warrior's greatest glory comes after his most abject loss. Did your father not tell you this?"

"My dad?" As Eddie said this, his head was bent in shame. His dad wouldn't have let Mattie throw the Spyglass; his dad would have seen that black mist before it had hit him.

"Yes. Your father is a great warrior, and were he here, he would tell you all warriors win and lose battles."

Eddie raised his head; his eyes were bright with tears, and he shook them away. The deep-brown eyes of the giant blue king bored into him, giving him strength. Deep in the pools of Gilgamesh's eyes, he saw his father looking out and heard him say, *Eddie, a warrior must remain strong of heart and keep the mission, even in the face of defeat.*

Gilgamesh knew the young *muktablu* saw his father in his eyes, for he felt the warrior strength of Sergeant Petersen resonate within him. "We will find your friends," he said, "for I know who has taken them. It is Abaddon, and he serves Marduk. Do not lose heart, my brother. We will find them and rescue all."

Eddie nodded and heard his father's voice. *Be strong in order to continue the mission.*

Before Eddie could respond, the words were caught in his throat by the terrible sight forming before him. The forest had transformed. The trees, now barren of leaves, uprooted themselves from the earth and flew up, with dirt from the forest ground clinging to their tendril roots as they swung up into the sky. Eddie and Gilgamesh were caught in the tornado of the rush of the forest trees that were wrenching themselves from the ground and were flying up. Eddie swung his scythe to form a protective barrier around himself and Gilgamesh. The trees flew up barren of leaves; they flew up and gathered into a mass of brown limbs, trembling in the air. Then a great roar sounded through the now treeless land, for the forest was no more, as all the trees had merged together. They formed first into the muscular arms and legs of a giant fifty feet or more in height, then the head of the giant who was Humawa. The giant's face was fearsome to behold, with eyes that were two evil leaves blinking in rage and hair made of vines with great thorns dripping with blood.

Humawa roared, "Gilgamesh, king of Uruk! You have dared to enter my forest. You bring a thief who steals the scythe of my servant the reaper!"

A great wind blew out the green flame in Gilgamesh's spear. The ground beneath Eddie and Gilgamesh shook as Humawa brought down his feet, stomping the ground. There was nowhere to run and hide in the desolate land. Humawa spat out thorns from his mouth that fell like shrapnel onto Gilgamesh and Eddie. Eddie swung the scythe to ward off the thorns as Gilgamesh wielded his golden spear. Humawa bent down with his great, muscular, wooden arms to grab Gilgamesh and Eddie; the ends of his fingers were roots, long and unyielding. The scythe's power seemed to lessen, for Humawa's humongous root fingers moved to wrap around them and crush the two in his grasp.

Gilgamesh called out, "*Muktablu*, keep the scythe in the air!"

Eddie obeyed and swung the blade in the air, just beyond Humawa's approaching fingers. He felt the weapon's power surge through his arms as the metal slashed through the air. Gilgamesh then raised his golden spear and struck the scythe's blade; the two weapons clanged. Suddenly a flash of light, like a spark, came forth. Both Eddie and Gilgamesh felt its strength vibrate from the weapons into their bodies. The spark, like a firefly, moved away from the weapons and fluttered in the sky. It grew and grew in size until it was a large silver flame of light.

The flame fell upon the wooden body of the giant Humawa. The giant bellowed in pain as the fire took hold and engulfed him in silver flames. Humawa howled as he was rendered into ashes—ashes that fell like rain onto Gilgamesh and Eddie. Then a silence filled the air. The giant Humawa was no more. Eddie and Gilgamesh were on land that was barren of any living thing. Not a blade of grass grew on the rocky earth below them for as far as they could see. It was flat and desolate land, topped with a granite-gray sky like an upturned bowl. Eddie caught his breath and saw too that Gilgamesh was awed.

"*Muktablu*," Gilgamesh whispered. "Humawa is no more! We have destroyed the giant."

The realization of this truth seeped into Eddie's consciousness. He, Eddie Petersen, had wielded complete control over the scythe. He was the weapon's master; and with such warrior strength, he could fight the evil that was sure to come against them; he could find Mattie and Geeta and Dr. and Mrs. O'Reilly...and protect Mr. Biddle. He started to form these words but was stopped. "Look, King!" he exclaimed. A glimmer of the silver spark no bigger than a firefly but sparkling like a diamond fell at their feet. The spark grew quickly. Gilgamesh and Eddie jumped back as great licks of silver flames rose from the ground. From the light a face shimmered—that of Nana, the wise sage woman of Uruk. Her black pebble eyes shone as she said, "Gilgamesh, long we have waited to hear from you. We know that you lost Enkidu to Humawa. Again you have found yourself in the forest of Humawa, and now you have destroyed the giant himself."

"Yes," said Gilgamesh. "But long has it been since I lost Enkidu to Humawa. And this young *muktablu* has lost his friends to Abaddon, here in what was once the evil forest of Humawa."

The flames grew further, and Nana spoke again, her voice low and guttural. "Gilgamesh, king of Uruk, the last of his people, I know everything that has happened. I speak to you from the Valley of the Dead, where the souls of the people of Uruk lay trapped by the Dark Master."

Gilgamesh's heart strained in pain. His people were trapped in the Valley of the Dead! "Help us with your strength, Nana. I must find Utnapishtim, who holds the secret to eternal life. And to do so, I must travel into Kurnigi, the land of darkness, and into the City of the Condemned, where lies my friend Enkidu."

The great wise woman spoke from the flames. "Pull with your spear two strands of wood from the scythe's handle and light them with these flames. Hold one, and the young *muktablu* shall hold the other."

Gilgamesh did as told; with his point of his spear, he slashed the handle of the scythe as Eddie held it firmly. The scythe shook, as if it felt the pain from the spear thrusting into its wooden handle. All the while Eddie felt the hypnotic trance of the silver flames and the pull of the old woman and her injunctions. Gilgamesh held two strands of wood from the scythe to the flames and lit them. He gave one to Eddie. Each small strand caught the cold silver flames and flickered in their hands.

Nana spoke a chant from the silvery flames.

> *With these bands of fire,*
> *forged from Death's one club,*
> *winds of fate,*
> *winds of terror,*
> *sweep these two warriors*
> *to the foot of the mountains*
> *of Mashu,*
> *so that they may find*
> *their way to Kurnigi.*

The strong winds grew around Gilgamesh and Eddie, and the flames that held the image of Nana disappeared. In their hands the flames that had caught on the strands of wood from Death's scythe increased, and a blinding white light enveloped them and took them up and then downward.

When they awakened, Gilgamesh saw that they lay at the foot of the impassable granite mountains of Mashu. These mountains grew straight from the ground, ten thousand or more feet high, impervious to encroachment. The granite was smooth like glass and therefore allowed no foothold. These mountains of

Mashu clearly allowed no entry, and there was no way to traverse over them.

Eddie's eyes traveled up the terrain. There was no way up, not even if he had the training his father had in repelling up sheer mountainsides. He saw Gilgamesh's eyes take in the mountains with a similar assessment.

"Four times the wind blows," Gilgamesh whispered, his spearpoint now flickering pale-green and silver. He pointed at the glass wall of the mountain. "Four chants that can break Mashu… if only I knew the spell!"

Eddie's ears were caught by a sound behind him. It was a soft sound, like that of a sigh but also a sound of movement like a curtain billowing in the wind. Gilgamesh's eyes showed that he also registered the sound, and he slowly turned away from the mountain toward it. Eddie moved quickly, his hands grasping the handle of his weapon, raising the scythe's blade as he spun around. There from the barren ground surrounding the mountain, like steam from the grates of a city street, rose the torn and tattered bodies of the wandering shapeless spirits freed from the forest of Humawa. They rose up and out, their images sharpening to show only their hollowed eyes filled with pain and confusion. They rose as a mass of eyes, the sound of their howls filling the air, revealing their confusion as to who now was master. The scythe, held by the Grim Reaper, had brought them to their bitter fate—this same scythe, now held by the yellow-haired boy, that had taken their souls. They had succumbed when they had wandered into the forest of Humawa—either in body or in slumber through the travels of their dreams—or their souls had been possessed when they were in mortal form by evil spirits that walked the land of the living and tempted those who surrender to their charms. So it was for these spirits of the land of Humawa called the wandering dead who had been laid trapped, for their souls were reaped and held buried in the ground of the forest to give the loathsome Humawa strength. These wandering spirits had been forced to bow to their master, the Grim Reaper, for the reaper held their souls. But the reaper was now no more. *Who is master? Who is master?* In a black mass, they flew out from the ground, like a spine-chilling wind of doom, their wails splintering the air with their anguish, and moved toward Eddie.

Eddie's eyes were open wide, for the black swarm of formless spirits was headed straight toward him. He held the scythe aloft and swung it around and around. "Backs to each other, king!"

Gilgamesh didn't obey this command, for he saw there was no defending against these creatures, in the thousands, who rose and were flying toward them, their song of sorrow loud. The sound of the dead rang in their ears, so loud that it was like sharp nails driven into their heads.

"*Muktablu!*" Gilgamesh shouted over the wails. "They are the dead of the forest of Humawa, come to seek revenge against the holder of the scythe who took them from their mortal lives!" As Gilgamesh uttered these words, the dead, who had flown up in a dark streak, now flew down, aimed like a rocket toward Eddie and Gilgamesh.

CHAPTER 12

the Bloody Sunday

Upon the frozen ground of Siberia, the shack that had once housed the Crone had risen again and held in its clasp the snake, who lay coiled in wait. Uri Gneezy awakened to the tremors of the agony of the defeat of the Grim Reaper. He shook his cobra head and in slow movements, resisting the cold, began to uncoil himself. In moments Gneezy emerged, his face containing the traces of his human form, the blue eye and green eye glimmering in the gloomy darkness of the shack. The snake tossed his head back, and the sharp forked tongue shot out and propelled the Black Book of Magic into the air. Its leathery pages opened at once, giving off the stink of decay. A sound, like a moan but deeper and more troubling, reverberated within the confines of the desolate hovel.

The Crone was shaken out first and dropped to the ground like a sack of rotten potatoes. She rubbed her crusty eyes and looked about, her mouth open, and there was only one snaggly yellow tooth as its lone resident. Then she heard the ominous sound of the Dark Master's displeasure and flinched as if hit.

The Iron Knight fell to the ground next but had the where-withal to immediately stand up, holding his baton in an angle and in attention. But even the Iron Knight was disconcerted by the strident sound of anger that surrounded them. He resisted the urge to flinch. He then saw the little pockmarked boy, Stal, fallen to the corner of the shack. The boy stood, his face set in defiance, his fists in the air, looking confused but determined for the fight.

Uri Gneezy uncoiled his body to its full length, his cobra head hitting the ceiling of the shack. The Black Book of Magic he swallowed whole. His blue eye and green eye flitted over his meager "army" below: an old Crone, a small pockmarked boy, and a pompous German.

The Dark Master's piercing red orbs surrounded them, and the shack was thrown into a red glow. The snake coiled himself down and bowed his head in supplication as the question rang through the hut.

Who is master?

Uri Gneezy felt terror strike each scale of his snake body as it shook to the question. "Marduk is master. It is you." Uri's voice was heard in slow hissess. The Crone flapped her almost tooth-less mouth in agreement, and the Iron Knight kept his head bowed, so appalling were the orbs of the master to behold. But the boy, Stal, the pockmarked boy whose soul was only recently given to the Dark Master, stared arrogantly at the red orbs and said nothing. What were red eyes to him when he had felt the red heat of his father's blows? *Stal.* He was Stal. Uri Gneezy saw the boy's arrogance, and his tail quickly whipped out and slapped him down. The boy, Stal, stumbled and scowled. The Dark Master's voice rumbled in anger, its force so great that it shook the shack and sent terror like electric currents through its inhabitants' bodies.

Who is master?

Everyone answered, even Stal, "It is you." The red orbs held them in a fearsome stare.

Who then holds
Death's scythe
if I am master?

Uri Gneezy immediately responded, "It is you, Dark Master, known by fifty names, revered as Satan, Devil...Marduk."
The Dark Master's voice rang with derison and anger.

Fool! How can it be so?
A boy now holds Death's scythe,
and a girl holds the Spyglass.
The dead have escaped
from the City of the Condemned.

Uri Gneezy heard the sounds of the Dark Master's displeasure, but this time it wasn't because of Gneezy's doing. If the dead had escaped the City of the Condemed, it wasn't the snake's fault. The control of the Grim Reaper and his scythe, and indeed the forest of Humawa, wasn't his but Ashurnasirpal's. It was from Humawa's forest that the souls were then plunged into the City of the Condemned. Now something had happened to change that. Control of Death's reaper had somehow slipped through the fingers of the beast—the treacherous beast who had stolen from him his prey of those precious to the child with the Spyglass. Here Uri Gneezy felt the first stirrings of triumph born from the Great Beast's misfortune, for to displease Marduk, to lose the spirits of the underworld and Death's scythe, the beast, stripped of his army of the dead of the underworld, surely now held no strength. He, Uri Gneezy, would rise and be all to the Dark Master, and with that would come power and glory. Marduk heard these thoughts, as he heard everything. His red orbs glowed again fiercely as he asked:

Tell me, snake,
how then is it
that I am master?

To this Uri Gneezy had no answer. The yellow snaggly tooth of the Crone shook in fear in its foul encasement.

The red orbs shone again, and the glow in the shack held a heat like that of the fires of hell. The snake's skin shriveled, and Stal cried out in pain as his skin shrank upon his own body. The Crone lay in a heap, moaning. The Iron Knight, his face beet red, perspired as he bit his tongue against the searing pain.

Uri Gneezy uncoiled himself against the pain and hissed, "Tell me, Master, what I am to do."

Marduk's voice shook the room.

You must capture
those who are the thieves
and their abettors.

> *Kill them,*
> *and bring me*
> *the Spyglass*
> *and the scythe.*

Uri Gneezy again looked at his meager force—an old hag, a boy, and a pompous German baron running to fat. Though the Black Book of Magic held the forces of Adolf Hitler's SS, he knew that it wasn't enough to overcome his two enemies. Uri Gneezy realized accurately that there were indeed two forces set against him—that of the meddlesome Biddle and the White Book of Magic and also the Great Beast, who now would seek to redeem himself to the Dark Master with full force and destroy Uri. "Tell, us Master," Gneezy said, "how are we to do so?"

Marduk spoke again.

> *Within the folds of time,*
> *before chaos,*
> *in this soil*
> *anger once*
> *raged strong in the*
> *hearts of man,*
> *and so their souls*
> *were ours.*
> *These will be your soldiers*
> *to command*
> *if you can keep time written*
> *as it once was.*

The snake's head shook in fear. *If you can keep time written as it once was.* He had Stal under his rule, protected from the grasp of good. But how would he find this time that the Dark Master spoke of? The snake knew he had to brave Marduk's wrath and put forth the question. "Master, what is this time you speak of?"

The red orbs deepened in color, and hateful sounds filled the air, the wails of those still held deep within the City of the Condemned.

Snake, know you not
the Bloody Sunday?

The snake felt the whips of the Dark Master's red orbs of light strike him, and he winced. Marduk spoke again.

Two fates are there—
one for those who succeed
and one for those who fail.
Succeed, and it will be sweet.
You shall become
lord of the City of the Condemned.
Fail, and you shall beg
for the circles of hell.

The red orbs faded, and the shack was again desolate in its gloomy, dim light as the forlorn wails faded away.

The cold Siberian wind lashed at the walls of the shack and shook it. The snake uncoiled himself and saw that the eyes of the Crone, the pockmarked boy, and the Iron Knight were upon him. The snake's tongue shot out against the roof of the shack, and from it the Black Book of Magic fell out once again. The snake's tongue turned the foul pages, as the Crone, the boy, and the Iron Knight looked on, shivering not from the cold but their encounter with the Dark Master. Greed and envy stirred in the hearts of man upon this soil; Gneezy again considered Marduk's words, and his reptilian head shook in palsied strokes. *Bloody Sunday.* Dark pages of misery filled the shack as he continued in search of the "time" of which Marduk had spoken. The pages, these pages of man's evil toward another, sprang up but were blurred at times, changing at others, dissolving into dust as they emerged from the Black Book. Uri Gneezy knew now that chaos had ensued truly, for never had evil in time emerged in this smudged and uncertain way. Yet he also knew the Dark Master thought that one time period remained vulnerable to the lure of dark forces.

Bloody Sunday. *This soil,* Marduk had said. There had been many bloody days in Siberia but not one Sunday of note. Then the realization struck the snake. *All of Russia.* The snake smiled, his blue eye and green eye blazing in sudden recognition. He pulled from the dark pages of history a specific time when the forces of greed and envy had stirred in the hearts of the peasant, the farmer, the worker, even the petty merchant who grasped for ever more treasure. Each had blamed the other for his troubles; they had worked both in unison and against one another. Yes, these souls would be ripe for the picking, Gneezy knew, as they had fueled the winds of anger in the hearts of man.

He pulled the bitter page out of the Black Book, and the force of its image, the teeming angry crowds in a cold Russian city square, shook the shack. The ground beneath them gave way. Into the opening earth they fell: the snake Gneezy, the pockmarked Stal, the Crone, and the Iron Knight, the reichsmarschall's baton still grasped firmly in his hand. When they emerged, it was upon the snow-covered streets of St. Petersburg, huddled against a biting January day in the relentlessly cold winter of 1905. There before a large stone gate, looming over the horizon, were tens of thousands of workers. They cheered on a man with a gray beard who was robed in the black garb of a priest and said with fervor, "We have come to present Tsar Nicholas our petition—a petition for the rights of workers, of ordinary men—that our bread should not be bought with a pound of our flesh!"

The crowds roared their agreement, some with fists punching the air. "Father Gapon!" they cried. "Our savior!"

Father Georgi Gapon wore the dark robes and tall headdress of the Russian Orthodox priesthood to which he belonged. Some in the church, those who stood beside the tsar, who were in the gilded churches of old, said Gapon wasn't a godly man, for he fomented anger among the people, not of agape or love of one's brother. But Father Gapon hadn't responded to his critics but his supporters. "A righteous anger have we," he had said, "for should we stand aside and fall to sickness and starvation because of the greed of those who hoard the gold?" So his strength had grown among the masses. He spoke of new ideas—that the sweat of their labor produced riches that were stolen from them by the landowners, the factory owners, the rich who grew fat by the blood of their labor. They, the people, came to understand that no man on earth should have more gold than he could hold in two hands. Such men should be cut down. All should be equal; no one among them should have more than the other. And all that was upon the land belonged not to the few but to the many. Comrades they were, not subjects to the tsar. This the people came to slowly understand was the truth. They had stood in subservience to the rich for too long. Anger formed in their veins when they saw how they lived in squalor while the rich, the nobility, the men with land and factories lived high upon the fruits of their labor.

Still others doubted him, for the tsar was also a godly man, and his power was given by the Lord. Even so, it would be good to have more wood for their hearths, more meat for their plates, and to be relieved of the constant sorrow of their babies being born dead or gone before three breaths were taken. Father Gapon had understood that new ideas were best delivered under the cloak of the old ones. The tsar was a godly man, he said, but perhaps the tsar, in his palaces, hidden away from the people, didn't know how his subjects fared. Shouldn't the tsar be told of their hardships? So it was that Gapon and his supporters had brought to the square of the Winter Palace so many tens of thousands with his petition. Gapon stood upon a small pedestal designed to place him above the others and give him the height to address the gathered crowd. Behind him he was ringed by priests who also wore robes, light in color, and held large crosses. Father Gapon again spoke passionately to the cheering crowd. "We shall move forward, march to the Winter Palace, and give the tsar our petition! For is not man made in the image of God, that one man should not be raised above another?"

The crowd cheered their agreement, and Father Gapon spoke again of their travails, of how they had been beaten down and robbed of the rightful fruits of their labor by the greedy rich owners of factories and land. Their anger at the inequities of their meager life when compared to the riches of the nobility could be felt; their wages bought less and less, though they worked more and more. Where was the fairness in this? Where was fairness when only the fewest of the few lived so richly while others starved? When the worker had nothing to show for his labor? Nothing! The anger rose within the hearts of those gathered.

Father Gapon never said that it was the tsar himself who was the greediest, but the unspoken word is often the most powerful, for the peasants in their thin and tattered coats only needed to look up to see the enormous edifice, a tribute to grandeur, that stood before them, the tsar's *Winter* Palace—only one of the many palaces of the emperor of Russia. They themselves lived in hovels that housed three families or more, one crowded upon the other. Always hungry. Always cold. The tsar and his family, however, lived in opulence, in not one but many palaces. Even the trains that took him to and fro were said to have been outfitted for the utmost comfort. A slow grumbling anger hardened the hearts of the men and women against the tsar, the nobility, and all who were rich—the many who had nothing, the few who had all. Father Gapon spoke of these inequities, calling for shorter work hours and higher wages; fair wages was all that was asked. The crowd roared their assent. Fair wages was all that was asked!

The snake Gneezy saw how this priest held the crowd under his sway, how they moved to his will. As the crowds moved past, their voices strong with anger, the snake felt the anticipation of battle, for in the eons he had traveled in time, back and forth, he knew he had only become stronger as humans in each era succumbed to the lures of evil. Again he thought of the strength he would have when that meddlesome Biddle, as he called himself, was gone. Uri Gneezy's skeletal head shook in anticipation. Now he would commandeer and bring to the Dark Master all the souls of Russia and the lands beyond. Then it would be but a small matter to destroy Biddle and those he protected with the White Book of Magic and bring the Spyglass into his hands. And at last the master would reward him. Power would be his, dominion over a multitude of souls. Uri Gneezy would rule a great swathe of the underworld as master of the City of the Condemned, and under his heel would be all those who had sought to hurt him.

The beast would suffer the most—this he would see to. These thoughts were so vivid in his mind that they stripped Gneezy's face of its human aspect, and slowly the scales formed and the head of the hideous snake sat on top of his emaciated body. The blue eye and the green eye in slits glittered voraciously at the thought of all of his enemies submitting to him.

The Crone's yellow snaggletooth shook again in her gummy mouth. She wished again and again that she never had allowed the greedy boy Uri that the snake had once been—much like this boy Stal—to come into her world. For had she not, the Black Book of Magic would still be in her clasp, and the promise of the restoration of her beauty would still be a possibility. Unlike now. Here she spat, the drool running down her disfigured face and over the thick hairs on her chin. How she hated the snake! If only...if only there was a way to destroy him.

Stal looked about the streets, confused and dazed. Russia. He never had been out of Georgia, and the great city streets of St. Petersburg felt daunting to him. So much had happened that he didn't know how to understand it. Only the river of rage that rode in the people's hearts—he understood this with a primal instinct. His greedy eyes took in the crowd. He saw how the priest held them in thrall, how the crowd hung upon his words and would do anything he said. Both a longing and a premonition of what he was to be filled the small Stal. Yes, it would be him soon, up on a stage—he whom millions would listen to and obey. Stal saw that the snake's eyes were upon him, as if his thoughts had been read.

The Iron Knight also felt the surge of energy. This he knew, for it was this strength that the Führer had taken into his fists and used as a whip to destroy the weak and make the strong submit to him. It was this strength that had made neighbor turn against neighbor. The Iron Knight felt it. Anger ran deep here. And though Hitler had been a fool, succumbing as he did to the false beauty of the Crone, a hag, the Iron Knight would become strong. He glanced at the pockmarked boy Stal who, when the story was written, was said to have had millions quaking under his thumb. This boy Stal, who stood with his mouth open, his ugly pockmarked face awash in wonder, would have to be managed, the Iron Knight resolved. But he was but a boy now, and his glory was one born of the Second Great War, not this one. The Iron Knight knew both wars, decorated as he had been in the First Great War. This story, unfolding right now, the Iron Knight knew well; it ran through his very veins. The story about to begin was seeded by rage in the hearts of peasants in the cold Russian streets of St. Petersburg. The Iron Knight's square jaw set further against the cold wind. He would aid the snake, yes. Plan the assault, take leadership of all of the Russian forces, and rise. *Yes, rise,* the Iron Knight thought.

Uri Gneezy turned to him. The Iron Knight's pudgy face flushed, for he was still caught up in his thoughts of glory and knew at once that the snake knew them. The snake smiled, his black forked tongue darting out. "In time, Iron Knight. In time." Gneezy pointed his bony human hand, so deceptively weak and innocuous, at the crowd and said to the Iron Knight, "All of Russia's military will be under your command. And we shall bring to his knees the filthy and foul beast Ashurnarispal, whose treachery cannot go unpunished, and seize control of the City of the Condemned. But for that we must gather the forces, reap the evil that is so rich here."

Father Gapon's words struck the winter air in loud and pious tones. "We ask in peace for this, for it is written, 'It shall come to pass in the harvest that you shall give one-fifth to Pharaoh.

Four-fifths shall be yours, as seed for the field and for our food, for our household and for our little ones.' "

The crowd cheered their support, impervious to the biting wind that drew over them. The cold was nothing to the privations of poverty under which they had labored. It was nothing to them, despite their worn coats and torn hats. They had come with the Lord's mission.

"We come in peace to the tsar and ask his holiness for mercy and generosity," Father Gapon said. "We ask in peace for what is rightfully ours. We ask in peace for the fair share of our labor, for bread and meat so our children do not starve. And so to the tsar, as it was to the Pharaoh, it should be one-fifth of the seed of our labor that is due and not four-fifths!"

The crowd of men, women, and children felt the truth of this in their hearts. Fairness was all they asked, and it was a God-given right. They linked their arms and sung a hymn, praising the Lord, praising Tsar Nicolas himself and asking for mercy.

"We march in peace!" Father Gapon cried out. "We beseech the tsar for mercy and justice! Fair wages is all we ask!"

The crowd chanted, "In peace we ask for fair wages!" From beyond, more and more ordinary people joined the crowd, until it seemed as if the whole of St. Petersburg was gathered to march upon the Winter Palace. In the air was the feeling of joy, for now Father Gapon spoke the words of the Lord himself. It was inconceivable that the tsar could turn a deaf ear to such holy pleadings. Gneezy had slithered close by, accompanied by his unholy trio: the Crone, Stal, and the Iron Knight. Neither Father Gapon nor anyone in the crowd had taken notice of these interlopers, for what was there to notice in this motley group? The sketetal figure of an old man, a pockfaced boy, an ugly hag, and a pudgy, blond, middle-aged man with a baton. But notice they might have, for it was the core of evil that stood so harmlessly in their midsts. They stood covered in the cloak of the mundane, as Father Gapon's rhetoric of peace fell like poisoned barbs into Gneezy's mind. His palsied head shook. No. Not peace. Never peace! An evil idea formed in his brain.

It was the sharp knifelike chill of the wind that woke Herman Biddle from the blackness of whatever evil spell had been cast upon him as he tried to enter Kurnigi, the land of darkness. He knew this cold well, for the biting winter Siberian wind had lodged in his memory from boyhood. Mesmerizing blue eyes were upon him, and Biddle realized that he was again in the encampment of the gypsies, and none other than Rasputin held him in his gaze. Grigori Rasputin, wearing the dark robes of a mystic, his long dark hair pulled back, and his face covered with a frizzy beard that fell onto his chest, looked every bit the mad monk, as he had been called by his detractors. But that Rasputin, the one of debauchery and trickery, was no more, not since the fateful events at the Devil's Shallow when the red-haired child with the Spyglass had freed the souls that lay captive there and brought the ancient souls of Nineveh to the Tree of Moreh. Since then, Rasputin had seen that his fate was to serve God, to be a righteous man, a holy man. All this Biddle knew, and he also knew that Rasputin's force was strengthened by mystical revelations, borne to him by dreams and visions.

Beyond Herman Biddle lay L. Rufus Wigglesworth, moaning under the cold. The few gypsies that were left surrounded him and lifted his great girth up from the cold ground where he had lain prone. Rufus's eyes seemed bleary, and Biddle knew that his mind was in a fog of confusion by their treacherous travel on the Path of the Virtuous. Where was Sir Henry? Biddle flinched at the thought of Sir Henry alone in the trenches of the City of the Condemned, and cursed himself for not being able to control their travels on the Path of the Virtuous. Sir Henry, however, had the strength of youth, and this, Biddle thought, was one comfort.

Herman Biddle stood unsteadily at first, the wind blowing his long cape back, gray now like the cold sky above. He had no words, for everything remained frozen in his mind, still and icy like the land he beheld. Siberia. Memories again of his youth, of running beside the Tura River with his brother Uri flooded him, and Biddle knew this place, Pokrovskye, was dangerous. Its treeless terrain, the cold hard ground, and beyond on the horizon, the ramshackle wooden homes, evoked the memory of his mother Alexa, her face pale with fright before she died on this very ground. Biddle felt the chill of memories so strong and heartbreaking that his body trembled.

"Come. Warm yourself by the fire, Dmitri." Herman Biddle heard his boyhood name uttered by the old gypsy woman, her dark eyes filled with kindness as she mistook his tremors born of fear for cold. "There will be time enough for the coldness of death that your brother Uri will bring upon us."

These words shook Biddle awake to the present dangers. "Uri. He is here, then?" he asked. Rasputin nodded grimly. This land of his boyhood, of when he was known as Dmitri Gneezy, frightened Herman Biddle, for in it Uri had held power over him. *Uri.* His brother's name echoed in his mind. Brother? That was so long ago; he had no relation to what Uri had become—slave to the Dark Master, a serpentine figure that moved through time, chasing him and wishing for his destruction, ever grasping for the Spyglass. Still the bonds that had tied them together in the womb could hold reign again if he didn't guard himself against such filial weakness. Biddle moved to the fire, its flames lighting his face with hollows, his thoughts holding him in silence again. This journey of the Path of the Virtuous, one he had avoided so steadily, would be his undoing. He saw how Rufus Wigglesworth was weakend, how he had to be helped by the gypies to be seated on a stone close to the fire, how his three chins quivered in his face, and how his corpulent body sank in resignation. Biddle feared that neither he nor Wigglesworth had the stamina for the Path's lessons, yet he *must* find the strength, for look now how they were all scattered: Mattie, Eddie, and Geeta. He feared they were somewhere in the dangerous depths of the City of the Condemned, looking for Dottie and Paddy. And Gilgamesh, the ancient king arisen again and in search of his friend Enkidu—what protection was he for the three if they entered Kurnigi, the land of darkness? Herman Biddle gave way to the feeling, the anguish.

"In despair," said the old gypsy woman, reading Biddle's thoughts, "there can be weakness. But so too there can be strength."

Rasputin looked at the thin figure that was Biddle and saw how the fire's light showed him to be an old man. "Since the red-haired child threw order to chaos," he said in low tones, "anger has risen like a great wave and seeped hatred and envy into the hearts of men. So it is that evil is ripe to be in its ascendancy."

The flames from the fire rose. Rasputin's mesmerizing blue eyes fell back into his head as he swayed under the trance from the movement of the prophetic flames of the fire. Visions fell upon him. Alarming visions. A bloodcurdling shriek penetrated the air, coming through the lips of Rasputin, and threw shivers through the spines of those gathered by the fire. It was the shout of pain of those being trampled. The images rode upon the flames, overcoming those who had gathered by the fire: that of a revolt, of the pounding hooves of horses ridden by the Cossacks, of blood dripping upon the faces of the innocent, of crowds falling under the swords of the Russian Imperial Guard at the Winter Palace.

L. Rufus Wigglesworth gasped in recognition. "Bloody Sunday! The fatal winter of January 1905. No! It must not be!" Wigglesworth stood suddenly, in a quick movement that belied his girth and shook his body, and turned to Herman Biddle. "Do you not see it? We must have Tsar Nicolas stop the carnage by the Cossacks of the people of St. Petersburg. Oh, Bloody Sunday, that hateful January day that augured all the misery to come for the next forty years! If there is no Bloody Sunday, then the evil of the two wars spawned by this seed will never be realized. Then perhaps time that is unwritten and given to chaos can be rewritten."

Rasputin's words came slowly, under the hypnotic lure of trance. "The tsar is not at the Winter Palace in St. Petersburg. He fell to the counsel of his advisors not to remain there. He is riding to Tsarskoye Selo, to the Alexander Palace."

Before them the flames rose again and dissolved into the blurry image of Tsar Nicolas wearing his blue uniform with gold buttons and his epaulets; his kind, handsome, bearded face bore suffering for his people as he was led to a guillitone. As quickly as it had come, the image dissappeared into the flames. Rasputin looked up at Biddle and Wigglesworth. "If the tale is told as it was written, there will follow much suffering and bloodshed. And then godlessness will grip Russia when Tsar Nicolas is martyred upon the guillitone."

Wigglesworth said, "Biddle, we must try."

Herman Biddle caught Wiggleworth's tone. Biddle had little hope, for any time that he and Wigglesworth had tried to defeat the evil events of time, the force of evil only gained strength. Nonetheless Biddle raised his arms and threw his cape, now gleaming and pulsating like a slate-gray ocean under a winter sky. He flung the cape forward and called out the words, which came out in spurts.

Enuma…elish la nab…u shamanu
shaplish…ammantum…suma…la zakrat.
When the earth below
and the sky above
had no name.

The White Book of Magic appeared, and the large pages that opened above them seemed flimsy and transparent. Though the bloodshed of the Night of the Broken Glass many years later, when they had been on the Second Stone, had been averted, Mattie had thrown time into chaos, and the story of creation, of humanity's existence, lay in tatters. And who was to rule the sky of heaven, to bring order to the cosmos also was unknown now. Therefore this chaos allowed Marduk the possibility of gathering more souls to evil, for that which was written had been unwritten, and all the souls of the world were vulunerable to capture by the lure of the dark forces. Herman Biddle saw how the White Book of Magic was dimming in power. Wigglesworth took note of the White Book of Magic and how it seemed faded, weak, and soft. The echo of the incantation's words hung in the air then rose up, scrambled.

La nab u enuma elish shamanu
ammantum la zakrat shaplish suma.

Biddle closed his eyes in pain at the destruction of the mystical chant, and with his arms raised under the torrent of the sharp words piercing his soul, he recited the chant again, his voice gaining strength with the intonations added by Wigglesworth, though the chant was but a whisper.

Enuma elish la nab u shamanu
shaplish ammantum suma la zakrat.

The wind rose from the cold ground, and the scrambled words took on shapes and forms, raining an evil vengeance like a torrent of locusts upon Rasputin, Biddle, Wigglesworth, and the small band of gypsies.

La nab u enuma shamanu elish
la nab u la zakrat suma la shaplish suma.

The desecrated chant fell like sharp knives upon their souls, a black and evil sorcery that now entwined itself with the words of the Enuma Elish so as to rob them of their power.

La nab u enuma shamanu elish
enuma elish ammantum shamanu
la nab u la zakrat suma la shaplish suma
shaplish ammantum zakrat.

The torrential assault of the scrambled words rose in the air against the chant. The pure words of the Enuma Elish fought a battle in the sky with the desecrated incantation. The war of the words was like a great lightning storm, with silver bolts of the chant dueling with the black bolts of the desecrated chant. The storm was so low in the sky that Rasputin, Wigglesworth, Biddle, and the gypsies felt the heat of the clashes of the bolts and put their arms above their heads in protection. Now the Siberian winter sky was streaked with the color of vengeance, of rust and blood, as the words gripped the small group by the fire.

When the earth below
and the sky above
will never be named
and all will hold allegiance to the One,
Marduk!

Then one black bolt that clashed with a silver one fell, and as it did, it moved like an arrow toward the old gypsy woman and pierced her chest. "O healer and creator of the eternal spring," the old gypsy cried as she flung into the fire two green stones, "divide the light from darkness, Tiamet, Tiamut...O mighty Mother Tiamat!" The old gypsy's incantation struck the evil words, and the fire exploded as a blinding white light rose. The good words untangled themselves for less than a few milliseconds from the desecrated chant, to the faintest whisper of sound, and a blinding-white light enveloped those by the fire as the sacred chant rang out.

Enuma elish la nab u shamanu
shaplish ammantum suma la zakrat.

The blinding light dissolved. Biddle, Wigglesworth, and Rasputin were gone. No longer in the sky was there a great battle. In that barren Siberian land, only the old gypsy and a few of the band remained. The old woman's eyes reflected the flames of the fire, her body's life force ebbing as the small band of gypsies held her. Before she died, she whispered what she saw. "Beware of the serpent in the path—a viper that bites the horse's heels that he should fall backward."

The pounding of the horses' hooves hit their ears. Gneezy saw at once the approaching Cossacks, the tsar's military forces coming from the Winter Palace. They were the mighty Cossacks of Tsar Nicolas II upon their horses, black against the gray winter light, charging forward with weapons unleashed toward the thronging crowd. The snake's head shook in pleasure as he took on full reptilian form. The evil of Bloody Sunday would happen intensely, viruluently, like a fire sweeping dry forests; the chaos of time hadn't changed the events, or so it seemed. Bloody Sunday would plant the strong seed of anger and hate and divide one man against the other. In this anarchy only evil could rule, for when no one man trusts another, the road to the plunder and control is smooth. In trust lay peace, and in peace lay the rise of souls to good, away from evil. So, Gneezy knew, this moment, this time, was critical for the capture of souls and for the seeding of anger that the tsar's assault on the protesting workers would spread like a poison through the world. And the world would turn to arms, country against country. Then and only then could evil rule supreme, for when anger drives man, he is most vulnerable to selfishness, most vulnerable to turn upon his brother and sister and give the keys to his soul to the forces of evil.

Seeing the armed tsar's soldiers approaching the crowd, Father Gapon chanted, "We come in peace!" To the crowd he said, "Resist not! We come in peace!" The crowd chanted the slogan. "We come in peace!" The banner of the cross was held high, and their signs said, Peace! Fair Wages! They only wanted their petition to be heard. The petition itself was held in the hands of Father Gapon, but among them, among the thousands, its words were etched in their souls.

O Sire! We are only the poor and beaten, so oppressed are we by the labor that lays upon our backs, on our wives, the old and crooked bones of our dying mothers and fathers, the small and twisted frames of our children. O Sire, we ask you, our ruler, to see as the Lord does, that we are all the children of our Savior. We ask only to be considered as men of blood and flesh. We seek from you our salvation from this burden of unceasing labor, hunger, starvation, and misery, for such is our plight that death itself would we welcome over another day on this mortal earth. We seek your salvation, O Sire. Do not cast a cruel and indifferent eye upon us, your faithful servants. Help us. Destroy the wall between yourself and your people.

Atop their horses, the tsar's soldiers stopped, uncertain, for they had been ordered by their superiors to quell the violence, yet there was no violence. They heard the words of those in the crowd, heard their words beseeching an audience with the tsar.

"Trample not our souls, for you shall sin against God. We shall go in peace, like lambs to slaughter, and our blood will be a stain upon you!" Father Gapon's eyes were shut as he spoke.

The Cossacks held back their horses. The leaders in the front stood before the teeming crowd on the bitter-cold gray day. The day was like night, for no sun shone. The snow upon the ground glittered a pure white. The horses snorted great clouds of wet breath into the air. The large crowd was now singing hymns. The soldiers saw Father Gapon, and his words fell upon them, chastising their violent intent. So the soldiers' horses were stayed, their swords drawn down. The leaders of the tsar's enormous military could subdue these ragged Russian peasants, though their numbers were large too. But why? For here in the thoughts of those who were in the front, facing the peasants, in the thoughts of the leaders of the Cossacks, was the fact that the people had come in peace. "Keep your weapons down!" the order went back. The great rustling of weapons to be drawn down rang out.

Father Gapon called to the crowd to stay back and reminded them that peace was their mission. "The God of heaven himself will protect us. Therefore we his servants will rise and claim our rights with peace upon our lips."

"Peace!" sang the crowd. "Peace!"

With alarm the snake saw what was happening, how Father Gapon controlled the crowd, and how peace and goodness could be used to win their demands from the tsar. Bile rose in his throat at the priest's words. *Peace!* Gneezy knew he had to act now; the crowd must be enraged for death and destruction to ensue. Then and only then could he grab their souls. The snake's scales glittered his malevelonce. He felt black and red under the sheen of green as he slithered speedily under the hooves of the horses mounted by the tsar's soldiers. The evil current rode through the entire legion of the horses as they reared up on two legs, frightened by the wickedness under their hooves, almost toppling their riders. A great confusion rose among the Cossacks as their horses whinnied in panic. The snake Gneezy slithered onto the horse of the Cossack leader, who was immediately paralyzed by fear at the sight of this giant reptile, its gleaming blue eye and green eye upon him. Soon the snake's forked tongue was around the neck of the soldier, strangling him.

"Give your soul to the Dark Master, and you shall feel no pain!" Gneezy hissed.

With bulging eyes and fear running through his veins, the Cossack leader assented as his spirit fell away. Gneezy pushed the soldier down, grabbed his sword, and slithered fully upon the horse, his body turning into the skeletal figure of a man, though his head was still that of a snake. He grabbed the reins and held the sword of the soldier and rode like a fury into the space between the soldiers and the crowd. He rode straight into Father Gapon, and fast as lightning, his sword plunged into the priest's heart. Father Gapon's eyes froze in shock as his lifeblood drained from him and death's rattle rose from his mouth. Gneezy pulled out the sword then backed the horse toward the line of the Cossacks. The priests who rushed to Father Gapon's side cried out in dismay and disbelief as they grabbed their dead leader. The crowd nearby, those who had witnessed what had happened, gasped in shock. Through the crowd the murmur rose—

"Father Gapon is dead!"

Gneezy, on horseback, turned in triumph to the crowd, his snake head shaking in pleasure. But it wasn't the face of the snake that was revealed to the crowd as Gneezy turned to them, so evil and clever was he. No. What was seen as the evil snake turned to the crowd was the face of Tsar Nicolas, grinning in demonic triumph as he held up the sword with the blood of Father Gapon. Through the crowd—from those who had witnessed the sword plunging into the heart of their leader, to those in the back who could see naught—like an electric current went the incredible news. "Tsar Nicolas has murdered our beloved Father Gapon! Tsar Nicolas murdered Father Gapon!"

The priests holding the dead Father Gapon cried out in distress, "Your Majesty! Why? We came in peace!"

Wearing the mask of Tsar Nicolas, the snake Gneezy spat out the word out in disgust. "Peace!" Then he hissed, "Bow to me, else you follow this vermin Gapon's path."

The priests shrank back, knowing at once that evil was in their presence. The snake Gneezy turned and rode swiftly toward the Cossacks, as the crowd behind him, stunned by the tsar's appearance and the murder of Father Gapon, cried out in anguish. Then they erupted in rage, "Tsar Nicolas murdered Father Gapon! His death will be avenged!" Holding bricks in their hands, they stormed toward where the Cossacks were mounted upon their horses. They turned their flags upside down and used the poles as weapons, plunging forward. Their ragged faces, tired with years of labor—even the faces of the small children who wore rags—screamed rage at the tsar. "Tsar Nicolas murdered Father Gapon!" The Cossacks turned in puzzlement to see the tsar riding fast toward them, waving a bloody sword. "Kill them!" he screamed. "They are traitors!"

The Cossack leaders upon the first horses hesitated, so unusual was it to have Tsar Nicolas among them. But the order had been given—"Kill!"—so the Cossacks unleashed their weapons at the oncoming crowd, who had but rocks and bricks in their hands as a defense against bullets and swords. Chaos ensued as the people were trampled under the horses' hooves, as their blood spilled upon the streets on this Sunday—this Bloody Sunday.

The snake Gneezy rode past the fighting Cossacks, straight onto the grounds of the Winter Palace.

𒐕𒅗 𒅗 𒐕

The Iron Knight saw that he would be crushed under the onslaught of the crowd if he didn't act. He saw how the pockmarked boy and the Crone were like flotsam in a stream, being carried by the crowd in their murderous rage. Should he save them? But were their souls not already dead? What was there to save? And then it hit him. The Cossacks were scattered through the crowd, and though they had weapons, there was no organization. He, Iron Knight, knew this was the snake's test. Were he to assume ultimate control, instead of the pockmarked boy, he had to show his strength. The Iron Knight swung his baton up and hit a nearby Cossack riding a horse. As the man let loose of his reins, the Iron Knight swiftly pushed him off and climbed upon the horse. Behind him he heard the angry calls of the crowd and felt stones fly past him. He rode briskly toward the Cossacks and called out an order, to form a semicircle, and the words that formed from his mouth were in perfect Russian. He observed how the reichsmarschall's baton glowed in his hands, how the entwining small serpents upon it seemed alive. The Iron Knight also saw how the Cossacks were mesmerized by the baton.

"Shoot!" he cried out, as the Cossacks surrounded the people on the street and followed his orders. The first of those hit didn't realize what had happened. Then more fell as the Imperial Guard shot again and again into the screaming workers. A river of blood filled the streets of St. Petersburg. And so too did the river of rage toward Tsar Nicolas rise in the hearts of those in the city. The Iron Knight's heart beat fast in exhilaration as he smelled the familiar sea-salt smell of blood. Soon he would be commander of the entire Russian army! His own bloodless body felt alive.

Within the crowds, pushed and pummeled forward, were the pockmarked Stal and the old Crone. The vengenance and hatred of the crowd didn't scare Stal, for he understood it well; he knew it as his own story. Tsar Nicolas had killed Father Gapon. But Stal had seen that it wasn't Tsar Nicolas at all but the snake Gneezy. The crowd, however, had been fooled. Who this Father Gapon was and why the crowd should be so enraged didn't matter, Stal saw at once. The snake had wanted this, wanted this blood-thirsty anger to be alive in the crowd's heart. The pockmarked boy had listened carefully to the directives of the Dark Master. He had wondered deeply how it was that he—only a Georgian boy—could be of such importance to the snake as to take him to make certain that his destiny of domination was realized. And it would be. This was his chance. The crowd was without a leader, and whoever was leader would rule mighty. The red-faced Iron Knight, Stal had known from the start, was his rival. He saw how the Iron Knight had pounced and taken control of the Cossacks. He must act, Stal knew, and seize control of the crowd, entrance them like that priest had. But how? For no one in this crowd would listen to him as he was—with his youth, with his smallness and ugliness. Then Stal felt the Crone's bony hand on his neck and smelled her foul breath upon him. "Come, boy. We must dis-appear." She pulled him against the wall of a building. Stal freed himself and forced himself to look at the frightful ugliness that was the Crone full in the face. "Crone," he said, "do you possess any power?"

The Crone's face first held surprise at the question then rec-ognition. She cackled, revealing the snaggly yellow tooth that had grown and lodged so lonely in her gummy mouth. "Ah. So what it is you want, *Pocky?*"

Stal scowled, and his rage immediately seeped into this voice at the old taunt. "Old ugly hag!" he spat out in fury at the Crone. "Better I should be pockmarked than have your foul face for eternity!"

The Crone, conscious of her ugliness, shrank back, her hands flying to her face. Her deep yearning for her lost beauty ran across her face before a black frown took it over. "You are no better than me! You and I live under the control of the snake, much like worms under a rock."

Stal immediately perceived the longing that ran across the Crone's face. In his short life, he had survived only by reading the faces of others for the violence to come—of the drunken sentimentality of his father before it flashed into rage, and the piety that filled his mother's face before she beat him mercilessly. These expressions he had read in order to live. So the Crone's yearning was as clear to him as if she had said it. "You are wrong there, Crone. The snake needs me," Stal whispered, as the Russian peasants raged past them, pushing him harder against the coldness of the building they were held against. "But you...you are nothing. What power can an ugly old hag have over others? That is what belongs to a beautiful woman, not to you."

The Crone flinched at these words. "You nasty boy! You are vile and vicious with your tongue, and one day it shall lash against you and destroy you. No power, you say? Watch, while I leave you here to suffer!" The Crone began to whisper a soft incantation in order to disappear.

"Wait!" Stal cried. "If I am to control millions and bring these souls to the Dark Master, should I not then become more powerful than the snake?"

Here the Crone stopped her incantation. Her eyes narrowed as she gazed at the pockmarked boy, for what he had said was true. The snake had plucked Stal out of time and kept him so that the boy would control millions upon millions of souls and give them over to the Dark Master. The Crone said, her voice even, "If I am to help you, you will have to restore to me what I want, for eternity."

Stal nodded. "You will have your beauty, not just skin deep but fully...for eternity."

The Crone bent her head low. "See here, boy. See here," she whispered, and the smell of her mouth was like the stench of an overflowing sewer. Stal forced himself not to wince. The Crone moved a crooked finger to motion him to move to a small, dank, dark alleyway away from the throngs of people rushing past. Once there, she pulled from her grimy dark dress two dried stumps upon whose ends were long and crooked black fingernails. "These are are the thumbs of an evil one...Abaddon is his name. They were given to me by the beast Ashurnasirpal even before I held the Black Book of Magic, when the beast needed me for a spell. This evil one, Abaddon, lived in the Grim Reaper's robe. Where he is now, I do not know, as the reaper is no more, and his scythe, the master says, is with the living. But these dessicated thumbs hold much evil."

The dried thumbs, with their long black nails, seemed alive with demonic power as the Crone held them aloft. They glowed black and blue, and they emitted a sound, a shriek, a wail, a long cry that spoke of fear and control. Stal immediately saw that these amulets were powerful, but he wondered why the Crone didn't use them for herself. Stal feared a trap. The Crone, hearing his thoughts, spoke, low and hissing. "The thumbs of Abaddon are strong, but my body is too weak to hold their power."

Stal felt certain the Crone was lying. "I will give them to you," she said, "but if and when you are powerful, and I ask for my beauty, and you do not give it, the spell in these thumbs will grab you and you will be driven down to the clasp of Abaddon and be his slave for eternity." Stal thought she was an old hag and he a strong boy. He reached to grab the dessicated thumbs, but the Crone quickly pulled them away from his grasp and secreted them in her foul dress. The Crone's hands, veined with age and with sharp yellow nails, were suddenly around his throat.

Stal felt the power in the Crone's fingers, and the nails that dug into his neck were sharp as knives as he was lifted off the ground. "Do not try to trick me, boy, for I can crush you to dust," she warned. "Swear your allegiance to me, Pocky. Swear it first, and then you shall have the evil power that lies within Abbadon's thumbs."

"I swear it!" gasped Stal, his legs dangling, for the Crone held the struggling boy aloft. "I swear allegiance to you, Crone! You shall have beauty for eternity."

When Stal said this, the Crone flung him down. As he scrambled up, he heard her words and felt their menancing undertone. "You will first become powerful, and when you are of such value to the Dark Master, the snake will be flung away. Then I will call upon you for the allegiance you have sworn to me. Then you will do as I ask of you. Do you understand?"

As the Crone held the dried thumbs aloft, their power entranced Stal. "Yes. I will do as you ask! I have have sworn so!"

The Crone then flung the thumbs toward Stal. They flew like two small malicious crows in an arc, and the long black fingernails each pierced into the space in his forehead between his eyes, the space that once had held his soul but now was empty. The Crone cackled as she saw the thumbs disappear. Stal felt a searing pain as the thumbnails drilled into this forehead, and then the whole of the thumbs disappeared completely. "Ah...

ah…" she laughed in surprised glee. "It is as it should be! There was no fragment of your soul in the Third Eye. So it is that the evil thumbs of Abaddon should lodge so well within you!" In truth the Crone didn't know why the power in the thumbs had risen now, for in the eons that they had been in her possession, she had tried but failed to awaken them. The boy must have some satanic force within him, the Crone thought happily, a force she would harness to destroy the snake. Upon Stal's forehead now was a mark—a faint black mark, like a thumbprint.

CHAPTER 13

Revenge of the vengeful spirits

Deep within his spinning black robes of mist, the evil Abaddon felt the weight of Mattie and Geeta being pulled into his web. The four black tendrils on each hand that had spun their way over the Spyglass were weakened. Without thumbs his grasp was doomed to be feeble, and the web he spun couldn't withstand the weight of the two girls. He bitterly cursed Ashurnasirpal for having stolen his strength from him. Abaddon's web gave way, and he and his prey plunged into blackness.

As the Spyglass twisted downward, she resolved revenge against Mattie. The Spyglass in her metal prison thought again and again with anger of Mattie—how she had thrown her right into the clasp of evil, how she had tried not once but twice to hurl her into the jaws of danger. The Spyglass's rage rose as she thought of how she had given one of her precious gold bands to bring Mattie back to life when she had eaten the forbidden fruit from the Tree of Knowledge. The Spyglass held firmly the strong thin rope that had entwined itself over Mattie, now upside down and redfaced as she dangled first in the air then was pulled into the slimy black mist that was Abaddon's web. Oh, that girl would learn who controlled who! Mattie's hands were held in a strong grasp by Geeta. Mattie cried out again, "Aaagh!" as she and Geeta were spun about and plunged with the Spyglass into darkness.

The darkness lifted as suddenly as it had come upon them. Mattie opened her eyes to see that she and Geeta had been thrown onto hard ground upon their stomachs. Before them was a massive stone archway with a heavy, dark, almost black wooden gate. This structure loomed large over them. The Spyglass was firmly glued to Mattie's hand, and she felt the iron force with which it clasped to her. The tendrils that the Spyglass had wound around her body were gone. Two giant beasts who guarded the gates snarled, and it was their sound that had first awakened Mattie.

Mattie jumped, her face red and sweaty with fear as she looked upon the monsters that growled at them—for there was no other word than *monsters* for these creatures of the night. They were giant beasts human only in body, one male and the other female. Their faces were like those of wolves, with two layers of bloody teeth that showed with each menancing roar. Around their heads erupted disembodied arms that ended in hands, their enormous fingers scratching the air. These two monsters, guardians of the gargantuan gate of stone and wood, howled and hissed at Mattie and Geeta, their arms ever elongating and their fingers reaching toward them.

"Geeta!" Mattie whispered, hoarse with fright, to Geeta, who lay nearby, not moving. "Get up!"

Geeta was awakened by the sound of Mattie's distress. She lifted her head and stared myopically at the large blurs before her, for her glasses were askew as usual. Geeta, who had been on her stomach, sat up and adjusted her glasses. She peered. When the monsters came into clear view, she emitted a loud gasp. Mattie, who had crawled toward Geeta, tugged at her sleeve. "Geeta, let's go!"

The girls quickly jumped up and ran away from the gate. Their sudden movement aroused large snarls from the dreadful ogres before them. The eyes embedded in their wolf faces were large, bulging bloodshot eyes—eyes that were sold souls bought by the treachery of their master. The eyes took in the forms of the two on the ground before the gates to Kurnigi. Words formed in their minds, the order of their master, the dreaded Prince of Wallachia. "Capture them!"

The monsters' arms elongated, and their fingers reached and grabbed both girls and lifted them. Geeta and Mattie screamed as the demon fingers wrapped around their bodies with a hold as firm as steel; their legs dangled in the air, and they felt the hold of the fiendish creatures threaten to squeeze the very breath out of them. But the creatures stopped, distracted by a murky, oily pool that formed before them. A black sheen, first spun as a mist, rose in a malodorous fog toward the monsters. It was the foul mist of Abbadon. He spun his body like a top, faster, faster, faster. In his movement, like the churning of milk that produces butter, Abaddon again found solid form. He rose up out of the slimy remnants of the reaper's robe and stood unsteadily, for this was the first time in centuries that he was upon his own two legs. These legs were sticklike and covered with greenish-gray scales. Abaddon was small and thin in form and short in height and gray in sheen. His black hair rose like a bristles of a broom above his head; his ears were elognated, almost like horns on each side of his face, with the symmetry of an upside-down triangle; his chin jutted out, and sharp teeth protruded from his mouth. Two gossamer black wings, like those of a bat, rose behind his back and beat silently against the air. He wore only a loincloth. So thin was he that his ribs stuck out of his bare chest.

Abaddon's yellow rodent eyes squinted up at the monsters that held the two girls in the air, as well as the Spyglass in the red-haired girl's hands. His thumbless hands immediately reached for the Spyglass, which made the monsters snarl. With a sychronized movement, they flung the girls up over the gate and into the shadowy land behind them, the land of Kurnigi, which they guarded. Then they bent their wolf heads, and with their sharp and bloody teeth, they bit into the handles of the wooden gates. Abaddon felt the cold breath of air from the shadowy land beyond as the gates opened and stepped back instinctively. This was Kurnigi, the land of darkness, where the Grim Reaper had flung the souls he had harvested. Abaddon also knew that within Kurnigi lay souls he had tricked when he had been in his mortal form and placed them into the clasp of the Dark Master. And now the reaper was gone; now the scythe lay in the hands of a living being, that yellow-haired boy. Abaddon feared the spirits whose souls he had stolen, spirits still trapped in Kurnigi. They were wandering spirits from eons past—this he knew—with revenge in their hearts against him. He had heard their cries when he was within the reaper's robes. Abaddon recalled how they had sworn that he would in time come into their realm and that they would break him and fill him with all their agony. And now Abaddon no longer had the robes of the Grim Reaper to protect him. He felt their vengenance against him rise like a cold gust, increasing in strength as it rushed forward and under his thin legs and whisked him into the land of wandering spirits and shadows. The gates then shut with a thunderous noise.

Hidden within the bowels of Kurnigi, within the dark tunnels of the deepest layer of hell, the Brotherhood of Evil stood in a circle within the protective web spun by the chanting of the seven desecreated names of Marduk.

Ankia-en-lugal,

Ugug,

Umum,

Tudu,

Udud,

Gar-gash,

Bilulu-en.

The sign of the Four, , that lay on their forehead pulsated with greed for power. So gathered the Four with the protective black web of treachery around them. Among them stood Khan of the Huns, whose legendary cruelty in the mortal world was well known—how he had beheaded his enemies, how he had subjugated people across the lands known to man through an iron rule. Next to him stood the Prince of Wallachia, born of nobility, with a taste for blood, and who drew pleasure from the pain inflicted upon his enemies, impaling them with small stakes. Within his dominion he had the unliving, who lived in the netherworld of life and death, from dusk to dawn, where they preyed upon the blood of the living; he was the Prince of the Unliving. They were souls caught by the prince for darkness but kept by him to prey upon mortals. The Duke of Muscovy, his soul as cold as the Russian winters, balding and pale, stern and foreboding, who considered only his quest for power and cared not even for the bonds of blood, stood in thought. And then there was the beast Ashurnasirpal, always the beast, in whose heart was held over thousands of years a bitterness and anger toward Marduk for his loss of earthly power. Ashurnasirpal now held very few souls under his command, and but for the tie that bound the Brotherhood of Evil, he would have naught. But it was he, Ashurnasirpal who had captured and held the prey, the two humans precious to the red-haired child who possessed the Spyglass. Each member of the Brotherhood was mesmerized again by the thought of overthrowing the others and being triumphant—grasping both the Spyglass and Death's scythe, and then in short order posssessing the Hidden Sister's Twin Tablet and overthrowing Marduk.

Greater than the Dark Master Marduk, I will rule, thought Khan of the Huns.

Greater than the Dark Master Marduk, I will rule, thought the Duke of Muscovy.

Greater than the Dark Master Marduk, I will rule, thought the Prince of Wallachia.

Greater than the Dark Master Marduk, I will rule, thought Ashurnasirpal.

They each read the others' betrayal once again, as if it had been spoken out loud. Only moments before, the four creatures in their circle of treachery had spoken in unison the desecrated names of Marduk, so as to doubly cover their activity against the red orbs of the Dark Master. The Brotherhood of Evil was such that loyalty was assumed only as long it was expedient.

It was Khan of the Huns whose sallow-colored hairless face tilted upward at the sound of the gates opening from the surface of Kurnigi. The large and protruding forehead wrinkled, and the askew almond-shaped eyes narrowed. Khan of the Huns snarled, and the ten small scorpions that were entwined like a living necklace about his neck moved in unison. "There is a change. Strangers have come into Kurnigi."

The Great Beast lifted his nose to the air and sniffed; then large flames erupted from his nostrils. "It is so," he growled.

The third member of the Brotherhood, the Grand Duke of Muscovy, his pale long face melting into a long beard, his bald head fringed by coarse dark hair, furrowed in further sternness. In anger the duke jabbed his pointed staff into the ground, and blood poured from it. "Who is who so dares?"

Ashurnasirpal, Khan, and the duke turned their eyes, brimming with suspicion, upon the Prince of Wallachia. The prince controlled the giant beasts that stood as guardians of the gates to Kurnigi and in whose heads were embedded the bulging, all-seeing, bloody eyes of those subjugated by him. And through those eyes, the prince guarded entry through the gates to Kurnigi. The prince smiled his pouty, red-lipped smile below a black mustache and embedded in a white oily face. He looked down his long aristocratic nose at his fellow brothers. The beast, the Duke of Muscovy, and Khan, with his sallow face set now in anger, moved closer to the prince. Treachery already! Had the prince formed forces that he was drawing on to overthrow them?

Khan snarled, "Do not think, Prince, that you can deceive us."

The prince smiled, unconcerned, as he patted his luxuriant mustache and flipped back one of the swirls of black hair that coiled about his shoulders, ignoring the threatening postures of his fellow brethren of evil. "Ah, brothers," he began, almost purring in conciliation, "are we not united in our quest to overthrow the Dark Master?" The Prince of Wallachia's unctuous words oozed through his inflated red lips.

"Tell us," said the beast, "how is it that you open the gates without our consent?"

The prince smiled again, looking well pleased beneath his signature foppish red-velvet hat adorned with the teeth of his enemies, and pointedly raised an eyebrow at the beast. "Yes, who is it that enters Kurnigi, the land of darkness, when now there is no reaper?" The prince asked the question, but it was clearly a taunt and an indictment of the beast for the demise of his servant, the Grim Reaper.

The beast snarled. He didn't enjoy the cat-and-mouse games of the prince, yet of all of the four, the beast now had the least power, having lost the souls the Grim Reaper had given him when Death's scythe had moved to the hands of the living yellow-haired boy. So the beast stepped back, recognizing his weakened position.

Khan of the Huns said in menacing tones, the dried bloody leaves upon his head shaking, "Do not toy with us, Prince." The Duke of Muscovy again plunged his forbidding bloody spear into the ground in agreement.

The prince smiled languidly to demonstrate that he wouldn't be hurried by threats and slowly pulled from his coat three bulging, bloodshot eyes of his enemies, which were his buttons. He tossed them from one hand to another, enjoying the drama. He then threw the eyes into the air as they twitched with fear. "Show them!" the prince cried.

The bulging eyes floated above the Brotherhood of Evil then formed a large oval ball of grayish light. From the light came the image of a brown owlet girl and a chubby red-haired girl being thrown by the guardians of the gates into Kurnigi—the red-haired girl who held the Spyglass.

The prince fluttered his hand up modestly then bowed. "The red-haired child and the Spyglass."

The Duke of Muscovy cried out first. "Well done!"

Khan smiled a very small smile of appreciation and said, "Yes. It is good."

The prince had pulled the defenseless red-haired child with the Spyglass into Kurnigi, and she was all but captured! Now all that was left was to seize the Spyglass from the child, a small task given the enormous resources of the legions of evil that Khan, the duke, and the prince held.

The beast remained silent. When he spoke it was not to give congratulations. He deeply resented the prince's grab for glory and understood what the prince was doing; he wished to become leader of the Brotherhood of Evil, to diminish the beast's authority. Ashurnasirpal snarled to himself, for what was there to congratulate? It was happenstance that the girl had come through the gates to Kurnigi, for the City of the Condemned below could be entered in many ways, not just through Kurnigi. The red-haired child had come because it was the beast who held in his clasp what was precious to her; it was he who taken her parents from the snake and set the trap. The other three were fools if they didn't see this. Still Ashurnasirpal no longer had control over who entered the City of the Condemned, as he had lost the souls captured by the reaper. He was now left with a meager force, the remnants of those who had in eons past sold their souls to him to give to the Dark Master. All these thoughts came in milliseconds, while the prince basked in the glow of congratulations and flipped his black locks about.

Then the beast caught something in the periphery of gray light emanated by the bulging eyes floating in the air. "Look," he said. He pointed to a small form that rose upon two scaly stick legs, with black wings rapidly beating against the pull into the land of darkness. This was a being that was being drawn and dragged into Kurnigi with a vengeance. He was pulled by souls who had been greedy, given to thievery and deceit, and who would have in time been within the Dark Master's realm. But they had been tricked into giving over their souls without reaping any of the promised earthly rewards. They were souls who wandered Kurnigi, waiting to exact their revenge against the one who had gravely wronged them in the mortal realm, the one who for eons had been protected—until now.

"It is Abaddon," the Great Beast growled.

"So?" said the prince dismissively and having duly noted (and resented) that no word of praise came from the foul fiery mouth of the beast. "Abaddon is nothing. He no longer has the Grim Reaper's protection. He will soon be tortured by the wandering spirits who roam Kurnigi and seek revenge against him."

The Duke of Muscovy nodded impatiently. "Yes. Yes. Let us grab the red-haired child now!"

"Abaddon is danger," the beast warned, staring at the gray glow.

The Prince of Wallachia grabbed the bulging eyes with one hand and flung them onto his coat. He shook his head impatiently and, in a commanding tone that the beast resented, said, "Say the chant to break the orb, beast, so that we may leave in safety." The beast alone knew how to release the orb so that Marduk wouldn't be able to smell the stench of the treachery of their thoughts once they were out of the web of protection. If the orb were broken without the protection of the chant, it meant certain destruction at the hands of Marduk.

Ashurnasirpal growled again. He saw how the duke and Khan held him with impatient eyes. He, the beast, had no other power other than the ability to release them safely from the orb. The beast wished they could rise to the surface of Kurnigi within the protection of the orb, but this could not be, for if they were released there, Marduk immediately would know of their secret ability to hide their thoughts from him. Here at least, deep within the bowels below the tunnels, the Dark Master's eyes and ears were dimmed, and his dominion over the creatures that crawled in the deepest parts of the underworld didn't hold the strength it did on the surface of Kurnigi. Even so, there was danger. Ashurnasirpal knew the Brotherhood would chance leaving the orb here in the depths without the protection of the chant, now that a prize so great as the Spyglass lay within their grasp. But still the beast ignored the prince's command and said firmly, "First Abaddon must be captured."

Khan of the Huns, with his ten small scorpions that were entwined in a living necklace about his neck, bristled in anger. "Beast, do you not know who it is you speak to? We command legions of souls. Abaddon is nothing. Speak of him no more! He is a cockroach who will be crushed beneath our feet. Now release us from the orb!"

The beast felt the sting of Khan's words. He, Ashurnasirpal, as a mortal king, had ruled over many more than this…this Hun had. Still the beast knew he held little power now and needed the strength of the Brotherhood. So he closed his small eyes shut, and from his nostrils came a flame, no longer red but yellow, a deep sickly yellow, the color of sickness, of jaundice. It rose from the beast's nostrils as he spoke words that were only heard as grunts to the others but were the words of cover—the seven desecrated names of Marduk, followed by the desecrated names of the Great Mother and words from the Tablets of Creation.

Bilulu-en,

Ankia-en-lugal,

Ugug,

Umum,

Tudu,

Udud,

Gar-gash.

Met-tie,

Met-tiu,

Met-tia.

Shamanu ammantum zakrat elish

la nab shaplish suma

la u Enuma.

As the grunts of the beast rose, the sounds splintered the black web that held them. The Duke of Muscovy, with his spear pointed upward, rose first. Khan of the Huns followed, declaring loudly as he flew up, "To Kurnigi and glory!" The Prince of Wallachia called to Ashurnasirpal as the three disappeared up and out of the tunnel, "Come, beast!"

The beast stood alone in the tunnel, no longer surrounded by the orb. The tunnel was so deep, so buried within the bowels of the City of the Condemned, that he knew it didn't command Marduk's attention. Even so, again he spoke the seven desecrated names.

Bilulu-en,

Ankia-en-lugal,

Ugug,

Umum,

Tudu,

Udud,

Gar-gash.

The orb appeared, its yellow glow enveloping the beast. He wished to gather his thoughts beyond the prying eyes of the Brotherhood. *Treachery.* His hairy body shook as the word shot through his mind. Abaddon was known to him as an underhanded sniveling coward whose untrustworthiness exceeded even that of the disloyalty inherent to those in the underworld. Abaddon also held in his black and shriveled heart anger and resentment toward Ashurnasirpal for what he had perpetrated upon him, for the beast had cut from him his thumbs, which had held his magic and strength. Here the beast snorted in lamentation. He should have killed that creature Abaddon and buried him deep in the Corkscrew of Terror when he'd had a chance, for even without thumbs, Abaddon couldn't be subjugated. As well, it was known that Abaddon had brought the Dark Master ten thousand souls, for the promise of control of the scythe. But the beast, through his servant the Grim Reaper, had controlled the scythe, not Abaddon. And the Dark Master wouldn't allow the beast control of Abaddon, instead keeping him captive within the robes of the Grim Reaper. But now the reaper was no more, and Abaddon had escaped and survived.

The beast stomped the ground with his hooves. Abaddon couldn't be trusted and was sure to plot against him. He worked for the Dark Master, and the beast didn't like his presence in Kurnigi. *What does Abaddon know of the Spyglass?* the beast wondered. *How is it that he is so close upon the heels of the two children that were thrown into Kurnigi?* The beast thought it was unlikely that it was merely happenstance that the red-haired child should be flung into Kurnigi at the same time as Abaddon. No. Abaddon was chasing the red-haired child with the Spyglass. Soon Abaddon, with his ways like the rat that he was, furtive and silent but ever present, would be upon him. Abaddon would insinuate himself into power. Surely the Dark Master knew that Abaddon now moved in the land of darkness. *But how much does Marduk know of the treachery in my heart?* the beast wondered, and shivered in fear. His animal eyes looked around the tunnel furtively. It was silent. Empty. The souls under the power of the other three of the Brotherhood of Evil lay above them. This deep tunnel, hidden from the eyes of Marduk, had been chosen by the beast for the Brotherhood to meet. And the desecrated chant of the names of Marduk with the power of the droplet was a shield, was it not?

The beast shook as he recalled how and from whom he had taken the droplet—the Crone, one who now was held in the power of the snake and therefore Marduk. The beast thought again of the Crone, who didn't know what the beast had taken from her; the Crone, who had been tricked by exchanging a worthless chant for the small magic in the black thumbs of Abaddon. Unbeknownst to the Crone, the beast had taken the droplet from her. The beast recalled how the Crone had cackled in triumph, for he had given over the amulet of the thumbs to the old hag when he had been at the nadir of his powerlessness, when first he had turned from man to beast. The Crone had said with glee, "Beast, oh beast, tell me who is the ugliest of all? Is it you or me?" And she had cackled her delight in the fall of the King Ashurnasirpal to a beast of burden. But the beast only had hung his head low and growled the words that were sure to please the Crone. "It is I," for his keen animal eyes had at once seen embedded in the tip of her long black nail the small trans-lucent golden droplet, so small that it was more a glimmer of light than liquid. But if one looked, one saw the sign, the ancient slashes, 𒀭𒈹𒁕 𒀭𒈹 𒀯, that flickered below the surface. The beast had been mesmerized by the droplet. *So it is true what the dead gods whispered upon their defeat!* he'd thought. The beast had dropped his head, as he didn't wish to bring the Crone's attention to the droplet, oblivious as she seemed to its existence. Now the beast thought again, *It is the droplet that fell from the eye of Marduk in the ancient battle when he and the other gods fought for who was to be the most powerful of the underworld.* The droplet held the waters of Apsu and Tiamet, who were said to have conceived Marduk and the Hidden Sister.

This, the beast knew, was told in the beginning of the true Seven Tablets of Creation, the story that lay buried so that the other tale, that of Marduk as invincible and all-knowing, lived while the true tale lay dead to the ears of all. This ancient tale had been lost and wasn't known to the others in the Brotherhood of Evil. But it was known to him, the beast, for once he had heard, deep in his palace when he reigned as King Ashurnasirpal, the voices of the dead gods. They wished desperately for the defeat of their enemy, Marduk, but for that they needed a member of his legions of the underworld to overthrow him. The dead gods whispered into the beast's ears that the kingdom he held in his mortal hands was nothing to what would be open to him if he helped them overthrow Marduk. They spoke of the Hidden Sister and how she clung to the other Twin Tablet of Destiny, whose whereabouts were known to an entity trapped in a Spyglass, and how they would share with the beast the power of both Tablets of Destiny. Then, when the beast had recoiled at the thought of so great and dangerous a treason against Marduk—even the thought of it rendered him at great peril—the gods told him of the droplet of weakness that had fallen from Marduk's eye in the Great Battle of the Gods. They tempted him with tales of how the possessor of the droplet, together with a secret incantation, could be rendered invisible to the eyes and ears of Marduk; after that it was just a matter of gathering others in the underworld of like mind to overthrow Marduk. Then the gods would be set free, and think of what power the beast would hold.

The gods had given the beast the incantation; all he needed was the droplet. "Seek it, for it is here, under your palace, that the droplet fell," they had told him. So the beast had succumbed. He had plotted and planned and had fallen, for he didn't find the droplet, but Marduk had read his treachery and turned him into a beast and held him as such through the eons. How it was that this smallest of droplets lay glittering upon the dirty nail of the Crone, the beast didn't know. But he did know that the Crone, incredibly, didn't know she held the droplet, so small was it that she didn't feel it. The beast knew she was greedy for her beauty, lost in the eons due to greed for more beauty and the power it held. The Crone was greedy for something else that she didn't speak of, something that had driven her through the ages, imprisoned in the cast of ugliness. The beast had kept his eyes steadily averted from the droplet, lest the Crone become suspicious.

The Crone knew the beast possessed the black thumbs of Abaddon that held dark powers. And as she had little power—only the small spells she had gleaned from others, and this was before the Black Book of Magic was given to her—she sought amulets from those who had fallen from the Dark Master's grace. "Do you have still upon you Abaddon's thumbs?" the Crone had asked, her face giving away her greed for them. "Yes," the beast had said. "I hold them still." The Crone had cackled, and a tooth, a yellow snaggly one, emerged from her foul gums as her desire for the thumbs grew. "Give it!" she said to the beast, and threw out her chants to mesmerize him. But the beast was too strong to succumb to her weak magic, for although the Dark Master had made him a beast, he hadn't stripped him of his strength. The beast had snorted fire from his nostrils, and the Crone had fallen back.

"Crone," he had said, "think not that I am weak of power because I no longer have the form of man." The Crone saw this was so. "This you seek, Crone," said the beast. Then the beast's tongue shot out, and upon the tip lay the two black thumbs of Abaddon. The Crone nodded as the thumbs glowed black and blue and showed themselves to be powerful with magic.

The beast pulled his tongue and the black-and-blue thumbs back into this mouth. He then spoke. "What can you give me for them?" The beast never once let his gaze fall upon the small translucent droplet upon her long black nail.

With feigned disinterest, the Crone said, "Abaddon's thumbs are trinkets not worth much, beast." The beast remained silent, and the Crone spoke again. "I have a few small spells. I will give you one spell for each thumb." The beast again remained silent. He was certain that the Crone didn't know the value of the droplet or even that she possessed it. Again he wondered how it could have fallen upon her person. The Crone said, "Come, beast. You know your amulets are not worth much."

The beast hesitated. "These spells—what will they do for me?"

The Crone cackled, "Why, beast, I have taken them from Apsu, the consort of the Mother Tiamet. They will make you strong and walk like a man rather than a beast." The beast knew the Crone was lying. He hesitated again and looked at how he stood on four hooves. The Crone didn't know he could walk on two hooves and have arms like a man should he wish. He bowed his humped shoulders as if in resignation. "Abaddon's thumbs cannot do that. They only hold the magic of deceit in them."

The Crone nodded. "Yes, they are small in their power, but I need their magic to add to what I have, so I'm willing to make an exchange."

The beast knew the Crone was lying about her spells. They were paltry in their powers, taken from mortals who had practiced dark magic on the smallest of scales. The magic in Abaddon's thumbs was stronger than anything she possessed. The beast sighed. "It will be so," he said, "for I long to walk on two feet, if only to be less of a beast than I am."

He opened his mouth, and his tongue shot forward, holding the two thumbs that were upon it. The Crone reached to grab them, and as she did, the very tip of the beast's tongue touched the droplet upon her long black nail, and it fell upon it. Quickly the beast retracted his tongue, feeling the sharp blades of the slashes in the droplet cut his mouth. The Crone wasn't aware the droplet was gone. She was mesmerized by Abaddon's black-and-blue thumbs and held them in her bony hands as she crowed with delight.

"Crone," the beast said, after the droplet had lodged like a burr into the side of his mouth. "Give me the two spells."

The Crone turned to him, her eyes narrow. "Two? I said one."

The beast growled, as if deeply displeased. Then the Crone took from the grubby folds of her dress a small wisp of powder; she opened her foul mouth wide, and from it was pronounced the incantation, words that were small and guttural in sound. The Crone then threw powder upon the beast and said, "Two legs to stand upon instead of four! Beast still but man more!"

The powder rose in the air, and gray dust fell upon the beast. It was in truth powerless dust, but the beast knew he must show the Crone that the spell held magic and thus warranted the exchange. The beast grunted and suddenly stood on two legs.

The Crone's face showed surprise, for she was sure that the dwarf who had given it to her had lied about his magical powers. Still, one never knew, and this was good, for now the beast would be satisfied he made a fair exchange.

The beast Ashurnasirpal grunted his thanks. "Though you gave me but one spell, Crone, it held the power of two."

So they had parted, the Crone believing herself to be the victor. And here the beast thought of the great irony, that the Crone should have sought power and gathered over the eons amulets and spells, until her humped back was weighted by them, when all she needed she had held in one small droplet.

Now, within the dark tunnels beneath Kurnigi, the beast possessed this droplet and also the dead gods' incantation that protected him from Marduk's eyes and ears. The beast wondered and worried often if the Crone ever knew how much magic she had held in the tip of her nail, especially when she had held sway over the Black Book of Magic. But she never gave any such hint, and the beast thought that the Crone knew not. The Dark Master, however, must have known that the droplet that could cover from his eyes treachery was held by someone. A great anxiety clutched Ashurnasirpal's heart, for he hadn't yet overthrown Marduk; he couldn't, for the might of the Brotherhood of Evil was still daunted by Marduk's power. And the dead gods had disappeared, said to have been destroyed forever by Marduk, rendered inert and powerless, for never again did the beast hear their voices once he had turned from man to beast. Still the beast worried. Did Marduk know he held the droplet? Could he have sensed it? The beast knew that the full power of the Dark Master wasn't known to him. But how could Marduk know of the Brotherhood, covered as they were by the desecrated seven names and the spell from the droplet that released the spell and blinded Marduk to them? Nevertheless, the beast thought, if somehow the Dark Master were to know their treachery now, before the Spyglass was in their possession, what would follow?

Fools! The beast was shaken from his reverie, thinking of the danger of Khan of the Huns, the Duke of Muscovy, and the Prince of Wallachia in the open sight of the Marduk as they tried to seize the Spyglass. The moment they did so, Marduk would read their treachery! The beast quickly muttered the chant to break the orb. Yellow smoke swirled from his nostrils up to the black web, which broke like thin glass. The beast rose up hurriedly through the broken orb. The Brotherhood above must not act now. The child must be lured into the tunnels beneath the City of the Condemned, and only under the cover of the power of the chant of the desecrated words of the names of Marduk could the Spyglass be wrestled from her, safe from the knowledge, and thereby the wrath, of the Dark Master. Ashurnasirpal flew up, through the tunnel's ceiling.

𒀭𒌋𒌋 𒀭 𒀭𒌋 𒁹

Eddie assessed the situation as this—trapped. Behind them was the impenetrable stone of the granite face of the mountain of Mashu. Sweeping toward them were the fiendish creatures of the dead. Gilgamesh, king of Uruk, wielded his mighty warrior spear against the onslaught of the hordes of the dead. His body arched as he thrust his spear forward. It flew into the swarm then flew back and fell at his feet, as if it was just a small stick in the wind.

"*Muktablu*," Gilgamesh said softly. "Behind me, quickly move now...so that you are sheltered in the front by me and in the back by the mountains of Mashu." Eddie saw the brave king of

Uruk's blue face set in warrior determination. Eddie stood his ground. He was a *muktablu* and would die with the king of Uruk and not stand like a coward behind him. Eddie's face was fixed in firm resolve to defend their position to the end. It was what his father, Sergeant Petersen, would do; no coward was the son of such a man. Eddie held the scythe aloft, swinging the weapon toward the oncoming onslaught of the amorphous spirits of the dead who echoed the chords of their wail of sorrow.

Who is master? Who is master? The cries of the long dead, their shapeless souls snatched from them by the reaper, surrounded Eddie and the king of Uruk.

"*Muktablu*," Gilgamesh cried urgently, "you must move now!"

But it was too late, for like a swarm of insects, the dead had moved in unison and soon would be upon them. *Who is master? Who is master?* buzzed the words of the dead.

Eddie and Gilgamesh's backs were plastered to the cold granite wall of the mountain Mashu. Eddie swung the scythe at the mass of the dead and saw that the king of Uruk also was swinging his spear but to no avail, for they moved fast, the dead now swirling and blurring until they were just one mass of movement, a tornado of souls moving toward them like an arrow toward a target. Like a tornado, the buzzing of their words stung their ears. *Who is master? Who is master?* The tornado was funnel shaped and a mass of blurred dark colors— iron gray, burgundy, ochre, and dull yellows—its point turned straight toward Gilgamesh and Eddie. The sound of the words of the dead reached a deafening pitch; the tornado's swirling, spinning mass now like the point of an arrow coming right toward Eddie and Gilgamesh. It moved with the force of thunder until Gilgamesh and Eddie were surrounded but not penetrated. Around them, over and under, was the whirling tornado of souls, a blending of the grays, reds, and yellows of the very forms of the wandering dead, that lifted Eddie and Gilgamesh up into the hollow of the tornado, and all around them were the dreadful sounds of the wails of the dead that rang again and again in their ears. Eddie and Gilgamesh were held up by the horrid winds born of the lamentations of the dead souls. They clung to their weapons as they were thrown about in the hollow of the mass of dead souls. Then a sound greater than that of ten thousand thunderstorms tore the air as the tornado of souls burrowed through the great granite mountain of Mashu. Then the sound ceased. Eddie and Gilgamesh fell to the earth and looked around in amazement. Felled in half was the great granite mountain of Mashu, slashed right through the center, creating a giant orange-and-yellow canyon.

In front of Eddie and Gilgamesh, the dead souls again rose within the canyon, now no longer one mass, as their bodies materialized slowly, one by one, then suddenly by the hundreds. Eddie and Gilgamesh held their weapons in a defensive position against the onslaught of the dead souls then exclaimed their surprise. These were the dead souls of children. Their cloaks and coats were upon some that were small children, others just at the cusp of blossoming into young adults, almost into the age of reason. They were the wandering spirit children, ghosts now but living once. Their spirits had been stolen from some of them in sleep, others when in a moment of despair they had made a blunder and bowed their heads to the temptations of evil, but goodness still lay in their hearts. Through the millennia these souls had been imprisoned within the dreadful forest of Humawa. Now they rose, freed from their chains as their master, the Grim Reaper, holder of the scythe, was no more.

All the wandering spirit children held up their hands toward Eddie to gesture that they meant no harm. Gilgamesh's face reflected surprise, and Eddie laid his scythe to one side. Then the spirits sang their song as one. The chorus began as their arms stretched out. They wept their tears of sorrow and sung the story of their unhappy fate.

We laid our heads down as the living
and awoke in the land of the dead,
the land of dark and sleepy shadows,
where dreams of grandeur
lay just beyond our greedy fingers.
As we clasped for riches,
our hearts stretched to seize
all that was powerful,
all that was mighty,
and we took the hand that held it.

Warm it was not, but cold.
The icy, cunning, evil,
bony fingers of the reaper
clenched us now.
And we struggled in vain,
for the reaper held us fast,
and the serpents that served him
coiled upon our whirling spirits
and plunged us into the dust and death.

We laid our heads down as the living
and raised it as the dead,

for our souls were stolen
by the reaper.

Our souls were taken
by the master of the serpent,
so have we wandered in this land
of unending night,
where our pleas for mercy lay frozen
in this land of darkness,
until you came,
holder now of Death's scythe
with the hand of the living.

The wandering spirits called a name, *Trina, Trina, Trina.* Then one among the wandering spirits came forth, a ghostly girl of eleven who wore a long skirt once of the finest wool, touching the tops of her ankles, now tattered and torn. Eddie's eyes widened with surprise; he never before had seen such a stunning girl. His heart was taken at once by her angelic aspect—her pale oval face, light-hazel eyes with dashes of emerald green, and her gleaming hair, which shone like polished dark wood, thick and luxuriant and held back by a velvet ribbon. Trina's large eyes brimmed with tears as she sang with grief and anguish:

Seven days is our
journey from body to spirit,
until the cold breath leaves us.
Seven times our souls
should be kindled.
Seven tears shall we shed
until we weep no more.

Seven steps must we take
until our we are freed
from this sad land of the cursed,
until we see the starlight
dancing upon our mother's brow.

Eddie's face was awash in wonder at this girl ghost, Trina; he felt her melancholy song reverberate in his heart. The phantom girl was bent in supplication, her head bowed toward Eddie. Behind her were the other spirit children, little ones with faces large with wonder, skin the color of caramel, eyes black as pebbles; others with hair the color of ravens, skin black and like a velvet night; some with hair the color of cornfields, eyes blue like the sky. Some had faces ruddy, some white, some yellow with eyes the shape of almonds. Some were teenaged in years, others much younger. Children who had succumbed to the reaper in sleep, in illness, in greed all cried out to Eddie. As the spirits looked to him, a silence surrounded them as they waited for the boy who held Death's scythe to speak. But Eddie hadn't done so, so overwhelmed was he by the plight of these spirits. Then the eyes of the angelic girl Trina held him again and beseeched him, her voice rising again.

O master who is living,
we beseech you to help free us!
O Master who is living,
who walks strong with the king of Uruk,
we beseech you to protect us
on our journey of seven steps,
where we must traverse
the dreaded land of smoke and shadows,
Kurnigi.

Eddie turned to the amassed spirits of the children, and his heart filled with their sorrow. He looked at the king of Uruk, Gilgamesh, as one tear fell down his noble blue face. "*Muktablu,*" said Gilgamesh, "the sobbing sorrow of these wandering spirits of the young dead strikes too my heart." Then he added softly, "We are also heading to the land of darkness, but to embark upon their journey of seven steps, which will lead these wandering children spirits to the Great Mother...*muktablu,* be warned, much treachery and danger will we face from the Dark Master. We also do not know the danger we shall bring upon our friends—the red-haired child and the brown owlet—who now lie in Kurnigi."

Eddie knew that Gilgamesh was warning him that what the wandering spirit children were pleading for him to do carried risks. *Risks are always part of a combat mission.* His father's words came to him. *But know this, Eddie—without the strength of the warrior, the weak will be crushed.* Eddie made up his mind. He held the scythe aloft and spoke the words that came from his heart. "Mission accepted."

The angelic girl's eyes turned to Eddie and brimmed with gratitude. The wandering spirit children lifted their arms in thanks, and their voices held the song of burgeoning hope. Eddie turned to Gilgamesh. "Let's go." He began the steps forward through the bottom of the canyon, the scythe held high. His steps were light and fast, as if he moved on air and not the ground. Gilgamesh was next to him, taking the same running-flying steps, holding his warrior spear aloft. Beyond them and fast approaching the end of the canyon was a shadowy coldness—Kurnigi.

𒁹𒌋 𒂍 𒁹 𒀭

Abaddon stood upon the cold and dark ground of Kurnigi—if it could be called ground, for it shifted from a solid form to a moving, living dust right under his feet. Above him was a dome of sky, gray and cold as steel. Silence reigned, an icy silence that filled the surface of Kurnigi, where nothing stirred. Then the disembodied arms and hands of those who had existed when their spirits were in mortal form—sliced from them and thrown down by Abaddon—stirred in the dust, fingers poking out and unfurling like sprouting seeds. These hands and arms first rose up and clutched at Abaddon's thin, gray-green, scaled ankles. They writhed in the dust and with skeleton hands, vengeance bleeding from their fingers. Abaddon jumped about the ground, moving about in dashes to avoid the creeping fingers of the vengeful spirits. He flapped his wings, but he didn't rise as the fingers of the dead grabbed him fast and held him.

"Aaagh!" cried Abaddon, flapping his wings hard, loosening their grasp and flying up. His yellow slit eyes flitted the terrain for a way out as he sought to escape his unlucky fate—no protection of Death's scythe, no reaper's robe. He turned toward the gates to Kurnigi beyond him and saw how they had shut tightly and prevented his exit. Abaddon spotted vipers, sharp of tongue, rising from the ground below him. Words formed in and around him, and the rodent-faced Abaddon squirmed in fear. These words were like echoes at first then rose again and again around the small and trembling creature that was Abaddon. The vengeful souls Abaddon had stolen from ancient times cried their chant of revenge, which poured into and stung his ears.

Abaddon, liar and wretch!
Weep as we have wept.
Sit as we have sat
in sorrow,
you who stole our souls,

you who thought he had conquered.
Wear upon your breast biting vipers
with poisonous tongues
so that your lips will
ever cry out lamentations,
for mercy is not yours.
Never given! Never received!

Mattie and Geeta fell into the shadowy land of Kurnigi as the words rained upon Abaddon. They dropped with the words upon the ground, amid the moving hands and arms of the vengeful wandering spirits. They fell where vipers were rising, small and gray, then black, then blue; the snakes coiled and uncoiled. "Yipes!" Mattie yelled as she stepped on a small snake. But the vipers didn't seek Mattie and moved quickly toward their prey—Abaddon just beyond, his wings flapping. He was pulled to the ground and jumped up and down on the dusty moving land, then flew up again. Abbadon's sharp face spoke of terror, the black bristles of his hair trembling as the fingers of vengeful spirits sought to grab him. Geeta's eyes widened behind her glasses. She looked up and saw that above them, from the gray sky of Kurnigi, like a dark cloud, loomed more spirits. "Mattie!" Geeta could only whisper, for the sight robbed the very words from her.

Mattie shook her hand in pain, feeling how tightly glued the Spyglass was to her hand. *It hurts!* Mattie thought angrily and shook the Spyglass once more. Then something in the periphery caught her eyes, and she looked up. There, dropping like a cold rain, were figures of men and women, their eyes hollow, their curses filling the air as they dove downward toward Abaddon, Mattie, and Geeta, bearing spears and swords.

But an even more ominous threat was emerging that Mattie and Geeta couldn't have fathomed, for the ground of Kurnigi shook again. And though not yet upon them, not too far away from Mattie and Geeta came to the surface creatures who hadn't done so for eons—the Duke of Muscovy and Khan of the Huns. These two rose from the depths of ground onto the surface of Kurnigi, followed by the Prince of Wallachia. The duke raised his forbidding bloody spear and, with khan and the prince, gave a bloodcurdling call. Soon from beneath the ground rose the legions of the duke's forces—soldiers from his reign of terror. "Ivan the Terrible!" they shouted. As well rose the enemies the duke had forced to surrender, whose souls were in allegiance to evil and whose bodies were bloodied and broken.

Then Khan cried his out own his call, and again the ground gave way to the onslaught of souls held deep within the bowels of Kurnigi. Souls from the ancient times of Khan rose up, holding their swords and clubs, finally freed from their prison in the tunnels beneath Kurnigi.

Finally the prince waved his hand in a flutter and gave a low growl. And so too did his sorrowful legions of souls rise from the ground of Kurnigi, some with tattered clothing of the artistocracy, some wearing the garb of peasants, others holding small sharpened stakes. The land broke beneath them as the spirits in allegiance to the evil trio of Khan, the duke, and the prince rose in a geyser of dead souls. Beyond them the dark clouds of Kurnigi dropped like rain upon Abaddon vengeful spirits bearing spears and swords so that they might seize him.

"See there!" the duke cried out, pointing to Mattie. "There is the red-haired child who holds the Spyglass!"

The prince's hideous buttons of eyes moved about his coat in glee as he clapped his hands. The duke kept his aristocratic reserve, but a faint sadistic smile flittered across his long face, as he thought of how easy it would be to pounce upon the child and nab the Spyglass.

It was Khan, with his moon face and lopsided eyes, that felt the force that surrounded the two children and understood the danger. "The creatures there—the red-haired child and the brown one—are living. We will not be able to break their life force."

The prince stopped his clapping and turned with a sneer to Khan. "No?" he said. Then he threw back his head and opened his mouth and gave a cry—if it could be called that; so deafening was this sound that it shook the air like thunder. The last note of the legions of the evil trio immediately coalesced into a black dervish of spirits; these dead were so strong that their collective souls were a force of their own. Then the prince flew into the swirling mass. "Come!" he called out.

The duke leaped up first, but Khan stood upon the ground for a moment. Where was the beast Ashurnasirpal? Was this trickery? Too easy was this, to capture the Spyglass from the girl child under the skies of Kurnigi—skies that had the eyes of Marduk ever lurking. The prince poked his face out of the spinning mass, his red pouty lips showing impatience. "Khan!" he beckoned.

"The beast is not with us," Khan said.

The prince shot out a hand to him. "The beast has no power. We rule now." Khan nodded. Yes. That was so. He grabbed the prince's hand and disappeared into the black mass, which immediately spun toward the girls.

Unaware of the fast-approaching black swarm of spirits, Geeta and Mattie hopped on one foot then another as the vipers and the bleeding fingers of the vengeful spirits moved like a rippling lake under them and toward Abaddon. Mattie's face was red and sweaty from the hopping. Geeta's braids were coming undone, and her paisley-patterned dress was covered with a patina of dust. Mattie gasped for breath. "The snakes don't want us!" she said in relief.

Geeta coughed as she tried to shake off the dust. Her eyes caught sight of the approaching maelstrom, a swirling mass of black, and the bloodcurdling cries that emitted from them. Then from the black mass Geeta saw the duke, his bearded face first, then his arms thrusting the bloody spear. "Mattie," Geeta gasped. "Look! That man is pointing a spear at you! They want the Spyglass, I am certain."

Mattie didn't know what to think, but it sure looked like that scary man was pointing the spear right at her! She shook the fixed Spyglass in her hand. "Spyglass! You rat fink! Get us outta here!"

The Spyglass remained firmly glued to Mattie's hand and saw only too clearly where they were—thrown over the gates and into the land of the dead. Kurnigi! The Spyglass felt waves of terror, and beneath those a fleeting thought, a painful splinter of a memory of the shadowy land of darkness. This memory stabbed the Spyglass with its relentless cold. *That stupid girl!* The Spyglass thought yet again of Mattie. She rued the day she had chosen her as her Mistress. *No!* The Spyglass started. They must leave, for eternal captivity in Kurnigi was the fate of all who entered. This the Spyglass knew—Mattie was a living soul; Geeta was a living soul. The Spyglass understood well what they were and what she wasn't, how she never would escape the force of Marduk if she alone were captured. The dark forces of Kurnigi couldn't easily overcome the power of the living; the living didn't belong in the land of the dead. The Spyglass understood that she had to stay close and firm to Mattie. No more would she let lapse her hold on the girl. Always would she cleave close so that they were never two but braided together as one; then she, Spyglass, would take control of Mattie, and the living soul would be hers. That was the plan but one that wasn't yet realized, Spyglass realized gloomily. But now what to do? What to do? She had no idea of how to leave Kurnigi, but leave they must. She tried to lift Mattie up but found herself weakened, unable to overcome the dark forces of the land of death around her. Mattie felt the Spyglass trying to pull her up but failing. Geeta observed how Mattie's arm jerked up then stopped.

The sinister mass of spirits revolved around Mattie and Geeta like a dark doughnut. It was a horrifying black circle of the dead, buzzing loudly, spewing cacaphonous sounds that spelled death. The dark mass moved closer and closer upon Mattie and Geeta but not fully upon them, for the force of their living, beating hearts repelled the evil trio and their legions, preventing them from touching them.

The prince, with his long black locks and pale face, emerged from the black miasma. He snarled at Geeta and Mattie, who were trapped in the middle. "Give us the Spyglass!" he said to Mattie.

Khan, with his lopsided face and necklace of scorpions, was tantalized by the Spyglass—it was so close—and his long greedy fingers reached toward Mattie with but were repelled by sparks. The Duke of Muscovy's bloody spear poked out of the black fog as he thrust it toward Mattie and Geeta. But the spear bent back against their life force. "Give it over!" the duke bellowed. "You are nothing against us!" Mattie and Geeta stood close together. Geeta saw there was a force around them that the evil couldn't penetrate. But how long could it last?

As Abaddon lay lashed to the ground by the dead hands that rose from the dirt, his greasy gray face shone with fear. His rodent yellow eyes darted here and there and fluttered. The vengeful spirits from above were now falling upon him, as a buzzing cloud of doom called out their bitter words.

Abaddon, liar and wretch,
weep as we have wept!

Beneath him, though his wings flapped up and down, the avaricious fingers of the dead had fully grasped him by his scaly ankles. Abaddon had seen the black of the spirits rising behind him and the khan, duke, and prince emerging from it. He saw how the trio sought not him but the girl child with the Spyglass, who stood with the brown owlet girl in the center of the black storm of spirits. But the beast Ashurnasirpal wasn't among them. At this Abaddon felt some relief, for the beast would want to capture him, now that the robes of the Grim Reaper no longer held him. He needed the Spyglass; it must be his. Abaddon struggled against the hold of the bloody fingers that grasped his ankles. He had to escape before he was blanketed into paralysis by the rancorous spirits that fell upon him. He must! But how? How?

Suddenly the ground shook as the beast Ashurnasirpal emerged from the earth of Kurnigi. He snorted fire from his dreadful nostrils as he saw the swirling black form of the legions of the khan, duke, and prince approach the red-haired child. He stomped the ground angrily. *Fools! Fools!* If they were capture the Spyglass here on the surface of Kurnigi, it would be for naught, for Marduk held power here. Without a doubt, Marduk would seize it from them and smell the treachery that was in their minds. Ashurnasirpal would have to overcome the children's will, subdue their living breaths, then grab the red-haired girl and the brown child and pull them both into his tunnels and trap them in the Corkscrew of Terror. Marduk would be told that the red-haired child lay trapped with the other prey. Then the beast would give the red-haired one a promise—relinquish the Spyglass, and the creatures precious to her would be released, as would she, back to the land of the living. All these thoughts rose in Ashurnasirpal's mind quickly and in pieces that were shattered like a puzzle; the beast thought this way as a protection, for each piece of the puzzle was innocous, and should the Dark Master have been listening, he would have been none the wiser to his deceit, or so Ashurnasirpal thought. The beast stomped forward and leaped into the black mist above.

CHAPTER 14

dance of satan

Abaddon smelled the stench of the beast and knew that if he didn't escape, the beast would capture him and keep him tortured and imprisoned. He struggled against the bleeding fingers on the ground that held his thin ankles and tried to pull him down, as well as the weight of the vengeful spirits, who soon would smother him. His wings were almost immobilized by the weight of the unforgiving spirits. Then he heard it. Abaddon's sharp ears pricked up. A sound. A chant. From far away. Someone in the land of the living calling to the dead. A call that Abaddon had heard many thousands of times when he had resided within the robes of the Grim Reaper.

Lake of corpses,
sea of spirits,
land of the dead,
those from the beyond,

I call to you.
Come to us. Come!

The words that formed in sound when they first fell onto Kurnigi now turned into a thin light with a hand embedded in it—a living hand reaching out. The avenging spirits that lay on him moved as if struck by a whip. Abaddon threw his bony four-fingered hands into the air to grab the hand. The force of the hand of the living pulled him up, and the vengeful fingers lost hold upon Abaddon. The spirits that had surrounded him, intent upon laying Abaddon to waste, gave way, groaning in dissappoint-ment. *Abaddon!* the dead called to him, as he was pulled up into the thin light. *Abaddon, we shall one day hold you in our hands and break you!* Abaddon, in the middle of the light, held fast with both hands, each of his eight fingers clinging to the hand of the living within the beam. The chant from the land of the living—*Those from the beyond, we call to you. Come to us! Come!*—rang out. His rat face, with its oily sheen, saw Kurnigi quickly receding below him. Then, as Abaddon flew above the whirling black mist, he glimpsed below the metal sheen of the Spyglass, and greed rushed within him. He calculated that there were nanoseconds left for him to grab the Spyglass. Abaddon ungrasped one index finger from the hand of the living and pointed it downward. The long black nail elongated as it spun downward, toward the middle of the swirling black mass. Fast, like the end of a whip, it lashed out to lasso the Spyglass within Mattie's hand. The Spyglass's eyes widened in fear; in an instant she dissappeared into the depths of Mattie's pant pocket. The lasso whipped toward and around Mattie's now empty hand and reeled her up.

"Aaagh!" Mattie cried in pain, for the lasso stung and dug into her as it wrapped itself around her fingers. "Geeta!" Mattie's legs were now off the ground. Geeta grabbed Mattie's ankle, and within seconds the two were up an out of the doughnut of the swirling black mist. Below them, Geeta saw the duke's angry face with his spear thrust up toward her, and through the swirling mass, the sinister faces of the khan and prince as the snarling animal aspect of the beast emerged. Mattie and Geeta were pulled up into the beam that held Abaddon and were blinded by a searing light as these words echoed in their ears—*Those from the beyond, we call to you. Come to us! Come!*

𒁹𒀭𒆠𒁹𒀭

Paddy O'Reilly stirred noisly in his sleep, little grunts of displeasure erupting from his open mouth up toward his bristly red mustache. Thoughts of that old wound ran through his mind; the fact his manuscript "The Eighth Tablet of Creation: Moving Beyond the Hegemony of Layard and Smith" had been rejected for publication by the journal was really quite unjustifiable. Indeed the criticisms were so far afield that that no one would call them constructive. Rather they were nothing but a wholesale slaughter of Paddy's core concepts. An academic's life was such that one had to develop elephantine thickness of skin to "constructive peer criticism." Further, the anonymity of the reviewer afforded for a sometimes harshly honest assessment, a process that Paddy himself as a reviewer knew only too well. Certainly one submitted manuscripts to journals to forward the scientific integrity of his subject area, and peer review was a critical aspect of the process. *Review—* not cut to shreds and spit back to the author with little in the way of an attempt to disguise the disdain the "peer" clearly felt.

What the state of academic journals was after the 1929 crash was a whole other matter. Yes, publication costs were high. Yes, they were in the midst of the Great Depression, and fewer and fewer universities were willing to take on the cost of a subscription, especially a journal covering an esoteric study, as to which Assyriology was increasingly relegated. And yes, yes, yes, there were very few members now in the American Society of Assyriology! And hence the *Journal of the American Society for Assyriology*—or *JASA*, as it was truncated—had fallen on hard times. Still Paddy's manuscript, so provocative in its title, "The Eighth Tablet of Creation: Moving Beyond the Hegemony of Layard and Smith," in no way deserved the scathing audience it had received.

His thesis was that George Smith had misread the Tablets of Creation and consequently misattributed to the ancient Babylonians the story of the flood. Moreover, as it was well known, Sir Henry Austen Layard had misidentified Nimrud to be Nineveh; Nimrud was Kalah, the ancient biblical site, of course. Both British Assyriologists had lost the forest for the trees, Paddy had written. And, Paddy continued, Smith was in truth nothing but an amateur, a neophyte with uncanny luck. Paddy's red mustache puffed out under a breathy snore. Strange that Smith should find the old dig of Layard's in Nineveh, its library in ruins, filled to the brim with stones, clay pieces, cement, bricks. Impossible that anything could be discovered now by Smith. Impossible certainly that Smith could have discovered the missing fragment of clay of the Gilgamesh myth. But he had. Smith had found the needle in the haystack on May 14, 1873 and funded by a newspaper of all sources, *The Daily Telegraph*, for all his expenses! Paddy thought of how he'd had to dig into the meager remains of an inheritance to fund his own expedition to

Nineveh. In the modern depression-gripped times of 1938, there was no newspaper interested in sending a young archaelogist to dig around the deserts of Mosul.

Smith and his luck had been the subject of little inquiry since 1873. Still, Paddy wondered, how was it from that small bag of ruins he had extracted that day in 1873, from the mess that was all that was left of Layard's archaelogical site of twenty-five years earlier, that Smith had pulled out the missing piece that completed the story of the great flood? A million-to-one chance, and Smith did it. Here in his sleep, Paddy again stirred. How was it possible for Smith to have such luck, when Paddy could find no support—not academic, not financial—for what was an even more stupendous prospect, finding the Eighth Tablet of Creation? He was neither an amateur with supernatural luck such as Smith nor an egotistical adventurer like Layard. Yes, he was treading dangerous ground to label Sir Henry Layard in such a way, but true it was. The man was a known swashbuckler in his dig days, known to have courted danger in his flirtations with the attractive harem women of the desert moguls.

That neither Sir Henry Layard or George Smith could appreciate what the Tablets that had lain in shards under their feet represented was another theme expounded by Paddy. Not like Paddy O'Reilly, PhD—his credentials and position at Columbia University as an established academic differentiated him from Layard and Smith who had held no such affiliations. Moreover, in their ignorance Layard and Smith had misled an entire field, thrown inquiry down a rabbit hole for decades. The story was older, by Paddy's reading, than the Babylonians. The true story lay in the memories of man more ancient than the Babylonians, recorded in the indecipherable language thought to be Sumerian, but as Paddy contended, older by thousands of years and of a heretofore unknown people. The mystery lay wrapped in what was yet to be discovered—the Eighth Tablet of Creation, the true story of the creation of humankind—which was why it was so critical that explorations of Nineveh were continued and that Assyriologists moved beyond the archaelogical hegemony of Layard and Smith. Paddy was enamored of the word *hegemony*, which spoke without restraint of scholastic imperialism forwarded by past works merely because of the fame of the writers.

So Paddy had written his article and sent it off to *JASA*. For his efforts toward breathing new life into the flagging field of Assyriology, however, Paddy hadn't been applauded. Rather for his heuristic efforts (*heuristic* was another word loved by Paddy, signifying how academic articles should have within them the seeds of further inquiry), he had been "rewarded" with a scathing rejection of his manuscript. He had taken the returned (and reviled) "The Eighth Tablet of Creation: Moving Beyond the Hegemony of Layard and Smith" with him to Nineveh and had stewed over the comments. Paddy had noticed with chagrin that his beloved word *hegemony* had been crossed out by the "reviewer" with a rather heavy-handed red slash. He suspected the reviewer was none other than L. Rufus Wigglesworth, PhD. Wigglesworth was the editor of *JASA*, and his disdain for Paddy's excursion to Nineveh and the search for the Eighth Tablet of Creation was none too disguised. "*Seven*," Wigglesworth had said to Paddy in a condescending tone, backed by that mysterious ally of his, Herman Biddle. "Seven days, Paddy, six for creation and one for rest. Seven Tablets of Creation. There is no Eighth Tablet, other than as a figment of your grasping imagination." The rejection was interestingly timed in its arrival: just on the cusp of his (yes, self-funded) Nineveh exploration in 1938, exhorted as a waste of time by Rufus Wigglesworth. Again this was another clue that the hefty hand of Wigglesworth had been at play in the rejection of the manuscript. Yes, Wigglesworth had used his editorial might and rejected his manuscript. Paddy bristled at this; shouldn't there be some degree of academic integrity?

"Paddy!" Paddy heard his name. *Odd,* he thought, *a female American voice. Here in Nineveh!* For his last memory was that he had taken a short shut-eye, a respite from the hot sun under which he had been laboring for hours. Paddy kept his eyes tightly shut. "Paddy!" He heard the tone sharp again and felt someone shaking him. He opened his eyes and gazed up myopically. A very attractive, slim, blonde woman was kneeling over him and straightening the glasses over his face. Paddy noticed he wasn't in his quarters in Nineveh but instead was looking up at the water-stained ceiling of an office. And underneath him wasn't his cot but a pile of papers upon which he was lying.

"Wake up!" Paddy heard the woman say.

Paddy grunted and formed the words, "Dottie…" It was all coming back to him now. His face hurt. The memory of the decapitated heads with large teeth biting him deep within the hellish tunnels, the river turbulent with creatures—all of it came at him in full force. "Aaagh," he said, a sort of swallowed scream and groan. So he hadn't perished, as he had thought. But where were they? Could there be more unspeakable events in store? Look what terror they, he and his charming wife from the future, already had confronted. He had been battered and beaten, trampled about and kicked. Oh, for the days when he had bemoaned a bad review of a manuscript! He felt his eyes close again, being pulled by memories. The red-slashed manuscript was a sore spot. Who was Wigglesworth anyway to make such judgments? An old fuddy-duddy with ideas still rooted in the nineteenth century, if truth be told. Wigglesworth was beyond his prime, decades beyond, Paddy thought rather ungenerously.

"Paddy!" the word cut through his descent into slumber like a knife. "Stay awake!" He felt Dottie tugging at him. "Please, Paddy, see if you can stand. We may need to run."

Paddy heard the fear in Dottie's voice. He lumbered up, wobbly upon rubbery legs. His eyes hurt; his head hurt. Even his bristly red mustache hurt. Everything hurt. Paddy reached out to steady himself on an old desk piled high with the detritus of decades of academia. How often he had sat at that very desk wondering at the mind that could work in such disarray. Suddenly the realization of where they were hit him. "Dr. Wigglesworth's office," he said. "But...how?"

Dottie shook her head and gazed around the office. It looked as if a great tornado had hit it—papers strewn about, bookshelves on the floor with their contents tumbling out. Paddy suddenly remembered. "It was here that I landed from Nineveh. Biddle was with me. And the children."

"Mattie and her friends, Geeta and Eddie?" Dottie asked.

"Yes...no...I recall only that presumptuous boy and the serious Indian girl. And we came upon Wigglesworth and Biddle too. A great wind blew...and then I was in a cave...perhaps tunnels. Then we met. Dottie, perhaps everything is all right! We're back in New York in the present!"

Dottie considered this. "Which present? Yours or mine? Nineteen thirty-eight or nineteen sixty-eight?"

Paddy considered this for a moment. It couldn't be both. "Well—" he began, but his words were cut short by a roaring sound that shook the room. Then webbed feet hit the desk and scattered the papers about as the rest of the person appeared. The body belonging to the amphibian feet was none other than that of George Smith. In an agile fashion, he jumped from the desk to the floor. He looked about to see the pudgy man and the blonde woman staring at him.

"Mr. Smith!" Paddy sputtered, irrationally wondering whether Smith was aware of how he had characterized him as an amateur bumbler in Nineveh in his manuscript "The Eighth Tablet of Creation: Moving Beyond the Hegemony of Layard and Smith."

Smith snarled a "Shh!" His lean frame was bent, his dark shaggy head tilted as if he were listening for something. His shrewd eyes scanned the office. His hands suddenly shot out, his palms flat, as if trying to feel the atmosphere around him, much like a mime would do in demonstrating the presence of invisible walls. Smith had assumed a wide-based stance, firmly planting his webbed feet on the paper-strewn floor, as if to anchor himself. *Most peculiar*, Paddy thought. Paddy began to open his mouth to form the words regarding where they were, but Dottie grabbed his arm, shaking her head. Who knew if this really was George Smith? So far it was unclear whether he could be characterized as friend or foe—though he had rescued Paddy and her—especially as his manner was so odd. He was more like an inmate of an insane asylum than a brilliant scholar.

Smith's gaunt visage—the scraggly, filthy beard upon his face; the eyes bloodshot and constantly shifting; his torn expedition clothes; the unshorn long, dark hair; and the grimacing, twitching face—suggested madness. Paddy and Dottie stepped back to allow him the room for movement, for George Smith, once heralded as a genius, discover of the Chaldean tale of the flood, decipher of the Tablets of Creation, was dancing a strange jig now on those frog feet, jumping as if the papers were hot as coals. Paddy assumed a protective hold on Dottie, for who knew what this madman would do next? Smith threw back his head, eyes squinted tight, sounds emitting from his pursed lips—gasps, grunts, long groans—in a rhythmic beat to the mad dance, knee up and out, the webbed feet keeping a beat. Paddy and Dottie glanced at each other; this must be lunacy born of confinement.

Smith was using his webbed feet as sensors for evil emanations. He had turned his palms up to provide a shield around them, as best as his little store of incantations allowed. And little there were too, now that he had bargained away much of what he'd had with the other prisoners of the tunnels of Ashurnasirpal. Smith knew they could still be imprisoned deep within the tunnels of Ashurnasirpal, in the Corkscrew of Terror, within the land of darkness, Kurnigi. He recognized from long experience held within the corkscrew that things were never what they appeared to be. Perception was controlled by the dark forces. The office must be a mirage, psychological torture, where hapless victims believed themselves to be out of the depths of Kurnigi, as the wish was so strong. But only when the heart skipped with joy at release would one find it was all unreal, and the cruel reality of the dank and bleak labyrinth of the land of darkness from which there was no escape once again would become real. Smith knew it was either the pudgy, moonfaced man with the bushy red mustache or the slight, prim-appearing blonde woman who had willed this image. But the fact that he was in it and aware was strange. Very strange.

The side entrance of a small, worn, brick building in New York City was entered through an alleyway. In front of the door was a poster. It showed a picture of a solemn, dark-haired, middle-aged woman whose hands were outspread; between them was a streaming beam of blue light. "Madame Lina, Psychic," it proclaimed. "Fortunes Found." On this cold, damp New York City winter Sunday in 1933, dysphoric, ragged men and women, who once had worn the robes of success but now walked with defeat upon their shoulders, paid their last hoarded coins to gain admission to hear Madame Lina. Those who entered did so surreptitiously, their rational selves ashamed that they would fall for what was sure to be psychic quackery yet having no other way to reclaim their fortunes, which had dissappeared in a flash when the stock market had crashed in October 1929. Truly Madame Lina was the last resort of hope for the desperate. And desperation was a theme so well worn in the minds of those in this time called the Great Depression.

This woman, Madame Lina, was whispered to be able to contact the powers of the underworld and channel them so as to reverse the wheel of misfortune toward fortune. What was true, what was false—who knew? Surely the crash itself showed the evil hand of underworld in the onslaught of bad luck upon the heads of the cursed. *And what about the strange occurrences where money finds its way to those who dance with Satan?* these men and women told themselves to bolster their faith in Madame Lina. And dance they would, if only the money could be back in their hands! Any pact, even with evil incarnate itself, would be worth shaking off the mantle of poverty. And so the thoughts went in their mind.

At the door to the building, a muscular man, thuglike in appearance, with short gray hair and a pugilist's stance, stood acting both as guard and collector of the entrance fee. The building, once a glittering outpost of the arts for the avant garde of the Columbia University set, had clearly gone to seed, mirroring the downward slide of those who now entered it. The stock market crash, that bleak October Monday in 1929, meant there was no money for indulgences, no money in fact for anything. Though 1929 had been just four short years ago, despair born of poverty and want had cast a heavy veil of despondency over the country. It oozed out of the worn faces of the men and women who now sat impassively, staring vacantly out at the black curtain before them.

The auditorium held two hundred seats at most, and less than a half were filled. The red-velvet cushions had been worn thin from repeated use, the wood floor scratched and dusty. The stage beyond showed the scuff marks, remnants of the marks of vaudeville acts, jazz bands, and small plays held there in happier days. Those days were gone, and now dejection issued out of the very boards of the floors, as did silence, broken by a cough now and again, the only signs that the men and women who sat on the worn seats were living beings and not automatons. There was none of the usual chatter, the prelude of anticipation to a show among the gathered. What was there to say anyway? They were all lost in their own thoughts and hopes, their own burning desire to be restored to who they had been, carefree and happy, when laughter had fallen from their lips, when there had been enough money for all their wants. *Money. Money. Money.* All gone now and in its place a gnawing hunger for what once was. So great was this want that they were willing to give away their last coins for the chance to again grasp fortune, even if, as it was whispered, that this dance with Satan meant the loss of the soul. In their once sensible minds, few in the audience had believed that money could be drawn from the ether, that Fortuna could be induced to place a kind hand upon their brow, but such were the circumstances after the crash. Hope, irrational grasping hope, was all there was left that their riches could somehow magically be restored, that dark magic could be used, that a pact could be made with the forces from the beyond to wave a wand over their bank accounts so that money suddenly would appear where there was none. There were those who had sworn that the spells of Madame Lina could do so, and the proof was in their sudden success: the job that appeared miraculously, the found money, the debt that was mysteriously erased. If fortunes could disappear in the blink of an eye, why shouldn't fortunes reappear just as quickly?

The heavy black curtains upon the stage parted. The lugubrious eyes of the men and women turned as one to the stage. Their hearts beat in anticipation. The stage was dimly lit and empty. Then a petite woman, with a pale moon face, a small pug nose, and dark hair that was braided back and worn in the style of the late 1800s, emerged from the shadowy darkness. "Madame Lina...Madame Lina...Madame Lina," the audience whispered in excitement. Madame Lina's entire manner of movement and dress spoke of the nineteenth century, an affectation to suggest her otherworldliness, that she didn't belong of the modern age of the 1930s but was a traveler from the past. She took no notice of the audience members, her movements indicating she was in a trance. She walked forward and stood still. The audience was hushed. Madame Lina's unblinking eyes, light-colored and slit like a cat's, looked above their heads and into the beyond. Her black skirt hit her ankles, to the tops of pointed velvet ankle boots, and about her shoulders was a dark wool shawl. Suddenly Madame Lina flung out her arms, and the shawl fell. The blouse looked to have been salvaged from the 1920s, flapper like and sleeveless. It accentuated the plump whiteness of her arms. Her moon face and arms were all that showed, a studied contrast to the darkness of both her clothing and the dim lighting of the stage. It was all manipulated to give the impression of a disembodied entity consisting only of a floating face and arms. Madame Lina's eyebrows furrowed tightly in concentration, as her lips began to move and whispered a guttural grainy set of vocalizations—the chant to the dead.

Lake of corpses,
sea of spirits,
land of the dead,
those from the beyond, I call to you.
Come to me!
Come! Satan!
Come dance with us, your mortal subjects,
and fill again
our pockets with fortune!

Madame Lina shot out her arms wide, like the wings of an eagle, as if she would at any moment fly up and into the audience. Between the arms, emanating from the fingers of each hand, first weakly then with strength, came streams of light that were purplish blue in hue, like ropes of an electric current. The audience gasped at the mystical quality of the purplish-blue light, and their excitement surged.

"Quackery!" a man suddenly shouted from the back, breaking into their rising hopes. He tore past the guard at the entrance and stomped toward Madame Lina on stage. Men and women in the audience showed their anger, for they didn't want the spell broken. Some tried to hold him back, grabbing at his dirty and torn suit. The man fought them off as he screamed, "Give me my money back, you fraud!" The muscular guard was now upon the pathetic man, grabbing him by the collar and dragging him out.

The man was sobbing as he screamed, "I gave you may last dollar! I have nothing! Nothing!" Some in the audience kicked the man as he was dragged past them. "Get out! Get out!" they cried, for they feared his maniacal shouts would break Madame Lina's spell, and their chance at the again grasping their fortune would lost. Others in the audience stirred as the man was pulled out of the theater, for they had feared in their hearts that Madame Lina was fradulent and that they foolishly had thrown away their last coins.

On the stage Madame Lina hadn't paid any attention to the crazed man; such was the strength of her trance. The purple-blue ephemeral light between her spread arms shone and grew in force and tantalized the audience, stilling their incredulity for a moment. Still there were many tricks by magicians, and this thought entered some of their minds, tricks of stage lighting that could produce this current. This notion could be read on the faces of the men and women in the audience, upturned with hope though restrained by fear and doubt.

Suddenly Madame Lina's left hand jerked down to the floor, and her impassive face broke in surprise. The purple-blue light moved and enveloped only her left hand and slithered up, encircling her arm. Within the light she felt something grab her hand, something cold and clawlike, and she screamed. The audience murmured in surprise. The purplish-blue light had moved and was over the left side over her hand and arm; they saw how Madame Lina was jerking about, as if from the force within the light. Her face contorted in fear. "Help me, Walter!" she shouted, as she fell to the floor. Her body was dragged across the stage as she tried fight off what had grasped her within the light. "Help!" she screamed. "Help me! Walter!" Was this a trick? Was it as the madman had cried out? No one rose to help her.

At the entrance to the theater, the muscular guard, Walter, whose name Madame Lina had shouted and who was in fact her husband, had just come back in after having kicked the madman to the streets and locked the door to the theater. Walter stood with a puzzled look and made no move to help Madame Lina. This jerking around the stage was new to the act, but then she was known to improvise as the muse struck her. Still Walter thought he heard something of genuine panic in his wife's voice and hesitated. Madame Lina had in prior "trances" called to Walter to save her, sometimes even screamed a bloodcurdling shout. It was understood that such theatrics were needed to demonstrate the strength of the dark forces. Walter shouldn't interfere; he recalled his wife's injunction, so he stood still. To the gathered men and women, in all her jerking about, there was increasingly something too much akin to the acts found in circus tents, frauds perpetrated by gypsies. The thrashing about didn't seem like something a psychic with a mystical tie to the beyond would do. It was too crude. A general sense of disapproval and disbelief rose in the crowd. Some in the audience booed and yelled, "Cheap trick!"

Madame Lina writhed about the floor, flailing about, screaming in pain. Was she being electrocuted? What had happened to the mechanism that controlled the light, the button on the floor? She tried with her free hand to remove her arm from the purplish-blue light light but was thwarted by a heat hot as a flame. In a quick flash, the clawlike thing that held her materialized out of the light. The hand was gray, long, and bony, with four black nails and no thumb. The hand wound about Madame's Lina's plump white arm, and the nails scratched her, leaving a trail of four long, bloody lines. Soon a rodent-like face emerged from the light, its yellow eyes alert, its black hair like broom bristles topping the head, its sharp ears darting out of each side of its rat-shaped skull, its long teeth protruding. The creature's sketetal body soon followed. It stood on bony, scaly legs, with feet that were bare and toes that held black toenails, sharp like the talons of a predatory bird, its black bat-shaped wings unfurling behind him. It was Abaddon, his small eyes scanning the stage as he scrambled up and stood unsteadily at first on his bony, scaly legs and stretched his black wings. The audience gasped; was it real? Who was the beastly creature who was now snarling and prowling about the stage? As he grabbed Madame Lina by the throat, she took one look and fainted. "Madame Lina! Madame Lina!" the audience called out. *Tell us the spell to regain our fortune!* But the psychic lay motionless on the floor and could give them no direction.

Walter, Lina's husband and protector, was almost all muscle and what little went for thought was marshalled toward perpetuating scams, and therefore he could only stand open mouthed at the goings on. His thoughts centered around the proceeds—were they going to have to split the take with this new man...or was it a midget because he was so small? The black wings in back looked amateurish. And how come Lina hadn't run this by him first? He would have said no. The take was too little to split. Plus the guy was overdoing it—too corny and unbelievable. Some in the audience held Walter's view and stood up angrily as they pushed their way past those seated. They were leaving and getting their money back. They had seen this kind of thing in circus acts, this baffoonery, this dance of "Satan." Look at how that rat-faced midget pranced about, flapping those rigged-up wings. Ridiculous. Those still in their seats were now tortured by ambivalence. Should they leave too? But was it real? If they left, their chance for restored fortune would be gone.

Abaddon's oily, sickly-gray, shiny face reflected dismay as he held up his two thumbless hands—empty! Where was it? Where was the Spyglass? He was sure he had grasped it in the depths of Kurnigi. His sharp rodent eyes flickered about the stage and into the audience. His eyes then caught the glint of something in Madame Lina's hands. Tendrils of purplish light were escaping from between her fingers. The strands of light zoomed over Abaddon. The light then streaked out over the stage, blinding those in the audience. Then suddenly Mattie and Geeta were sliding down the light. Abaddon, who had grabbed Madame's Lina's hand to ensare the light, snarled. Madame Lina's eyes suddenly fluttered open. She saw the thin, scaly creature with black bristling hair, a gray countenance, pointed ears almost like horns on each side of his face, and a bare skeletal chest. He wore only a loincloth and danced about her, flying low with his black wings. Madame Lina whispered fearfully, "Satan…" and fell away to unconsciousness once again.

Abaddon's keen ears had caught a sound; he turned his head and saw Mattie and Geeta thrown out of the light onto the stage. His greedy mouth opened, revealing the sharp black teeth. He squealed in glee. The red-haired child had the Spyglass! Now it would be his! Mattie and Geeta had fallen with a thump and lay unconscious at the edge of the stage.

Those in the audience blinked their eyes, adjusting to the effects of the receded blinding purple-blue light. They saw the girls, the brown one and the red-haired one, who had fallen upon the stage. "Gypsies," said someone. "Gypsy smoke and mirror tricks." "Seen it a million times." "Cheater!" "Trickster!" These cries were hurled at the unconscious Madame Lina. Even the ones who had held fast onto hope, in the face of what looked like a bad circus act, could no longer hold on to their credulity.

The blinding purplish-blue light was too much of an obvious trick. All were now up, disgusted at themselves for believing, and angry at Madame Lina. They would get their money back! Some vowed to thrash the man who had taken their money, Walter, if he didn't give back their coins at once.

Abaddon flew up near the rafters of the stage. His thin, naked legs treaded the air like water, and his hands were outspread. The four-fingered hands were flung downward, the black nails elongating into eight black rubbery ropes. He then flung up his hands; the ropes fell away and were no longer part of his fingers but were eight lassos in the air. With deftness he grabbed the ropes with his two hands then braided them into one rope, at the end of which were eight sharp points of black fingernails. Abaddon flung the rope toward Mattie to lasso her firmly into submission.

At the edge of the stage, Geeta and Mattie were unsteady, dazed by their slippery journey down the purplish slide of light. "Yipes!" Mattie cried, as Abaddon's rope hit her and the small eight-pointed end stung her arm. "Jump!" she said to Geeta, pointing up.

Geeta looked up to see Abaddon flying above them. "It is that…creature who roped you before!"

The girls jumped off the stage, escaping the grasp of Abaddon's lasso, and tumbled into the audience. There pandemonium had ensued. Now all anyone wanted was their money back. Mattie and Geeta fell to the floor of the auditorium. They were kicked by the rushing feet of those leaving the theater to reclaim their money; the men and women who had so eagerly given their last stash now feared that those who came upon Walter first would take their money too. Elbows edged into the ribs; some people fell, and others kicked them aside in the rush to get their money back. Getting their money back was all that mattered!

Abaddon flew down and alighted off the stage, his head swiveling about his thin neck. The black bristles of his hair vibrated, antennae to seek out his prey. Where was the red-haired girl? He arched his scaly legs forward, jumping onto the heads of the scrambling audience as if they were steppingstones, his clawlike feet leaving bloody marks upon them. The men and women screamed in pain, flailing their hands in the air to ward off the creature that jumped upon their heads. Geeta rose from the auditorium floor, her arms up to fend off the blows of those rushing by. She was jostled back to the ground by a plump man and looked up to see the sharp talons that were Abaddon's bare toes piercing the head of man right above her. "Aaagh!" the man cried out. Geeta grabbed Mattie, who had been struggling to stand upright, and pulled her down. She pointed up at the clawed feet of Abaddon flying above them. "We must keep our heads down!" she told Mattie. Mattie nodded, her face red and sweaty. She still felt the sting of that creepy whip. They hunched their bodies down and zigzagged their way in crablike movements between the adults.

Abaddon's yellow eyes, in that slate-gray rat face, flitted over the crowd. He flung his lasso in a frenzy over the heads of the men and women upon whose heads he was jumping from one to another. The sharp-pointed end of the rope was aimed at those below him as he perched on their heads. Screams—anger mingled with fear—rose from their throats as they rushed to escape the hellish auditorium. A foul smell and a dusky gray-black smoke emitted from Abaddon, the smell of death that he carried from his long ensconcement in the Grim Reaper's robes. It choked those around him. Out! Out was what they wanted!

Geeta and Mattie were carried to the entrance by the crowd. And there Walter, who had locked the door, was besieged.

Hands grabbed at him, some at his arms, some at his throat. "You swindler!" "You cheat!" They shook Walter in a fury, and the coins fell from his pockets. Those in front grabbed them and stole the coins that belonged to the others. They thumped their shoulders against the locked doors, for Walter was in a heap at their feet, the key lost now, having fallen from his pockets when he was shaken mercilessly by the men and women. Their anger rose like a hot wave and consumed the crowd. "Give me back my money, you charlatan!" they shrieked at Walter when his eyes fluttered open. "Get your circus monkey off us!" they cried, referring to Abaddon, who was snarling and vaulting from head to head. Abaddon lashed his black rope, striking those below him with sharp strokes. Soon the combination of the stench and whips led to an opening in the crowd below. Crouched on the head of a particularly tall man who was desperately trying to shake him off, Abaddon caught a crablike movement. There was the red-haired girl crawling like a cockroach right next to the brown owlet! He yelped in triumph. The way was clear.

With precision he threw down the rope and neatly snarled Mattie's torso. Mattie felt the pinch of the rope as it spun around her and squeezed her abdomen. She struggled against it, but Abaddon's rope was strong in its hold. It lifted her until she was swinging horizontally above the scrambling people below. Mattie had felt the pull of weak hands on her feet before she was swung into the air; they had tried to hold her down to no avail. She heard but couldn't see Geeta below her, shouting to those around her to help her grab Mattie. "Geeta!" Mattie screamed. Geeta was jumping up and down, trying desperately to grab Mattie, but it was too late. Mattie was being reeled up like a fish on a line. When her eyes turned upward, they were met by the rat-faced Abaddon, his black teeth bared in his anticipation of grabbing the Spyglass.

𒀭𒈾𒆠𒀭𒁹

George Smith stopped the recitation of his chants. They were still in the mirage. His webbed frog feet were still now, and he turned his eyes toward Paddy and Dottie. "Which of you willed this?" he demanded.

Dottie and Paddy, now with their backs to the wall, having been the audience to Smith's mad dance, looked at him warily.

"Willed what?" Paddy asked, puzzled, rubbing his face, painfully aware of the bites upon him. His once bushy red mustache lay limp below his nose.

"This!" Smith shouted. "This fantasy place!"

"Fantasy place!" Paddy continued, ignoring the pinch to his arm by Dottie to be quiet. "Why, I'd hardly describe Dr. Wigglesworth's office in that way." *Really*, he thought, *how the mighty have fallen*. The great George Smith, indeed, and to think Paddy had been reviled for having the temerity to criticize Smith and his 1872 and 1875 interpretations of the Gilgamesh myth and its relation to the biblical Noah and the story of the flood.

"Paddy, be quiet," he heard Dottie whisper.

Smith's eyes darted about. "Dr. Wigglesworth? Who is he?" For Smith didn't need to be told they were in an office; that much was obvious. Both Paddy and Dottie remained silent. Smith looked about guardedly. An office was an odd place to be sure; it must have to do with the pact the pudgy man and the blonde woman had made. It was imperative that he know the details of the pact so as to be able to defend himself. Smith picked up papers here and there, glancing at them, flinging them down as he spoke. "What did you sell to the devil for your soul?" he asked.

Dottie was immediately offended. She said sharply, "We *did not* sell our souls. The Lord is upon each breath we take."

Smith's eyebrows shot up in surprise. Were they that stupid, these newcomers to Kurnigi? Did they not even know they had been condemned to hell as a payment for their pacts—whatever it was in their mortal form they had sold their soul for? Smith had aided them as newcomers, as he could see they had small bits of magic still about them; it was useful to school the uninitiated into the world of Kurnigi and as a payment take what little they had in the way of capital—the spells and amulets they brought to the underworld. Here Smith's mind stopped, and he took in a sharp breath. *Unless.* And that "unless" would explain why he was in this unlikely place. The wishes of the condemned were often fantastical landscapes and not a mundane, dreary office. Smith took a quick jump close to Paddy and Dottie, who had nowhere to go, as they were already backed up to the wall. Smith sniffed at them; Paddy and Dottie were revulsed. What a degradation of a once great man! Dottie wondered at the man's (if he was still that) demise. And Paddy thought ruefully, *George Smith, brilliant Assyriologist, translator of the story in cuneiform of the tale of the flood, who made the audacious statement that the Old Testament tale of the deluge was a Hebrew adapation of the ancient Babylonian story! This man, who deciphered the secrets of "The Epic of Gilgamesh," who found the missing piece of the tale of the flood, a fragment among broken pieces buried in the earth in Nineveh.* That man, that scholar and legend, was now sniffing about them like a wild animal!

Smith shook his shaggy head in disbelief. He was astounded. "You are living!" Before Smith could take this in—that living beings had entered Kurnigi, and not just Kurnigi but the deepest part of that hell, the Corkscrew of Terror—the room shook. Into it fell someone. Someone that made Dottie gasp. Made Paddy wonder. And someone whom George Smith immediately flung his body toward in a murderous rage.

When the call of the living had sounded in his ears in Kurnigi, Abaddon knew full well it had been heard through the dark land, and he was certain it had been heard by the ten thousand vengeful spirits who sought to destroy him. He knew he had to act fast. He had to grab that Spyglass before all his enemies came after him—the revengeful wandering spirits; those who ruled Kurnigi, such as the Prince of Wallachia, who held power over the unliving that walked the earth; and most terrifyingly the beast Ashurnasirpal. Abaddon was perched on a rafter, squatting to balance himself, as his bare feet with their black talon-like toenails burrowed into the wood of the beam, his black wings still. The long rope was curled around the red-haired one, and she was swinging over the crowd. His yellow eyes focused intently upon Mattie as he reeled her up. He didn't want to lose his prey again.

Mattie felt Abaddon's hot and fetid breath and stench from above. The weird lasso brought her closer and closer toward the creepy, nasty monkey man. She saw his vile yellow eyes staring down at her; his oily, gray-sheened, rodent-featured face topped by the black spikes of hair; and those long bony hands that grasped the rope that bound her. Mattie felt the rope tighten over her arms and around her stomach. She was swaying horizontally above the stage but below the rafters and was like a puppet controlled by Abaddon. She felt rather than saw the mad rush of people below her. She heard Geeta's voice somewhere in the midst, telling her something—something she couldn't understand. Mattie struggled fruitlessly against the tight hold. She felt the cold and heavy metal body of the Spyglass deep within her pocket in her plaid pants, hitting her thigh. Mattie thought of how being Mistress of the Spyglass was a big fat lie. She wasn't Mistress at all. She thought of how the Spyglass was always letting her down; how many times the Spyglass had tricked her, had left her to get hurt, wouldn't help Eddie or Geeta, never came when called! She recalled how the Spyglass had done nothing to help her find her mom. In fact the Spyglass had made everything worse with her selfish ways. Mattie felt a great surge of anger at the Spyglass. "You rat-fink, two-faced Spyglass!" she screamed.

Mattie pushed against the pull of Abbadon, who was reeling her up toward him. She thought of her mom being held by that evil snake Gneezy, and her strength swelled against Abaddon's hold. She had to find her mom and rescue her. The Spyglass was no good; all her magic did was foul things up. But there was that nice blue king, Mr. Biddle, and Dr. Wigglesworth. Plus Eddie now had a weapon, and Geeta was a gypsy princess. They didn't need that stupid Spyglass at all. First chance she had, she was going to throw the Spyglass again, or let that monkey guy take it, let him become Master of the Spyglass; he'd learn quick enough what a heap of trouble it was. Mr. Biddle had been right all along; the Spyglass was evil. So her thoughts went. And they went not unheard but heard.

The Spyglass was awakening to these treacherous thoughts of her Mistress. Yes, she had chosen badly this time—very, very badly. And she had weakened herself by giving up one gold band for

Mattie. The Spyglass had stolen from Marduk his rightful prey, for those who ate the poisonous fruit of the Tree of Knowledge went to evil. But she, Spyglass, had interfered, had shed one of her three precious gold bands of protection so that Mattie would live. What the impulse had been that had driven such stupidity, the Spyglass couldn't now understand. She, Spyglass, had given up her one band that braided her with Mattie, that braided their fates forever, or so Spyglass had thought before Mattie flung her into danger, not once but twice. Twice! Oh, what folly! And now she was weakened to two bands of gold. And to what end was her sacrifice? Only to be flung right into the jaws of destruction! Her memory of who she was remained murky. She had felt hopeful when Mother Tiamat had called out, "Daughter" to Mattie. If Mattie was the daughter of Tiamat, then she held the other Twin Tablet of Destiny, so Spyglass had believed. But now Spyglass knew. Mattie was no more the daughter of Tiamat than any other soul she had occupied over time. No. The wretched red-haired girl was just a stupid mortal like all the others. Mattie had been a disaster.

But Spyglass had to have a human soul in her full control, that much she knew, before she could regain her memory. A pure soul was what she needed, and pure souls who could be manipulated to do as she commanded were hard to come by. In fact Mattie was the closest to a pure soul, with naïveté that allowed for taking control, that Spyglass ever had occupied. But she, Spyglass, was no closer to controlling and assuming full possession of Mattie's soul than when she had revealed herself to Mattie in that dark attic in Hackensack, New Jersey. It had all seemed so simple then, before the stupid girl had catapulted them onto the Path of the Virtuous and scrambled time to chaos.

Oh, what to do? What to do? Spyglass was frozen in indecision, deep within Mattie's pocket, for to reveal herself now would mean the sharp claws of Abaddon might grasp her. Who knew how much power she had to thwart him? All this wretched chaos that Mattie had begun—eating from the Tree of Knowledge, having turned upside down and uncertain the story of creation, having thrown the River of Time into chaos, having brought them onto the Path of the Virtuous. *Oh, that silly girl!* Spyglass reproached herself for the millionth time for having chosen Mattie as the vessel for her salvation.

Abaddon dug his sharp talon toenails farther into the wooden rafters. He grunted and pulled with all his strength, his hands pulling the rope up, against the struggling Mattie, whom it held around her middle and who swayed hither and thither below. He felt the girl's strength of opposition to his force. In the pandemonium below, Geeta fended off the blows of elbows and bodies in their frenzied rush to leave. Hands greedily grabbed the coins flung to the floor in their shaking of Walter and at the same time pushed toward the front to escape the cursed auditorium. Geeta kept her head up and shouted to Mattie, "Call the Spyglass!" Though the Spyglass was duplicitous, surely, Geeta thought, it wouldn't allow Mattie to get into the clutches of that creature of evil above! But that was exactly what looked to be happening. Geeta tugged at the people rushing past her. "Please, help my friend!" she cried to no avail. "It's locked!" Geeta heard people at the front, by the entrance door, call out in a panic. The stench, that of the smell of rotting bodies, emanating from that circus creature above, now perched on the rafters, was filling the place. People were gasping to breathe. "Slam against the door!" Some of the stronger men pushed their shoulders against the auditorium door, but built in the days of old, made to be sturdy, this door was thick and couldn't readily be broken. Others pulled the dazed Walter, shaking him like a ragdoll and demanding the key. But the key was lost, trampled somewhere upon the floor.

What to do? What to do? Spyglass, above, lay mired by indecision. Mattie dead could destroy all her hopes for freedom and power; she needed the protection of her human soul. But. But. And the thought crystallized. Mattie surviving would surely destroy her, for the girl had all but promised to fling her into oblivion the first chance she had. Spyglass made her decision. She wanted out—out of the Path of the Virtuous. Impossible it may be but doubly so if she stayed with Mattie. She needed a new soul and couldn't have one with the current Mistress still alive. Spyglass knew they were no longer in Kurnigi but once again in the land of the living, called by the chants to the dead. Yes, Spyglass resolved, Mattie must die. That was only way. Then Spyglass would find another soul, here in the land of the living. She would choose one whose will was weak and pliable, as a first step. Yes, a pure soul was needed for finding her memory, for finding the Daughter of Tiamat and for becoming whole, but now wasn't the time. What Spyglass needed now was any soul who was willing to be taken over. She didn't have time to lure a mortal with shining promises of power and gold. It had to be done now. Who here was open to possession? Spyglass opened her eyes and saw below her the prone body of Madame Lina and saw too that the stupid woman had left the door wide open for her soul to be taken. The Spyglass had heard the call to the dead coming from her lip—*Lake of corpses, sea of spirits.* Madame Lina would do for now. She could be manipulated, the Spyglass thought.

Down below on the stage, Geeta pulled the black Card of Time that Mr. Biddle had given her and flung it up toward Mattie. But as before, it boomeranged right back into her hands, slick and blank. There was no magic in the card. Geeta looked up helplessly at Mattie above the stage and nearing the rafters, where that evil creature was perched and pulling her up. Mattie was struggling against the rope that the creature was tugging. Her face was so red, and she looked so fatigued, Geeta at once observed. Then she saw the Spyglass fly into Mattie's fingers, which were just outside the grasp of the binding ropes. Geeta felt a surge of hope.

𒁀𒌋𒁉𒂍𒁀𒌋𒀸

"Scoundrel!" George Smith lunged at the man in an attempt to choke him and, failing, flailed at him with closed fists. The man was a swashbuckling handsome fellow, dark hair swept to one side, clean shaven, muscular, and dressed in expedition garb of the mid-1800s. He jumped back, escaping the wild, flailing blows of Smith, from his arms and the strange frog legs.

"You've gone stark raving mad, Smith!" the man said, in the crisp English of a British aristocrat, as he deftly ducked the blows.

Paddy and Dottie pushed themselves farther against the wall, as the two men faced each other, one determined to fight, the other warding off the blows; one powered by the strength of youth and vigor, the other driven by insanity. Paddy's mind was spinning. Could it really be? And in his youth? "Dottie," Paddy whispered, his eyes wide behind his glasses, "don't you see who it is?" He looked at Dottie, who didn't appear to recognize the man but was fully alerted to danger. Her hands firmly pressed Paddy's arms, holding him back lest he was tempted to enter the fray. Smith appeared to be a lunatic. The other man, Dottie thought, did seem familiar.

George Smith jumped, using his webbed frog feet as a weapon, thrusting one toward the man's handsome square jaw. But the man was quick and laughed heartily at this move as he grabbed Smith's ankle and pitched him to the floor. Smith struggled, his body, one leg, and two arms thrashing about, raising up a flurry of manuscripts and yellowed papers of long ago.

"I shall let you go, Smith, if you will stop this nonsense," said the man, still holding Smith's ankle securely.

Smith struggled a bit more then gave up. He snarled, "Look at what has become of me! And all of it, all of it I lay on your head, Layard!"

Paddy heard the name. So he was right. "Sir Austen Henry Layard himself!" Paddy whispered to Dottie. In the flesh but young. Looking like the sketches from Layard's manuscripts about Nineveh and his expeditions. Sir Austen Henry Layard in the flesh! My! My! Paddy was in awe. Despite all his talk of the "hegemony" of Layard, in actuality he much admired the man.

Layard let Smith's ankle go and grabbed an arm, all in quick moves that jerked the gaunt Smith up easily, and held firm. He demanded, "What do you mean, you lay it upon my head?"

Flattened to the wall, Paddy and Dottie watched the encounter. "Sir Austen Henry Layard!" Paddy whispered again, awestruck. Dottie's eyes were wide, for she too had studied the great man's works, such as "Nineveh and Its Remains" and "Discoveries at Nineveh." What budding Assyriologist hadn't? Still she hadn't spent much time researching Layard's form in his youth. He was much more striking in the flesh, with dazzling movie-star charisma that sketches of the man didn't convey. Unconsciously Dottie patted her hair to fix it; such was the effect of the handsome shape of Sir Henry Layard upon women. Still she held firmly to Paddy's arm as she felt him about to move toward Smith and Layard. "No, Paddy," she whispered. "It may be the devil's trick."

Smith fought Sir Henry's hold to no avail, his dark wild hair rendered even more disheveled by his scrambling about on the floor of Wigglesworth's office. With mad eyes Smith turned to Sir Henry and shouted, "I beseeched you to help me when I lay trapped in the godforsaken land of darkness! You heard my pleas night after night in your dreams, yet you ignored them!" His haggard face and form, the scraggly beard embedded with dirt, and the torn clothing were a study in contrast to Sir Henry's tanned and muscular form, his crisp bearing and pristine khaki expedition clothing. Before Sir Henry could protest the characterization as false, Smith's eyes rolled back into his head, and he said in guttural tones, *The ša nagba īmuru, the story of the unknown mysteries and known now as the story of Dup Shimati. It is not as it was thought. The dark underworld lives. And I fear I will soon be plunged and imprisoned beneath the black earth, for the forces of the Dark Master surround me. I feel the evil breath of the curse of King Ashurnasirpal II upon me, his hooves treading on my neck as I awaken in sweat each night...and the shadow of the snake behind him.* Then Smith turned his eyes, hot with wrath upon Layard. "Now you will see for yourself what the power of the underworld holds as it treads upon *your* neck."

Unnerved by the words, Sir Henry let loose his grip on Smith. "It was not I, but you, Smith, who made a pact with the devil himself. You made a pact to enable you to decipher the Chaldean tale of the flood, so that fame and fortune would land upon your mortal head. You made the dirty bargain. Now you have to keep it."

Paddy's wide eyes turned to Dottie. That very theory had been bandied about by Smith's detractors, and here was Sir Henry

Layard giving voice to the charge. Paddy's words were halted by the explosive words that erupted from Smith.

"Lies!" Smith spat out, and brushed off some papers clinging to him. He shook his shaggy head furiously and shouted, "I made no such bargain!"

Sir Henry snorted and said in mock belief. "Of course not. Naturally any uneducated English clerk who leaves school at age fifteen could easily learn cuneiform and would know that the sun had been darkened to eclipse in Nineveh in 703 BC and decipher the story of Jehu's payment to Shalmaneser, thanks to knowing when that eclipse had occurred."

Paddy thought the very same thing. He was going to add his agreement but was pinched into silence by Dottie. He yelped a bit, but neither men took notice of him.

"Layard...forgive me, *Sir* Henry," Smith spat with disdain, as he moved warily away from him, his webbed feet feeling still for emanations of evil, "my gift was heaven born, while you were gifted only with *dubious* charms of flirtation." Smith stopped suddenly. He moved his palms toward the ceiling, and his eyebrows shot up in fear.

Smith flailed his arms and stamped his webbed feet upon the paper-strewn floor. He threw his head back and emitted a sound, a yowl. Sir Henry watched Smith's movements, pained now by the man's lunacy. "Smith," he began, "you've suffered greatly, I see."

Paddy shrugged off Dottie's grasp. They were in the presence of the great Sir Henry Layard, discoverer of Nineveh himself! Really, such an opportunity to hash out his theory of the Eighth Tablet could not—must not—be passed up. "Sir Henry," Paddy said, moving toward the man with his hand out, "my name is Dr. Paddy O'Reilly and—"

Layard's ears caught the name. He turned toward Paddy. "You," he said, pointing his finger at him angrily. "You, sir, have caused a great deal of trouble."

Abaddon's eyes caught sight of the Spyglass glittering in the red-haired child's fingers, and he salivated in anticipation. He knew enough not to try to cheat the Dark Master by keeping the Spyglass. He had learned what treachery toward Marduk brought from the long years he had been imprisoned within the robes of the Grim Reaper. Soon it would be in his hands and the Dark Master, who sought the Spyglass, would at last make him master of the tunnels. Yes. Then the beast Ashurnasirpal would fall under his foot. Abaddon grunted as he reeled up the rope that bound the red-haired girl. Mattie felt the Spyglass clasped in her hand and tried to throw it down. "Get away from me!" she sputtered. But the Spyglass had glued herself firmly to Mattie's hand.

In her resolve to dispose of Mattie, a coldness emanated from the form of the Spyglass. The cold chill went through Mattie, and she felt the Spyglass jerking her up. Mattie struggled against the draw. The Spyglass then pulled harder, countering Mattie's resistance, yanking her toward Abaddon above. Once they were there, she knew Abaddon's sharp claws would grab Mattie, and the Spyglass's plan was to fall away. Then Abaddon would drop Mattie, who would plummet to the floor. Given that the distance, the Spyglass estimated, was at least fifty feet from the rafters to the stage, it was certain that the fall would kill her. Yes. Mattie would soon lay dead. Then the Spyglass would be released. She held fast to this grim and gruesome plan as she propelled Mattie toward the rafters.

The mayhem below had reached epic proportions. The stench given off by the fumes emanating from Abaddon, the close confines of the bodies of those pushing against one another, the futility of trying to escape from the unbudging side door all lead to frustration. Some pushed on the locked door at the back of the auditorium to no avail. Others screamed at Walter to open the door—Walter, who lay on the floor unconscious. Geeta felt the heat of anger and panic surround her. Her blood froze at the actions of the Spyglass. The Spyglass was taking Mattie right up into the grasp of the evil monkey creature! Geeta ran toward the stage, jumping onto it and trying to find a way to thwart the Spyglass. She cried out, "Mattie, throw away the Spyglass!"

Mattie was trying to do just that. She tried to unclasp the Spyglass, but her frozen fingers wouldn't move. Her face grew redder, and her frizzy red hair became even frizzier by her exertions. Mattie was now almost in the grasp of Abaddon, who had wound her toward him and just below the rafters. The hot breath, the foulness of it, hit her squarely in the face. The stench was almost so great that Mattie thought she would faint. She felt the Spyglass jerking her right into the monkey man's clasp. "Rat fink! Rat fink!" Mattie cried out, as she tried to shake off the Spyglass. Abaddon's sharp teeth were now near the hand that held the Spyglass.

Geeta jumped up and down on the stage, trying to grasp at Mattie. She pulled the black curtains, thinking there must be some way to hit the creature above. But the curtains didn't budge. *Oh, it cannot be! It cannot be!* She saw that her friend was within inches of the clasp of the evil creature, who held her trussed and bound like a animal. Geeta gasped; his mouth was near the hand that held the Spyglass, ready to chomp off her fingers to get the prize. The black Card of Time didn't work, and she had no gypsies to help her. No Mr. Biddle. No Eddie. No kind king of Uruk. Geeta had nothing. And this realization felt like a swift kick to her stomach.

Abaddon's sharp black teeth were now upon Mattie's fingers. She was just below him, the rope holding her horizontally, his mouth at her wrists, inches from the Spyglass. The Spyglass saw her moment; she was going to disappear just as the teeth came near her. She'd fall toward the stage so that Abaddon would fling Mattie down and jump to grab her, the Spyglass. *Soon...soon Mattie will be no more,* thought the traitorous Spyglass. And she would escape into the body of the stupid, pliable Madame Lina. And kill her too, she would, once they escaped from Abaddon, for an impure soul was like a flimsy paper bag that ripped apart easily.

𒀭𒌋𒀭𒌑

Paddy sputtered at Sir Henry's angry words. "Me? Cause trouble?" Then he thought with a blush about the manuscript and what he had written, "...Moving Beyond the Hegemony of Layard and Smith" and how he had characterized Sir Henry as an "eogtistical adventurer." Was it possible that the great Sir Henry Layard had read his work? But how, given that Sir Henry had died in the late 1800s and Paddy had submitted the manuscript to *JASA* in 1938? Still, time was so unpredictable—witness that he was standing next to his bride of the future—so perhaps it was time to clarify his thesis. "Sir Henry, scholarly ventures must be pure of ego, so of course you must concede that the Eigthth Tablet of Creation brooks no scholarly timidity."

Sir Henry's eyebrows shot up in surprise. "What's that you say?"

Dottie interrupted; this wasn't the time to bring up the Eighth Tablet of Creation, which she knew to be a matter that long had obsessed him. "Paddy, no…"

But Paddy, undeterred, shrugged off Dottie's hold and went blithely on. "When I called you an egotistical adventurer, naturally I meant no disrespect. In 'Moving Beyond the Hegemony of Layard and Smith,' I—"

Sir Henry's eyebrows were knitted in incredulity. "What the devil are you talking about?"

George Smith cried out sharply, "Shut up, you fools!" His head was cocked in one direction, listening for some unheard sound. "Don't you hear it?" Smith jumped onto the desk.

From beneath the building, the sound of darkness was swelling. It was the clanging of the chains unleashed of the eons of dead souls, the vengeful wandering spirits. The sound pierced the air with wails.

Abaddon, Abaddon!
We seek that liar and wretch!
Weep shall he
as we have wept!

The melancholic chant rose like a damp and cold fog as the dead souls emerged, snaking through ground below the basement of the old building and up through the floor of Dr. Wigglesworth's office, seeking Abaddon. The rodent-like creature had fled Kurnigi to the land of the living, for Madame Lina had called to the Sea of Dead Spirits; she had unlocked the gate between the land of the living and the dead with her chant and allowed Abaddon to escape. So came they did, thrown up from Kurnigi into the time to where Abaddon had run. They followed the scent of Abaddon to the land of the living and into which Dottie, Paddy, Smith, and Sir Henry also had fallen into the year 1933, as the Corkscrew of Terror had unraveled open.

Dottie shrieked as the papers below, a calendar depicting the days of October 1933, flung up from an unseen wind and turned into ghostly hands that grabbbed her ankles. Pulled downward to the floor by these very same hands, Paddy was stopped midsentence in his disseration to Sir Henry. He now lay thrashing about, overrun by the dead souls, who grabbed him as leverage up and out of the floor, overrunning him first with their hands then their feet. Paddy's mouth was open in astonishment, much like a great, big, bloated fish thrashing about on the floor of a fisherman's boat. "Aaarr…aarrr!" Paddy garbled out a shout.

George Smith stamped about the desk with his frog feet and flailed his hands to fend off the rising dead and their grasping hands. Some had eyes bloodshoot and teemed with anger; others were decapitated bodies, some missing limbs. They were young and old, and all rose with a vengence, snarling fircecly, prowling about, looking for the hated one.

Abaddon, Abaddon!
Cheater! Torturer!

It was Abaddon who had tricked them here, ten thousand souls of the land of the cruel Ashurnasirpal, the beast who could rule over them no more. They had been cheated by Abaddon in their mortal lives, their souls stolen for the Grim Reaper. And they had waited for eons to exact their revenge against the sniveling, cowardly Abaddon, who had hidden within the robes of the reaper. But no more! No more! For Death's scythe was held by the living; the reaper had been crushed into dust, and the forest of Humawa lay in ashes. The souls now filled the room, those with eyes searching, searching, grabbing the living souls, touching their heartbeats to feel once more the warm rhythm of life.

Sir Henry Layard quickly grabbed a chair and, after breaking it upon Wigglesworth's desk, wielded the wooden leg as a weapon. No stranger was he to an onslaught, though in the past the assailants had been living beings. But no matter. He was adept at fighting. The weapon went through the ghostly bodies of the dead souls, but the phantoms moved away from Sir Henry. Dottie felt the ghastly coldness of the dead hands, their fingers reaching into her body, grabbing her heart with icy fingers. She shuddered at this close touch of the dead and fought the woozy feeling that was overcoming her. She was going to faint. Her legs gave way. Sir Henry quickly made his way to Dottie as she was falling. He grabbed her by the waist and pulled her up and out of the grasp of the denizens of the dead. Their fingers retreated from her heart, though she lay limp, her eyes fluttering as she moved in and out of consciousness. Sir Henry threw Dottie's slim frame over his shoulder and, with his free hand, manfully fought off the onslaught of spirits. "Back! Back!" he shouted, as he swung the wooden chair leg like a sword at the dead souls rising from the floor. The spirits moved away and flew about the room, hitting the ceiling in confusion, like birds trapped in a closed space.

They hovered around Smith, who hands spun about him faster and faster so as to create a space of wind about him. Then he shook his shaggy head as he shouted, but his voice was lost in the shrieks of the dead souls. "You, Layard, will now know how the dark world rules! Let us see who it is who dances with Satan!"

On the office floor, Paddy continued to thrash about as the revengeful spirits flowed over and above him like waves. He had felt their coldness enter him and had almost given way when his eyes caught the glimpse of Dottie thrown over Sir Henry's shoulder. Paddy felt the hot stab of jealousy, and this awakened him at once. Scoundrel! The wife-stealing cad! Paddy shot up; though upon wobbling legs, he was nonetheless fully awakened by anger. His heart beat wildly, his hands slapping at the fiendish spirits swirling around him—they who were released from Kurnigi and bent upon vengenace and were flowing up from the ground below and rising up and over him. But the ghastly vision of the rising dead paled in comparison to the image—a red cloth to an angry bull—of his beloved Dottie grasped so intimately by that...that...womanizing adventurer!

"Hands off her!" Paddy shouted at Sir Henry. More dashing than ever, Sir Henry held Dottie over one shoulder and battled the spirits with his free hand, deftly wielding the wooden chair leg.

Dottie was his wife, Paddy thought, battered about by the storm of the rising spirits. He moved toward her, fighting them off, shouting, "Hands off her, you scalawag!" Why, as her husband, Paddy should be the only one to hold her and defend her, not this...flirtatious wife-nabbing scoundrel!

The spirits hit the ceiling and flew up and down, wailing their fury, spinning around and around. Perched on the table, Smith wildly flailed his arms, lashing out at the spirits as if they were gnats. Sir Henry wielded the wooden chair leg as if it were Excalibur itself, a warrior knight of old beating off the ghosts to save the damsel in distress.

Paddy huffed and puffed his his way toward Sir Henry, the exertion reddening his pudgy face. "You...you...cad! Give me my wife!" he sputtered, the bites on his moon face shining brightly, the red mustache bristling with indignation.

Layard cried out, "Grab a stick, man, and fight!" Henry Layard felt the adrenaline rush through his veins. His eyes were bright with excitement. He struck here, struck there, and successfully fended off the spirits, the stick going through them but creating enough of a wind to repel them.

Paddy lunged at Layard and slipped, falling like a big blob to the floor. "Aarrgh!" he growled, trying to regain his balance but to no avail, for the storm of spirits was a growing tornado, the wind of its evil spinning around Sir Henry, Smith, Dottie, and Paddy. It formed a force that lifted them into the air. Sir Henry held Dottie firmly over his shoulder as he felt his feet lift. Smith screamed the yell of lunacy as he was drawn up. And Paddy cried out, "Dottie!" as his chubby legs were sucked into the whirling mass. The spinning spirits then tore through the ceiling of the office and flew up into the starless black sky of New York City.

𒀭𒈾𒁹𒀭𒊩

"Oh!" Geeta gasped, as she squinted her owl eyes up into the rafters from the stage floor. She jumped and jumped to no avail—the small, flying, evil creature had Mattie in its clasp. Beneath the stage was the rabid mass of people trying to push their way out, their shouts and screams filling the air. Geeta again yelled for someone to help her, but it was useless. Oh, how could she loosen the hold of that creature? Geeta ran to a chair on the stage and tried to hurl it up and aim it at Abaddon, but it was heavy and didn't budge. Abaddon had Mattie in his grasp, and his sharp black teeth were over the fingers that clasped the Spyglass.

Rat-fink Spyglass! Mattie thought, and anger filled her and blew away every speck of fear she might have felt had she considered her situation. But Mattie's ire was raised; Spyglass had pulled her right into danger, into the very jaws of that hideous thing with bat wings! Mattie felt the strength of the Spyglass, bent on destroying her, she was sure. "I hate you, Spyglass!" Mattie shrieked, and tried to unclasp her fingers to drop it. Abaddon saw the movement and bit her hand. Mattie felt the sharp black teeth pierce her skin and recoiled. In that moment the Spyglass fell loose from her fingers. Then, as Abaddon tried to grab it, the Spyglass spun downward toward Madame Lina. Spyglass felt the gloat of triumph. All was going as she had planned, for Abaddon immediately had dropped rope that held Mattie aloft, and she was plummeting to the stage. Mattie screamed, her face red, her frizzy hair like a halo of orange around her head. She struggled against the ropes that bound her. She had no ability to position herself, as her body was wrapped tightly. Thoughts zoomed through her head as she fell, and she remembered what Eddie had said before when they were falling—*Assume airborne position to break fall!* Mattie tried to bring her knees up but couldn't.

Abaddon quickly jumped off the rafter and flew toward the Spyglass. In response the Spyglass zigzagged down. Mattie had to die before the Spyglass could take possession of a new soul. Geeta felt the beats of horror fill her heart at the sight of Mattie all bound and tied and falling down, down. "Oh, my God!" Geeta gasped, her owl eyes in shock. Mattie was going to hit the hard floor of the stage and surely perish upon impact! Geeta noticed that the Spyglass was zigzagging down beneath Mattie but made no effort to save her Mistress. Indeed, Geeta thought, it seemed the Spyglass was actually moving *away* from Mattie. Oh, what deceit this was! The Spyglass looked like she was trying to have Mattie killed!

Geeta ran and frantically pulled at the prone woman on the stage, the psychic Madame Lina. The woman had magical powers; she had pulled them out to this place from the dark place of the underworld. "Please wake up!" She shook Madame Lina, whose eyes were fluttering as she muttered, "Sea of spirits." Then her eyes opened but soon rolled back into her head. Geeta shook Madame Lina again, but she fell back into a faint. Oh, where was Mr. Biddle? Where was Eddie? Tears rolled down Geeta's face. *Stop. You must not*, she commanded herself. But the tears still flowed, as anguish stabbed her heart in quick thrusts. This Third Stone of Anger was going to destroy Mattie. Then the floor beneath her feet began to move.

Those in the auditorium screamed. The ground below shook like thunder. A cold wind was mounting, churning, and throwing the men and women below upward and around, as if they were specks of dust. The draft from below tossed Mattie in her descent sideways and held her in a jet stream. It threw hither and thither the Spyglass. Abaddon flew toward the Spyglass, his greedy hand stretched out, the four fingers with their long black nails scratching the air. Below Abaddon, still on the stage floor, the unconcious psychic fluttered. Madame Lina's strength had been drained by pulling the three from the land of the dead, her first-ever successful experience at what she always had pretended to be able to do—contact those from the beyond. Now the presence of spirits about the land within the cold wind were real, unleashed by her call to dead. Madame Lina moaned as she felt the impure breath of evil ones. "Sea of Spirits," she gasped. "They come."

Fiendish images took shape in the wind; they took the form of faces, ghoulish faces, some streaked with blood, some yellow with fever, others red hot like the flames that had burned them in life. They came holding the forms of their battered bodies as they were when they had left their mortal form. They rose, pushing over and past Madame Lina, who was besieged. The spirits flew past Geeta, tossing her to the stage floor. With alarm that creature of evil, Abaddon, heard their cries. The dead souls wailed their delight upon seeing Abaddon batted above in the wind of doom and spoke their merciless prophecy.

Abaddon, Abaddon!
Liar and wretch!
Soon you
shall weep
as we have wept.
Ten thousand tears!
Abaddon, Abaddon!
Lakes of fire,
cauldrons of boiling pitch,
minotaurs that devour the damned—
this will be your fate,
O Abaddon,
black crow of deceit!

Abaddon was pummeled about by the icy wind, his black wings wildly beating. Still he kept his yellow rodent eyes firmly locked on the prize below. He scrambled in crablike movements against the force of the spirit wind to move downward and snatch the Spyglass. He knew that once he had the Spyglass in his grasp, Marduk would give him all. Then he would take his talon black toes and pierce them into the necks of the vengeful spirits once more! He would harness them into submission. He would prevail once more. The ghouls raised their dead hands and stretched their fingers toward him, each fighting the other to be the one to grab the rat-faced traitor and torture him themselves, for they had waited eons for this moment. They had nursed the manner of retalitation against he who had condemned them to horror of the land of Kurnigi. *Cheater! Traitor! Deceiver!* They howled. Abaddon was quick and sly and retained the tricks of old learned from the reaper. He was now a foul gray vapor, dodging the grasp of the ghouls, the outlines of his body and face in wisps of smoke. Those vicious black nails raked the air about him and left streaks of blood in their wake. He moved down toward the Spyglass, his hands and nails retaining their solid form so as to grasp the Spyglass firmly.

The jetty of wind that held Mattie moved in a serpentine manner, flinging her about. Amid the chaos of the howling spirits, Geeta beseeched, *Oh, ThaTha! Help me! Help me!* So strong was the storm that she could barely see Mattie buffeted above her. Geeta heard her old ThaTha's voice. *In the battlefield for the soul, whether there is to be eternal order or chaos in the cosmos, one who fights her dharma loses, not just for herself but for all.* Dharma. Geeta heard the words. Dharma. Duty. She didn't, however, understand the message.

CHAPTER 15

twin rivers of darkness

Uri Gneezy rode hard and fast upon a great black stallion, brandishing the bloody saber that only moments earlier he had plunged into the heart of the workers' patron, Father Gapon. Gneezy's snake face was masked by the form he had assumed when he plunged the sharp point of the sword into the priest's heart, that of Tsar Nicolas II, His Majesty. So it was that the snake wore the blue tunic, the golden braided ropes, and the epaulets of the emperor of Russia. As the evil serpentine creature rode away from the square toward the Winter Palace, a great river of blood flowed through the streets of St. Petersburg, mounting in proportion to the rage in the hearts of the peasants against Tsar Nicolas for his murder of Father Gapon. The night sky was black and littered with but a few small stars and a dimming moon. It bore a stark contrast to the white snow that lay thick upon the streets and that gave off an eerie red glow of Bloody Sunday. The grimly stained snow reflected the gore and blood more than it had been written for that January Sunday of 1905, before the River of Time had plunged into chaos.

Uri Gneezy's forked tongue shot out into the air to feel the vibrations of the pain and to ascertain that all went as he wished. Gneezy had felt with satisfaction the anguished cries of the workers behind him as he had ridden off. "Tsar Nicolas has murdered Father Gapon!" These workers, the old and young who had come to the square, many in tattered black coats, beaten by the icy wind of winter on the injunction of their beloved Father Gapon, were gathered around the fallen priest. At first there were only the gasps of astonishment, but soon their hearts filled with anger. "Tsar Nicolas has murdered Father Gapon!" Their shouts rang through the streets of St. Petersburg. The crowd was now frenzied by their desire to exact revenge upon the tsar and the Cossacks. They had come in peace, holding crosses and the images of Christ, singing songs of loyalty to the tsar and asking only for their just due for their labors, only to have Father Gapon killed in cold blood, skewered with the imperial saber by His Majesty, whom they had just moments ago praised. Never would this day this Bloody Sunday in January in 1905 be forgotten! Never! Never! Father Gapon lay bloodied and dead upon the ground, his black priest robes wet with his fresh blood, his sharp bearded face stiff in death, frozen in an expression of surprised horror.

From Gneezy's long forked tongue slicing the air, the Black Book of Magic sprang out. Its reptilian-textured pages flapped against the night air like a vulture's wings. "Show me the Iron Knight!" Gneezy commanded, for he had to know that the Iron Knight had fulfilled his promise as a warrior. Images of the martyred Father Gapon flew up. Men lifted him up gently and carried their martyr's limp and bloody body high, tears streaking their faces. They cried, "We came to bring peace, but now we will bring the sword!" The snake's eyes brought what was happening into near and sharp focus. He saw the pudgy, red-faced Goering, Iron Knight as he called himself, having thrown off the Cossack leader and taken hold of the stallion, and shouting orders for the soldier to shoot and kill the protesting workers. Yes. The Iron Knight had assumed full control—the Iron Knight upon a black steed, brandishing a sword and leading the Cossacks in a ruthless slaughter of the workers. Tsar Nicolas's soldiers plunged their swords into the helpless workers below; they raised their black whips and beat the crowd; they shot their weapons and with satisfaction saw the peasants fall. They came, hundreds upon hundreds, against the tsar's men, throwing their rocks, shouting revenge for the slaying of Father Gapon, even as their blood, and not that of the Cossacks, marked the white snow red.

In the flotsam of the crowd the snake saw Stal escaping from the battle with the Crone. It didn't matter that the pockmarked boy should be so cowardly, Gneezy thought. Stal wasn't needed after all. The Iron Knight was stirring rage and pitting Cossack against peasant. Soon the streets of St. Petersburg would be filled with a second river of darkness, filled with the blood of brethren who fought brethren. Uri Gneezy was thrown back suddenly, and his steed whinnied in fear under a thunderous roar, a splintering of the earth. Chaos. The Black Book shrank and disappeared into his snake tongue.

Gneezy saw the blackness in the sky deepen and the stars begin to fade. Before him the fast-approaching, dull-red, immense Winter Palace blurred and was overlaid with the image of another Winter Palace, bright and hopeful, painted blue and white. Sounds of laughter and happiness filled the air then were silenced. Then dark shadows of despair fell again over the palace. Time was asunder. Gneezy's thoughts ran faster than the hooves of the black horse upon the snow-covered cobbled square. The ground beneath him shook again. Light could prevail over darkness, Gneezy's snake mind realized. The souls once grasped by Marduk could be lost. Uri Gneezy recognized this. It had to be now. Tonight. The peasant workers had to have their anger churned into a murderous pitch this night. The real Tsar Nicolas must be killed in order to bring bloody rage fully into the land.

The Iron Knight had fomented anger that would spread like a virus across the land—peasant against Cossack and soon tradesman against farmer and nobility against one another. The Dark Master didn't care about the divisions of man; Cossack, peasant, worker, landowner, and nobleman were all the same to him. The gold that man held so dearly as marking a man's worth above the other was in truth of no value, for all souls were the same and could be equally blackened, regardless of whether there was gold in their pockets. The ground quaked again—time in chaos. It had to be now, the snake realized. This night had to bring to the Dark Master the souls that in time past had taken years. The Iron Knight would churn the crowd further with his brutality, and the Cossacks and Hussars, the cavalry of the Imperial Army, would be provoked into a murderous rampage. The workers and the soldiers would nurse their anger at the other for their fallen and vow bloody vengeance. The Iron Knight was proceeding as he should. Then it would be that Marduk, in one fell swoop offered by the open gate of anger, could seize possession of millions of souls.

The rage toward Tsar Nicolas by the people, who were being slaughtered in cold blood by the Cossacks in the square that fronted the immense Winter Palace, had reached a pitch. The revered Father Gapon, who had preached peace, had gathered the workers—some just coming into manhood, others children; men and women; the old and young; tens of thousands—in the streets, braving the bitter January gusts. The year 1905 was still in its infancy. "May the New Year bring us respite from the back-breaking yoke of labor," Father Gapon had told them. "They, the merchants who steal the few rubles we earn for old bread and spoiling meat; they who own the factories and take our very lifeblood so that they may live in splendor while we live like dogs in hovels. These are the things Tsar Nicolas can reverse. Surely, if we are the children of the land, the tsar who rules over us as a father should not wish to see us suffer so. There is one way to end the inequity—to appeal to the goodness of Tsar Nicolas." Father Gapon had told them of the His Majesty's godliness; there was no one who held closer to his heart Lord God Jesus Christ than the tsar. The tsar could be prevailed upon to hear their requests through a petition. They would come but in peace, not with anger upon their lips but the song of the Lord. "'Who so hath the world's goods and beholdeth his brother in need, and shutteth up his compassion from him, how doth the love of God abide in him?'" Father Gapon had recited from the Bible. And so they had come by the tens of thousands. Father Gapon had told them that Tsar Nicolas surely would listen; certainly he would, as holder of such immense power given to him by God. But the tsar hadn't. Instead Tsar Nicolas had come on his mighty black steed and thrust a saber into the heart of their beloved Father Gapon! These thoughts further fueled their anger. The peasants threw stones at the oncoming assailants; others kicked the horses, risking being trampled under their hooves.

The Iron Knight thrust his reichsmarschall's baton sideways across his tunic. Then he pulled from his side a sword, held it high, and shouted, "Traitors to Mother Russia! Who joins me to avenge these traitors to the tsar?" The tsar's soldiers, hundreds upon hundreds, roared their assent. The Iron Knight knew this would be his glory. He wore not metal armor but instead a white satin coat that was fur lined. If he could have looked at a full-length mirror, he knew it would show him the handsome manly form of a soldier. The rolls of fat were well hidden, and he thought that his indulgences in mortal life were of little note now. He glanced at his wrists, where the coat ended in cuffs of luxuriant sable. The Iron Knight saw the gleaming buttons of gold and braided loops and knew the total effect was one that gave him a royal presence.

Tsar Nicolas's army felt the strength of this new Cossack guard leader who wore no beard, had fierce blue eyes, and was leading the bloody charge. Who he was, they didn't know. This nameless man, the soldiers whispered, may have come from the court of Kaiser Wilhelm, the tsar's cousin. But could a German be trusted? The rumors flew rapidly; it was said the new colonel had been a secret *leib-gvardia*, a bodyguard for His Majesty and the imperial family and was a blood relative. Most incredibly, the news that Nicolas himself had killed Father Gapon had flown through the ranks. They who had witnessed it said the tsar upon his black steed came fast and plunged the royal saber with the Russian eagle upon it straight into the traitor's heart, for Gapon was now called a traitor, a spy bent upon destroying Mother Russia who had blasphemed all that was holy! And they also had seen the tsar ride like the wind past them, brandishing the bloody sword in triumph as he moved toward the Winter Palace. The tsar's soldiers plunged into the crowd with bloody vengeance, brandishing their whips at the crowd, unleashing their weapons.

Uri Gneezy's cobra head shook with anticipated triumph as he galloped toward the Winter Palace. The gore behind him was taking its full and hideous shape. The Dark Master would prevail fully on this Bloody Sunday of 1905. A thrill ran through Gneezy's body, and the horse beneath him jerked under the weight of evil. Russian against Russian—no better way to have man commit evil than in the heat of anger against his brethren. Uri Gneezy knew this only too well. Anger in mortal men was the quickest way to open their souls to the clasp of the Dark Master.

Gneezy would take that army of souls of the tsar's soldiers and the peasants and workers alike and plunge deep into the tunnels of the treacherous beast Ashurnasirpal. He would pull the beast up like a rodent burrowed in a dirt hole. Then Gneezy would capture the Spyglass as well Death's scythe, for he was certain that red-haired child and her friends must be deep in Kurnigi, seeking to rescue the prey—that fat man and the yellow-haired woman. The snake would return both treasures to the Dark Master Marduk. Gneezy knew not to swindle the Dark Master of his due, for look at the fate of the beast who had done so, forever trapped in the body of an animal and enslaved to Marduk. Yes, Marduk would be holder of all destiny, all-powerful. For his reward, he knew the Dark Master would let him rule supreme the tunnels of Ashurnasirpal and also Kurnigi, the land of darkness, and all of its power would be at his fingertips. No more chasing Biddle across the eons, always losing the Spyglass and condemned to endless cat-and-mouse games, for the first to be crushed to dust would be his brother Dmitri, or Herman Biddle, as he was now called. Gneezy's snake face flickered as his forked black tongue hit the cold air in satisfaction.

Gneezy was now fast approaching the palace, and the cobra face receded until once again it was covered by the mask of

Tsar Nicolas. The snake dug his spurred boots into the sides of the horse to move it fast across the entry, right into the Winter Palace. Gneezy fiercely whipped his black stallion and flew past the astonished sentry guards at the Winter Palace, who never had seen the tsar ride in a military action or not surrounded by a retinue of Cossack escorts. Gneezy's imperious wave and the somber bearded face so well known to all as His Majesty were enough for them not to dare question his passage.

Uri Gneezy knew time was short; he had to get the souls of the tsar's men firmly committed to evil. The real Tsar Nicolas must be found and killed tonight by the peasants so they could believe they had exacted their revenge. In turn, across the land, the Cossacks would butcher the peasants. So it would be that the waves of anger would be ridden until all were killed and their souls captured by the millions for the Dark Master. Each would be pitted against the other so that no man trusted another and suffering reigned mighty. Then and only then, in the divided empire would the souls fall into the hands of Marduk as easily as ripe fruit. The country would run with the blood of darkness. But all of it must happen now, for the River of Time was in chaos, and events that would have moved slowly toward the capture of the millions of the souls of Russia and beyond had to happen now, this night. Now. Bloody Sunday. In the Iron Knight, Uri Gneezy knew the seed he had planted—to grab power over the tsar's army—had blossomed as he had wished.

Gneezy rode fast into the Imperial Guard's stables, brandishing the bloody sword high above his head. The stables on the grounds of the Winter Palace were crowded with men dismounting their horses. The men in the stables gasped. Yes, it was. It must be, for he wore the blue tunic of Tsar Nicolas, the gold bands across his shoulders, and the red swash tied around his waist. No one doubted that it was Tsar Nicolas himself. The Cossacks in the stables were astonished. Never before had the tsar himself come down like this, and without his protective squadron around him. This also was puzzling because the leaders had been told that the tsar had left for the Alexander Palace to join the tsarina. But then the Cossack leaders knew the life of Tsar Nicolas was under threat by the mounting discontent among the many peoples of Russia: the peasants on the farms, the workers in the towns, even the land owners. So it was that plans changed many times over so that only a secret few knew where the tsar and his family were at any given time. The tsar's route also was guarded by the *sotnias*, squadrons of armed men who accompanied the royal family. Everyone knew that the tsar himself was no great fighter. Many of the men of arms thought secretly that Tsar Nicolas was too soft, too womanlike, rather like a warrior. He also bowed to the counsel of his wife, the tsarina, and many secretly thought it was Empress Alexandra and not Tsar Nicolas who was in truth the supreme ruler of all Russia. Thus the appearance of the tsar riding the black stallion was confounding. He also seemed different, though none could say how.

"Sire!" they exclaimed, startled by His Majesty's presence in their lowly environs. Those upon their steeds scrambled down from their horses and bowed their heads. Just moments before the tsar had arrived, a messenger had told them that the gathered workers had to be put down, for they were attacking the tsar. So the men had begun to prepare by taking up once more their weapons. Incredibly too, the messenger had said that it was the tsar himself who had taken control and killed Father Gapon. Now here was the tsar with his sword dripping with blood and brandishing it in the air!

"Your Majesty," Orlov, a stocky, red-bearded, high-ranking Cossack leader sputtered. He appeared bright and crisp in his uniform, the gray wool cloth clearly unsullied by battle. He came forward, his head bowed.

"Fools!" Gneezy shouted. "Why are you not at the square? Why do you sit here grooming your horses as your fellow soldiers fall under the attack of the peasants?"

Orlov was cowed by this direct question; he dared to lift his head and flinched under the tsar's stare, under the strange eyes—one blue, one green, of which he hadn't heard. Orlov had once seen the tsar close up, when his regiment was given commendations; he hadn't observed the strange eyes then. Through the lines of the men behind him confusion rode back in waves. Tsar Nicolas himself was in the stables! The majesty of his dress, the royal blue of his uniform, the shining gold buttons and ropes, the deep red swash around his waist intimidated them. Most had seen the tsar only from a great distance. The sight of the tsar brandishing a bloody sword also was incredible.

The Cossack leader sputtered, "Your Majesty, it was I who ordered the men to put away their weapons. When I saw in the square that Father Gapon had led the workers in peace, we came back here."

"Father Gapon, you say, came in peace?" Uri Gneezy hissed, as he pulled at his horse, which whinnied and threw its head back, aware by primal instinct that evil rode it. Some of the soldiers nearby heard the strange hiss, the vibrations of which traveled in notes of fear down their spines. Those close by would swear they had seen another face under the face of the tsar—that of a snake. Then Gneezy snarled, "Peace like this," and swung his sword at Orlov's neck. The Cossack leader staggered back, stunned, putting a hand to his neck, from which blood flowed like a stream. Then he gurgled a death cry, for it was obvious, as he fell down, that his head had been severed from his body. The others around the Cossack leader froze. A chill and silence born by terror stilled the stables. Though there were hundreds of men, not a whisper was heard. Uri Gneezy whipped the side of the horse hard, forcing the animal over the fallen man and into the crowd of the soldiers, who parted as he swung his sword.

Gneezy hissed, "They come to cut my throat, which this coward called 'peace.' And this turncoat ordered my soldiers to stay back. Who else among you is such a traitor? Who else among you is such a coward?"

The Cossacks prided themselves upon their bravery, their loyalty to Tsar Nicolas. Traitor, yes, it must be so that Colonel Orlov incredibly was, for it was he who'd had them stay back, and was it not the tsar himself who had to defend against an attack? Uri Gneezy then proclaimed, "This sword now holds the blood of two traitors to Mother Russia—Father Gapon, whom I stabbed through his treacherous, deceiving heart, and this vermin who lies dead before you." The men murmured, for the tradition of the Cossack was long, their loyalty to the tsar unquestioned. This man, Orlov, fallen at their feet, his head sliced off his neck, never had been suspected to be a traitor, many thought. But why should Tsar Nicolas butcher him with no provocation?

"Are you men of valor?" Gneezy said. "Men sworn to defend our sacred land? Or are you cowards, sniveling like this traitor upon the floor that the enemy comes in peace?" Gneezy flaunted the sword high. "Who joins me in defending the greatness of Russia against the black-hearted traitors to our beloved land—some of whom are tradesmen with gold overflowing from their pockets? They who complain that their work is too hard? That money must be handed to them for doing nothing, while you shed your blood so that you may work?"

The honor of the army, the beloved lands of Russia—these were words that meant much, meant all that was sacred to their hearts. All this was now under threat, to be destroyed by the petty demands of those who were frightened of hard work. And also hadn't the Cossacks before them laid their lives down for the tsar for generations? And hadn't the blood of their brothers flowed unchecked in the foreign land of the Orient? Here now was awakened among these soldiers of the Imperial Guard a pride they hadn't heretofore felt—pride in a leader, this Tsar Nicolas not shirking from battle but thrusting forth, a man of strength who rode so hard and fast. Perhaps it was true that Orlov was a coward and traitor, as the tsar had said, for look at the fine goods he had come into and how his gray tunic was never sullied by battle. Look at how Orlov had stood back and given orders but never dirtied his hands! Yes, they thought, the tsar had rightly struck down a cowardly traitor.

Uri Gneezy tossed back his head and laughed, for he heard their thoughts clearly. The Cossacks heard the laugh and believed it to be the one of joy, of their great father welcoming back his errant children. How strong he looked, they marveled. Tsar Nicolas and their beloved honor must be almighty, must be victorious against the dirty, greedy workers roused by vermin like Father Gapon. They roared their assent as they snatched up their weapons. Gneezy hissed in satisfaction, the serpentine aspect of his face glimmering under the face of Tsar Nicolas. At long last the battle would be won. He would hold power over all of the tunnels of Ashurnasirpal and the inhabitants of the underworld. Power he had sought through the eons. Power thwarted again and again by Herman Biddle, who would be crushed to dust once and for all.

The snake, however, had made a crucial error, for his ego, the grandiose visions born of his own anger nursed as a mortal and carried through the eons against his brother, known then as Dmitri, known now as Herman Biddle, had blinded him to treachery—treachery he soon would come to understand and that came in the form of Stal.

CHAPTER 16

the prince of demons

In the dank, dark alleyway of a St. Petersburg street, with the pandemonium of death buzzing just beyond it, a demon was rising—a demon Uri Gneezy had ignored when mesmerized by the close grasp of power in his hand, for evil's great weakness is self-absorbtion. Stal's head jerked back and twisted. He yelped in pain. The sounds around him were sharpened, the shouting of people falling to their deaths, the shots, the cries of the Cossacks. But there was a scream, a bloodcurdling wail that was worse than anything else. Stal realized with a start that it was coming from him. The black-and-blue thumbs of Abaddon the Crone had thrown into his forehead had penetrated deeply and sent lashes of pain through him. Then, as if he were a corkscrew, his head rotated one way and his body another. Stal felt the wicked darkness of the fingers coursing through him, wringing him like a wet cloth. His eyes bulged, and then he felt his body stretch. He groaned in agony and shut his eyes against the excruciating pain that bore through him, pulling and pulling him, until he felt it would destroy him.

Then it stopped, and Stal opened his eyes. He saw that instead of the twigs that were his legs, he had the strong legs of a man, covered in gray wool pants. His arm, formerly broken and twisted, was straight. He looked at his hands and spread them, and the two thumbs of Abaddon glowed black and blue upon them. He wore a thick gray coat with a black belt made of small snakes twisted and biting one another. Upon his head was a wool cap, thick and warm. Black brows arched in an evil expression upon his pockmarked face. But it was his eyes that were the most fearsome of all, for they smoldered red in anticipation. Stal's body was surging with the strength and impetuousness of young manhood. Upon his lip he felt the bristles of a mustache.

But something else had happened; the power of the old demon cave gods had been awakened within Stal. The mixing of the deep evil that would have risen in the mortal Stal, the seedling of his cruel being, unfurled and grew, fed as it was by the demonic power within Abaddon's thumbs. The darkness of Stal's soul, combined with the wickedness in the thumbs of Abaddon, gave him fiendish power. Wickedness was awakening, evil born from the misery and darkness of those imprisoned within the thumbs. When Abaddon had held the thumbs, he didn't know that Marduk had placed his enemies inside them—the old, old gods of death whose forms were drawn by man in caves when words were just being formed by mortal man. Those demon gods had been older than the gods of the wind, thunder, and rain who had been worshiped by generations of those who had lived in the valley between the Tigris and Euphrates Rivers and in their arrogance had betrayed Marduk first when he battled the Great Mother, known then in all her power as Tiamat, to overpower him and grasp for themselves the sky of heaven.

But the old gods of primitive man had stayed with Marduk—they who had risen to power when the whispers of the Spirit over the Deep had become silent and man was relegated to the vessel of a mortal form; when the knowledge of eternal life was clouded; when mortal man grasped at the shiny things of the illusory earth in a cruel and unending dance of life and death and couldn't distinguish what was good from what was evil. It was those old cave gods of destruction who had been first Marduk's allies in the battle for the sky of heaven against Mother Tiamat. But in the time of Abaddon's mortal life—almost a millienium before Jesus Christ would walk the earth, when they found that Marduk's promises to them of their old glory, of mortal man's worship to strengthen their waning spirits, had never been realized, not in the tens of thousands of years that they had waited—it was then they had raised their opposition to Marduk. Treachery had risen in these ancient evil ones of dark caves, and they sought the counsel and help of the dragon gods and the fallen angels who lay trapped by Marduk under the Palace of Ashurnasripal to align for power. Together, with the other forgotten mighty gods, they were known as Asaru-alim-nuna.

Marduk's strength, however, was such that these old cave gods with no worshipers were whispers in the wind, for Marduk had fully overcome and laid them and as well as the gods of destruction of the Tigris, the Euphrates, and the Indus Valley to obscurity. And Marduk had thrown the ancient evil ones of the cave inside the thumbs he had given to the greedy Abaddon, trapping them in a wicked soul. Inside Abaddon's thumbs it was certain that the old gods would have no power, as they never would have their names spoken by mortal lips. When the thumbs were cut from Abaddon's hands by King Ashurnasirpal II, Marduk had done nothing, for the Dark Master knew that the desire for power clouded the brutal mortal King Ashurnasirpal's eyes, and the powerless cries of the old gods wouldn't be heard by him. So it was that the thumbs had remained a prison for the old gods—from the living hands of Abaddon, to the beast Ashurnasirpal, to the Crone. So they had stayed in the hands of the beast and the Crone, who had tried mightly to find their power but couldn't, for true power lay in the awakening of evil of a black soul when chaos splintered the earth, when the stories of old could rise again, when mortal man would raise his eyes once more in confusion and plead to the gods of old for mercy.

Stal's eyes went back into his head, and he felt the pull of spirits as he heard the call of demons and felt the might of the underworld surge through him. *Asaru-alim-nuna!* Words he didn't know—words that been held deep in the memories of those deeply etched in hell—sprang from his lips. "Asaru-alim-nuna!" Stal cried, his eyes shut and his body shaking with the vibrations of the demons' strength rising through him. The boy turned into a man as he was pulled by the demonic old cave gods, the words again and again upon his lips. "Asaru-alim-nuna! Asaru-alim-nuna! Asaru-alim-nuna!"

Terror vibrated through the Crone's body, shaking her like a ragdoll. Stal was calling the demons of old, calling the demons who had once tricked Marduk! And he, the Dark Master, had turned one upon the others and taken from each their power. Where these old gods lay now, the Crone didn't know. But to call the old demons with Marduk's eyes and ears about them was surely to court the fiercest wrath of the Dark Master. *Oh, stupid boy!* the Crone thought, and her mind moved rapidly to ways to save herself.

Deep within the treacherous caves beneath the tunnels of Ashurnasirpal, where the beast had just stood with the Brotherhood of Evil before he rose up to the surface of Kurnigi, the old gods heard Stal's call to them. For the first time in the eons, these forgotten mighty ones rose—those who were the ones to first take the form of the serpent in the Garden of Eden, who were the first demons of darkness, now forgotten and powerless as dust. It was they who had been called. *"Asaru-alim-nuna! Asaru-alim-nuna!"* The walls that surrounded the Brotherhood in the depths beneath the tunnels were made not of earth but of those who once had reigned supreme as gods. They were old demon gods whose presence hadn't been detected by anyone deep within the caves. Not the beast. Not the khan. Not the prince. Not the duke. Nor to any who lay in the grasp of the khan, duke, prince, or beast. There were layers of darkness and perfidy, layers upon layers that wound upon one another with the thread of deceit and disloyalty like threads that made the weaving, for underneath the souls harvested from mortal men were the other enemies and traitors to Marduk. They were the shadows of the old gods worshiped no longer by mortal men and therefore having lost the power given to them by such adulation. The old gods, once glorious, once had held the power of the rivers and oceans; their eyes had moved with the force of the wind and the light of the stars, and mortal men had feared and worshiped them. They had won man's soul first then lost it, and thus began the battle among the demons for who were to be the mighty ones.

Then it was that Marduk rose among them, turned one demon upon another, and seized their power. He had told the demon gods he would lead them in the battle against the Great

Mother, who had interfered with man's fate, stolen from them the souls won fairly over by the demon gods. Marduk had told them, Asaru-alim-nuna, the oldest of the demon gods, that they would rule supreme, as was their right, over all the demon gods, and soon too would they hold the sky of heaven. But the demon Marduk had tricked them, and turned them upon one another. So it was in that division that Marduk found strength and took from each their power. He held them captive, broke their sacred spears, took the songs and chants from their lips. He took from them their godly forms, reduced them to broken bodies, and built this dungeon deep beneath the earth and buried their voices forever.

From their dismal place, imprisoned in dirt and stone, a slow rising chorus began. It was the groans of those held within the walls, now awakening, now heard. Long tongues shot out from the walls. "Asaru-alim-nuna! Asaru-alim-nuna!" The true mighty ones had been called at last, and the walls shook. Then the walls whispered, and behind them their forms could be seen—those of broken bodies, bloody hands, skeletal forms, and shadowy eyes. The old gods, hidden and imprisoned in the rocks and clay of the walls, were now summoned, as Marduk's orbs dimmed and the souls escaped from the City of the Condemned. Death's scythe was now held in the hands of the living, they could see once more.

They made out the forms of the Brotherhood of Evil. Now the old gods' ears sharpened as the strength of their foe Marduk waned, and they found they could hear once more. The first words they heard in eons were those of the Brotherhood, their plots and plans to take the reins from Marduk. The power of the Dark Master was ebbing, they exulted. And the metal amulet, the Spyglass, was in Kurnigi. But greater still than the treacherous plans of the Brotherhood of Evil to destroy Marduk, they heard the thoughts of the beast as had stood alone when the others had departed. They had heard the beast snort and tread his hooves upon their heads as his thoughts rang through the air. These were thoughts the beast believed were hidden, but in truth echoed in silent vibrations in the dank cave. The beast had risen up out of the cave to the surface of Kurnigi, innocent that the knowledge had been imparted to those who would use it well against him.

Now the old demons knew that it was the beast who held the droplet fallen from the eye of Marduk in the Great Battle with the old gods. The droplet had held the potent birth waters, sweet and bitter, of Apsu and Tiamet, who had conceived Marduk. The beast didn't know the droplet's full powers; not only could it blind Marduk from the stench of treachery, but within the clasp of the old gods, Asaru-alim-nuna, once the ancient chants were spoken, it could be used to drain Marduk of his being, for the droplet held Marduk's birth water. Their chants could turn the birth water and thereby Marduk himself into dust. Then they, Asaru-alim-nuna, would hold one of the Twin Tablets of Destiny. And with that they would seize possession of the metal amulet, the Spyglass, and squeeze from it the secret—where to find the Hidden Daughter, the sister of Marduk, so they could clasp to their demonic hearts both Tablets. The Great Mother would then fall to dust. Soon mortal men as well as the dead souls would worship them. Their oceans would rise and fall; the rains from clouds and the very night and day would come at their bidding. Mortal men would once again fall to their knees and offer sacrifices to them. And these old gods would write the story of creation. They would reach their hands up to the touch the sky of heaven; the infinite blanket of stars and suns would be theirs. *Theirs!* But to do so, they needed to be released from the captivity of the cave; they needed to be remembered and called. And the time had come at last. They had been called.

The voices from the walls whispered:

> *He, the beast Ashurnasirpal, who hides from Marduk,*
> *will we hold in our power*
> *and take from him the droplet.*
> *Then the Twin Tablets of Destiny*
> *shall soon be upon us.*
> *Upon our breasts they shall lie,*
> *and Marduk, who conquered*
> *and laid us to waste,*
> *will no longer reign supreme.*
>
> *He will soon weep*
> *in fear and tribulation*
> *when we grasp him in our hands*
> *and lay him asunder,*
> *and the demon Marduk's*
> *lips will speak our name*
> *as he bows his head to us.*
> *"Asaru-alim-nuna!"*
> *Mighty ones will we be!*

Asaru-alim-nuna, Asaru-alim-nuna—the true mighty ones, they who had tempted man in the Garden of Eden, who had taken his soul in the bargain and lost it. Long black tongues shot out from the walls again and reverberated to the sound of their name from the land above—the land of the living but spoken by one of the dead. The old gods had long sought the release that would come when evil called them. Into Abaddon's thumbs Marduk had imprisoned others who had fought him for power and lost—the primitive cave gods of death. The thumbs had grown in demonic power as they held the pain and agony of those Abaddon had tortured. To Abaddon these Asaru-alim-nuna didn't appear, for they knew him to be too weak and greedy to be a vessel for their release, and he also was deaf to their brethren, the cave gods of death, trapped in his thumbs. Abaddon also had allied himself with their enemy, Marduk.

The black-and-blue thumbs Abaddon had held so dearly eventually had been sliced from his hands by King Ashurnasirpal II. To the king, successor as son of Tukulti-Ninurta, in the eight centuries before Christ, as the beast was known in his mortal form, the old gods had turned. They knew the depth of depravity of this King Ashurnasirpal, how he had used the bodies and bones of his enemies to build the walls of his palace, pulling the eyes from those who had seen too much and chopping off the ears of those who heard too much, or the legs and hands of those who had grown too fast in power. In his mortal form, King Ashurnasirpal had shown the world cruelty it hadn't known. So the old gods of destruction knew of his harshness and reveled in it, for they thought in this mortal they had found a kindred spirit. Ashurnasirpal had inflicted much suffering in the old lands—invading Aram, conquering the Aramaeans and all the peoples between the Khabura and the great Euphrates, leaving the rushing water red with blood. The old gods imprisoned in the tunnels beneath the Palace of Ashurnasirpal had rejoiced at the slaughter and how this mortal king had boasted of the massacres—how he made puppets of old men's heads, cutting ears, noses, and lips off until they bled to death; how the dead had been advertisements of his rapacious cruelty, left in broken heaps, the decapitated heads posted as trophies of his bloody glory; how he had burned people alive and destroyed their temples with flames. Yes, this one, the old gods trapped under the tunnels had thought possessed enough evil to rise against Marduk. So the old gods had spoken to Ashurnasirpal in his mortal form, through his dreams of the droplet. They had lured him with the promise of power greater than he had known as a human—power only the Dark Master held. This Ashurnasirpal, the old gods thought, would be their vessel for release. "Search," they had told him in whispers in his dreams, "in the tunnels," for they knew the droplet had fallen from the eye of Marduk. Ashurnasirpal had been cursed by greediness, trying to deceive Marduk and grasping power greater than the Dark Master.

As he grew in strength, the mortal King Ashurnasirapal became pompous and thereby careless and foolishly didn't cover his thoughts from Marduk. Soon his greed would betray him and bring upon the old demon gods and himself the wrath of Marduk. Deep into the tunnels of Kurnigi had the Dark Master secreted away the old gods, for he knew from the beast's thoughts—which Ashurnasirpal foolishly hadn't covered with the desecrated chants—that the old gods had spoken to him. So driven were they by Marduk deeper and deeper into the Corkscrew of Terror that they were but rock and dirt in the dank caves where they lay still, deaf and blind, where no sound they uttered was ever heard, by the dead or the living. Until now.

Now the old demon gods could seek their vengeance against Marduk. The shadows of the old gods with no followers rose up, weak like broken thunder.

Asaru-alim-nuna!
Asaru-alim-nuna!

They rose from the walls to he who had called them. *Stal.* He would kneel before the old gods and have mortals pledge their souls to them once more. Their forms would move from weakness into strength, like a small stream that joins the great ocean. The Mighty Forgotten Ones, filled the tunnel walls with their dusky images. First to take clear shape were the mightiest among them: the horrendous aspect of Nergal, god of destruction, with the face of a dragon, sharp in teeth, and with the body of a giant. Then came Namtar, demon of tribulation, bearing dark winds of pain; Lamashtu, demoness of forgetfulness, rising like a gray fog of confusion; and Zaltu, goddess of conflict with eyes of lightning bolts that shook the earth. These first forms of the Asaru-alim-nuna called the Four Terrors rose from their millenniums-long imprisonment from the walls of tunnel, forgotten no more, mighty again.

Asaru-alim-nuna!
Asaru-alim-nuna!

Yes, Stal would now clasp the demonic magic of the Saber of Shadows and wield death through the steel of sword that held both deception and darkness.

Asaru-alim-nuna!
Asaru-alim-nuna!

The black-and-blue thumbs of Abaddon upon Stal's outreached hands stabbed the St. Petersburg sky, a dusky dome to the Bloody Sunday killings below. The Crone cowered in fear against the wall of the alley at each utterance by Stal of the call to the old demons. What would Marduk do to them? How could she escape? Stal shouted the words but didn't know why.

Asaru-alim-nuna!
Asaru-alim-nuna!

The words rose from his throat, awakened by a deep memory—a memory that sprang from the black-and-blue thumbs of Abaddon into Stal's lips. The stars above, which had glittered against the black velvet night, were fading. He felt his red eyes roll back farther into his head as his body shook. Stal's thumbs glowed black then blue. From these thumbs images emerged— stick drawings of fiendish figures, drawings of death, of agony of terror that lifted from the thumbs and rose like vapors into the sky. The horrific demon drawings shook the sky with their evil, flashing eyes. Then Stal saw from these eyes bolts of light that formed into a saber flying down toward him. Its arched blade gleamed a ghostly gray metal with small black slashes. The little black snakes weren't inlaid in the sword but were writhing over the blade.

"The Saber of Shadows," the Crone gasped. She had heard of this mystical dark weapon, forged, it was said, in times of old by the demon gods Marduk had battled, but she never had seen it. Its magic lay in the handle, which was unequaled in the terror it could cause, mighty in battle if the holder had the strength to control it. The handle was made of four bones, of the jaws of the four dragon horses ridden by the old demons of strife and death. Here was the Crone's way out of Marduk's wrath and the snake's clasp. She would be Mistress of the mighty weapon! With it she would she slash the reptilian neck of the snake and grab back from him the Black Book of Magic.

The Crone reached her gnarled hands toward the sword and cried:

Nergal, Namtar! Lamashtu, Zaltu!
O deliverers of strife and death!
Bearers of destruction,
cast into my hands
the Saber of Shadows.
Give into my clasp
this sword of darkness!

The saber flew about, just above her grasp, and these words filled the air.

Seek do we our new master.
Thumbs of black and blue
has he.
Pocked is his face, and
so marked is his soul.

The Saber of Shadows fell into Stal's hands. One hand upon another clasped the handle, the black-and-blue thumbs glowing as they touched the sword. Stal heard the Crone groan in disappointment. His eyes blurred, and his mind was groggy. He knew he had spoken dark, demonic words; he had felt their bitter taste upon his tongue. But he didn't know their meaning. He only knew he had fallen into a trance, and the words had sprung from his lips. Then the sword had fallen into his hands. As Stal grasped the sword tightly by its bone handle, its force ran like a current under his fingers. The saber felt as if it could at any moment fly from his hands. It felt both hot like a flame and cold like ice. Stal was aware keenly of the power of the weapon, and with the thumbs of the demons upon his hands, nothing could thwart him from crushing those in his way and stepping into greatness. But how? He was only one boy—no, a man now, but still just one man. Why would the peasants listen to him and make him their leader?

Stal held the saber aloft and hesitated. Then he slashed the air with the weapon, and it formed streaks of gray light. The blade was strange—metal but not, for it glowed a dusky dark ominous light. Stal didn't know what this rapier was, where its strength lay. But though he didn't know the weapon's power, he had seen the greedy look in the ugly hag's eyes and knew it was more than just a sword. He felt its power like the writhing of a great serpent under his grasp. Stal thought of the snake Gneezy, the power he held writhing and growing, overpowering all. Yes, this sword was given to him by the forces of the underworld to make him mighty, he was certain. He didn't know how to harness its strength, but he was certain the Crone did by the way she had called to it. Stal didn't trust the Crone, knowing instinctively that the old hag was duplicitous to the core. To reveal his lack of knowledge would be a weakness, but ask he must. He said, "I heard you call this sword the Saber of Shadows. Tell me its magic, Crone."

The Crone wavered. She heard Stal's thoughts. The boy—for it didn't matter that he was now in the form of a young man; to her he was nothing but a pockmarked cockroach—didn't realize the power he held. She had felt the deep stab of disappointment when the Saber of Shadows didn't come to her. The words of the snake Uri Gneezy rang in her ears—*This boy Iosif, when his heart turned black, when he became a man, would boast he was made of steel. This Stal, it was written, would rule with terror and turn one against another, and our master would reap their souls to fill the Book of the Dead.*

Stal's heart was already black. But he and not she held the saber with its power of darkness. The Crone decided it would not be he who ruled with terror but her. Stal could be controlled by her, *would* be controlled by her. She would tell him what she knew of the weapon, for she was certain he would soon learn of it anyway. Better that she should have him relying upon her for direction. Knowledge was power, and this power she would wield. With sharp eyes Stal noted the flicker in the Crone's face. He couldn't read her thoughts, but her expression told him to be wary.

"Tell me, Crone!" Stal said, and his pockmarked face glinted with the cruelty that soon would come to fruition. "Or perhaps I can discover it for myself by slashing your ugly body in half?" Here Stal wielded the Saber of Shadows toward the Crone, who flinched and moved away from the sword.

The Crone's yellow snaggletooth rattled in her gummy, odorous mouth with displeasure. "I told you, boy, that if you betray me, I will exact my revenge." She raised her bony fingers toward him to cast a spell. Stal raised the saber against it, hitting the spell and seeing it fall to the ground in sparks. The Crone snarled and pressed her wrinkled lips firmly closed.

"Speak, Crone," Stal said, his voice now like steel, "or truly I will slash you to pieces." The shadowy gray light hit her gnarled hand, and she cried in pain, not in her mortal body for she had none, but pain that vibrated through her form as notes of warning.

"It is the Saber of Shadows," the Crone hissed, "whose blade was forged from the lightning and thunderbolts of the gods of old."

Stal said softly, "Asaru-alim-nuna."

"Yes," the Crone said but dared not utter the name of the demon gods, fearing the wrath of Marduk.

The demon gods, Asaru-alim-nuna, had chosen him. *Him.* And he had a power that made the Crone fearful. He saw how the Crone cringed at their name as Stal spoke it again, savoring the syllables. "Asaru-alim-nuna."

The Crone despondently fell back against the wall of the alley. Betrayers—the snake Uri Gneezy when he was only a mortal Russian boy, and now this cobbler's son. Her black eyes caught sight far off of the Iron Knight gathering strength from the Cossacks. Where was the snake? Gone, she realized. The Crone felt the first beat of hope. The snake was gone. Here was her window of opportunity. "The old demon gods, who carried death upon their breath," she said. "One side of the blade, when waved, casts the shadows of deception, and the other side the darkness of Death. Its handle is made from the jaws of the Four Dragon Horses of Terror."

Stal slashed the sword in the air again, reveling in the power. The Four Dragon Horses of Terror. A sword of dark magic for a prince—for he was now a prince, not a small, helpless, poor son of a Georgian cobbler and a washerwoman. *A prince of demons,* Stal thought. But the thought didn't go unheard.

The Crone snickered to herself. *This idiotic boy thinks himself a prince.* The boy was now in a young man's body but remained stupid and greedy. The Crone heard the longing for power in the pockmarked one; he was early still to the yearning for power, and the Crone knew that once a little power was in his grasp, it would inflate his head and be his undoing, for in ego there lies much opportunity for failure. It would be easy to control him through his grandiose yearning. The Crone bowed her head, as if now in supplication to a new master. "Prince of demons," she said, the words accompanied by puffs of foul breath.

Stal held the sword aloft and said, "Saber of Shadows." As he slashed the air, ominous, rumbling sounds flew out of the weapon, and he felt a deep satisfaction. He, Stal, held demonic powers. "Ah, so it is a saber of control, of the peasants beyond, with its shadows."

"Yes, you are the master of the saber. You must go and proclaim yourself the leader of the peasants. They will obey the prince of demons," the Crone urged.

Stal moved out of the dark alley and into edges of the Winter Palace square. He didn't trust the Crone's soft voice of supplication; he wasn't as stupid as the old hag believed. But move into the hearts of the peasants he must. He was struck by the grandeur that lay ahead of him. The square was massive. Though thousands had gathered, the square's breadth and width swallowed them. It made them small and insignificant in the face of the symbol of wealth and power that lay ahead of them—the tsar's Winter Palace and the hundreds upon hundreds of mounted soldiers there. The Winter Palace was an enormous structure of dull red with gold baroque gilding; a large onion dome sat atop the Grand Church on the palace grounds. The palace was daunting in size, with a thousand rooms, it was said, maybe more. Its splendor spoke of the unimaginable wealth of the tsar—wealth that none who gathered shivering in the cold, none who now lay dead under the stampede of the tsar's army could have envisioned even in their most grandiose dreams. The sky was becoming black, and no light from above shone upon the square. Throughout, even in the streets that bound the square, the air sounded with the cries of the peasants whom the Cossacks had shot. Mayhem reigned. Shops nearby were being looted, stones thrown, people shouting, as the salt smell of blood filled the air.

Stal stood at the edge of the darkness in a boundary of indecision. The power he'd felt moments before seemed insignificant, somehow daunted by the might and gold of the tsar in the form of the Winter Palace ahead. Stal felt his poverty again, his meager status. He stood just outside of the alleyway with the weapon in his hand, this Saber of Shadows, this sword of darkness. He cursed himself for his ineptitude. He knew he moved awkwardly, not with the strength of a man, for he was still new to a man's body, and walked like a mere boy. Stal observed how the Cossacks in the distance upon their horses cracked their whips into the crowd to keep them back. Other soldiers shot into the crowd. The screams were deafening. Many times Stal was pushed by men, women, even boys and girls as they ran toward the oncoming horses. The people were falling beneath the horses' hooves; the peasants and workers were armed only with stones and bricks. Still they rushed at the horses, the young and the old; even old hags that looked as ancient as the Crone herself—they too were charging at the horses. Far off was the Iron Knight, galloping here and there, shouting orders to the tsar's soldiers.

When the Crone emerged from the dark alley, she was greeted by the cacaphonous mixture of sounds: death, terror, anger. The blood flowed from the fallen, and the scene beyond them spelled bedlam. She had crept slowly behind Stal and saw how he stood like an idiot, holding the great Saber of Shadows as a boy might hold a toy weapon. For surely, the Crone thought, it was Abaddon's thumbs and the sword that held the power, not their bearer. Stal was but a stupid boy whom she would soon bring to destruction. She would chop Abaddon's thumbs from his hands and take possession of the Saber of Shadows. The Crone, however, didn't know why the thumbs of Abaddon had such demonic strength, for they never had shown much magic while in her possession. In fact they had shown none. She had felt tricked by the beast Ashurnasirpal, for the thumbs were nothing but dessicated, odorous, black-and-blue sticks secreted within the folds of her dingy skirts. Yes, Stal was nothing but an ignorant Georgian cobbler's boy plucked before his time, before mercilessness would have run through his veins as a man. Now, though in a strong man's body, and though he held aloft the demonic saber, he didn't know how to wield its power. She saw how he stood, looking dimwitted, with his mouth gaping at the scene before him. So it would be that the Crone would be the puppeteer, and the power of the Saber of Shadows would be hers— by proxy through the puppet Stal but hers nonetheless. First the boy-man must be made ruthless, to feel the thrill of the blood of mortal men upon his hands, to pull into his thumbs more and more demonic power. But under her rule would he be, under her sway. Then she would possess the Saber of Shadows. The thoughts of her plan flurried again through her mind—cut Abaddon's thumbs off Stal's hands and soon slice off the cobra head of the snake Gneezy then snatch for herself the Black Book of Magic.

Stal heard the Crone, who was now beside him, cackling. He knew the old woman had treachery in her heart, but their fates were linked until he fully knew how to wield the Saber of Shadows. Then he would make good on his promise to slash her in two, for he didn't fear her threat to exact revenge.

Suddenly the Crone pulled at a short man in a torn coat who was hurling rocks at the approaching Cossacks. The man shook her off. "Old woman," he said, "leave me be!" He winced at her smell. The Crone dug her yellowed nails into his arms, and the man angrily pulled her off and threw a stone at her.

"He!" the Crone said, clutching another man's coat as she pointed at Stal. "This one is your savior!" Stal winced at the word.

Stupid hag—what was she doing? The Crone cried out to no one in particular, as the crowd moved like a wave of rage through the Winter Palace square and toward the tsar's soldiers. "Your savior is here!" the Crone called out. This second man pulled the Crone's hands off him and, noticing Stal nearby, sneered. "This pockmarked one is a coward," he said, "clinging to the skirt of an old hag."

Stal heard the old taunt and blushed at the man's indictment. It was true. He had the power of demons running through him and felt its current, yet he stood like a dimwit with the Crone hawking him like a fisherwoman did her catch. The man pushed the Crone hard, and she fell to the cold ground. The Crone wailed piteously, "You have hurt me...I cannot stand." *Boy, come here to help me. Then slash the throat of this cockroach!* The Crone called this order to Stal's mind. In this way, the Crone believed, the masses would see the power of Stal, his bloodthirstiness. A crowd formed around them, but Stal knew this wasn't the way of strength. Several in the crowd chastised the man for pushing an old woman down. Others chuckled at the pockmarked one holding the sword.

One large man with hair that was bushy and black and a beard equally fearsome stepped forward and pushed Stal. "Give me that sword," he commanded. He went to grab the Saber of Shadows from Stal, encircling one of Stal's arms with a vice grip and using his other hand to reach for the sword.

The Crone stood up and pulled at the man's coat. "No! Leave him be!" she cried pitifully. *Kill him now, Stal!* She commanded Stal through his mind.

The man shook off the Crone. By now an even larger crowd had formed around the large man and Stal. "What is happening?" some in the crowd asked, while others wondered aloud,

"How did that young man come to have such a sword?" The sword appeared to be worth many rubles, gilded and gleaming as it was. "It is the son of a rich man come to cut our throats!" they cried. Then the burly bearded man called to the others, "Let us take his sword and cut this rich man's son to pieces! Do you see how fine a coat he wears? And the weapon he carries against us?" The big man had caught hold of Stal firmly and sneered, "Pockmarked coward who hides behind an old woman! *Pocky!*"

The old taunt was like a flame set upon dry tinder. It enflamed Stal, bringing him a vision of how short and small, pockmarked and ragged he had been, a poor boy in the Gori Church School for rich boys. He had been a charity case brought about because his mother Keke had *begged* the church. He had worn dirty, tattered clothes and had hidden his nails, which were embedded with dirt, ashamed at how unclean and odorous he was compared to the wealthy boys who bathed daily and wore clean clothes. His mind was flooded with memories of how he had pushed his head down and moved through the clot of schoolboys, their fists striking him on all sides. He recalled their laughter and slurs. *He's nothing but a filthy, lice-ridden coward! He drinks the dirty water his mother brings home after cleaning the floors! Pocky!* The taunts of his boyhood tormenters ran like a current of anger through him. Stal's rage burned through him. The desire to kill them had throbbed his veins, but he had bit back his anger, knowing that were he to give in, they would pummel him to a bloody mess.

But not now. He was no longer that small boy beaten down by the rich bullies. He was the prince of demons. He was Stal. He cried out, "I am Stal!" His hate and anger coursed through his body, strengthening him, and he pushed off the vice grip of the burly man who struggled to grab the Saber of Shadows. Stal twisted the Saber of Shadows away from him and jabbed one thumb in quick succession into both of the man's eyes. The current from the black-and-blue thumb flew into the man. He fell down to the ground, where his beefy body thrashed about. The man shook as if bolts of lightning were jolting him.

The crowd backed away, hushed. They saw Stal's red eyes gleam in anger as he held the saber aloft above the man. The current of rage was strong. He never would be a sniveling coward. *Never.* He was Stal...steel...*Stal.* Far beyond him, near the enormous front of the Winter Palace, Stal—now with the sight of demon eyes—saw the Iron Knight, riding strong, giving orders as Tsar's Nicolas's men trampled the crowds. The desire to be in command surged through Stal.

The large man, still writhing upon the ground, pointed a finger at Stal, as others held him back. "The devil is a rich man," he growled. "You will be nothing soon, as the masses rise against you."

Stal heard the words of accusation, that he was a rich man. He knew the grinding wear of poverty, of wanting what the wealthy boys in his class had: warm coats, shoes without holes, food when your stomach raged with hunger and not a ruble was to be had for bread. Rich man. Yes, in his mortal form, he'd felt anger toward rich men, not for their wealth but because Stal himself did not have it. He'd felt angry that the toss of fate had made him a poor boy in ragged clothes and his taunters rich boys. He'd felt angry that the beguiling and rich Trina never would be his, because he was grungy, lice-ridden, and pockmarked. Not now. Not now. He was a demon now, a *prince of demons.* He had black magic and more power than a rich man with gold ever would. Even the tsar's opulent palace was nothing compared to the power he held. Stal realized he had let his old mortal emotions, of insecurity born of poverty in the face of wealth, control him. Such emotions were to be used, not felt. He heard his mother Keke's voice, meek with the words of God, caution him, *Anger opens the door for the snakes of hell to enter your soul.* Anger.

The peasants felt the anger rising like waves of heat from the strange young man with the glowing red orbs. They felt his rage, his power, his hatred and cast wary eyes upon him. "It is the devil's work," some in the crowd whispered, and fell back. "Let us move from here." The men and women, worn with care and worry, backed away. The Crone was near Stal; he could smell her. She was saying something, but he knew her counsel was worthless. He shut his mind to the Crone's voice. But his mother's voice rang strong. *Anger opens the door for the snakes of hell.* Yes, Stal would open the doors of anger for these peasants and ride would they to hell, ride behind him, their master. Was that not how the snake was strong? He could be even more powerful than the snake. He *would* be more powerful. Stal strode directly toward the crowd as they moved away from him. He held the Saber of Shadows aloft and waved the glistening blade of light.

"I come to help you throw off the chains of your confinement by the rich!" he shouted. "Soon the work you do won't be like that of a beast of burden but of the man who rides the beast!"

These words stopped them. They were words, some whispered, that Father Gapon himself had said. Others pointed ahead to the crowd in the distance that was falling by the hundreds under the hooves of Tsar's Nicolas's army. "Do not listen," these others said. "Move forward to kill the dirty Cossacks and avenge the death of Father Gapon!" "Do you not see how our brothers ahead of us lie dead in the snow, fallen under the weapons of the tsar's army?" Still others, seeing the slaughter of their brethren beyond, scared of death themselves, wondered whether they would become such lambs to slaughter. Was there not a better way? Some in the crowd pressed near. Who was this young man, strong with anger flaring in his eyes? How did he come by this sword? There was something about this sword that repelled them, that frightened them yet drew their respect.

Stal saw that while some in the crowd had left him, others stayed. He needed just a few; then soon it would be many. And this thought came to him from wisdom he was yet to gain—*One death is a tragedy, a million a statistic.* The stupid priest Gapon's death must be capitalized upon, and then the tragedy would lead to a million deaths. A million souls to control. And power greater than that of the snake or the pompous Iron Knight. He, Stal, would be ruler of all of Russia.

Stal shouted, "Is it not in the interest of the landowners, the merchants, the factory lords to control you?"

The large bearded man who had been blinded by Stal's thumbs, wobbling still from the effects of the bolts, shook his head and said, "He is a spy, a rich man's son come to trick us!"

Stal heard the words and smiled inside. Saber of Shadows. Yes, he realized, the man was a fool, ready to be used. "Who among you, comrades, hides like a wolf in sheep's clothing?" he asked, as he lunged toward the large bearded man and slashed his sword at the man's coat with one side of the Saber of Shadows, which cast its deceptive spell. The blade cut the worn, dirty coat and revealed beneath it a rich black wool coat, pristine with shiny gold buttons. "It is not I who is the rich man, comrades, but he who accuse me so," Stal said. "See what he has in his pockets!"

The crowd of people roughly grabbed the protesting man. "He is Satan!" the bearded man screamed. "Look at how he tricks you!" As he did, gold coins fell from his pockets. The crowd was furious. "It is you who tricks us!" they said. They kicked him with anger at every landowner, every shop merchant who had tricked them. They kicked him until he fell unconscious.

Stal's words, arrows of deception, fell upon the crowd of peasants. "Who doubts that I come to lead you, sent by fate after Father Gapon was slayed?" The crowd murmured. Beyond them rose the death cries of their brethren, slaughtered by the Cossacks. Still their hearts were checked by fear and doubt. Yes, the man had showed them a traitor; still there was something about him—his pockmarked face, eyes that shone like...like those of the devil.

Stal said, "'Like sheep you have gone astray, have turned to your own way, and therefore the hand of inequity lays upon your brow.'" The young pockmarked man had spoken the words of the Lord! And Stal heard their thoughts. He knew well the words of piety, having heard them so often repeated by his mother and the Georgian priests. Stupid were those who held their heads meek in submission to God, he thought, for they always received a sound kick to their heads. "Is it right that four-fifths goes to Pharoah?" Stal called out. "Rise, comrades! Rise against the rich who keep the fruits of your labor." He shouted, "Do not turn a blind eye to the prophet who arises among you, known to you as he gives you the sign of wonder." And here some in the crowd were unnerved. Their hearts beat the words, *Satan, Satan, Satan,* but although these words were wrong, they listened to the pockmarked devil.

Feeling the power of his words, Stal knew he had entered the minds of these workers, these foolish peasants. "No man shall be able to stand against you. Every place on which the sole of your foot treads shall be yours." Stal's red eyes glowed demonically, and his pockmarks seemed to bore deeper into his face, like great black holes. "Satan," he heard some in the crowd whisper.

The words the Crone had cried out when the Saber of Shadows had first appeared flew from his lips as he called out to the old gods and goddesses of destruction, "Nergal! Namtar! Lamashtu! Zaltu!" The Saber of Shadows suddenly surged, and fell to his feet. The saber formed a shape that lifted him into the air, and he heard the cries of astonishment around him. He was riding on a giant blood-colored animal with the head of a dragon and a horse's body. The black bands upon the beast's neck glowed, and from its neck three more dragon heads sprung out. And soon the beast was four-headed, snarling to show ghostly white teeth shaped like daggers flecked with blood. Stal gripped the reins of the fearsome four-headed dragon horse, and when the black-and-blue thumbs of Abaddon touched them, the beast stood still. The crowd near Stal backed away fearfully. *Satan.* It was *Satan,* for Stal's eyes glowed red; his pockmarked face shone with pure evil. Then the saber appeared again in his hand. Stal displayed it and slashed gray beams in the air. He saw the crowd move away, as they whispered that he wasn't a man of god but a satanic force.

In a distant part of the square, pandemonium raged, and their cries pierced the shocked silence of those witnessing the sight of Stal in the air. Those peasants were ignorant of the demon that had risen on the edges of their riot, as they threw meager rocks at the tsar's horses; they knew not yet of Stal, so far away was he. But those he faced now, stopped by the appearance of the sight of the four-headed dragon horse, must be turned to him. The four-headed dragon horse now snorted great flames of fire. Some near the beast shuddered and turned indecisively. Should they be pummeled to the earth by the hooves of the tsar's men or follow this…this demon?

Thoughts formed in Stal's mind, and he shouted them into words—words he knew would have been his when he eventually grew into manhood, words that were now his from that memory yet to be formed. "The downtrodden were we but no more, for why should a rich man have all the gold? Why should some shiver in the cold under ragged cloth clothes while others have ten wools coats in their homes?" The strange pockmarked demon was speaking the words of Father Gapon.

Stal thought with certainty, *If you tell them what to think, they will,* for people were sheep, and he had read their hearts, filled with anger and envy. The Saber of Shadows had given him the power of deception. So the the ugly, stupid Crone had been right. He was their *savior*. Soon they would believe that good was evil and evil good. The giagantic four-headed dragon horse snarled. Stal felt the power of his rhetoric upon the growing crowd, and his words found the burning need in their souls.

Stal shouted, "Why should we roam the streets like starving dogs, smelling the rich broths and meats boiling in the homes of those who rule us? Why should we fall under the feet of the ruling class? We who have the strength of numbers? We who have the strength of will?"

Like a thick blanket, the gray light from the saber befuddled the crowd's thoughts. It seeped into their souls through their rage, their anger at their miserable poverty and those responsible for it. Their fury grew against those who held gold coins. Why not them? Why did their work give them nothing? Why were they no better off than the animals in the field? Why was fortune not at their grasp? They must slice the throats of the rich and grab for themselves what was after all theirs! That was the way. Stal heard these thoughts and rode the four-headed dragon horse in the air around the men and women.

Then he turned his fearsome beast toward the tsar's men. "Come comrades!" he exclaimed. "We shall kill the Cossacks and Tsar Nicolas himself and take all his gold, which is rightfully ours!" He raised the blade of his sword, and from it flew gold coins. The tattered men and women grabbed them greedily then turned their eyes toward Stal. *He is not Satan, surely, but one of God, for look how he gives*, the crowd thought, *and asks for nothing.* "Who is he? Who is he who fights for us?" those who hadn't seen the rise of Stal asked. "He fights for us against the Cossacks," some answered. Then he heard others say, "He is Stal, who comes to avenge the death of Father Gapon." Still others proclaimed, "He is Stal, sent to us from the heavens to overcome the tsar and his men who oppress us!" Finally Stal knew he had his army, for he heard in the screams of the peasant workers the cry of vengenance.

CHAPTER 17

asaru-alim-nuna—RISE of the forgotten mighty demons

Gilgamesh held his sacred spear aloft, toward the cold and shadowy darkness that was Kurnigi. He felt the strength of the spear forged by the eleven warrior gods; mighty was it in strength, and written within it was the story of valor. It gleamed a golden color with a tip that held a sharp, flickering, emerald flame. Gilgamesh had surged beyond the young *muktablu* to see what they would have to confront, leaving just behind him Eddie and the wandering children spirits. Deathly fingers of frigid air reached out in grasping tendrils, and a shiver ran through the king's giant blue frame. Gilgamesh turned around to tell the young *muktablu* his fears and saw him holding Death's scythe, arching it toward Kurnigi. But though the young warrior held the scythe firmly in his hand, Gilgamesh saw that the boy's eyes and heart weren't upon the coldness rising just beyond them but upon the angelic girl, the wandering spirit. Gilgamesh knew the heartbeats of first love beat their alluring rhythms in the young *muktablu.* He also knew the danger of this, for the *muktablu* was from the land of living and the girl from the land of the dead. As well, the *muktablu* didn't know exactly what he had agreed to when he had said he would travel the journey of the seven tears of which the wandering girl spirit had sung. Gilgamesh heard the words chanted by the wandering spirit children behind him and shivered.

> *Seven days is our*
> *journey from body to spirit,*
> *until the cold breath leaves us.*
> *Seven times our souls*
> *should be kindled.*
> *Seven tears shall we shed*
> *until we weep no more.*
> *Seven steps must we take*
> *until our we are freed*
> *from this sad land of the cursed,*
> *until we see the starlight*
> *dancing upon our mother's brow.*

The sad land of the fallen souls, Kurnigi. Though Gilgamesh was three-quarters god, he was also vulnerable as he was one-quarter mortal. *As I am a son of Lugalbanda, my blood holds death within it,* he thought, *but so am I three-quarters god, as the son of the goddess Ninsun, priestess once of Shamash.* Still the awfulness of Kurnigi drove daggers of trepidation into his heart.

Kurnigi was the land of no return, land of darkness and despair. Gilgamesh felt the pangs of sorrow for all the troubles of his people of Uruk, of how it must be for them and for Enkidu to wander in darkness. He must find Enkidu, lost to the shadows of death, and give to the people of Uruk eternal life, as Nana, the wise priestess of Uruk, had told them in the depths of Kurnigi. As the coldness of Kurnigi grew closer, it brought to the surface all that was dear to him. Gilgamesh remembered Nana's kind and wise face, brown and wrinkled like a walnut, ancient in age; she had worn the robes that told the story of the fate of the people of Uruk, how they withered under evil winds of disease. Again Gilgamesh thought of the brave Enkidu, his mortal friend, wracked with the ravages of the virulent disease that had descended upon Uruk—the valiant Enkidu who wouldn't let Gilgamesh journey alone into the forest of Humawa. And there, so many eons ago, Enkidu had taken his last mortal breath and plunged into the land of darkness. Where was Enkidu to be found, trapped somewhere in the endless depths of Kurnigi in the City of the Condemned? First they must find Utnapishtim, the old sage who held the secret to eternal life, lost to the dragons who ruled darkness and death—the secret herb of eternal life that would allow his people to again see the rays of light. Gilgamesh knew he must complete the journey that had begun thousands of years ago but was stopped as he lay trapped in the fragments of the Tables of Creation. *The Tablets of Creation.* Gilgamesh wondered where Mother Tiamat's fiendish son Marduk had hidden the true Seven Tablets of Creation that celebrated her and how impossible a task it was to find them. And where was the Hidden Daughter of Tiamat, who held the Twin Tablet of Destiny, that of light?

These thoughts troubled Gilgamesh greatly, for each task was enormous, and together they rang of the impossible. He had only his spear—mighty with the strength of the warrior gods true, but meager it seemed now as the cold winds of Kurnigi blew toward him. The cunning metal amulet of the red-haired child held much mystery and evil trickery, and perhaps it was as it was said, that the spirit in it knew where the Hidden Daughter lay. Gilgamesh thought now of how the red-haired child with the metal talisman and the brown owlet had been pulled to Kurnigi. He feared that Marduk may hold them now in his grasp. The eyes of the gentle Gilgamesh, king of Uruk, brimmed with anguish. He shook his long ropes of wild black hair, and his braided beard that fell upon his chest also quivered. Again he looked with worry at the young *muktablu*, whose head was bent toward the wandering spirit girl called Trina, his eyes filled with adoration.

Eddie heard the king speak into his mind, *Muktablu, beware of the wandering spirit girl,* but he ignored this. The king was a worrywart and needed to be a stronger warrior and not so afraid of everything. *Trina.* Eddie savored the name in his mind. *Trina.* She was a wandering spirit; he knew this. There was something unreal about her but not in a scary way like a ghost; something was just *different* about her. If he had known the word, Eddie would have thought, *Ethereal,* for Trina was a spirit in form, not blood, flesh, and bones. Trina was gentle and good; this Eddie knew by instinct.

The wandering spirit children sang behind them as they floated up and around Eddie and Trina in a protective half circle.

We laid our heads down as the living
and awoke as the dead,
in the land of dark and sleepy shadows,
in the land of misery and dread.

Then the spirits saw the land of Kurnigi looming before them. Eddie felt their waves of fear, and the spirit children uttered loud moans, as when the grips of a nightmare freeze all movement against danger. They floated back, cowering behind Eddie and Trina.

Trina spoke their thoughts softly. "We fear the rising land of darkness, fear its grasping hands that may soon be upon us. We fear that we shall be pulled into its depths, never to be released. Yet we must journey through it if we are to be freed."

"Don't worry," Eddie said. "I'll protect you." He felt the valor in this, to be the protector of the weak—this was his MOS. He raised Death's scythe, and the weapon that once had belonged to the land of Kurnigi swayed. Eddie felt the current of its awfulness writhe through the handle straight into his fingers like a python uncoiling. He used both hands to subdue it. *I am master!* he called out in his mind. Then he said confidently to Trina, "It'll be OK. We're going to find my friends, and we'll get you where you want to go too."

Trina smiled, and the smile suffused her face with light and hope.

Eddie wanted to ask her how and when she had become a spirit. He knew it must have been a long time ago by how old-fashioned her wool skirt looked. It was from another time and another country—not 1968, not Hackensack, New Jersey, like him. But Eddie couldn't find the right words and felt awkward about asking someone how they had died!

Trina spoke as if she heard his thoughts. "I am from the country of Georgia. We are not Russians, as others think, but our own people. My father was a merchant. I lived in a fine house with my mother and father. Though we were not Christians but Jews, we were never scorned. Then one day, when I was outside the church school, I was possessed by an evil spirit that my body could not hold. It was then I was taken and pulled into darkness, to wander as a spirit."

Eddie felt a deep sadness for Trina. "Oh," was all he could think of to say.

Trina again looked upon him with eyes filled with gratitude and wonder. "You are so young to be a *muktablu*."

Eddie paused. He wanted to say he was almost twelve, but that sounded ridiculous. Time had changed, and he knew he had as well since Mattie had found the Spyglass, since they had begun the journey on the Path of the Virtuous. He wanted to tell Trina all this—how he had yearned to be a brave warrior, a protector of the weak; how he had grasped Death's scythe and wondered whether he was strong enough to possess such a weapon. Instead Eddie said nothing, mesmerized as he was by Trina's hazel eyes with the little dashes of green; her hair, dark and smooth, that was tied back with a worn velvet ribbon; and her face that was so... gorgeous. This was all Eddie could think. He wanted tell Trina how he had grown strong on this journey that had begun so long ago in the basement of Sears in Hackensack; how his father was a warrior, somewhere in the jungles of Vietnam and commanded a platoon; how brave his father was and how much Eddie had learned from him. But all this lay caught in his mind, and his tongue seemed incapable of saying anything. Trina looked at Eddie again, and her eyes dropped down shyly. Eddie's heart beat a little faster. *She likes me!*

"*Muktablu!*" Gilgamesh's voice, loud with panic, broke into Eddie's thoughts as he ran back toward him. "See what arises before us!" The king thrust his spear at the approaching doom. There was movement in the dark wall of shadows that was Kurnigi—a wall that was both shadows and stones, a wall of beings that was moving toward them with a thunderous force.

Abaddon, Abaddon!
Liar and wretch!

The surface of Kurnigi was in chaos. The beast Ashurnasirpal had been battered by the rising wandering spirits, vengeful in their quest to grasp Abaddon. The Brotherhood of Evil had swirled in a black mist around the red-haired girl and the brown owlet child, only to let them fall from their grasp. The beast had snorted angrily as his hooves thudded into the ground of Kurnigi, away from the spinning stupidity of the Brotherhood of Evil. Abaddon had heard the call of the living and escaped through it, and the beast saw how he had lassoed the red-haired girl and the owlet who clung to her. *Fools!* The beast Ashurnasirpal pounded his hooves again. Khan thudded next to him with his followers behind, his large, askew, almond eyes surprised by the thundering sounds that rose around him on the surface of Kurnigi.

"Beast—" Khan began.

But the beast snorted a warning, a large foul flame that sizzled as it went through his wet nostrils. "Quiet!"

Khan's anger showed upon his face; he was not to be spoken to by a foul beast of burden in his manner! He was Khan of the Huns! But before he could give voice to his displeasure, the Duke of Muscovy and the Prince of Wallachia were upon them, sliding out of the spinning mist above. Their followers—the cruel legions of those who tormented and tortured others and had pledged themselves to the prince and duke—spun out wildly, thrown by radiating forces to the earth below them.

The ground of Kurnigi split into a wide chasm with a sound like the jarring shriek of the dead. The Brotherhood of Evil were tossed first into the ground that lay asunder then upward by a force that rose beneath them. Cries exploded in the air.

Asaru-alim-luna!
We have risen,
mighty once more
and not forgotten!

Beneath them the old demons were gods rising up, and upon them the Brotherhood of Evil fell and were carried, up and out. Some were missing limbs, some heads; some rode creatures that had three legs or were headless; some produced thunder and rain from their mouths, others maggots. Thousands upon thousands rode up and out. Some had the heads of rodents, others scorpions, others faces of bones. All were ancient forms who once had held man in fear and had received flesh and blood as sacrifice. Some had pointed ears and faces like dragons; some possessed scorpion tails that ended in sharp points; some rode upon strange steeds that were wolf in face, and equine in body; others rode tremendous black flying sea creatures, serpents, or crocodiles. These ancient demon gods of death and destruction let loose upon Kurnigi. They rose, and all around them, the Brotherhood of Evil were batted about and heard the cry of the demons.

The prince of Demons
frees us!
Asaru-alim-nuna!
Mighty are we once more!
Asaru-alim-nuna!

These old demon gods rose up with a fury from the dark depths of Kurnigi. They rose in blind ferocity. They rose and collided into one another, crashed into the still rising vengeful wandering spirits in search of Abaddon and cried out again and again:

Abaddon, Abaddon!
Liar and wretch!

The groaning chaos that was the black rising wall of stones and spirits of the old demon gods moved up and out of Kurnigi. They moved as a force—a seething collision of the cold winds of the old demons with the hot winds of doom of the vengeful spirits. The old demon gods screeched again and again in their terrible voices, old and hoarse, voices that hadn't rung in an unknown number of millennia.

Asaru-alim-nuna!
Mighty are we once more!
Asaru-alim-nuna!

The beast heard the words. He instinctively felt for the burr on the side of his mouth; the droplet remained. He couldn't stay here; he knew the old demon gods sought the droplet but didn't know he had it—not yet. In the chaos of the collision of the old demon gods and the vengeful spirits seeking Abaddon, there was the opportunity for the beast's escape, for the demon gods moved away, like a great black wave, from the vengeful spirits. They heard the cry of the prince of demons, to whom they would travel. The beast jumped into the rising wind of the vengeful wandering spirits near him, away from the demon gods, and was taken upward.

The Prince of Wallachia, batted hither and thither by the wind, saw the beast escape. He called to the others, "We cannot let the beast go! For see how he is already tricking us by his escape!" The prince plunged into the wind of the vengeful spirits with his followers, and soon the khan and duke, along with their legions, leaped into the maelstrom of spirits.

But the beast didn't fully know who and what the old demon gods were, for they were all so different in appearance. The oldest ones had just awakened from the stone walls that had imprisoned them deep within the labyrinth of the tunnels. They had risen last from the now still ground of the underworld to see that their brethren demon gods had left them to writhe upon the gray ground of Kurnigi. Even among the old demon gods, they were held in low regard, thought to be just above maggots in their place in the song of death. These demons of death and destruction, older than the cave gods even, were so old that mortal men didn't worship them but had known their presence as one knows primeval fear. They hadn't drawn their images but instinctively had recognized them as the creatures that moved silently and unseen in the seas where they swam. These ancient demon gods had heads that were of sharks upon bodies of pythons; their skin was scaled and the color of the murky depths of still water. It was they who smelled the droplet in the mouth of the beast. They rose up into the air, as silently as they had in the days when they lived in the sea; they then slithered into the wave of the vengeful spirits.

𒐊𒐖𒐚𒐖𒐊𒐖

Red orbs rose in the sky and cast an eerie light upon the gray, smoldering bleakness of Kurnigi and upon the spirits that remained there, moving like maggots upon carrion. These were the sundry spirits of the underworld tossed up and out of the depths of Kurnigi who were neither followers of the Brotherhood of Evil nor victims of Abaddon; nor were they old demon gods. From the reaches of the sky over the splintered land of Kurnigi, Marduk's eyes glittered over these remaining spirits. Kurnigi, the land of darkness, was falling asunder with the escape of so many spirits, but Marduk's power was great, for he still held his Twin Tablet of Destiny firmly to his breast. Marduk had seen the beast Ashurnasirpal plunge into the mass of escaping vengeful spirits. But the beast was stupid and cursed with shortsightedness. Marduk didn't know the extent of the treachery plotted by the beast and didn't care, for in the eons the beast had schemed against him time and again, only to have his effort result in the gain of Marduk and the further loss and degradation of the beast. So it was that Marduk was content to have the beast spin his plots again, as he knew they would fail once more. No power did the old demons have, nor would they ever, Marduk vowed, for once caught again, as they would surely be, the Dark Master would crush them to dust and fling it into the abyss, the dark and powerful force of evil that held no form, no substance. In doing so, however, Marduk would lose them as his inhabitants of the underworld, but at least they never again would be able to rise against him.

The souls of darkness always would be under the dominion of the Master of the Dark World. He would remain that master, the old demon gods would see soon enough. The old demons gods had tried but lost their right to rule the Dark Underworld. Marduk had fought and won this right; he had plunged Mother Tiamat into obscurity and made it so that humanity had uttered her name in its desecrated forms—Tiamet, Tiamut; then it was forgotten. She became nothing but an ancient tale, a powerless myth, while he Marduk rose and had in humanity's minds names upon names: Baal, Satan, Bile, Azazel, Ravana, Dagan, Mormo, Mictian, Balaam. In those who didn't believe in the spirit world he had his strongest allies—those who lived righteously in selfishness.

Marduk's red orbs shone brighter with his anger and bitterness toward the Great Mother. She had given just one Tablet of Destiny to him and left the other in the hands of his sister, the Hidden Sister, the Hidden Daughter of Tiamat. He bemoaned that the Great Spirit had given free will to man; but for that, Marduk could have grabbed their souls with brutal force. But for that.

Chaos was reigning in the world of light and darkness. The escaped condemned souls were Marduk's and Marduk's alone and soon would be brought back, and new souls would be added to his tally—new souls that the serpent was cultivating greater than time had written it as destiny before. Death's scythe soon would be returned to him, for no living being could hold it under his sway. The Spyglass would be taken away from the forces of light and reveal the whereabouts of the Hidden Sister. Then soon Marduk would possess both Tablets of Destiny. Then the sky of heaven would be his, and he would be the all-powerful one.

The thief, that red-haired girl protected by the wizard and the White Book of Magic, would be destroyed, and she and Biddle would be thrown into the black abyss of nothingness. The River of Time had been set to chaos, but this new story of mortal souls would be written so that he, Marduk, ruled supreme, and darkness would rule with an iron fist. The red orbs shone again in evil pleasure. Yes, like a tower of dominos the story of light would topple. But Marduk, in his arrogance, had forgotten that the strength of one's power was held at its weakest point. He didn't know that the beast Ashurnasirpal possessed the droplet that held the tale of his birth or that the demon gods sought it.

Mattie's head hit the top of the rafters. Then she was thrown to the side, then pulled into the torrent of wind created by the vengeful spirits. She was spinning like a top; her head felt dizzy and hot. The screams of the living, which combined with the dead, richoted in chilling notes in the shabby Harlem auditorium that had just moments before been the dominion of the fraudulent psychic Madame Lina. It was now filled with the vindictive spirits of those who sought Abaddon. Chaos reigned, the dead with their fierce gales enveloping all, ghouls crazed with vengence and moved to hot rage by the sight of Abaddon, who had tricked them in their mortal lives to surrender their souls, cheated them of the mortal pleasure that was purchased, and plunged them into the worst depths of Kurnigi. Their anger raged and erupted in volcanic proportions. The spirits collided into one another, each frenzied by the desire to seize for themselves Abaddon and throw him into the Corkscrew of Terror. It was the fury of the rageful possessed with one goal—to capture and torment Abaddon with all manner of cruelty, for he should suffer tenfold what they had endured. They roared in frustration when Abaddon took on the form of vapor and escaped their grasp.

The Spyglass was battered by the force of the malevolent wind beneath her. She felt the power of the fury of the condemned souls against Abaddon. She thought of herself first, last, and foremost, and her ruthlessness knew no bounds. Only once, in a moment of an emotion that she didn't understand, had she saved Mattie by giving her one of her precious gold bands. *Mattie*. That silly girl she had just abandoned to be destroyed by Abaddon. As she was buffetted by the rising winds of the dead, doubt raised its head in the mind of the ever duplicitous Spyglass. What was she thinking? The new soul she sought was that of the false psychic, Madame Lina, who lay on the floor unconcious to all. That stupid woman couldn't withstand the magnet that the possessor of the Spyglass became to the forces of the evil underworld. Madame Lina would break at once, and Spyglass would become prey to any grasping hand. And also the Spyglass could foresee the imprint of the snake Gneezy upon Madame Lina's hand; the snake would only too soon wring the neck of a Madame Lina and capture the Spyglass. Madame Lina didn't have the wizard Biddle with the White Book of Magic, protector of Mattie and de facto of the Spyglass.

She had willingly surrendered Mattie to Abaddon. Fear stabbed her. *Mistake, mistake, mistake,* she chastised herself. Grabbing any soul might do in times that were not treacherous, but such was not the present. In letting Mattie to fall to the clutches of Abaddon, in abandoning her in the service of a plan to get a new soul, Spyglass was now caught in the whirlwind of the dead and without the protection of a living soul. Without such a soul, she knew she would be pulled down to Kurnigi within the maelstrom of the spirits. And then she would fall right into the control of the snake Gneezy then Marduk. Spyglass shuddered.

Hidden in this metal prison, she had escaped that fate in the past and had sought to take over a soul she could possess. If she could find such a soul, it would free her and bring back her memories regarding who she was and where the Hidden Sister was. The Spyglass knew that Marduk sought her for this knowledge and that he wished to grasp both Tablets of Destiny. But that knowledge was elusive; it lay under the depths of her memory, and the Spyglass couldn't bring it to the surface. She needed freedom from this metal prison and to be possessor of a soul. Then Spyglass knew she would have free will and with it the ability to bring back the memories formed when she also had a soul, before she was trapped in the metal tube—but by whom and why, she couldn't remember, such was the power of the curse of her imprisonment. If Spyglass could possess a soul, she could destroy the Hidden Sister and grab the Twin Tablet of Destiny from her. But now it seemed all over, swirling as she was in the sea of the dead and surely soon in the grasp of darkness.

The howling of the winds of the spirits blew stronger and stronger as more and more dead souls rose through the earth into the theater. The force pulled up the seats bolted to the auditorium floor, ripped the curtains from the rafters, lifted the very boards of the stage, and dashed the scrambling men and women against the walls. Geeta was caught in a whirlwind, her thin legs moving in rapid bicyling movements to keep from being flung to the walls. Amid the chaos of the howling spirits, Geeta beseeched, *Oh, ThaTha! Help me! Help me!* So strong was the storm that she could barely see Mattie battered about above her. Geeta heard her old ThaTha's voice. *Know that the splendor of the sun that shines forth in the universe, the moon that brightens the dark sky, and the fire, which burns brightly, are the entire One. The ocean of the mortal world has neither real truth nor order.* Geeta's eyes brimmed with tears. *Oh, ThaTha,* she thought, *these words are wise but are not helping to save us!* Her black braids whipped out in the wind, and her vision blurred behind her thick glasses from the tears she steeled herself to control. She had to use ThaTha's message to save her friend. *There is no one here to help Mattie but you,* Geeta thought. *You must not cry. It is time to think in a rational manner and not let emotions cloud your judgment.* Again Geeta heard ThaTha's words—*In the battlefield for the soul, whether there is to be eternal order or chaos in the cosmos, one who fights her dharma loses, not just for herself but for all.* Dharma. Geeta's head spun. Dharma. Duty. Her thinking remained foggy.

Oh, what a disaster this was! Why couldn't she understand ThaTha's message? *One who fights her dharma loses, not just for herself but for all.* Who was it that ThaTha meant? How was she fighting her duty? Geeta thought, *Oh, you must guide me, ThaTha! I am lost.* Then ThaTha's voice came to her again. *When despair stares you in the face, when the obstacles seem insurmountable, realize, Geeta, that all is Maya.* This situation was utterly impossible. That was the reality.

Flying above Geeta, the evil Abaddon was being chased by horrific ghouls and had transformed from material form into a black vapor, barely discernible and careening toward the Spyglass. Mattie remained bound by the ropes with which Abaddon had lassoed her. She was horizontal and revolving around and around. She felt the gale pushing her about, and the screeches of the vengeful spirits filled her ears. The sounds were wild and angry, the atmosphere dark and smoky. Where was Geeta? Mattie thought only of that mean thing with the rat face and yellow eyes that had those long black nails and how it could hurt Geeta. How small and skinny Geeta was, and how her glasses were always lopsided on her face so that she couldn't quite see what was in front of her. And there was no Eddie to protect Geeta. Geeta was book smart—she could get straight As and knew all the words in Mrs. Elmwood's fifth-grade Vocabulary Garden—but she didn't know how to fight.

Mattie's thoughts spun with her body. She had to save Geeta! But how? Here Mattie felt resentment rise. Look at all the trouble that Spyglass had caused. Oh, that Spyglass! She felt such anger toward the Spyglass that it overtook any fear she had. She twisted her head down and struggled against the ropes that cut into her arms. She had to get free. Mattie pushed against the tornado-force winds to fall down to where she thought the stage was. She had to find Geeta, get her to cut her free, and maybe they could run out of here. *Find Mr. Biddle. Find Eddie.* These thoughts passed through Mattie's mind as her body was thrown about in the winds of churling chaos of spirits above, below, and around her. Then something cold and metal hit her head. The force threw her into the path of a falling rafter, into which her head banged with a fierce force. First Mattie saw stars; then her eyes rolled back as she fell into unconsciousness.

The Spyglass was startled as she collided into the head of a living creature. Mattie! In a quick flash Spyglass burrowed herself into Mattie's frizzy red hair. Mattie, in her unconsciousness, didn't register the Spyglass. Abaddon's keen yellow eyes alighted upon the Spyglass. Seeing where the Spyglass had burrowed, he turned into material form again. With his claw hands, he grabbed Mattie's hair, his nails raking her head, searching for the Spyglass. Mattie was oblivious to the pain. The Spyglass felt the nearness of Abaddon, inches from her. Mattie had to be awakened. She had to take posession of her, become her Mistress once more, as Spyglass drew from the living soul the energy for her power. The Spyglass's eyes glistened in determination, and bolts of light shot from them. Abaddon's claw hands drew back. He snarled at the pain, his bat wings flapping behind him. But it was just momentary. He again plunged his long black nails into Mattie's head, scraping her scalp, despite the bolts that the Spyglass threw at him. The Spyglass's eyes widened in fear; she needed Mattie awake in order to harness her full power. *Stupid girl!* she cried out. *Awaken!* But Mattie lay inert. The forms of the vengeful spirits saw that Abaddon was above them. Their cold fingers reached up, and in a mass they sprang to grab him.

Sir Austen Henry Layard was borne high by the winds of fate figuratively and more immediately by the ghastly spirits that had risen and thrown them over a strange city that glittered below. The night sky was starless and moonless. He clasped hard the unconscious female he had hefted over his shoulders. He felt something hit his face, cold and slimy, and saw the vague outlines of the frog-like foot of George Smith. *Ah, Smith, what bargain you made with Satan, that you should be so plagued!* Then he thought, *It was you, Henry, who knew of the fires of heaven as you called them, the divine vengeance and wars between the gods when you unearthed the mound of rubbish in Nineveh.* He also had known that under the mounds were the subterranean passages of evil. He had heard the moans of the dead and the snarls of the wild beasts of the darkness that guarded those tunnels. He had known that the passages were haunted yet had drawn the map of them born of the journeys he had taken while in sleep. But in the search of the forbidden, he had found her. *Her.* Oh, to see her eyes, pools of dark brown, again! Those eyes had held him enthralled; in the very beats of his heart, he knew her as his true love, from lives he had lived and no longer remembered but had seen reflected in her eyes. *Lady of my soul.* Sir Henry Layard was roused out of these thoughts by the grasp of a hand upon his ankle—a living hand.

"You...you...scoundrel!" He heard the gasping utterances, which he knew to have come from Paddy O'Reilly—the ill-fated O'Reilly, whose bumbling expeditions and curiosity had led to these catastrophic events. "Dottie!" he heard the man cry, and the woman upon his shoulders moaned in response. Sir Henry felt his body being jerked down and heard Paddy O'Reilly scream. He felt the spirits, a great foaming whirlpool, swirling down fast into the building below them. The colliding vengeful spirits were such that Sir Henry could no longer see what was below him. He heard the splintering of wood and felt bricks flying below.

Pandemonium reigned all around Geeta on the floor of the deathly auditorium. Her glasses were askew, her braids hitting her face like whips as the spirits roared about her. The sounds of the shrieking spirits had grown to deafening proportions, their battered forms by the hundreds filling the theater; the people around her pushing, screaming, trying to escape. She saw glimpses of the familiar frizzy red hair and the creature with the four fingers grabbing Mattie's head, but Mattie wasn't moving. A startling thought grasped Geeta's heart—was Mattie dead? Cold ghostly fingers, belonging to snarling spirits, with sharp teeth and bloody faces were pulling the creature whose hands had burrowed into the hair of Mattie, who lay unconscious. Geeta's heart was pounding hard. "Mattie!" she screamed. Oh, what to do!

The Spyglass saw her chance. The vengeful spirits wanted Abaddon, and Abaddon they would have. She summoned all the power she had and threw out bolts of hot flames toward the evil rodent-faced creature. Then the flames enveloped Mattie, melting the ropes that bound her. The heat brought Mattie back to consciousness. "Aaagh!" Mattie's cry caught in her throat, as her eyes saw flames all around her. She flapped her hands and legs. *Free!* She was free! Then she felt something clinging to her head, and as her hand went up, immediately in it was the Spyglass. Spyglass looked straight into Mattie's eyes and shed elephant tears, full and as false of contriteness as such a creature of manipulation that she was could produce. Mattie's eyes narrowed, and she went to fling the Spyglass away. But Spyglass wasn't going to count only upon pulling Mattie's heartstrings. No, the Spyglass made her sure her metal body had small curved nails that plunged into Mattie's hand and secured themselves firmly. "Ow!" Mattie cried out in pain. Her face was red and hot, and her hand hurt where the Spyglass had plunged her nails into her. Abaddon's grasp on Mattie was lost, pulled as he was by the vengeful spirits on one side and thwarted by the hot flames on the other. The cold hands surrounded Abaddon about the neck, and the spirits laughed in triumph.

Abaddon! Abaddon!
Wretch and fiend!
Suffer will you now!

Geeta heard the words of her old ThaTha and grappled for their meaning. *Maya. Illusion. Maya. Illusion. What is real is unreal, and what is unreal is real.* How was this an illusion? To emphasize that point, the ceiling of the old auditorium cracked wide open as the floor below move backward and forward and split. Geeta felt her legs give way as the ground below her opened, and the people in the auditorium screamed as they fell downward. Above her the roof of the building exploded. Then Geeta felt a volcanic force lift her and throw her up high in the air. The cold wind hit her face sharply as more and more deadly spirits erupted from the ground around the theater. They went through her, chilling her very soul. Geeta saw Mattie being tugged up by the Spyglass, who was again in her hand! Mattie was alive, and this thought filled Geeta with relief. "Mattie!" Geeta called out then remembered when Mr. Biddle had spoken to them through their thoughts. *Mattie, beware the Spyglass!* Geeta thought. *She tried to have you killed!*

Spirits released from Kurnigi rose from the ruptured ground below; they rose up and out of the roofless auditorium and hit the swirling spirits who clasped Abaddon. They carried with them Mattie and Geeta. All rose from the torn auditorium into the starless, moonless New York City sky. Within them they held the beast, followed by the Brotherhood of Evil. It was a whirlwind of anger—a force that, once released, held unimaginable destruction, much as a shattered atom does. Abaddon felt the cold, clammy grasp of hands upon him, death hands that would exact a ruthless revenge upon him. The rat-faced Abaddon's yellow eyes bulged. His bat-like wings flapped helplessly, kept down by the vengeful spirits who clasped him.

Sir Austen Henry Layard felt the force of the eruption in the building below. They were above in the sky, carried by the current of spirits. He cried out to Paddy, "We're doomed to be captured by these ghouls!" George Smith, just beyond him, was being drawn into the vortex of the churning spirits, for right in front of them, rising out of a roofless building, were thousands of souls churning in a whirlpool of death. Then they collided right into the mass of vindictive spirits rising from the auditorium. Sir Henry felt himself become unbalanced by the tugging of the foolish Paddy O'Reilly upon his leg; he was losing the grasp upon the woman he held. A gust of wind turned Paddy's pudgy body completely upside down. "Aaagh!" he cried out, and let go of Sir Henry's foot.

Then the yellow-eyed demon Abaddon saw his escape, for flying toward them upon the winds of hate were more vengeful souls but who held living creatures. Abaddon had learned the tricks of the condemned when he had been imprisoned within the reaper's robes. He remembered those whose forehead was marked with death who had tried to cheat the reaper; in the twilight of their life, they would clasp hard the living soul, and thus delay their entry into Kurnigi. The creatures of death who held Abaddon would be powerless—at least momentarily—if he could adhere himself to a living creature. Then Abaddon felt it, the warmth of the blood that ran in a living soul as it hit the spirits who held him. The beats of the living heart rang in his foul, sharp, horned ears. It was Paddy. The ghostly souls drew back surprised, and Abaddon seized the moment. He used one free hand, and his four foul black nails reached out and plunged into Paddy. Paddy yowled in surprise.

The beast Ashurnasirpal, within the vengeful souls that rose up, saw Abaddon in the midst, holding on to the one that was his prey. And the beast snorted in great anger and plunged upward toward them, fighting the crazied ghouls.

Below him the Brotherhood of Evil saw what beast was doing. The Prince of Wallachia held his velvet hat to his head in one hand, and the other pale bloodless hand with its vile rings with bloody eyes reached out to the beast. "Beast!" the prince cried out. "Seek not Abaddon now, for see what is below us!" There below them rose the ancient primeval demons—the ones with bodies of pythons and heads of sharks—in a straight path. The python bodies of the demon gods sprang to wrap themselves around the beast Ashurnasirpal. Though they were but seven in number, they had in their shark mouths a thousand sharp teeth open to capture him. Khan's almond eyes bulged at the strength of primordial evil that emanated from the demons. He wondered what it was that the beast held that these serpent demons sought. As did the duke. And as did the prince. And each of the Brotherhood of Evil wondered how he could wrest it from the beast. The duke's spear plunged into their python bodies, and the prince threw his stakes into the demon gods. All their attempts were to no avail, for the demons gods wrapped themselves more firmly around Ashurnasirpal.

Amid the storm, the Spyglass felt her power grow, as she was bound with Mattie again. Escape—they had to escape from here before Abaddon came toward them again. But how? For they were caught in a torrent of vengeful spirits. Mattie angrily shook the hand that grasped the Spyglass so she could drop it. Then she saw the webbed feet of George Smith fly by. *The flying frog!* Mattie thought. Her mother must be nearby. Somewhere within the churning chaos, Dottie heard Paddy's yell. It awakened Dottie, who lay upon the shoulders of Sir Henry Layard. She reached her hands out. "Paddy!"

Tossed about by the spirits, Sir Henry strengthened his grasp. "Madam!" he cried. "My grasp will loosen if you struggle so!" But Dottie's eyes were keen, and looking down below, she caught a horrific sight—Paddy below her, a creature with flapping batlike wings and a rodent face, with its teeth sunk into Paddy's arm. The creature's leg was in the mouth of the beast who had captured him, and the engulfing serpent sharks were winding their bodies around the beast.

"Paddy! Paddy!" Dottie called out. "Oh, please help him!"

Mattie heard her mother's voice above her, somewhere in the black New York City sky, where dim forms were lit by the ghostly spirits who whirled in chaos. "Mom!" she called, and struggled to move toward the voice. Mattie fought to fly up against the spiraling chaos of the spirits. She saw the dim outlines of her mother flying above her, over the shoulder of someone; it wasn't her dad. Her mother's arms were reaching downward. "Mom!" Mattie called out again. A great funnel of energy grabbed her, and below her Mattie saw Geeta's braids and then her small, thin, brown face looking up. She felt a wave of relief.

Geeta was rapidly being moved up by the current—a current that was something beyond the force of the spirits that drew them up into the sky. She saw Mattie, like her, being pulled up, and as she moved up, she saw the beast holding Abaddon and Paddy O'Reilly. *Mattie!* Geeta called to her in her mind. *Your father is here! He has been captured by the creature!* Mattie turned downward to see Geeta just beneath her, in the funnel of energy that was taking them somewhere.

Mattie pointed the Spyglass toward Paddy and said, "Spyglass! Get him free!" The Spyglass's eyes were turned downward, beyond Paddy, and looked in horror at the scene of the Great Beast Ashurnasirapal in the clasp of hideous creatures and Abaddon holding the mortal Paddy. But why should she do anything? They could all destroy one another—that was best! The silly girl didn't understand that the beast, like Abaddon, was their enemy. Mattie's eyes narrowed as she saw that the Spyglass did nothing. She threw her body downward, pointing the Spyglass right at Paddy, feeling how the Spyglass struggled against her. *No,* the Spyglass resolved. *I will show this girl who is Mistress and who is slave. She will obey me!* Then the Spyglass jerked Mattie up.

Geeta saw all of this, moving as she was into the spiral of current that held Mattie. She was pulled into it and found herself being sucked upward, just a few feet below Mattie, who struggled against the Spyglass's hold upon her hand.

The eyes of the Brotherhood of Evil turned as one toward Mattie, who was pointing the Spyglass at the captured Paddy, in the teeth of Abaddon and in turn in the teeth of the beast Ashurnasirpal. Their eyes were taken away from the sickening sight of the serpent sharks binding Ashurnasirpal. The red-haired child was here! They saw the Spyglass in her hands. But without Ashurnasirpal's protective chant against the eyes and grasp of Marduk, even if they possessed the Spyglass, it soon would be lost. But here greed outweighed caution. They jumped in unison to grab Mattie, flying against the swirling ghouls, toward the current that was carrying the red-haired one with the metal amulet clasped to her hand.

Waves of terror ran through Geeta when she looked up to see was happening just above her, the Brotherhood of Evil inches away from grabbing Mattie. Oh, but if Geeta really was the princess of the gypsies and had magical powers to save Mattie! Then ThaTha's words rang in her ears. *Maya. Illusion. What is real is unreal, and what is unreal is real. The power of the universe is in your grasp.* Geeta grabbed the black Card of Time from her dress pocket, the Card of Time that had remained inert. *What is real is unreal, and what is unreal is real.* She flung it up into the air. *The power of the universe is in your grasp.*

"Card of of Time, take form and take us away!" Geeta cried.

The black card flew from her hands like a crow against the current that held her. It turned and fell downward to Geeta, black and slick. Still just a card. Geeta saw the Brotherhood of Evil struggling against the spirits, their hands outreached toward Mattie, surrounding her on all sides.

"Card of of Time, take form and take us away!" she cried again.

The card turned transparent like glass then transformed into a flying hourglass. Geeta gasped. Oh, no! It was taking the form of time! No…no…but it was too late. The hourglass was permeable and flew straight into Geeta and enveloped her into its shape, and then it flew straight up into Mattie and engulfed her. Both girls fell plop down to the glass floor of the giant hourglass. Outside the hands of the Brotherhood of Evil reached into the flying hourglass where the two girls were now held, but they hit glass, for now the hourglass was solid. The angry faces of the duke, prince, and khan surrounded them. But though Geeta and Mattie were safe from the evil grasp of those beyond them, they were trapped in a giant hourglass. They stood up as the sands of time poured onto their heads from above and gathered and grew at their feet.

Mattie's mouth opened in alarm. "What did you do?" she asked Geeta.

Geeta's eyes were wide, stunned as she was by the transformation of the Card of Time. She sputtered, "It was the Card of Time." The snarling faces of the Brotherhood of Evil flew about them, their hands striking the hourglass. Then it turned, upside down then right side up again. "Aaagh!" both girls cried, for now the sands of time poured over them with a vengeance.

Mattie shook the Spyglass. But even Spyglass, had she been willing, couldn't release them from the hourglass, for the Card of Time had come from the White Book of Magic. Geeta's heart sank as she choked on the sand that filled her mouth. Oh, what a perilous thing time was. Again Geeta heard ThaTha's words. *In the battlefield for the soul, whether there is to be eternal order or chaos in the cosmos, one who fights her dharma loses, not just for herself but for all.* Dharma. Geeta's head spun. Dharma. Oh, what did ThaTha mean? Then the current increased in force and spun the hourglass until Geeta and Mattie saw nothing outside of their sphere, only blackness.

𒀭𒄑𒉆𒊩

The beast Ashurnasirpal felt the strength of demon sharkpythons as they wrapped around him and sunk their teeth into his body. He kept his bull teeth upon the scaled leg of Abaddon. The beast caught sight of the demon creatures, their murky scaled bodies. Who were they? At first he had thought they were emissaries of Marduk, sent to capture him. But their smell was strong of death, foul and sharp. And then a memory awoke in him. Ashurnasirpal felt the first stirrings of understanding, a deep primitive memory. By this instinct he knew it was the droplet they sought, though why he didn't know, for in his grasp the droplet only served to hide him and the Brotherhood of Evil from Marduk. The beast sensed these creatures sought the droplet as a wild hungry animal does its prey. But he wouldn't give it up so easily. He sunk his teeth deeper into the scaly leg of Abaddon, who in turn kept a firm grasp on Paddy. Then with his tongue he found the droplet. Yes. The droplet. They would never have it. He would say the chant, for it would protect him. Though it would also show Marduk what he held, there was no choice. He then whispered the desecrated names of Marduk.

Ankia-en-lugal,
Ugug,
Umum,

Tudu,
Udud,
Gar-gash,
Bilulu-en.

The words that had formed through clenched teeth upon Abaddon were heard by the demon shark-serpents, and they fell back at the sound. A yellow cast fell over the beast, Abaddon, and the hapless Paddy, who cried in pain.

Ankia-en-lugal, Ugug, Umum, Tudu, Udud, Gar-gash, Bilulu-en. The words had formed into the ancient symbols and wove around the yellow cast. The serpents heard the desecrated names of Marduk, who had imprisoned them, and unwrapped their python bodies from the beast. Their bodies, long and fierce, swam in the air around the Ashurnasirpal and twisted up in unison—the seven ghastly creatures of the murky, slimy depths. Quickly they rose toward the words that slashed the air around the beast in a web of protection.

Ankia-en-lugal, Ugug, Umum, Tudu, Udud, Gar-gash, Bilulu-en. The seven serpent sharks opened their mouths again but not to bite. Words formed from their teeth, and they said, "We are Ankia-en-lugal, Ugug, Umum, Tudu, Udud, Gar-gash, and Bilulu-en. And to he who first calls us after our long sleep we belong."

The beast's bull face wore astonishment at the serpent-sharks. He had unclasped his hold on Abaddon, who with Paddy, was suspended in the yellow orb, and both looked fearfully at the great python-sharks that swam just outside. These seven serpent-sharks of the murky depths swam in a circle around the yellow web, opened their mouths with a thousand sharp shark teeth, and spoke with heads bowed to the beast. "We submit to you,

Master." Before the beast could respond, a thunderous sound filled the air. He saw above him the red glowing orbs of Marduk. *Though I see you now, beast, I have heard your treachery, and for this you will pay.*

But Marduk's promise of torture was not to be heard, for he spoke as if he still ruled all. The red orbs of Marduk glowered in surprised displeasure as the sky shook. From the land of Kurnigi, the great foes of Marduk, Asaru-alim-nuna, had risen, and Marduk's orbs dimmed. Then the shroud blackness fell onto everyone and engulfed all who were flying in the night sky—from the Brotherhood of Evil; to the beast and his new servants; to Abaddon; to Paddy, Dottie, Sir Henry, and Smith; and to all the vengeful spirits who had risen. The River of Time rang in notes of chaos and threw them into the destiny that would no longer wait. The Great Battle would now begin.

CHAPTER 18

the cape of ša nagba īmuru

Herman Biddle's cape glittered from within, as the cold wind blew it back from his shoulders. If mystery held a color, if the mythical could be said to pose a hue, then this cape did so, for it was like that of a reflecting moon upon a placid night ocean hinting at the depths below, at a power that could be unleashed but was held in abeyance. Biddle knew the Russian landscape by instinct, though he could see none of it now. He heard a train in the distance. It must be the royal train moving toward Tsarskoye Selo. Was Tsar Nicolas on this train? The silvery-white horse he rode upon pounded the snow-covered ground with a fury that made his teeth clatter.

There was darkness all around, offset only by the glow of the animal he rode and the cape that flew behind his shoulders. Biddle held tightly to the reins as he glanced back and felt relief. Wigglesworth and Rasputin were mounted similarly upon silvery-white horses, riding fast against the cold wind. Herman Biddle didn't question how they had come upon horses; the chant had been potent, and he knew that time was short. The Path of the Virtuous had thrown him and Wigglesworth away from Kurnigi. Where were Mattie, Eddie, and Geeta? Could the king of Uruk protect them?

In the velvet blackness, Biddle felt a sharp chill stab his soul. Who knew how the events of Bloody Sunday had progressed, altered as everything now was by the River of Time churning in chaos? It must be the royal train, carrying the tsar, or the chant wouldn't have sent them here. The tsar rode the royal trains, heavily guarded, and he and his family were rarely at the largely ceremonial Winter Palace in St. Petersburg. Still chaos had churned events, and whether the tsar was en route, away from the Winter Palace, or already at Tsarskoye Selo and the Alexander Palace was unknown. These thoughts ran swiftly through Herman Biddle's mind. The tsar had to be brought back to St Petersburg to the Winter Palace square to appease the Russian people, to give the peace they asked for. Biddle prayed that the events of Bloody Sunday hadn't occurred; that he, Rasputin, and Wigglesworth were arriving before Father Gapon made his plea, before the Cossacks shot into the unarmed crowd. Biddle felt the stab of alarm; for events to turn in the direction of lightness, away from the evil of the Dark Master, Tsar Nicolas had to make Father Gapon his ally and have peace reign. The tsar must not blunder, as he had in the story as it was written in the times past. Then the tsar would never be martyred; then the godlessness that filled Russia with its bitterness, its bleakness could be averted.

Then maybe those other events could be prevented, those whose history was written in the blood of millions, felled in the world war that didn't end all wars but only set the stage for the next one. Perhaps horrific next conflict could be averted, World War II, when evil ruled supreme and souls were given over to Satan by the millions by their leaders, when Russia seized lands under fierce coercion, when a ruthless man with a pockmarked face ruled with an iron fist. No, not iron—he was of steel, impenetrable to the agonies of others. Steel. The hand of the Dark Master, the force of evil that had written the story with that blood, had garnered so easily the millions of souls that now were the strength of its wickedness. He had snatched their souls from the dry, dusty world, where God had been banished, and where agape, pure love born of empathy for another died under division, was replaced with suspicion by each man of another. Biddle's brow furrowed in worry. Had they changed much on the Second Stone when the Night of the Broken Glass was thwarted? For it seemed that the hand of Gneezy was strong upon them. Though Uri Gneezy didn't have the Spyglass, the beast Ashurnasirpal held Dottie and Paddy in the land of darkness, Kurnigi. Paddy and Dottie were lures that Marduk would have his minions keep imprisoned to get Mattie into their trap. Biddle thought woefully of how by now it may well be that held Mattie, Geeta, and Eddie were held captive somewhere in Kurnigi, for they had traveled there with the king of Uruk. Could he harness the power of the White Book of Magic and somehow find them again?

Biddle glanced back again to make certain Wigglesworth was still mounted upon the horse and saw the portly figure teetering upon the animal. The first thing Rufus Wigglesworth registered with alarm was that he was on a horse. The second was the deep, biting cold. Wigglesworth pulled to one side, but the horse seemed unaware that he was its rider. His corpulent body wasn't made for equestrian ventures, a fact of which he was only too aware. He felt rather than saw Biddle come by him, for he didn't dare look to his side, lest he fall from the beast.

"Biddle…I am no horseman!" Wigglesworth yelped, as the horse galloped forward.

Rasputin moved deftly near Wigglesworth and directed, "Hold the reins tighter!"

Rasputin held firmly his own steed. The dark night filled him with wonder. "Bloody Sunday, 1905!" this the sorcerer who had fallen with the wizard Biddle had cried out. Had it happened? If this was the time they traveled back to, it would be, Rasputin thought grimly, at least a decade before his influence upon the tsarina had begun, for that had happened when he had cured her son, Prince Alexei, of the bleeding disease. But that time was ten years into the future, if it still existed, and the boy Alexei was now but an infant. How could he, Rasputin, a peasant monk in the eyes of His Majesty, have any influence upon him? For even the times that were to come—if they came or perhaps had come, Rasputin didn't know—the tsar was never a receptive audience to his premonitions, not like the tsarina.

Biddle himself felt the sharp cold steel of premonition as he noticed the sky. Black. No moon. No stars. The blackness spelled danger, sinister tidings that he didn't wish to consider. His mind said the words, *I am not be afraid of evil tidings. My heart is steadfast, trusting in the Lord,* but his heart still beat to the rhythm of fear.

Biddle threw his question into Wigglesworth's mind. *Rufus, the night sky. Do you notice something?*

Wigglesworth heard the thought, but he couldn't look up as he feared doing anything more than cling to the reins of the animal that ran with such lightning speed. Then he glanced quickly to register the sky above them for the first time. Wigglesworth shivered, though it wasn't the cold that made him shake. *When the moon no longer rises, when the stars sparkle no more.*

"What has happened?" Rasputin asked, looking at the sky. "There is no moon. There are no stars."

In the night sky, the faintest of outlines of an oval face appeared. Biddle said, "Stop" and stayed his horse. Rasputin followed and grabbed Wigglesworth's reigns to stay his steed. "Anunitu," Biddle whispered. He knew her appearance, and its faintness confirmed his worst trepidations. They turned their heads upward to the gloomy heavens. As Biddle spoke, a softness fell over them, enveloping the three in protection, and time stood still.

It was the goddess of the moon, Anunitu, a delicate silvery outline translucent against the opaque sky. She said in foreboding tones:

When the black velvet
of the night sky
cradles me not
and cannot hold the silver light
of my gleaming face,
when the moon no longer rises,
when the stars sparkle no more,
they will soon be
upon the land of mortals,
called by the
prince of demons.
Evil demon gods of old,
Asaru-alim-nuna,
will rise again.
Asaru-alim-nuna,
the forgotten mighty ones.

Her almond-shaped eyes, streaked with bolts of silver light, turned toward Wigglesworth as she spoke the words.

Ša nagba īmuru!

The moon goddess Anunitu's face wavered, and from her eyes fell two tears that melded into one, falling like a beam of light downward. Then her face dimmed and disappeared until the sky was black. The beam of light spun into a small silvery-gray ball in the air. It then opened like a bird stretching its wings, falling as a cloak, soft like the finest cashmere, above the shoulders of Wigglesworth, the silky silver underbelly shining. The soft silver gray was alluring in its promise of depth as it hinted of ever softer and darker tones; the color was that of the sky ominous before a storm. The cloak fluttered over Wigglesworth's shoulders, and Herman Biddle looked at him. But Wigglesworth's eyes were shut in pain. Biddle spoke to him through his mind, saying what Wigglesworth knew. *Rufus. It is time now, my friend, to be the bearer of the Cape of Ša Nagba Īmuru.*

Wigglesworth trembled, and the folds of cape still hovered, waiting. He heard Herman Biddle, but his thoughts only ran to the words of Anunitu, goddess of the moon, *Asaru-alim-nuna— the forgotten demonic mighty ones rise.* He knew they were the old demons who had first tempted man in the Garden of Eden.

Time now stood still, but Herman Biddle knew that the protection the moon goddess gave them soon would shatter. Time would then grab them with all its fury, and the evil that was to descend would do so. *Asaru-alim-nuna.* Biddle now realized how futile his attempts had been to avert a destiny of destruction. He had spent so much time, hidden in the basement of Sears in Hackensack, New Jersey, plotting and planning with Rufus

Wigglesworth. They'd made journeys back and forth from past to present, to untie the knots of evil, thinking that to bury forever the alluring Spyglass would close the door to the robbing of free will from man by the dark forces. He thought ruefully of how doomed all his efforts had been to destroy the Spyglass, to keep the prying eyes of Paddy O'Reilly, which had been so close to the truth of the Tablets of Creation and the secret of the Cape of Ša Nagba Īmuru, from breaking open the Pandora's box they now faced. His efforts to protect Mattie, Geeta, and Eddie from the serpentine Gneezy and the dangers of the Path of the Virtuous, to stop them from continuing on the Path had been for naught.

The River of Time now roiled in chaos; this Mattie had done in ancient Nineveh when souls belonging to darkness had been stolen for light. It couldn't be undone. The war between the forces of light and darkness, of good and evil, raged, and light was losing. What had happened that unleashed the forgotten mighty demonic ones, Asaru-alim-nuna, Biddle didn't know. He didn't know that the hands of the living—Eddie's hands—now held Death's scythe, and so the spirits held in the land of darkness had churned upward and out, and the demons of old had broken forth. And Biddle didn't know the creature Abaddon had flown into the land of the living and grasped at the Spyglass, who now sought to destroy Mattie. He had no idea that the dark events of Bloody Sunday were raging more horrifically than he or Wigglesworth could have imagined—and that the prince of demons was Stal. But Biddle heard the heartbeats of doom and their song of the death of man; Wigglesworth could not shirk this task.

Rasputin observed the two old men on the silvery horses next to him. He felt the stillness of time. The horses shook their heads, and from their nostrils burst puffs of air that turned into intricately patterned crystals that rose upward. He saw the beauty of the silvery-gray cape and how the old sorcerer had quaked in fear as it fluttered, waiting over him. The silence of the land, in truth, frightened Rasputin. He had traveled in his own time since the Second Stone, when Tsar Nicolas as martyr had risen over the ancient land of Nineveh and spoken his prophecy—that the Path of the Virtuous had to be traversed for the story of creation to be rewritten. But then Rasputin was thrown back in time again with the small band of gypsies, to a time when the tsar's mortal heart still beat, and two old sorcerers had appeared once more. Rasputin didn't know whether or not he remained in a mortal body. He only knew that time had twisted and turned; that a force beyond his understanding rode the land and had taken him with it. Still, when the spell cast by the captivating moon goddess dispelled, would it still not be Bloody Sunday? And would the prophecy be fulfilled—that the blood spilled would be much greater—if it were true now that evil was to reign supreme? But Rasputin kept his thoughts to himself, as he pointed to the silvery cloak that floated in wait over Wigglesworth's shoulders. "This cape," he said. "What is it?"

Herman Biddle remained silent. Wigglesworth's voice was faint when he finally spoke; he clutched the horse's reins tightly. "The gods of old, those ancient gods of light, wove the Cape of Ša Nagba Īmuru." Then Wigglesworth fell silent. The story of the Cape of Ša Nagba Īmuru was known to him and Biddle alone. It held the fury of the seas, and woven into its threads was the story of the earth and of man's fragile existence and that of his soul. It also held a mystery within which was embedded the secret. How had it gotten to this, the release of the old demon gods, Asaru-alim-nuna, who first tempted man into evil? The sound of time for man was at an end, which also meant all that was good and light would fall if in the final balance the souls were tallied to darkness.

Donning the Cape of Ša Nagba Īmuru meant carrying an enormous burden—the fate of the souls of the world. Wigglesworth was certain that his worn, old shoulders could not bear it well, that he would break under the weight of the cape and the souls he was to protect from evil would fall. The mortal vessel, which he had taken, was now weak, and in addition he had gone through many lifetimes already, and his soul was dimming, but the journey had only just begun. The Path of the Virtuous couldn't be tread by the faint of heart. It couldn't be tread by those who wanted to thwart their destiny. The Path of the Virtuous, the unrelenting Eight Stones of which they were but on the third, must be treaded to the end—if it could be. Wigglesworth knew that all he and Biddle had done in their travels through time in the name of protecting the sanctity of man's soul had all been for naught. Asaru-alim-nuna, the forgotten mighty ones, would soon traverse the land, as the moon goddess's prophecy foretold. They would rise in demonic power and shut out lightness. If so, all would be lost—the souls of man, and then…Here Wigglesworth trembled in fear. The Cape of Ša Nagba Īmuru demanded much, for its softness was deceptive. Wigglesworth, in a time when youth was his, in those many lifetimes ago, had been pledged its protector, if such could be said of a thing of destiny such as the Cape of Ša Nagba Īmuru. In that time, eons prior, Wigglesworth had held the White Book of Magic, when the division of light from darkness began first to dim, and goodness became more and more elusive to man upon the earth.

Rasputin saw the old portly sorcerer's face deepen in anguish and knew there was more to be told, and to which he would not be privy. He looked to Wigglesworth then Biddle with quizzical eyes. Rufus Wigglesworth cast his gaze to Rasputin, saw the clear intensity of eyes that once had mesmerized for deceit, and knew this man who had changed his fate from evil to good would be their ally. Rasputin would be needed in this long journey, needed for the Great Battle, the last horrific one, that they were now plunged toward headlong as they journeyed on the Path of the Virtuous.

Wigglesworth then quietly said in a voice that came from the past:

Ask me whence and upon what time
the fury of the oceans' might in darkness drowned the land.
Ask me when the thunder of the evil ones,
Asaru-alim-nuna,
rose from the blackness, stones shattering upon the earth.

It was when the demon gods,
Asaru-alim-nuna, rode mighty
and threw their arrows red with venom:
hatred for the other.
Flung their spears brimmed with poison.
Hatred for their brother,
the demon poison
hatred for the Great Mother.

The demon gods who rode the land,
Asaru-alim-nuna,
threw did they their mischief
in fragments like black sand.
pitted was it now
Man's once unsullied heart, souls once pure and clean.

Ask me when the wild and terrible sounds
of these dragon demon gods,
Asaru-alim-nuna,
splintered the air of Eden.
And to that I will tell you,
when man opened wide the portals to his soul,
took the demon gods' bargain,
took the deceptive, shiny fruit,
took the glittery fruit of temptation.

Lured was man by the demon gods' promise;
greater would man be than the Great Mother.
He would now be the creator, the maker of the living,
and for this to the demon gods man gave his soul.

Then tumbled did he from the gardens.
To the earth plunged he did.
With a heart that beat in mortal rhythms.
And man learned too quickly
of the folly of the bargain he had made.
Though man could give life,
it was in death that he paid.

The poison of the demon arrows
was filled with envy and greed,
was filled with pride and need.
So it was war and vengeance,
an endless dance of bloodshed,
souls bruised and blackened,
fallen to the demons' fierce and dreadful grasp.

Then man cried out to
their forsaken Great Mother,
cried in endless lamentation,
"O save us from the demon gods
Asaru-alim-nuna!"

And the Great Mother heard man's cries,
their notes long and high.
As she grieved for her children,
her tears sprang from the sky
and flooded all the land,
that the Asaru-alim-nuna
may be destroyed,
that the story of man's creation
could be written with a new hand.

But the demon gods' bargain
was not so easily undone
"Their souls are ours," cried Asaru-alim-nuna
to the greatest of the spirits,
the nameless, faceless, all-powerful one.
And so the Great Spirit spoke,
"To man was a soul given
that in unfair temptation he did sell.
To man now I will give free will.
Choose he shall where his soul shall go,
into the light of heaven or the darkness of hell."

Then the Great Spirit warned,
"The demons' poison arrows,
filled with envy, greed, pride, and need,

will fill the heart of man with desire
that he must overcome.
Choose will man to hunt one another
or to live in love and peace.
And to light or darkness
will so follow the souls of man."

But again warned the Great Spirit,
"*So shall it be for all eternity,*
when it is finished,
whether light or dark is victor,
no more for mortal man.
Then shall it chime the sound of time."

A great silence followed Wigglesworth's last words. Rasputin was stilled by the enormity of the tale. *Whether light or dark is victor.* Wigglesworth's eyes shut, and his shoulders bent, though the cape still fluttered above his shoulders, waiting for the sign that he would be the wearer. Although it was in material light as a feather, in spirit it was heavy as lead. Biddle knew how heavy was it—this weight of responsibility that his friend Wigglesworth would assume as wearer of the cape and knew too that his old friend feared his ability, but he spoke into Wigglesworth's mind nonetheless. *All the wrath of the forgotten demons in this time of chaos will rise against us to thwart us on the Path of the Virtuous. Shall we ignore our destiny, surrender softly to this evil night, and let darkness clasp the mortal soul, Rufus?* Biddle asked, for he saw that Wigglesworth was cowering. With fear came weakness, and with weakness all would lost.

Wigglesworth gingerly touched the edges of the Cape of Ša Nagba Īmuru, which fluttered over him, waiting. He felt the softness of its touch, its warmth infuse him. Wigglesworth threw his arms up, and his three chins shook. He called, "Ša Nagba Īmuru" to the cape. The cape fell over him, and the power of the cloak and its mystery coursed through his body. Now it was he who would be protector of the secret. Wigglesworth said, "'In the beginning God created the heavens and the earth. The earth was without form, and void; the darkness was on the face of the deep.'" He Who Saw the Deep was *ša nagba īmuru*. His eyes were bright and gleaming, and if one looked in them, it was almost as if the glittering universe was reflected back. Then his eyes turned black.

The sound shattered the land as the soft blanket of the moon goddess' protection gave way. Time formed again, and they were three once more, mounted upon silvery steeds on the cold and frozen winter Russian soil. It was Rasputin who heard the noise of the hooves behind them first. He turned to see fast-approaching men on horses from all around. These men surrounded Biddle, Rasputin, and Wigglesworth and pointed their weapons at them. Then one among them rode toward them with a vengeance. Rasputin's eyes widened in surprise. "Your Majesty..." But Rasputin's words were caught in this throat by the terrible outlines that shimmered under the face of Tsar Nicolas. It was the face of a snake. Then this snake spat out a long tongue, forked and black, that struck Herman Biddle across the face and hissed, "Dmitri."

CHAPTER 19

the martyr

Upon the bloody, frozen ground of the Winter Palace square, Stal, the pockmarked prince of demons, took his fearsome sword and sliced off three of the four heads of the dragon horse, which each fell to the ground. Each head then transformed into three mighty red dragon horses. "Mount the horses so we shall overcome the Cossacks!" Stal shouted to the peasants. Three burly workers jumped upon the dragon horses. Stal swung his sword, and from the small snakes upon it, whips and sabers flew into the hands of the those on the horses. Then he waved the Saber of Shadows again, and the snakes upon it transformed into swords that flew into the hands of the crowd. Stal then shouted a cry of triumph and pushed his dragon horse forward, toward the Cossacks. He slashed his blade in the air as the beast rode forward, fast like the wind. The peasants on the dragon horses behind him followed, brandishing their weapons at the Cossacks.

Stal felt the blade strike the neck of a Cossack and the thrill that came as he saw the head roll across the frozen ground. He sensed the rush of power surge from his thumbs, flood through him from the dragon horse through its reins and into his body. He screamed a spinechilling cry, and everywhere near him Cossacks fell. Stal felt but didn't see a crowd swell behind him. Then they moved toward him, risking being trampled by the Cossacks; they waved a banner—once white but now soaked with the blood of their martyr, Father Gapon—a banner with the sign of the cross on it. "Our savior!" they cried. Stal's red eyes burned in anger at the cross. He pulled at his great dragon horse. He knew this symbol of meekness, the sign of the cross, must fall in order for him to rule. The followers of Christ, Stal knew, could be persuaded to believe that their travails on earth were noble burdens to be borne with silence, with docility. They would turn the other cheek, like his mother Keke had. Stal's anger grew and burned fiercely in his eyes. The sign of the cross must be destroyed.

"No longer will you be the rich man's beast of burden! No longer will your blood run to fill the tsar's coffers with gold!" Stal shouted. He waved the Saber of Shadows to the side of deception. The saber cast its spell upon those on the ground, and the spell grew stronger with Stal's words. They held power for the eyes to see black as white, and white as black. Stal slashed the sword through the air again. "Pick up your sickles! Pick up your hammers!" From the saber rained sickles and hammers that fell straight into the hands of the peasants.

"No one among us is greater than the other! Comrades are we!" Stal declared. He swung the evil sword at the banner and slashed it. The sign of the cross fell and transformed into a sickle and a hammer. The peasants who held the banner felt the demonic force of Stal run through the cloth, for at once they felt strength and power. Yes, comrades. No more meek sign of the cross; no more prayers for the life after this one, but food, hearth, and gold, here and now upon this earth! The meek did not inherit the earth, Stal knew; the strong did.

"The sickle and the hammer, for all comrades!" The peasants shouted in triumph, circling Stal, who rode upon his mighty dragon horse. They handed the banner to two peasants who rode upon the dragon horses that had formed from Stal's steed. The bloody banner now turned fully red, and the sign of the sickle and the hammer shone in gold. The peasants behind Stal shouted again, brandishing their sickles and hammers, charging toward the Cossacks.

𒀭𒅗𒌋𒁹𒅗𒌋𒀸

The dark mass of the dead that was Kurnigi—of shadows and stones transforming into a wall of demonic beings that moved like a great wave, a thousand feet high—fell with a thunderous force onto Eddie, Trina, Gilgamesh, and the wandering children spirits.

Asaru-alim-nuna.
We, the mighty demons, rise!

As the dark wall approached, Eddie grabbed Trina's hand; it was soft like silk, and while he felt that it was spirit in form, there was substance underneath it. The force grabbed them and took them upward. Eddie held on to the scythe with one hand and the ephemeral Trina with the other. He could neither see nor hear Trina or the wandering spirit children. He only felt Trina's hand, the silky soft hand that wasn't substance but like a soft wind that whispers its sweet perfume. He heard Gilgamesh call to him,

"*Muktablu!* Keep a firm hold on your weapon!" Eddie knew only this—that his heart beat wilder than it ever had and that protecting Trina was a mission that he wouldn't fail. The black waves of evil of the rising demonic beings, all of the old mighty, pulled them down and up in a great tsunami of darkness.

When the darkness finally lifted, the sounds of hooves of horses fell hard upon Eddie's ears. They were in the middle of a raging battle upon a frozen and bloodied ground. Eddie held fast to Trina's hand, as they tumbled to the earth, missing the horses' hooves. He scanned the surroundings. "Stay low!" he told Trina as he hunched down. Eddie caught sight of the Cossacks in the distance, with their red uniforms. And beyond he heard the cries of battle. Where were they? The chill of the Russian winter wind went through him. The sky was black, and the light around them came from yellow gaslights, but this Eddie didn't know. All he felt was blackness and the dim lights that threw ghastly shadows. From the sky fell more and more of the wandering children spirits onto the cold Russian ground.

Gilgamesh stood upon the ground, stabbing the sky with his spear. "*Muktablu!*" he cried. "See what falls!" The old demon gods swirled in the air then rained down like locusts upon the land. Gilgamesh held his spear high and moved close to Eddie. The released demon gods fell from the sky, colliding with one another and against the living mortals who were battling on the ground. Gilgamesh looked in confusion at this battle—Bloodshed and bodies falling. He felt the cold upon his skin. "The mighty demon gods of old have arisen," Gilgamesh said to Eddie. "We have entered the land of the living and not Kurnigi."

Suddenly a demon wave of black spirits whirled around Gilgamesh, Eddie, Trina, and the wandering spirits, as they had caught the smell of Death's scythe. Eddie was now in defense mode; he had unclasped Trina's hand and firmly grasped the scythe with both hands, shielding her with his body against the circling demon gods. He felt the fear of the wandering children spirits rise behind him, as the demon gods raked the air around them with their sketetal death fingers. Gilgamesh jabbed his warrior spear toward the circling black spirit gods. Their forms were of scorpions, of snakes, of rodents; some upon human bodies, some with mutated forms. They all rushed forward then were repelled by the force of Gilgamesh's spear and the power of Death's scythe in the hand of the living.

In the sky the Four Terrors formed. There, Gilgamesh saw with fear what was falling. "*Asaru-alim-nuna, muktablu.* The evil demon gods have risen." Eddie looked up and saw the aspect that was Nergal, god of destruction, with the face of a dragon, sharp teeth, and with the body of a giant. Then Namtar demon of tribulation emerged, bearing dark winds of pain. Then came the long-haired Lamashtu, demoness of forgetfulness, her gray locks spreading like a fog of confusion. Finally Zaltu, goddess of conflict, arose, her head with many sides, all with eyes of lightning bolts that shook the earth. The Four Terrors, released from their millenniums-long imprisonment from the walls of the tunnels, forgotten no more, mighty again, sought their retaliation against Marduk.

𒈨𒌓𒈨𒁹

In the godforsaken Russian night, Gneezy's snake face shimmered with ever more evil under the mask of Tsar Nicolas as his tongue sprang forward to hiss again, "Dmitri," the hated name of his hated brother. Herman Biddle couldn't move. He saw the gleaming blue eye and green eye filled with hate flicker at him in the milliseconds before Gneezy's tongue sprang forward, hissing, "Blood of the dragon viper's poison." The dark spell fell upon him as he felt his arms and legs turn leaden. The men behind Gneezy, the tsar's Imperial Guard, with their swords unsheathed, waited for their orders to kill the three, their horses' snorting black moist puffs of air. Quicker than flashes of light, the snake's forked tongue lashed Rasputin and Wigglesworth's faces. Both felt the snake tongue sting them and the poison of evil that was upon that forked tongue enter their beings. Biddle struggled against the spell of darkness, but the more he did, the deeper it fell upon him. To his dismay he saw from the corners of his eyes the blurred visions of Rasputin and Wigglesworth upon their horses, immobile like statues. His gaze fell upon Uri Gneezy, the same one with whom he had shared a womb, whose heartbeats he once had heard as clearly as his own. But it wasn't the same Uri, Biddle knew. He also knew that his failing was that he had given in to the false belief of brotherly love. But though the snake held them in his black spell, he hadn't grasped Biddle in order to kill him; Biddle knew there was something that held Uri back. Biddle's window of opportunity would be short; he had to act in concert with Rufus. But he couldn't speak into Wigglesworth's mind, for his tongue was heavy and bloated in his mouth from the snake's poison, and his mind was sinking deeper into a fog.

The snake held Biddle under his hypnotic gaze; he hissed with pleasure as he saw the work of his spell upon Biddle and his foolish allies. Gneezy's words rang silently in Biddle's mind. *A pleasure it will be to have you plunged deep into the labyrinth of Kurnigi for all eternity.* The snake had to fight his desire to break out of the skin of Tsar Nicolas and grasp Biddle with his great serpent body and hurl him into the depths of hell. But the snake couldn't reveal his true self yet, for the Cossacks, now in the hundreds, had ridden behind him from the Winter Palace to this spot. With a speed they had never before experienced, they had ridden upon the wings of the Black Book of Magic that the snake had called to silently as soon as his forked tongue had felt the heartbeats of his brother upon the land. That sound had drawn him to where Biddle, Wigglesworth, and Rasputin stood when the spell of the moon goddess was broken.

The Cossacks had to believe that Gneezy was Tsar Nicolas for the land to be plunged brother against brother, for division to occur, and for the conquest to take place. If he were to turn into his serpentine form, he knew their allegiance to him as the tsar would be broken. Wait he could, for Biddle and his two allies were frozen by his dark spell, which rose as hisses and black sparks. So it was that Herman Biddle was mesmerized and help-less. Rufus Wigglesworth also felt the snake's poison in his blood. *O moon goddess, I have failed you so soon,* he thought. But then he stilled his mind, for he saw the snake's eyes dart toward him.

"Plunge your swords into the traitors!" Gneezy shouted to the Cossacks. The tsar's soldiers, with their unsheathed swords, rushed forward. However, the snake had erred. His spell was fragile, and his words and movement shattered it. In that millisecond, Biddle raised his cape blue as the ocean and uttered:

Enuma elish la nab u shamanu
shaplish ammantum suma la zakrat!

The blue light enveloped Rasputin, Wigglesworth, and Biddle in a flash, and where they once had stood were the three silvery horses, empty of their riders. Then the silvery horses also disappeared. The Cossacks looked in astonishment at the empty space. The snake shook upon his horse with rage at himself for his error. *Biddle!* He cried silently. *Escaped you have, but for the moment.* Then Gneezy turned toward the Cossacks. The story of the disappearing traitors flew through the ranks. They saw Tsar Nicolas before them, his strange blue eye and green eye flashing with anger. The snake hissed, "Black magic. The followers of Gapon worship the devil. We must kill them all." A cry of assent rose up.

𒀭𒂍𒀭 𒁹

Tsar Nicolas II's long aristocratic face, framed by brown hair and a trimmed beard, frowned in concentration. He sat with his eyes shut tightly as he whispered chants to awaken the long dead. In front of him was a small candle on a dark table that flickered under the vibrations of the royal train as it hurtled toward Tsarskoye Selo. Tsar Nicolas used these solitary moments to seek the counsel of his ancestors in how to rule. The royal train carriage was luxuriously upholstered in silk and leather; the ceiling was polished oak upon which strange images were cast from the candlelight. Tsar Nicolas smelled the blood first—the salty sea smell—that was the last sensation Tsar Alexander II had experienced as he died on the snowy ground. It was that smell of death and violence that always preceded the arrival of the spirit of his grandfather, Alexander II. Nicolas opened his light-blue eyes and felt horror at the vision forming before him. He gasped, for Alexander II came not as he had in the past to Nicolas II when he proudly had worn the great coat and red-banded cap of the Imperial Guard and showed strength and valor. Instead Tsar Alexander bore the wounds of the assassination attempt that had proven fatal. Upon his face were burns; his legs were shattered, his pants splattered with blood. There were great gaps in his face, the once aristocratic nose broken, chunks torn from the jaw, blood where once his signature mutton chop whiskers resided, the receding hairline embedded with small pieces of gravel, the high-necked blue tunic darkened with bloodstains—all showing the effects of the bomb that had killed him.

Tsar Nicolas stood up in alarm. "Grandfather, why have you come to me in this gory form?"

The ghostly form of Alexander II spoke. "Nicolas, see my wounds and know them as yours, you who will be the last emperor of Russia."

Nicolas recoiled at the forewarning. "Last emperor, Grandfather? What is it you speak of?"

Tsar Alexander grimaced. "Blackness lies like a smoky mist upon man's soul. Before the night's end, the snow shall be blanketed with blood. And too shall you die."

Shaken by the prophecy, Tsar Nicolas grabbed the table and thought at once of his wife and children. "Alexandra, the girls, and little Alexei."

The old tsar shook his head. "None of the Romanov dynasty will remain from this night forth, as holy Russia plunges into godlessness."

Tsar Nicolas shook his head. "For myself, I care not. You must tell me, Grandfather, how I am to protect my wife and the children. You must!"

The vision of Alexander began to fade, and his words were garbled and faint, but Tsar Nicolas heard them—"You cannot escape your destiny, the prophecy of Saint Seraphim"—before Tsar Alexander disappeared.

Tsar Nicolas stared at the empty space where the vision of his grandfather had spelled the bloody prediction. *My destiny. Saint Seraphim's prophecy of my fall from power, for the destiny of martyrdom.* Tsar Nicolas's heart cried out in pain. How would he protect Alexandra and the children? How? His family was now in Tsarskoye Selo. *Safe,* he thought. His hands trembled at the thought of their deaths. No!

The train shook, and Tsar Nicolas grabbed the table to steady himself. The candle fell to the floor, and its flames rose high, not red but blue in light. From them appeared three strange figures—Biddle, Wigglesworth, and Rasputin. The tsar's eyes widened. Two were old and wore capes. One of the capes glittered like the ocean under a full moon; the other was silvery and gray. The other man looked like a poor monk, wearing a worn black robe tied in the middle with a rope. This one had eyes that mesmerized. Tsar Nicolas stood staring wordlessly at the figures he believed to be messengers from his grandfather.

"Your Majesty," Herman Biddle said. They had seen the form of Tsar Alexander II that had just disappeared in the blue light. Tsar Nicolas must have had his future told by the old tsar. "We have little time. Please listen," Biddle said. He then waved his cape and threw out a Card of Time. "See. See what it is that happens." The card showed the bloody battle at the Winter Palace square.

The tsar's face fell. "What is it that you show me?" he demanded.

Now Wigglesworth spoke, not looking at the Cards of Time that told the tale as time had once written it. Wigglesworth instead saw the horrific images that were upon his eyes. The Cape of Ša Nagba Īmuru gave him the power to see events as they unfolded, as the mortal wearer bore the burden of it, helpless to change these events, just as mortal man held knowledge of his death but could not avert it. He saw that the Winter Palace square was now brimming with violence, more upsetting than what the Cards of Time showed. Wigglesworth saw dark forces falling upon the square and anger rising exponentially in the hearts of the peasants. Hopelessness stabbed him. *Are we too late?* Wigglesworth thought, desperately sending the message to Biddle.

Biddle heard Wigglesworth, and his voice quavered as he spoke. "Bloody Sunday. We have come to warn you, Tsar Nicolas, and to ask you to help us avert the evil that will fall not just today but stain the world for a millennium."

Tsar Nicolas stared at the images on the cards that unfolded before him. "Cossacks killing unarmed peasants. Why does this happen?"

Biddle spoke again. "We don't know how it started. But this day, this Bloody Sunday, begins one knot of darkness that descends upon Russia and will spread like a black stain across the world. You must go to the Winter Palace square and accede to the demands of Father Gapon."

Beside him Wigglesworth shook again but couldn't speak what he saw. The sickle and hammer upon a banner. A pockmarked rider upon a dragon horse, brandishing the Saber of Shadows. Wigglesworth moaned inwardly. Thus was the onerous burden of the Cape of Ša Nagba Īmuru to its wearer, knowledge without power to act, to speak and warn. Wigglesworth turned to Biddle's Cards of Time, which revealed what had occurred before the River of Time had been set in chaos. Clearly Biddle didn't know the depth of Uri Gneezy's wickedness. Wigglesworth, who saw the rage of the peasants, also didn't know what had set it ablaze like a wildfire upon dry tinder. He saw what was happening but didn't know what had happened before—that Gneezy had killed Father Gapon as he wore the face of Tsar Nicolas, that Gapon's followers rose now against the tsar's men, that blood ran unchecked upon the frozen ground of the Winter Palace. He didn't know that the peasants now called Stal, the prince of demons, their leader.

Rasputin's eyes took in the events of the Card of Time as they unfolded before him. The bloody revolt. He felt the pain of it all and remembered the events as they had been written, as they showed now upon the wizard Biddle's cards. He knew that soon Tsar Nicolas and his family would be executed, and Russia soon would fall to godlessness.

Rasputin shivered at this knowledge. "Your Majesty," he said, "you must come and do as they ask in order to protect your family."

Tsar Nicolas looked at the strange man, familiar somehow, with the piercing blue eyes. He looked Russian, but the old caped men were wizards, he was sure. *Wizards, messengers from the beyond.* Tsar Nicolas felt all the confusion of the strange situation. Could his grandfather's prophecy be prevented? The train's wheels hummed, and Tsar Nicolas felt their vibrations under his feet. The candle's blue light enveloped the train car.

"We must go now, Your Majesty," Biddle said.

Tsar Nicolas turned to the tall, thin, old wizard who had spoken. "I will come with you," he said, "but my family must be protected."

Herman Biddle paused. It was written the family would be executed in 1917. If Bloody Sunday could be undone, their executions also would be undone. But Biddle was ignorant of the devious crime of the murder of Father Gapon by Uri Gneezy wearing the mask of the tsar and didn't know what treachery Gneezy had set forward.

Wigglesworth said, "Biddle."

Biddle turned to see Wigglesworth staring out, his eyes turning black. The vision in them of what was to come made Wigglesworth recoil—masses of peasants plunging sickles and hitting with hammers the prone body of Empress Alexandra, her children lying dead at her side. Wigglesworth's tongue was frozen; he couldn't speak of what he saw. Biddle saw pain cross his old friend's face. Rufus now wore the Cape of Ša Nagba Īmuru and bore the burdens of the visions it showed, of the knowledge of deep mysteries that bore into the soul of mortal man. *Do not fall prey to the visions of the cape,* Biddle spoke to Wigglesworth's mind. *What you see for the future does not have to be.*

"Come," Biddle said grimly. He flung his cape forward to envelop them and launch them out of the moving train into the blackness of the foreboding night sky.

𒁹𒅆𒂅 𒂖 𒁹𒅆 𒀹

On the ground beneath the night sky, Uri Gneezy stayed his black horse to see a blue flash over the train and knew at once that it was Biddle bringing the real Tsar Nicolas to the Winter Palace. He hissed in pleasure. What a fool was Biddle! Bringing the tsar to be butchered! Now the peasants would kill Tsar Nicolas to avenge the death of Father Gapon. And the tsar's men would retaliate in full force. Gneezy hissed again in glee. *Divide and conquer in anger.* How stupid was mortal man. No opportunity was richer to cultivate the souls of man to evil than when man held in his heart anger toward another. Soon the Dark Master would reward Gneezy with his due, for time indeed had been rewritten; chaos was working well for Marduk indeed.

"To the Winter Palace square!" he called to the Cossacks. Then he flung out his tongue, and a great black wind rose under the horses' hooves and sped them toward the square.

𒀭𒈾𒁹𒀭𒈾𒁹

Within the great expanse of the Winter Square, the giant dragon horse that Stal rode raised its fiery head toward the sky and moved toward the fearsome demons that spun and fell from the sky. Below him the chants of the peasants rang between the bloody screams of death. "Sickle and hammer! Workers' power! Workers' strength!" Anger clouded their vision, for though demons were falling upon the earth, their own vengeance had risen strong; blood was what they wanted. They screamed and raised their sickles and hammers against the Cossacks, and the Cossacks fought back amid the shower of falling demons.

A cyclone of demon gods circled Eddie, Trina, Gilgamesh, and the wandering children spirits. It made a circle of evil energy that repelled the battle of mortals from them. The Four Terrors who had fallen now called:

> *O prince of demons,*
> *whose call we heed,*
> *to whom we gave saber and steed,*
> *we call to you now*
> *to take from this mortal's grasp*
> *Death's scythe into your clasp.*

The dragon horse that held Stal galloped toward where the Four Terrors filled the night sky and rode past the evil ring of the whirling demons. Eddie heard the pounding of a gigantic animal, and when it stopped, he saw that upon it rode someone not a lot older than him, no more than eighteen. Eddie heard his father's voice. *See and assess your enemy; his weakness is your strength.* Eddie took in the intel—a rider whose eyes blazed red in a face that was pitted with black pockmarks. The enemy combatant's weapon was a sword covered in small snakes; his hands had thumbs that glowed black then blue. *Where is this guy's weakness?* Eddie wondered, his hands holding fast to Death's scythe, which now writhed with an evil force that vibrated under his hands.

Muktablu, beware, Gilgamesh spoke to Eddie's mind. *This demon rider holds the Saber of Shadows.* Eddie saw the sword, how it flashed a gray-and-black glow. Gilgamesh raised his spear toward Stal. His ten feet of height put him close to the height of the savage dragon horse that Stal rode. Gilgamesh stabbed his spear at the beast, which then fell back.

Stal raised the fiendishly gleaming Saber of Shadows as the whirling Four Terrors—Nergal, dragon god of destruction; Namatar, demon of tribulation; Lamashtu, demoness of forgetfulness; and Zaltu, goddess of conflict—blew around them and filled the air with the stench of the long dead and the dark winds of pain. Stal felt the current of the Saber of Shadows hum under his hands, and sharp stings of pain filled the black-and-blue thumbs. Stal knew he must obey the order the demon gods had given him. He looked down from the height of his dragon horse and saw the tall blue warrior with the spear and the yellow-haired boy who wielded the scythe, and just behind them, spirits of children, the weak and frightened dead. This would be a small first task indeed, for the Stal knew his demonic strength easily would overpower the two. He slashed the Saber

of Shadows toward the yellow-haired boy. "Give me the scythe!"
Stal demanded. "Or die."

𒀭𒌋 𒂍 𒀭𒌋 𒀸

In the outer reaches of the Winter Palace square, near the
palace itself, the Iron Knight's ruddy, fat face reflected the exhilaration of the conquest. He, resplendent in the uniform of a
Russian colonel, was indeed the Iron Knight of old. He moved at
a rapid pace, brandishing the saber, shouting orders for forma-
tions, the old orders from when he had been a hero of Germany
in the world war, the first one, the one yet to come. But here,
in death, he would achieve more—more than he what he had
hoped for when he had plotted for Germany, when that erratic
Hitler had given away the keys to power to the snake, all because
of the lures of a false beauty. The Iron Knight pushed away the
thoughts of what had happened when all his plans for the Führer
were shattered, when he himself became nothing but a pawn
under the control of the snake Gneezy. Now all was changed. He,
Iron Knight, would soon command the entire Russian army and
have the mighty Cossacks, the Hussars, and the millions of army
worker bees of the tsar's force under his thumb!

As he urged the Cossacks on, in the distance he saw a skir-
mish then felt the winds rise as the demon gods fell. *What is
this?* he wondered. Then he thought perhaps it was the snake's
black-magic call to serpents to aid him. He didn't notice the rise
of the prince of demons, the boy Stal, whom he had dismissed.
He didn't see that power was growing in the pockmarked boy.
When the sickle hit one of the tsar's soldiers near his line, and
the horse fell in a bloody heap, and the soldier also was felled,
the Iron Knight wondered who had given these peasants their

weapons. Still they were nothing compared to the weapons and sabers that his men—and here the Iron Knight paused to savor the words, *his men*—possessed. "Fire!" he screamed, and rode his horse front and back. "Fire at all on the ground!" A barrage of weapons fired at once into those on the ground, producing a cacophony of horrific cries mingled with the firing of the guns.

Above the battle unfolding upon the bloody ground in the Winter Palace square, four riders on silver horses appeared in the sky. It was Biddle, Wigglesworth, Rasputin, and Tsar Nicolas. The tsar cried out in agony at the sight—peasants with sickles and hammers raised against the Cossacks, and his men in turn with their weapons impaling or shooting those beneath them. As the horses flew downward, Biddle saw the banner in the hands of two peasants who rode beasts that were of Satan, with their dragon faces and teeth flecked with blood. More fearsome than the beasts was what the banner held. Biddle paled at the sight. Wigglesworth whispered, "We're too late. The sickle and hammer already have replaced the sign of the cross."

Biddle's heart fell; he now knew there was no chance for Tsar Nicolas to plead for peace, no chance for him to agree to the demands of Father Gapon. That time had come and gone. Peace wouldn't survive in the midst of this volcanic anger. *The evil chain of events has started, but in strength a thousand fold from what had been written. The tsar must be protected,* Biddle said to Wigglesworth in his mind. Wigglesworth merely nodded, his heart clutched with fear. Wordlessly he pointed to where the mighty evil forgotten demon gods were falling like locusts toward the ground. Then he whispered, "Asaru-alim-nuna. The forgotten mighty demon gods have risen to take the earth and mortal man once more." Biddle's blue eyes filled with pain. He shook away the defeatist thoughts that were starting to rise.

"Rasputin," Biddle called to the monk, "keep close to Tsar Nicolas, to protect him." But the tsar couldn't be held back. Biddle cried, "No! Your Majesty! Keep back." But it was too late. Tsar Nicolas was upon the ground. He raised his hands to the Cossacks nearby and commanded, "Stop! Stop this carnage!" For his heart couldn't stand the sight of such slaughter. The Imperial Guards near him, seeing the tsar, were confused, for wasn't the tsar in the Winter Palace stables? And hadn't the new colonel, the German one, given the orders to fire upon the peasants?

Biddle landed on the ground, followed by Rasputin then Wigglesworth. Biddle made the move to wave his cape. They must leave this place, into the Space-Between-Time, and form a new plan. "Your Majesty! Stop!" Biddle cried, as he saw Tsar Nicolas.

The tsar turned his horse toward Biddle. With deep anguish his light-blue eyes looked at the bloodbath. "You cannot stop destiny," he said. Tsar Nicolas rode his horse straight into the middle of the peasants with sickles and hammer then called to them, "Why is it you hate so?"

The peasants were stopped by the bearing and dignity of the tsar. They felt their poverty in his presence; they saw the magnificence of his royal-blue coat, the shiny red belt, the gold braids that adorned his shoulders, his long aristocratic bearded face, and his cap with the gold cross. The sight of the cross upon the tsar's head again incited anger in their hearts—the cross, the one they had borne with their poverty, the one they had carried upon the counsel of Father Gapon to urge the tsar to hear their cause, only to have their beloved priest be killed by this one, this tsar. One among them cried out, "You, who killed Father Gapon in cold blood, dare ask us why we hate?" They hit the tsar's horse with their sickles and hammers. The horse whinnied and fell forward, throwing the tsar to the ground as he whispered, "Because iniquity shall abound, the love of many shall wax cold."

The Cossacks nearby came to protect the tsar, but their horses were stopped by the peasants' weapons. They reached their hands up and wrung the Cossacks to the ground, the imperial sabers falling from their hands. A peasant picked up one of the swords. Rasputin jumped off his horse and ran into the crowd. "No! Do not harm him!"

The force of hate and anger, however, was too strong; arms grabbed Rasputin and held him back. They didn't harm him, for they saw by his tattered robe that he was poor like them. "Brother," the man who held him said, "stand back as justice is done, as the will of the people is done."

Rasputin struggled against their restraining arms. "This is not of God's will! It is the work of Satan! Do you not know that he that loveth not his brother cannot love God?" But his words were lost in the shouts.

The tsar stood up, and in a quick movement, the peasant with the Cossack's sword plunged it into Tsar Nicolas's heart. The bloodstain spread across the royal blue of the tsar's coat, an omen of the stain of anger and vengeance that would soon spread across Russia. The peasant pulled out the sword and raised the bloody weapon, declaring triumphantly as the once mighty Tsar Nicolas fell to the ground, trampled by the feet of peasants, "Father Gapon's death is avenged!"

Blood poured from Tsar Nicolas's heart as he lay on the frozen ground, his heart beating its last mortal beats. Rasputin broke through the throngs, and the sight crushed his heart, for there lay Tsar Nicolas at death's door, only a small movement showing the faint vestiges of life.

Several other workers, now armed with sabers wrung from the hands of the slain Imperial Guards, shouted and went to plunge their swords too into the heart of their oppressor, the tsar. But Rasputin held the tsar, and his body was a shield to their swords. The peasants drew back, repelled by the fierceness of Rasputin's glare. They saw in the monk's eyes something that frightened them. "Stay back!" he commanded, his eyes shining with anger then dismay. He held the dying tsar in his arms, the royal blood marking the monk's dark and dirty robes. "Look at what you have done!"

In the Winter Palace square, where the blood of peasants and Cossacks still flowed as they struck and killed one another, lay the dying Tsar Nicolas. Those immediately around Nicolas, the emperor of all Russia, were stilled. The tsar would soon be dead, felled by them. The enormity of their act hit them. Who would now rule Russia? The cruel face of the pockmarked man rose before them, and terror shot through their veins.

𒀭𒊏𒀭𒊏 𒀭

Gilgamesh pushed past Eddie to face Stal. He cried to the whirling demon figures circling them and the pockmarked one they called "prince of demons." "Demon gods of old, we fear you not!" he cried, then struck the the Saber of Shadows with his mighty spear. A loud burst of sound followed. Then the Saber of Shadows sent sharp daggers of light toward Gilgamesh that hit him again and again. Gilgamesh staggered back, and the pain caused him to drop down. Eddie sprang forward and wielded the scythe at Stal. "*Muktablu!*" Eddie heard Gilgamesh cry out in alarm. "Stay behind me!" Gilgamesh heaved himself forward, but it was too late. Stal moved forward with a vengence. The

Saber of Shadows sent three bolts of light in succession that hit Eddie's arm, chest, and face. Eddie fell to his knees. This pain was unlike anything he'd ever experienced, so sharp and fierce. He held fast to the scythe; he couldn't lose the weapon. *Pain is just weakness. Let it leave your body.* Eddie heard his father's words as he felt his consciousness leave him.

The giant hourglass that, just moments before, had held Mattie and Geeta in New York City in 1933, spun in the black sky as the ground below them took form. They were now flying above the Russian night, the Bloody Sunday night of 1905, over the tsar's Winter Palace. All around them, instead of stars, they saw figures of the vengeful spirits falling downward. The sands of time swirled inside the hourglass and fell upon Geeta and Mattie. Mattie saw her mother, hoisted over the shoulders of a strange man, as well as the flying frog man, all flash by her. "Mom!" she cried out, as she saw her mother fall to the ground below.

"Oh!" Geeta gasped, for just beyond the hourglass, flying around them, appeared the seven serpent-shark demon gods.

"Jeepers!" squealed Mattie. "Look out!" She pushed at the hourglass, hitting it with the Spyglass, who remained firmly lodged in her right hand. The serpent-sharks, primitive beings though they were, recognized the entity that resided within the Spyglass. They were now upon the hourglass, their mouths open, showing their thousand sharp shark teeth and lunging to grab it. The Spyglass recoiled. She threw out bolts of light that flipped the hourglass up and above serpent-sharks. A wind blew up, seizing the seven creatures, and flung their writhing bodies to the ground.

The hourglass twirled high above in the night sky, holding Mattie and Geeta. "Oh!" shouted Geeta. "Look below! It is your mother!" The hourglass turned upside down to pour the sands of time upon them.

"I can't see!" Mattie cried.

But the Spyglass could, glued as it was to Mattie's hand. The Spyglass saw the terrible serpent-sharks and the bloody violence below. *It's the work of Marduk,* the Spyglass thought. *Chaos to conquer.* And the snake Gneezy couldn't be far behind. They must leave here before the Dark Master came. Spyglass felt herself strengthen, drawing energy from Mattie's mortal soul.

Mattie felt the vibrations of the Spyglass's thoughts as the hourglass turned again and the sand poured through the hole away from them, then turned again. Mattie thrust her arm with the hand that held the Spyglass and plunged the Spyglass into the hole to plug it. The hourglass twirled again but now without the sands of time falling upon Mattie and Geeta as the Spyglass was an effective cork. Geeta hit the side of the hourglass in an effort to escape, and Mattie was dangling; her hand was still glued to the bottom half of the Spyglass, the top of which was in the hole that was now plugged. Mattie struggled to get loose and said to Geeta, "I can't let go of the Spyglass!" Geeta pulled at Mattie's arm to no avail.

The sands of time fell hard upon the Spyglass and bore upon her memory. *Sand. The sand that buried me once in the desert ground of Nineveh. Sand. Sand. Sand.* The Spyglass panicked as claustrophobia hit her. *No! No! No!*

Hidden by a ring of now silent peasants, the dying Tsar Nicolas whispered a verse from the Book of John in the Bible. "'God is love; and he that abideth in love abideth in God.'" Then his mortal body was no more. Rasputin turned to the peasants, his hypnotic eyes glittering in accusation. He lifted one hand, palm toward them, dripping with the blood of the tsar, and said, "Behold, your house is left unto you desolate."

"The tsar is dead!" Throughout the Winter Palace square, news of the tsar's death rang loud. The Imperial Guards and Cossacks who followed Gneezy, wearing the mask of Tsar Nicolas, didn't know he was the false one, he with one green and one blue eye, and they entered into the edges of the bloody chaos that was now the Winter Palace square. "How can that be?" those who had followed the false tsar cried. "Look! His Majesty rides before us!" All turned to the figure beyond, whose horse spun toward them. There, upon the black steed, they saw only an old man dressed in the clothing of the Imperial Guard, an old man whose eyes flashed green then blue. The Cossacks who had followed Gneezy when he had worn the mask of Tsar Nicolas shook their heads in surprised confusion. "Come!" the remaining battered Cossacks called. "See how the peasants are armed and kill our soldiers! Come! Draw your weapons!"

As the tsar's men rode fast past him, the sunken and skeletal face of evil that was Gneezy smiled. The real Tsar Nicolas was dead, and blood flowed fast. Cossacks killing peasants. Peasants killing Cossacks. The Dark Master Marduk would be pleased indeed. So many souls would rise to darkness and be plunged into the netherworld. As the power of darkness rose, the White

Book of Magic would fade, and soon Biddle would have no powers left to protect him. Soon indeed all that he, Uri Gneezy,
should have had would be his—Biddle crushed to nothingness,
the beast brought under his control, and rewards of power and
glory beyond the imagination bestowed upon him by the Dark
Master; Uri Gneezy would rule Kurnigi.

The horse beneath him shook in fear as the snake form took
shape upon it, the blue eye and green eye glittering with evil.
The snake Gneezy slithered off the horse onto the ground; his
scales, green and black, shone with anticipation. He grew gigantic in size as he sped across the ground, oblivious to the hooves of
the Cossacks' horses as they sped toward the thick of the battle.
Then the snake jumped up, startling the rider upon the horse
and stopping it from riding forward. The snake spat out its long
forked tongue and hissed at the man, "Iron Knight. It is time to
capture the souls we have harvested."

The Iron Knight's ruddy face registered the order and wondered how the snake could be so oblivious. The snake was no warrior, for he didn't recognize there was an enemy force at work,
and right before his face. "Master," he said, pointing beyond, to
where demons were raining from the sky, "what of them?"

The snake Gneezy turned his cobra head and saw the demon
gods dropping in a storm from the sky. He heard the old demon gods,
thousands now, falling like enormous hailstones. The demon gods,
in their macabre forms—with bloody teeth, sharp nails; in the bodies of serpents and dragons, of scorpions, of creatures of the water;
slimy and foul of smell—all cried in joy at their release from their
imprisonment in the walls of the tunnels of Kurnigi.

Marduk, who once conquered,
who laid us to waste,

will soon weep
in fear and tribulation,
when we grasp him in our hands
and lay him asunder.
And the demon Marduk
will bow his head in submission.
Asaru-alim-nuna.
Mighty ones are we!

The snake Gneezy shot his head up farther. *Asaru-alim-nuna.*
The blue eye and green eye narrowed. He didn't know the
origin of these demon gods. He didn't know all the intrigues
of old, as he hadn't held the Black Book of Magic for eons as
the Crone had. *The Crone.* The snake hissed. The Crone would
know. The Iron Knight saw the snake's head move up and down
in palsied movements. The snake hissed again; he would find
the Crone and wring her throat to learn what this falling of
Asaru-alim-nuna meant and how to conquer these demons, for
the demise of Marduk only meant his demise. And that could
not be. The snake grabbed the Iron Knight with his long tail, as
the horse beneath him fell. They shot into the sky then down to
the ground, toward where the demon gods dropped.

The peasants who had crowded around the dead tsar drew
back. Rasputin's words rang in their ears. *Behold, your house is left
unto you desolate.* The monk pointed to the sky. Above them, risen
now from his mortal body, was the spirit of Tsar Nicolas in all
his great majesty: his gleaming blue uniform, his kindly bearded
face, and the gossamer gold wings that showed him to be an

angel now. The man with the bloody sword dropped the weapon, and the peasants around them gazed in amazement as the tsar appeared in the sky above the bloodied Winter Palace square. Tsar Nicolas's spirit spoke to them the words of John the Baptist, spoke into their minds and hearts, *If a man say, 'I love God,' and hateth his brother, he is a liar; for he that loveth not his brother, whom he hath seen, how can he love God, whom he hath not seen?*

The peasants near the fallen mortal body of Tsar Nicolas cried in pain and now, too late, recognized that they had been driven to evil by a servant of Satan, the pockmarked one who called himself "Stal." The spirit of Tsar Nicolas faded into a bright white light.

Rasputin stood defiantly, holding the tsar's body in his arms. The peasants stood back, and one said, "We will call for peace." They turned toward the raging battle and cried to their fellow peasants, tradesmen, and workers to stop the slaughter. Among them also were Cossacks who had seen the tsar's spirit form fly over them and heard his words. They dropped their swords and cried to their brethren to stop the slaughter. But a volcano, once it has erupted, cannot be stopped. The anger and hate raged forward, and those who tried to stop the battle did so in vain.

Rasputin felt a sword pierce him in the back and felt only a small surprise. He crumpled, still holding the body of the tsar. As he died on the frozen, bloody ground, his spirit rose toward the sky. Below him he saw other souls rise, translucent bulbs of light that came from the bodies of Cossacks and peasants who had spoken for peace and laid their mortal bodies down for it. The other Cossacks and peasants, those who held fierce hatred for one another in their souls, rose up, and then great grasping skeletal hands took them into the ground, to their eternal hell within the land of Kurnigi. So it was that the battle ended, and all the mortals who had raised their hands against one another, who had hunted their brothers, were fallen. An eerie silence filled the Winter Palace square.

Biddle had ridden upward, into the sky, on his silver horse when the battle was raging; he threw back his cape in the air as the battle ended. Then he saw it fully; Nicolas, the last emperor of Russia, lay dead, as did Rasputin. A light that formed into a beam flew past Biddle into the heavens. Few souls rose to the light, while many were soiled and pulled downward. Biddle felt anguish at his failure. The Path of the Virtuous was a cruel teacher; its lessons weren't for the weak of heart. Anger, the Third Stone, was a brutal beast that rode hard upon man's soul, luring and destroying it. Bloody Sunday hadn't been averted; in fact it was worse in scope than Biddle could have imagined.

If this were so, what was the fate of Mattie, Geeta, and Eddie? Were they imprisoned somewhere deep within the folds of Kurnigi? Biddle feared that Gilgamesh, though king of Uruk and three-quarters god, wasn't enough to protect them against the evil that sought the prize of the Twin Tablet of Destiny, the Tablet of light. Biddle felt deep sorrow at the carnage below.

The Cape of Ša Nagba Īmuru flew back from Wigglesworth's shoulders and lifted him and his horse up into the sky. Wigglesworth saw the rise of Satan's will in the hearts of mortal man below. Then his black all-seeing eyes gaped at the sight beyond him—that of the prince of demons, the pockmarked young man with red glowing eyes, ready to pierce Eddie with his sword. *Biddle,* he said in his mind. *We must fly down now!* Wigglesworth shook the Cape of Ša Nagba Īmuru, which cast an eerie light upon them both. *Come!* he said, and the light pulled them both, horses and all, toward Stal, the prince of demons.

𒐊𒅆𒐊𒐊

Stal was in triumph. He would crush this yellow-haired boy with ease and pluck Death's scythe from his hand. The prince of demons, upon his fearsome dragon horse, raised the Saber of Shadows to stab Eddie but was stopped by a spirit that moved to deflect the blow away from the boy.

"Iosif," Trina said, her hands raised toward him.

Stal was shaken by the sight and the call of his name. *Iosif.* He looked down from the back of the giant demonic beast and saw the familiar angelic face of his boyhood longing. *Trina.* The cries of the demon gods faded into garbled sounds. *Prince of demons! Prince of demons! Take Death's scythe from the mortal's grasp!* Only her name, *Trina*, floated in his mind, and his eyes took in her beautiful pale oval face, the light-hazel eyes with dashes of green, and her hair, shining like polished dark wood, so smooth, thick, and luxuriant, held back by a ribbon. *Trina.* And Stal was once more mesmerized.

𒀭𒈾𒀭𒁹

The night sky gave way to the red glow that emanated from Marduk's red orbs. He heard the prophecy of the demon gods. But they had forgotten that Marduk still held power over the underworld. The red glow filled the sky and cast its light into the hourglass that imprisoned Mattie and Geeta. The heat of the orbs surrounded the spinning hourglass to penetrate it. Though the hourglass was a creation of the White Book of Magic, the powers of light and goodness were fading, and this Marduk knew. The red orbs shone more to melt the hourglass; when it did, the red-haired thief would fall to the ground to be grasped by the snake Gneezy and spirited away to the underworld. There, whatever protection Mother Tiamet—here he defiled the Great

Mother's name, for he hated her—had given the Spyglass would fail; then the Hidden Sister would be located, and both Tablets of Destiny would lay upon his breast, as they always should have. Then the sky of heaven would be his. The red orbs shone again. How stupid were the demon gods of old to think he could be so easily overcome. *Prince of demons!* That one, Stal, was his, brought to him cheaply by the snake. They would see this soon enough when they were felled by their "prince." The beast Ashurnasirpal he also saw, with the serpent-sharks swimming about him, and the foolish trio—the duke, the prince, and the khan—who followed him. They too would be duly punished.

𒀭𒁶𒁉𒀭𒁹

Mattie and Geeta shut their eyes against the light; they felt the heat like a flame upon their skin. The Spyglass, plugged in the hole of the hourglass, also felt the heat. The heat, in her claustrophobic panic, brought to the forefront of her memory her burial in the hot desert sand of Nineveh. The Spyglass felt the energy of the mortal soul that was Mattie; there was hope. She turned in her sand prison; she spun, and the sand turned colors: purple, yellow, orange. The colors infused into Mattie's arm and throughout the hourglass. It shone in contrast to the heat of the red orbs. Mattie struggled against the Spyglass's hold. "Help me get loose, Geeta!" she cried out, and Geeta tugged on Mattie's arm.

𒀭𒁶𒁉𒀭𒁹

The snake Gneezy slithered around the dark and dank alleyway, beyond the edges of the peasants who crowded around Stal, the prince of demons. The red-faced Iron Knight, now upon two feet rather than the might of a warhorse, appeared petulant as he flaunted his sword in the empty alleyway. Why were they there and not upon the battleground? Moments before, he had been glorying in battle as the leader of the entire Russian army, and now he stood alone with the snake in a dark alley. The snake hissed, "Crone."

Then, from the shadows, the Crone appeared, clearly pulled there against her will. The Crone hunched her repugnant head into her body. "Crone," the snake hissed again. "Asaru-alim-nuna." The Crone flinched. "Tell me," said the snake, wrapping his python force around the Crone's body. He took her in his tail and flung her up. Then the snake grew again, moving its giant cobra head close to the Crone's face. "Tell me."

The Crone opened her foul mouth, the lone tooth shaking in the terror she felt. Did the snake know of her treachery? She willed herself not to think. "Master," she said, "it is the demon gods of old, those who battled Marduk and lost. They now rise to exact their revenge, though how they escaped from Kurnigi, I do not know."

Gneezy hissed again. "How do I destroy them?"

The Crone gasped. Was the snake so stupid? "Destroy them, Master? Why, that is not possible. They are gods of old."

The snake hissed in displeasure. He threw the Crone down, who whimpered upon the dirty pavement of the alley. "Crone," he said, "if I find you have deceived me, the terrors you feel now will pale by comparison." He turned to the Iron Knight. "Come. We will get the pockmarked one, Stal, and crush these demon gods." The snake shot out of the alleyway, leaving the Crone upon the ground. She then stood. The snake was indeed stupid. And here she felt hope rise in her. Stal was the prince of demons and held the power of the Saber of the Shadows. He would cut the snake Gneezy in two. Then perhaps she would be free of his hold.

Outside the alleyway, Stal remained mesmerized by Trina. "Iosif," she said again, her palms up beseechingly. *Iosif.* The name rang in his ears, and the mortal memories filled him with Trina, her striking face, and the longing that once had beaten in his heart and pounded in his ears. Stal looked down to see Trina, her face angelic. The dragon beast that carried him shook, and the demon gods around Stal cried out for him to kill the yellow-haired boy and seize Death's scythe.

Eddie was quickly losing consciousness, so deep and penetrating was the pain. He heard the rustling of Gilgamesh behind him, also felled. *Pain is weakness leaving the body. Let it leave, and you will be strong.* Eddie heard the words of his father, Sergeant Petersen. *Let it leave.* He willed himself to go with the pain and felt it rise out of his body. *Trina.* His eyes saw the lovely Trina in front of him, shielding him as she faced the pockmarked enemy atop the giant dragon horse. *Trina.* Eddie stood up against the pain. His grasp on the scythe tightened as he stumbled forward.

"Eddie!" He heard his name and looked to see Biddle and Wigglesworth descending toward him upon silver horses gleaming against the now red sky. He saw that the orbs of Marduk were beyond and that Biddle and Wigglesworth were in danger of the evil that lurked behind them in the form of Marduk. "Look behind you!" he cried to them.

Marduk's dark-red orbs glowed strong and enveloped Biddle and Wigglesworth, keeping them pinned to the sky. Biddle saw

Eddie holding Death's scythe and losing his battle against a pockmarked demon riding a dragon horse. "Wigglesworth," he called, "we must help Eddie." The searing heat of Marduk was almost paralyzing.

Then the sky was torn asunder, as the Four Terrors rode up: Nergal, god of destruction; Namtar, demon of tribulation, bearing dark winds of pain; the long-haired Lamashtu demoness, with her gray locks spreading like a fog of confusion; and Zaltu, goddess of conflict. All were vengeful now against the Dark Master who had imprisoned them; they would be forgotten no more, but mighty again, and it would be Marduk's turn to be thrown into the walls of the tunnels beneath Kurnigi. So the battle between Marduk and Asaru-alim-nuna began. Marduk's fierce red orbs shook the black sky against the winds of the Four Terrors who called forward more and more of the long imprisoned dead souls. This battle in the sky was evil against evil, but in the battle of dark against light, evil was now the victor, for below, on the frozen Russian ground, the souls of mortals moved to the underworld. Darkness was in its ascendancy, for there was always chaos before great victory—this the Dark Master knew—and under the forces of evil, knots in the time of mortal man only knit stronger.

In this maelstrom, Biddle and Wigglesworth were released from Marduk's ferocious hold. The vengeance of the Four Terrors created a whirlwind that threw Biddle and Wigglesworth off their silver horses. The horses careened downward. Flying toward Biddle and Wigglesworth was the hourglass that held Mattie and Geeta. It was filled with multicolored sand on one side and Mattie and Geeta on the other, flailing about. Mattie and Geeta saw the figures of Biddle and Wigglesworth being battered by the winds of the Four Terrors. Biddle reached to grab them with his cape to no avail as the hourglass spun away. *How miserably we have failed, Wigglesworth, in our task!* Biddle bemoaned.

The beast Ashurnasirpal fell hard to the frozen ground of the Winter Palace square. The serpent sharks slithered around him, swimming in the air toward their master. The beast snorted and shook his head to clear it. He saw the dead mortals on the ground and the dead souls of the wicked plunging downward. But didn't see the snake or Abaddon. Where was the wretch? Soon Abaddon, whose grasp on Paddy had been lost in the wind, tumbled down, followed by Paddy. A strange, sickly, yellowish light encased them and suddenly broke. Ashurnasirpal saw the scurrying movements of the rodent creature flapping his wings. Abaddon, with his gray-green pointed face, flew above the beast and was drawn by a magnetic force to the edges of the Winter Palace square, where Stal rode. Following closely were the vengeful spirits, calling out again and again, *Abaddon, wretch and thief!*

Paddy fell and was blubbering upon the ground. The beast recognized him and ordered the serpent-sharks, "Hold tight this prey." One of the seven serpent-sharks wrapped itself around Paddy. "Good God!" Paddy cried in horror. Then he felt the stings of the serpent-shark demons' tails, which had sharp talons at the end. His thoughts, however, didn't reside with his pain but with Dottie. Where was she? Was that wife-stealing cad Sir Henry Layard still holding her? The thought made him struggle with futility against the increased strength of the serpent-sharks. Then fell his beloved Dottie, still clasped by Sir Henry, followed by Smith, his webbed frog feet up in the air.

The beast Ashurnasirpal cried in delight that both prey—those who were precious to the red-haired one who held the Spyglass—had fallen so easily into his grasp. "Bind them!" he commanded the serpent-shark demon gods, and they wrapped their python bodies around the struggling Sir Henry and Dottie, and also George Smith, whose eyes were mad with fear. The beast grunted. Soon the red-haired one would be in his clasp and the Spyglass his. First that, and then he would deal with Abaddon, for the vengeful spirits were sure to capture him and plunge him into the depths of the tunnels beneath the City of the Condemned.

The serpent-shark demon gods swam around Ashurnasirpal. *Master, master, master,* they called in warning. The beast felt the grasp of hands upon his hooves, and saw the trio rise from the ground. It was the Brotherhood of Evil. The Prince of Wallachia spoke first as he took form. "Forget us not, brother, for still we ride with you." The duke and the khan materialized around him and saw the serpent-shark gods baring their teeth at them. "Tell them, beast," they said. The beast grunted for the serpent-sharks to move back, for the Brotherhood of Evil still had power that the beast needed in order to take the Spyglass, hold both Tablets of Destiny, and overpower Marduk. They saw how the sky above them turned blood red with Marduk's fearsome orbs.

"Let us go now!" the prince cried. "Do you not see Marduk?"

The beast snorted in anger. He saw the red sky, but he also saw the hourglass with the red-haired child and brown owlet girl in it. The red-haired child was close by; they had to grab her. But then he saw how the red orbs glowed, and along with them, he saw the Four Terrors. "Call the chant!" Khan cried to the beast. Ashurnasirpal, touching the droplet in his mouth, whispered the seven desecrated names of Marduk.

Ankia-en-lugal,

Ugug,

Umum,

Tudu,

Udud,

Gar-gash,

Bilulu-en.

The serpent sharks swam toward him and spun. A yellow light enveloped the beast, the Brotherhood of Evil, and the prey they held—Dottie, Paddy, Sir Henry, and Smith—and they all disappeared. But they didn't disappear without notice, for Marduk had heard the request of the Brotherhood of Evil to call a chant and also had seen the serpent-sharks spin around the beast. It was then that Marduk knew that the beast held the droplet. The red orbs dimmed beneath the assault of the Four Terrors.

𒁹𒌋𒌋 𒁹 𒁹𒌋𒌋 𒀸

"Trina," Eddie gasped, "move away." He raised Death's scythe toward Stal. The demon gods who were screaming for Stal to seize the scythe drew back, and Stal was awakened from the trance in which Trina had held him. He swung the Saber of Shadows again as Eddie wielded Death's scythe. The clashing of the terrible weapons produced a deafening sound. Trina cried in alarm as Eddie shouted in pain when the saber's vibrations traveled into his body. He stumbled down. Trina ran toward him. "*Muktablu!*"

Stal raised the Saber of Shadows again, this time with the blade of darkness bared, to plunge its point into Eddie. *Roll! Roll!* Eddie heard his father's command and rolled. *Weapon up!*

Sergeant Petersen's voice called the command. Eddie raised Death's scythe as his father's voice called, *Engage!* He felt the strength of his father through him, and the scythe was no longer resisting him but obeying him. He thrust the weapon at Stal's saber and struck it; he saw the pockmarked rider of the dragon horse flinch. Then the Saber of Shadows hit Eddie again and filled him with searing pain. Still Eddie didn't let go of the scythe.

Trina came toward him, her eyes sorrowful, and behind him he heard the wails of the wandering spirit children and the soft cries of warning of Gilgamesh, who was struggling to stand. "*Muktablu!*" he said. "I will...come."

Eddie's arms were seared—bloody and raw—but he still held on to the scythe. Trina whispered, "You are hurt." His eyes were blurred by pain. Then the images flowed slowly. He saw Trina bending over him. *Trina.* No harm could come to her; he couldn't bear it. He felt his love for her surge and saw it reflected in her eyes, and it beat again in his heart. Something was happening to his heart and soul; his love for Trina was deep and old. He knew then that he had loved her before, had known her before, and he realized that this love, this endless love, had led kindred souls to find one another again and again in the sea of time. Trina's eyes showed this recognition. Eddie saw her change before him, grow older, into the young woman she never was as a mortal. Her hair was longer now, and her face more captivating, and in her eyes Eddie recognized the woman he had once loved, lifetimes ago. And the recognition changed him too.

Then the arm of the pockmarked one reached forward and grabbed Trina, lifting her onto the dragon horse. Stal held her tightly—Trina, now a dazzling young woman, the perfect princess for the prince of demons! Into Eddie's mind Trina spoke,

Muktablu, leave this place and save yourself. But Eddie closed his mind to the message, for all he saw was Trina grasped by the pockmarked demon Stal, and the sight was too unbearable. He lunged forward with Death's scythe.

"*Muktablu!*" Eddie heard Gilgamesh cry. "Stay back...I will take this demon." Gilgamesh held up his spear to deflect the blows of the Saber of Shadows. He saw Eddie's bleeding arms and how he plunged again and again against the blows of the Saber of Darkness, how Death's scythe hit the saber but left Stal still holding Trina tightly to his side.

Stal slashed the sword toward Eddie and saw that he was no longer a boy. He grasped Death's scythe, now held in the arm of a young yellow-haired man. Eddie plunged forward again. "Let her go!" he screamed, and hit the saber fiercely. The ground beneath Eddie shook, and the scythe missed its target.

The great serpent body of the snake Gneezy formed upon the ground and with its tail went to grab the dragon beast that Stal rode. Eddie lunged the scythe at the dragon beast. If he could hit the creature at the right angle, the pockmarked demon would fall, and Trina could be rescued. He thought only of Trina, not of the danger of the snake Gneezy and the attention Eddie brought to himself. The snake turned toward Eddie and saw the scythe. Gneezy hissed, and his tongue shot out to grab it. Eddie jumped back and swung Death's scythe at the snake.

The snake's head shook in anger. "Give me the sword, cockroach, that I might cut this one to pieces and take Death's scythe!" he demanded of Stal.

Stal, prince of demons, snorted, "Move back, snake, or I will strike you too! I am the prince of demons and will soon grasp Death's scythe for myself!"

"You!" hissed the snake. "You are nothing but a pockmarked insect who serves me!"

But here the snake was mistaken, for Stal was now a prince, and the demon gods surrounding him sprang to grasp the snake. The snake Gneezy saw their power. The Black Book of Magic sprang from his forked tongue in the sky. The Black Book, in its scaly binding, shook as the snake leaped into it, shaking its head at Stal and hissing, "Traitor are you now, you pockmarked roach. We shall see how you fare when the Dark Master holds you in his clasp." Black snakes sprang from the book and grabbed the Iron Knight and Crone below before it shut and disappeared.

The dragon steed shook, and the prince of demons on it only laughed, and as he did, the other dragons that had formed from the one head, which once had held the peasants, came now. Their furious hooves sprang upon Eddie, and though Death's scythe struck them, the creatures' hooves and fire hurt him. Gilgamesh battled beside Eddie, stabbing his spear at the monsters. Gilgamesh saw with surprise how Eddie was no longer a boy but a man of eighteen years. The king lunged his spear at the beasts to keep them away.

A great wind formed, and Stal shook upon his dragon steed but held firmly onto Trina. Then the figure of a gaunt Buddha formed, enveloping the sky with light. It neared Biddle and Wigglesworth in the sky, still held in the winds of the Four Terrors, who fell back. They were repelled to the ground, where Stal was grasping Trina upon the dragon horse.

As the Buddha spoke, more and more Buddhas filled the sky: some fat, some thin, some male, some female, some with faces that could not be seen—all in a meditative pose, covered in saffron-colored robes. Then a chant rose and vibrated through the air over and over.

Eight precious stones,
eight matters of the soul
rise like the wind of wrath.
Eight stones of suffering.

The sound of the Buddhas' chants rang repeatedly through the sky.

Fear, hate, anger, bitterness, envy, duplicity, greed, and despair.
Five stones remain.
If you can cross them,
you will find the Seer of Truth.

The winds of the Buddhas grabbed the hourglass that held Mattie and Geeta. The hourglass was filled with a hurricane of multicolored sand. The Spyglass resisted the pull of the Buddhas, which she felt and heard. Spyglass threw her will against the pull of the Path of the Virtuous; she wanted nothing more to do with this treacherous journey!

Geeta saw the figures of Biddle and Wiggleworth pulled into the great light that was the Buddhas. Was that Eddie below? She felt a stab of fear, though she didn't know why. She saw Mattie pushing the hourglass to move away from the light. "No!" Mattie screamed. "We have to stay here and find my mom. No!" The harder Mattie pushed, however, the more the hourglass shook and moved into the light. Geeta's black braids whipped about as the hourglass spun higher and higher, away from the ground and into the pull of the Buddhas. Geeta heard ThaTha's voice again. *In the battlefield for the soul, whether there is to be eternal order or chaos in the cosmos, one who fights her dharma loses, not just for herself but for all.* Then the light from the Buddhas blinded and absorbed Geeta and Mattie.

On the ground below, the great wind of the Buddhas moved down to Eddie and pulled him up. Though he was a young man now and held that strength, he nonetheless was pulled upward. The wandering spirit children moaned in pain. Gilgamesh also felt sorrow at the sight of Eddie moving up into the light of the Buddhas above; the young *muktablu* had been like Enkidu, a friend, a brother. But Gilgamesh saw that Eddie's fate lay with the spirits that had wrenched him up from the land. Eddie struggled hard against the Buddhas' pull. He wouldn't leave Trina to fall into the depths of Kurnigi, to be imprisoned by the pockmarked demon. Eddie's love for Trina was strong; he fought against the wind, slashing the scythe toward Stal, kicking against the force that drew him up. As the winds of the Buddhas rose in strength, Eddie's will rose as well. *Airborne!* Eddie heard his father's command. He rolled his body down and broke the force of the Buddhas as he jumped toward the ground. The Buddhas' light dimmed and faded. Eddie had escaped their grasp, tumbling as he was through the air to the ground.

Gilgamesh's large hand grabbed Eddie as he fell to the earth. Eddie sprang up to lunge at Stal, whose grip on Trina remained strong. With his other hand, Stal swung the Saber of Shadows. "Trina, grab my hand!" Eddie shouted. Trina struggled against Stal's tight grasp to reach him.

Above them a buzzing sound like a swarm of mosquitoes filled the air. Then the flying rodent figure of Abaddon, chased by the vengeful spirits, flew into Stal. Abaddon's yellow eyes saw his thumbs upon the hands of the pockmarked demon. He flew down then bared his sharp teeth and plunged them into Stal's left hand. Stal, still holding Trina tightly, shouted in agony and swung the Saber of Shadows to fling away the creature.

The red orbs of Marduk still flashed ominously in the night sky. Marduk's eyes glowed, and he cried out that it was he who was the master of the underworld, and the vengeful spirits that escaped had but one place to return to, Kurnigi, for the imprint of their sins couldn't be erased, and their sentence to the land of darkness was for eternity. And so too would he imprison the Four Terrors and all the Asaru-alim-nuna. Then Zaltu, goddess of conflict, with her many-sided head and eyes of lightning bolts, hurled her bolts toward Marduk, as the fogs of confusion rose and the winds of the Four Terrors shook the red orbs in the sky. Marduk's red orbs weakened against the might of the Four Terrors, who bellowed, *Marduk! Destroyed shall you be!*

As the red eyes dimmed in the sky, Marduk thundered his prophecy.

Triumph shall you for the moment,
Asaru-alim-nuna,
but soon you shall wonder
how quickly your
prince of demons
laid you asunder,
for he is servant not to you but me,
as soon you shall see!

The vengeful spirits flying about Abaddon, whose teeth were sunk into Stal, cried out, for the Four Terrors fell onto them from above. Then below, from the ground, rose the fearsome and many forms of Asaru-alim-nuna. Suddenly the cries of all of the mighty forgotten ones—with their broken forms; their giant bodies of scorpions, skeletons, and dragons—hit the air with their long tongues and cried that they were forgotten no more. *Asaru-alim-nuna!* Their cries cracked the air with triumph.

> *O Marduk, Dark Master will you be no more,*
> *for our poison demon arrows*
> *into mortal man's heart have struck,*
> *filled with envy and greed,*
> *filled with pride and need.*
> *So will it be war and vengeance,*
> *an endless dance of bloodshed,*
> *as man will hate one another,*
> *as man will kill his brother.*

> *And rule we shall Kurnigi,*
> *land of darkness and the dead,*
> *land of misery and dread!*

Eddie's heart beat hard as he ran toward Trina, the scythe reverberating with the rhythms of evil, pulling him toward the call of the mighty demons. Then the ground beneath them gave way under the weight of evil. It split suddenly into a deep canyon from which rose a force that pulled the demonic creatures into the darkness, into the Abyss of Blackness. Gilgamesh's blue face deepened in anguish under the frightful prophecy of the mighty old demons, and behind him the wandering children spirits wailed as they were pulled into the darkness. The king of Uruk shook in fear at sight before him, the gruesome Abyss of Blackness, which lay underneath even the deepest bowels of Kurnigi and held an awfulness that silenced the soul.

Eddie stumbled against the great rumbling of the earth. Before him Stal, upon the gigantic dragon horse that also carried Trina, fell when the ground beneath them gave way, and they disappeared into the black void below. Eddie shouted, "Trina!" as the chasm was closing.

"No, *muktablu!*" Gilgamesh cried in alarm, for he saw what the young warrior was going to do. "It is the Abyss of Blackness!"

But Eddie's heart and mind were open only to one thing—Trina. He jumped into the abyss as the ground closed over him.

End of Book Two